To Capture A Highlander's Heart

THE TRILOGY

Teresa J. Reasor

COPYRIGHT © 2013, 2016 by Teresa J. Reasor

Contact Information: **teresareasor@msn.com**

Cover Art by Tracy Stewart
Edited by Faith Freewoman

Teresa J. Reasor
PO Box 124
Corbin, KY 40702

Publishing History: First Edition 2013

ISBN-13: 978-1-940047-09-6
ISBN-10: 1-940047-09-9
Print Edition

Table of Contents

To Capture A Highlander's Heart

THE BEGINNING
A HIGHLAND MOONLIGHT SPINOFF
SHORT STORY

Teresa J. Reasor

Scotland 1330

GABRIEL EYED THE bedclothes and other garments spread on the bushes around his hut. He approached his cottage with a combination of caution and curiosity. The wee folk had visited his home while he was away again? This time they—she—had been cleaning.

In the months since the visits began, his surprise and pleasure had melted into wariness.

The fresh baked bread, the herbs tied with a scrap of ribbon, his mended shirt, though appreciated at first, now made him feel…obligated. Whatever was given, there would be a price to be paid later. Were these small gifts the bait? Would the trap be sprung today?

The scent of stewing vegetables and meat wafted to him before he reached the door. Shoving open the portal, he ducked his head to clear the lintel and swept the cabin with a quick, questing look. His clothing hung upon pegs, his wooden plates and bowls, now washed, were stacked on the shelf. The hearth, swept clean of ash, boasted a newly laid fire. The stew he smelled bubbled in a pot balanced on the iron stand above the flames. Aye, she had been cleaning—and cooking. He breathed an oath. Who was she? And what was she about?

GRACE TUCKED THE empty basket beneath her arm and raised her skirts to climb the steep hill to the village. She had bolstered her nerve to announce her presence, but one look at Gabriel's expression had shriveled the urge like a dried pea, and she fled. Why had he been angry? What had vexed him so?

Her steps flagged, and she stopped midway up the hill to rest amongst the wild hyacinth blooming along the path. Setting aside the basket, she plucked one of the clustered blossoms and raised it to her nose to enjoy in its fragrance.

She was nothing like Tira, the woman he had once loved. She could not give him beauty, but she could mend his clothes, clean his cottage, and cook his food.

She could bear him children.

And she would do it with a love in her heart that would make the offer sweeter.

If only he could *see* her.

She studied the work-roughened fingers that grasped the flower's stem. But why should a man such as he settle for a homely little mouse when he could have beauty as well?

Her love was no small thing. Was that not a prize worth more than a pleasing face?

She lay down amongst the flowers, and their scent embraced her. If men's bellies were full and their clothes mended, did they ever think of love? Mayhap not.

Then why would she not do as well as any other woman?

But for him to consider her, she had to make him *see* her. But how? And if he did and turned away? Pain grabbed her throat and threatened her composure.

At the snap of a nearby twig, she jerked upright.

A gasp escaped as the object of her thoughts emerged from the stand of trees and came to a halt in the clearing. Black trews hugged his muscular legs. He wore the shirt she had mended for him beneath a leather tunic that clung to his torso and emphasized the width of his chest and shoulders.

Grace scrambled to her feet, her cheeks hot.

Gabriel's long strides seemed to eat up the distance between them, and with every step her heart beat a flighty rhythm.

"Good morn, lass."

The deep timbre of his voice, with its hint of raspiness, sent delightful chill bumps down her arms. She fought the sudden breathlessness making it difficult to speak to him for the first time. She swallowed and forced her voice to work. "Good morn."

His dark brows, angled in a V over the straight slope of his nose, hinted at the anger she had recognized earlier. His neatly trimmed beard, darkening the lower half of his face, outlined the sensuous curve of his lips.

"How long have you been here, lass?"

"Only a wee time."

"Have you seen anyone about? Has anyone passed you on the path?"

She shook her head. "Nay." He was hunting for the person who had been in his hut. He was not happy about their trespass— her trespass.

He nodded once, a quick jerk of his chin. "Good day, then."

As she watched him ascend the hill, Grace hitched a despairing breath. All he saw when he looked at her was Lady Mary's maid, not a woman. For a man who was known as one of Alexander Campbell's most fierce warriors, he was as blind as a hairy coo in a snowstorm. She climbed the path behind him.

GABRIEL TOPPED THE rise and looked down into the village. There were few people about, and none of them women. Who was she? Where could she have gone?

At the whisper of skirts behind him, he turned and waited for Grace to come abreast. His attention dropped to her basket. The ragged container looked familiar. Was it not the same one that had held the loaves of bread someone had left for him? Shock punched the breath from his lungs, and his eyes leapt to her face.

"Who sent you, Grace?"

Pain whipped across her features. She straightened her shoulders and met his gaze. "No one sent me."

She strode past him and started down the path to the village.

In two paces he caught up and matched his long strides with her shorter ones. "Why would you clean my hut and prepare food for me, lass?"

"You are not dull-witted, Gabriel."

From the bite of her tone, nor was she. He studied the tender slope of her jaw. She had a small heart-shaped face, dominated by large, dark-lashed eyes. Freckles sprinkled across the bridge of her nose.

"Grace." He grasped her arm, compelling her to stop. "You are a wee, young lass. Too young to waste your youth on a man nearly half a score older than you."

"I am a score and one year old. Old enough to be a wife. Old enough to be a mother."

Surprise held him immobile.

"I am not the same young, ignorant girl I was when first I came here to Castle de Sith. Lady Mary has taught me to read. And though I have not grown in body, my mind has grown, and I am more than I was. Good enough for you or any other man. If you canna believe that, I have made a grave mistake in my judgment of you."

Gabriel's face flushed at her tone and his jaw grew taut. "And how many other men have you been cooking and cleaning for, then?"

Color stormed her cheeks and her eyes narrowed. She swung the basket, hitting him in the shoulder. Reeds, fragile with age, splintered, and the vessel collapsed. As she broke into a run, she hurled the wreaked container with a backwards sling.

Only his quick reaction kept it from smacking him in the face. He eyed the basket. Dry bits of debris flaked away to scatter upon the ground. All the thing would be useful for now was to feed his fire.

He studied the angry twitch of Grace's hips while she stormed down the path toward the castle. He frowned at the response that ran straight to his groin.

The bread had been fresh, and the stew he tested before leaving the hut had been well seasoned and tasty. But marriage seemed a steep price to pay for them. And marriage was what she was after. But why him?

It was after he had supped on the stew Grace cooked that he looked around his small cabin and noticed how her light touch about the room had changed the cluttered space. And how contentedly the food rested in his belly.

As he climbed into his bed, the soft scent of soap and greenery on his threadbare sheets wafted over him. Grace had washed and hung them on the brush outside his door to dry.

Gabriel punched his pillow and turned on his side. 'Twas nonsense. She was too young for him. To wee for a man as large as he.

His response to the tight swish of her hips when she stormed down the hill, however, gave a lie to the belief. He had never thought of her in that manner. Before. But now it was all he could think about.

GABRIEL'S EYES NARROWED while he watched Grace's braid swing back and forth like a pendulum at the small of her back. She whipped the length of tartan fabric from around her shoulders and hung it on a peg at the door.

In the four days since their conversation, every word she had spoken wove through his thoughts, triggering feelings he had tried to deny but could not. Fed by the knowledge that she had already been inside his home, he found himself envisioning her in his hut, preparing a meal, mending his shirts, sleeping beside him. The images had taken root in his mind and whetted his desire for something more…substantial…than imaginings.

He had hoped to speak with her at the evening meal, but she accompanied Lady Mary to attend a sick child in the village. Now she had returned, he saw his chance and rose from his seat. He quickened his pace across the great room while she slipped between the heavy wooden tables crowded with men finishing their meal.

A long, muscular arm whipped out from one of the tables and caught her about the waist. Bruce Campbell dragged her down onto his lap.

Grace stared at the clansman, her eyes large and startled.

Too far away to hear what was said, Gabriel bore down on the couple in time to see Grace shake her head and push against Bruce's shoulder.

The other men at the table laughed, and her cheeks flushed berry red. She pushed against the edge of the table and attempted to lever herself out of his grasp, but the man held on. Ignoring her struggles, he buried his face against her neck.

With the speed of a loosed crossbow bolt, an emotion Gabriel had never experienced shot through him. *Mine!* The word reverberated through his entire being.

Outrage fueled his temper, while every protective instinct in him took aim at the man holding Grace. As he reached them, he gripped Bruce Campbell's wrist and peeled it loose from her waist. He grasped her forearm and, with an easy tug, plucked her free of the man's lap.

Pushing her behind him, he turned to face Bruce. Irritation clouded the clansman's face as he half rose. Gabriel shoved him back into his seat and thrust his own face close. "I'd hate t' split your head over a woman, but I will do it if you press the matter, Bruce."

The surprise on Bruce's face, as well as those of the other men at the table, brought Gabriel's temper under control. He had as good as laid claim to the lass in front of the entire company.

For one long, tense moment, silence reigned.

Bruce spread his hands in an acquiescent gesture. "There are always other lasses, and I winna have t' suffer a broken noggin' t' have them."

Gabriel nodded. "'Tis a wise decision, my friend." He turned to capture Grace's hand and tugged her toward the antechamber on one side of the great hall.

✳

GRACE'S BREATH SHUDDERED and hitched while Gabriel tugged her into Lord Campbell's antechamber. With the door finally closed behind them, he released her and began to pace the room, his movements agitated.

He had fought for her. Fought over her. What if he had done so simply out of kindness? She struggled to suppress her excitement.

A huge table and chairs dominated the room. Just off center sat a basket filled with wild hyacinth blossoms. Wary of the anger still vivid on his face, she moved to touch the flowers and stir their fragrance.

"Your basket dinna survive your treatment," Gabriel said. "Since 'twas my fault, I thought t' replace it."

"Oh—Gabriel—" Grace's heart beat a frantic rhythm. Tears blurred her vision and her fingers dwelt upon the lip of the new basket. No man had ever given her a gift. But what if she should misunderstand his meaning?

"Do the flowers please you, then?"

"Aye." Her attention focused on him as a small niggling hope bubbled up inside her. "Aye, a great deal"

"That day upon the path, you were lying amongst them—" Color touched his cheekbones. "I have been thinking about that."

He *saw* her. He finally *saw* her. Joy whipped through her, and she smiled.

His gaze settled upon her lips, and his features took on an intent expression filled with heat and promise. "Walk with me." He offered his hand.

Her heart beat a heavy rhythm against her throat as she grasped it, and the heat of his callused palm warmed her hand while he drew her from the room to the front entrance.

Gabriel paused upon the stone stairs just outside the great hall door. "Why me, Grace?"

Grace breathed in the cool, moist air, relishing the scent of hay and livestock, of smoke and freshly turned earth.

She averted her eyes. If she looked at him, she could not broach the subject. "You loved Tira. You loved her son, and cared for him as though he were your own. A man with so generous a heart—" His grip tightened upon her hand and her voice died.

Gabriel raised her face with his fingertips beneath her chin, his features set and serious. "'Twas not love, Grace. I ken nothing of love."

She did not believe that. "You knew enough t' care for a fatherless boy who needed you. And 'tis not just loyalty that holds you here at Lord Campbell's side."

"I canna hope t' live up to the man you believe me to be, Grace."

"'Twill not hurt you t' try."

His quick, surprised expression dissolved into laughter.

"'Twill do no good, should we not please each other in other ways," he said a moment later, a smile still curving his lips.

The emotion she read in his expression left her breathless, and stole the strength from her voice. "And what would you be speaking about?"

Gabriel's arm slid around her waist, and he pulled her into the shaded alcove next to the door. His arms tightened, aligning her body with the long, lean length of his. His eyes scanned her face, a look in their depths that hurried her heart. His lips covered hers.

After the first moments of surprise passed, a sweet sensation of pleasure swept through her. Grace slipped her arms up his back, holding him close while the soft pressure of his mouth moved upon hers, his beard soft against her cheeks. The height and breadth of him offered her, at first, a sense of protection, then something else. Suffused with an aching need to be closer, she rose on tiptoe and curved her body into his.

When he drew back to look down at her, Gabriel's cheeks were ruddy, and his breathing unsteady.

She pressed her hot face against the coolness of his leather tunic and reveled in his gentle touch as he smoothed her hair.

"Does that please you, lass?" he asked, his voice husky.

"Aye." She drew back. "For now." She slipped free of his arms and skipped down the stairs.

STILL ADDLED BY his own response to the sweet taste of her lips and the shy inexperience of her kiss, Gabriel eyed Grace when she turned to look over her shoulder at him.

"'Twill take more than a gift and a kiss, Gabriel."

The challenge he read in her expression brought a smile to his lips, his heart thumping. "Aye, I can see that."

It would be marriage or nothing.

He would not have wanted it any other way.

She offered her hand, the gesture a dare. He leapt down the steps to capture it.

To Capture A Highlander's Heart

THE COURTSHIP
A HIGHLAND MOONLIGHT SPINOFF NOVELLA

Teresa J. Reasor

Scotland 1330

GRACE SCOOPED THE thick porridge into a wooden bowl and gave it a suspicious sniff. Had the cook burnt it? Surely not again. She drizzling a small helping of honey over the substance and stirred. Seeing no improvement in its consistency, she frowned.

"I wouldna eat that, lass," Gabriel said from behind her.

At the sound of Gabriel's voice, her breath caught and her heart raced. She struggled to suppress the outward expression of her response before she turned to face him. His dark hair, tied back with a leather strip, bared the strong, masculine bones of his face. His closely trimmed beard, as dark as his hair, outlined his lips, drawing her attention to them and reminding her of the kiss they had shared on the steps outside the castle. *Her very first kiss.*

A tingling heat raced down her body to settle in intimate places. She dropped her gaze to the bowl. "It could serve other purposes besides food. Perhaps mortar to hold together the stones in the west wing."

Gabriel grinned. "I shall suggest that t' Alexander. 'Twill save work for the men and may protect the cook from certain attack. The worse the food becomes, the more their tempers are tested." He stepped forward, closing the distance between them. "Will you break your fast with me, Grace?"

That he asked instead of demanded sent a sweet rush of pleasure through her. "Aye, I should like to join you."

"I have more than enough food for both of us," Gabriel said, motioning to a table on which sat several wooden bowls.

Vividly aware of every digit of the hand Gabriel rested against the small of her back, Grace allowed him to usher her to a seat upon the bench. The great room was filled with Alexander Campbell's warriors, all eating and talking at once. The rumble of their deep voices sounded like thunder as they rose and fell in conversation.

"Did you hear the news, Gabriel?" Artair, one of the older clansmen asked from down the table, then continued without pause. "Robert the Bruce entrusted Lord James Douglas with carrying his heart t' the Holy Land."

"Who told you this, Artair?"

"'Twas Duncan. He has just returned from Castle Lorne with news."

Gabriel frowned. "'Twill be Scotland's loss when Black Douglas leaves our homeland. He's a fierce warrior. But the Bruce chose well. I have no doubt his dying wish *will* be carried out."

Grace had heard several tales about Black Douglas. But now that the king was dead, all of Scotland seemed to have become afflicted with a feeling of dread. What new trials awaited them?

Gabriel peeled a hard-boiled egg and set it before her with a thick slab of bread. Grace studied his features. He was loyal to the king, Lord Alexander Campbell, and to Scotland. Should the call to battle sound, he would be among the first to answer it. Fear suddenly stole her appetite and made eating impossible. She accepted the crock of honey and drizzled a wee bit over her bread, hoping the sweetness would make it palatable despite her upset.

Two of the men wandered over to join the discussion. Bruce Campbell propped his booted foot upon the bench, and, leaning down, braced his forearms across his knee. "And when Douglas leaves, a Highland warrior and leader such as he will carry some of the heart of Scotland with him, along with the king's. We will have lost a well-versed warrior, something we shall need when the English make their move. And 'tis no doubt they will, sooner or later."

"Alexander fought for the Bruce for half a score of years. I will wager he is as skillful in battle as Black Douglas, or any other leader," Gabriel said. "'Twill be Alexander that I follow."

"Let us hope none of us have t' leave this valley t' make war upon the English again," Artair said.

To Grace, the older man's words seemed the only wise voice at the table. Why were men so eager to fight? The scar that ran the length of Artair's arm from beneath his jerkin to his wrist looked raw and red, though it had been some time since the injury had happened. The near loss of his arm may have made him appreciate the danger and lent him a more cautious stance.

"'Twould be my wish t' avoid a conflict, but not at the expense of having the English boot of tyranny upon m' neck," Gabriel said.

All three men nodded in unison. Bruce Campbell's eyes strayed to Grace.

She looked away. It had not been so long ago that Bruce Campbell had grabbed her in the great room and nuzzled her neck as though they—Her feelings of outrage, of helplessness returned each time she saw him.

After a few more minute's discussion, Bruce Campbell straightened and wandered away. Grace drew a deep relieved breath. "Would you like something t' drink, Gabriel?" she murmured.

"Aye."

She rose to serve him, but he moved more quickly and motioned for her to retain her seat. He strode across the great hall to a table to collect two tankards and a pitcher of milk. He brought the cups to the table and filled them, then set aside the jug.

No man had ever served her. Once again her gaze rested on his face as she voiced her thanks. Afterwards silence stretched between them.

"Do you really think the English will come now our king the Bruce is—gone?" she asked.

"I believe we will have to struggle anew to maintain our separation from them."

Did that mean he would leave and stand ready to act on behalf of the next Scottish sovereign, the king's young son? Or rather his advisors, for the boy was just a wee lad.

What if Gabriel did? What if she never saw him again? An ache settled in the pit of her stomach. She swallowed the bite of bread she had taken and set the rest aside.

Gabriel ran a hand down her back to her waist. "You will be safe, lass."

Grace shook her head. "'Tis not myself I am concerned for, Gabriel. 'Tis for you—and the other men."

His brown gaze settled on her face. Color stormed her cheeks and she reached for the tankard of milk.

"Grace," his deep voice, spoken so soft and husky, set her heart to flight. He ran his fingers along the braid that hung down her back. It took all her control to remain stationary beneath his attention. Every time he looked at her, touched her, she wanted to press close, to feel his tall, manly frame against her. Her heart was lost to him, but what of his?

When he took her hand and gave it a reassuring squeeze, she focused on his long fingers, strong and callused from honing his skill with bow and sword, and from controlling his mount's reins. He was a warrior. Nothing would ever change that.

To change him would make him less than the man she'd come to love.

She fought the urge to rest her head against his shoulder and glanced upward to find him watching her. He traced the curve of her cheek with the back of his fingers. His smile brought an answering one to her lips. "Mayhap I shall teach you how t' use a bow, eh?"

"Lady Mary is very skilled with one."

"Aye, she is."

"'Tis difficult t' feel as though you are powerless again'—" she paused not wishing to say "men" for fear of insulting him—"an enemy."

"Bruce Campbell will never touch you again, Grace. You need not fear him."

So he had noticed how uncomfortable the man's presence made her. "Aye. I know. I dinna wish t' be a source of discord between you. Think no more about it."

He raised a dark brow.

She offered him an uncertain smile, and, catching a glimpse of Lady Mary as she disappeared up the steps to her room, sighed. "I must go. Lady Mary will be awaiting me."

"'Twill be midday before I will return t' the castle from patrolling the valley. Will you meet me at my cottage? I have something for you there."

The idea of being alone with him stole her breath. What if he wanted more—once they were alone? She had thus avoided—more—with anyone.

Since she was under Lord Alexander's protection, serving as Lady Mary's maid, she knew that assured the men would always be careful in how they treated her. And as Lady Mary's personal servant, she held an added advantage. The men might look, talk and even grab, but they would not use force for fear of reprisal.

Gabriel had been patient and caring with Tira's son, and the village children always flocked to him to be lifted high and swung about. The other women in the village oft watched him longingly.

But for the moment, he wanted her. She saw it in the way he looked at her, heard it in the way his voice grew husky when they spoke.

And Gabriel would do nothing to hurt her. "Aye. I will meet you there."

GABRIEL WATCHED THE gentle sway of Grace's hips as she climbed the stairs.

She was so untried. So innocent. And he, a warrior more than ten years her senior, had seen too much, experienced too much. What did the lass see in him to offer him such trust?

His eyes dropped to her untouched food. She'd barely nibbled a crust of bread after the talk of war had interrupted their meal. Concern and fear had been plainly written on her face as she'd gazed up at him.

If the call came and Alexander Campbell answered it, Gabriel would follow. He had no other choice. He owed the man his loyalty, his life. Alexander had taken him as an untried boy and taught him how to survive. And now he provided him with food, shelter, and a place in this valley to call home.

But Grace deserved a man who could stay with her, warm her bed, help with raising their bairns—not a warrior who would follow his lord into battle. And mayhap, in doing so, lose his life on the battlefield.

The kind thing to do would be to end her hopes and dreams now, before her affections grew too strong.

Everything in him rose up in protest at the thought. To deliberately hurt her…

And to deny her desires would mean he would have to toss away his own. And he could not deny he wanted her.

She'd wasted no words that first day. She wanted marriage, a guidesman who would offer her shelter and security. And affection.

In the beginning, burning with the first rush of desire, he'd taken up the gauntlet.

But now with the rumblings of war on the horizon…

"Gabriel. Do you mean t' sit about all day dreamin', or will you be joinin' us?" Artair asked.

"Aye, I am coming." He rose from his seat, scooped up the slice of bread Grace had barely touched, finished it in three large bites and washed it down with milk. Gabriel motioned toward the group of seven men who sat together at one of the large wooden tables. They rose as a group, collected their weapons, and filed out the tall doors of the great hall to the courtyard beyond.

"He has gone daft over a wee lass," Bruce Campbell said with a grin as he elbowed him in the ribs.

Unwilling to be the brunt of his teasing, Gabriel shot him a frown. "'Tis the rumblings of change that concern me, Bruce. With the king's death comes uncertainty."

"It does no good t' dwell on somethin' you canna change," Artair said. "What comes will happen whether you dwell on it or nay. 'Tis better t' live each day as it dawns and be grateful t' be alive and breathin'."

Artair spoke the truth. Gabriel's duty was to keep the clan safe. He needed to take one moment at a time. But should he and Grace decide to wed, what would happen if he were killed?

What would she do then?

As long as Alexander Campbell lived, there would be a place for her here at *Caisteal Sìth*. The thought gave him some peace and eased some of his concerns, but not all his doubts were resolved.

The stable boys were cleaning the stalls. The heavy smell of manure and horses filled the air inside the structure. Gabriel saddled his gelding and led him out into the fresh summer air. The other men straggled out. He mounted his horse and turned it toward the front gate, grinning at the sound of the men rushing to catch up with him.

Outside the castle walls, the loch, blue-violet and deep, stretched down the valley. Gabriel paused to breathe in the scent of lush greenery and the water before turning his mount west. They worked their way along the loch's banks and looked for signs of trouble. Nearly a league into their patrol Gabriel recognized the subtle traces of others having passed close by. He paused to dismount and knelt to study the tracks pressed in a patch of mud, his eyes narrowed against the late morning sun. "They have turned east but are in no hurry," he said to the men sitting astride their horses. "Mayhap they are passing through and dinna mean t' stop. But they will pass close t' the village."

"Do we sound the alarm then, Gabriel?" Tobias asked.

"Nay not yet. But we will catch up t' them and discover who they are and what they are about. If it's mischief they are bent on, we will 'encourage' them to leave Campbell land."

GRACE PAUSED AT the window and strained to see the sun's position through the obscuring clouds. Gabriel would be hungry when he returned. She had packed her basket with some of the cold meat and bread from the castle kitchen and a large wedge of cheese she had purchased from the village dairy. She reached for her tartan shawl and wrapped it around her shoulders.

She ran her hand over the handle of the basket. Since she'd had no family, she had learned that gifts were a rare and wondrous thing. Since coming to her service, Lady Mary had given her small things, on special occasions, and she treasured every one. But the basket coming from Gabriel meant *much* more. He had given it to her after she had destroyed the last one by hitting him with it. She smiled as she recalled that afternoon. When he'd insulted her, it had seemed to please him that her reaction had not been meek or mild. And she had captured his interest.

If she hoped to keep his favor, she had to overcome some of the uncertainty she felt when near him. Squaring her small shoulders with determination, she took up the basket and left her room. Her feet flew down the narrow stairs as she made her way to the great hall. She suppressed the urge to skip as she let herself out the side door and wandered through the front gate on her way to the village. Her heart raced more from the fact that she would be seeing him than from her eager flight.

She slowed when the path reached the village, lest she appear conspicuous in her eagerness. She paused atop the rise that led down to Gabriel's small cottage and smiled when she spied a lone horse tied to one of the small shrubs outside his door.

He was here waiting for her. Heat from excitement flushed her cheeks and her breathing quickened. She controlled the urge to run, but by the time she arrived at the small rock-paved patch of ground in front of the doorstep, she was out of breath anyway.

Pausing a moment and smoothed back the fine feathery strands that brushed her forehead, she once again straightened her shoulders, tapped at the solid wood door, and after a brief pause it swung inward. A stranger stood before her, his clothing worn and dirty, his jaw unshaven and his hair askew. A frown touched her brow. "Who—?"

The man grabbed her arm, jerked her into the house and slammed the door.

THE LONGER GABRIEL followed the trail, the more his stomach knotted. Grace? Had she gone to his cottage? If she had, she would be alone. And in the direct path of the riders. He tapped his heels against his mount's flanks and quickened the pace.

Half a league away from the castle the invader's trail turned toward the village. Gabriel kicked his mount into a gallop and the men followed suit, falling into single file behind him. Gabriel's horse stretched out, his powerful haunches bunching beneath him, his hooves sending up clods of mud. Gabriel bent over the animal's neck as they dodged beneath branches on the narrow path. The pounding of the horse's hooves mirrored the rapid beat of his heart and seemed to whisper hurry-hurry-hurry. With every fiber of his being, Gabriel focused on getting to the village and his cottage as quickly as possible.

GRACE PERCHED ON the edge of the wooden chair. Her eyes darted around the room frantically in search of anything she could use to defend herself. His hands had roamed over her body while he searched for a weapon, and he had found and taken her small dagger. She shuddered against the crawling sensation his touch had left behind. He had pawed her hair, her cheek and even squeezed her breasts while she fought against him. He had been intent on more until he'd seen the food in the basket.

The man across from her stuffed half a chunk of bread into his mouth, followed by huge bite of ham. His cheeks bulged. His jaw flexed and she glimpsed bits of half-masticated food as he chewed noisily with his mouth open, smacking meaningfully when he glanced her way. She looked away, sickened by the greedy way he ate. He looked at her, as though he thought of ways he might take a bite out of her.

The stench emanating from him of horses, sweat and other foul things filled the small hut. Her stomach roiled and she pressed a hand to her lips.

"Where would yer man be?"

"He has gone t' the castle and will return in a short while."

The man raised the tankard of ale, drank deeply, slammed it down and swiped at his mouth with a shirtsleeve stiff with filth.

"What business does he have there?" He flipped a sliver of meat into his mouth then sucked the grease from a finger embedded with dirt.

Bile crept up her throat; she swallowed it back and raised her chin. "He is one of Alexander Campbell's men."

His hand came to rest on the dagger next to the bowl from which he ate.

"You are on Campbell land, stealing Campbell food. He winna be pleased."

An ugly smile spread across the man's face, revealing teeth black with decay. "I will stick him like a pig. And then I will stick you with something more impressive than this dagger."

Grace shivered. Once the food was gone, he would do just that. Her heart shrank with fear. "I have some cheese." She rose and reached for the basket. He leaped to his feet and tore it from her grasp. The wedge of cheese tumbled to the floor and he snatched it up. Grace shoved against his shoulder, sending him tumbling back into the chair. He rocked back, his boot hitting the table, and it jumped, sending his tankard over the edge and spilling milk across the hard-packed dirt floor.

Grace lunged for the door, and jerked up the latch.

Gripping the edge of the table, the man lunged to his feet. In two strides, he was on her. She heaved the solid door back and hit him in the face.

He gave a startled yelp, but his fist gripped the tartan she had looped around her shoulders. She jerked free of the cloth and wiggled out the door, pulling it shut behind her. A misty drizzle fell, wetting the stone walkway embedded in the clay before the cottage. Her shoes slid on their slick surface and she waved her arms for balance as she danced to keep her footing.

The man's bellow of rage echoed behind her and spurred her faster toward the village. Her slippers sank in a marshy spot at the base of the hill and she jerked her feet free, leaving her shoes behind, and took to the path in her stocking feet. A stone bit into the ball of her foot and she stumbled. She gritted her teeth, and, hiking her skirts up to her knees, ran for all she was worth.

Midway up the slope, her skirt was grabbed from behind and the full weight of her attacker struck her in the small of her back, slamming her forward and down. The heavy bulk of the man drove the breath from her lungs. One large hand pressed down between her shoulder blades, holding her face-down in the mud, while the other wrestled with her skirts.

She wiggled like a seal, a shriek of outrage and terror tearing from her as she clawed at the sparse grass on the path in an attempt to break free. When he touched her thigh, she screamed and heaved upward, dread twisting her stomach.

"Did you think you could leave without serving me, lass? Is that how you treat a guest?" he hissed against her neck. His rank breath made her gag. His hand shoved against her thigh making room for his knee.

The sound of horse's hooves was almost lost beneath the heavy beat of her heart and her cries of denial. A large chestnut horse topped the rise above, its hooves cutting into the mud and shooting up clumps of muck as he pounded down the hill toward them.

The man swore and staggered to his feet. Grace rolled off the path just in time to avoid the horse as it thundered past. A large figure launched himself from the back of the animal and struck the marauder chest-high, and the two toppled like trees and rolled down the hill.

GABRIEL STRADDLED THE fallen man and hammered punch after punch into his face. With every blow he recalled Grace clawing at the ground, struggling to escape, and the man between her thighs about to rape her. As the man's attempts to defend himself ceased, the red haze that filled Gabriel's vision slowly dissipated.

He became aware of Grace's fingers digging into his arm, "You must stop, Gabriel." Her cheeks and hair were muddied, her clothing sodden and caked with filth as well. Tears streamed down her cheeks.

His fingers, stiff from being clenched, were reluctant to straighten as he released his grip on the man. He flexed them while he fought the urge to continue pounding the wretch's face into the ground. His knuckles were red with blood, his own and the other man's. He wiped them off on her attacker's shirt, leaving streaks across the grungy fabric.

A single rider trotted down the hill. Gabriel staggered to his feet. Artair looked down at the man's limp form. "You didna save any for the rest of us, Gabriel. You have left a trail behind you. Have you killed this one, then?"

"Nay, he still breathes," Grace said. "He can be taken t' the castle and given care."

Gabriel turned at her words, but bit back his protest.

"Are you hurt, lass?" Artair asked, a frown wrinkling his broad forehead.

She hugged herself and shook her head. "Nay. I fell in the mud."

She shook. Her braid hung wet, and muddy clumped against her shoulder. Her large gray eyes looked dark and haunted.

Had the man hurt her? The thought triggered a sick feeling in the pit of Gabriel's stomach.

"Warm yourself inside the cottage, Grace. I will accompany you t' the castle once we have taken the thieves t' Lord Alexander."

After a brief pause, she turned and limped down the path to the hut.

Gabriel took a step after her, then hesitated, torn between duty and desire.

"You have done enough, Gabriel. See to the lass. We will haul this vermin to the castle with the rest." Artair's gaze followed Grace's progress down the hill, his features grave. "Did he harm her?"

"Nay. But he meant to."

Artair spat on the ground. "I will take my time seeing him t' the castle. Mayhap he will die and leave the rest of us better off without him."

Gabriel shot him a look and a nod. "I will see t' Grace and take her t' Lady Mary."

Gabriel snatched up his horse's reins and tugged him down the hill. He found Grace's shoes stuck in the mud and his jaw tightened. It was no wonder she limped. He bent and pulled the slippers free.

He secured his mount inside the small shed at one side of the hut, and, dipping a bucket of water from the barrel next to the door, dunked her shoes into it until the worst of the mud dropped away. He set them aside, and paused to wash his hands until his knuckles stung. He ignored the discomfort and filled another bucket, then knocked before entering the cottage, lest he startle her.

Grace opened the door, her expression anxious. She held a cloth in her hand and had wiped her face clean.

Feeling awkward he held up the bucket. "I have brought more water."

She stepped back for him to enter.

His gaze swept the room, settling on the bed for a moment. Its surface looked as it had when he'd left. He had actually spread the covers into some kind of order. So, at least he had not assaulted her there. Aside from an unpleasant smell, the rest of the cottage looked as it usually did. The remnants of some bread and meat lay on the table.

"He ate the food I brought," her voice wobbled.

He had to ask. Not knowing for certes was like lye eating at his insides. "He didna harm you?"

"Nay. You came—in time."

Relief raced through him in a wave and he drew a deep breath. He stepped forward to pour the water into the large pot on the fireplace and set the bucket down. He went into the bedroom area of the small cottage and retrieved the shirt she had mended not too long ago. "I will go t' the castle and ask Lady Mary t' gather you some clean clothes." He offered her the shirt and she took it. "There is a pelt there at the foot of the bed." He pointed toward the animal skin. 'Twill keep you warm until I return."

He should have arrived here sooner. He should have protected her. He turned to leave.

"Thank you, Gabriel."

He glanced back over his shoulder. The uncertainty in her expression drove him toward her. He crushed her close, cupped her chin, and raised her face to his. Though he wanted to clamp his mouth to hers and kiss her until the gut-clenching guilt and helplessness passed, with an effort he set aside his own needs to see to hers. He pressed his lips against her forehead. When she slipped an arm about his waist and clung closer, he tightened his hold.

THE DOOR CLOSED behind Gabriel with a snap. Grace drew a deep frustrated breath and shook her head. He had wiped away all the horrible moments and made her feel safe simply by holding her. That had ended when he jerked away and took his leave.

She turned and caught her reflection in the small metal disk over the washbowl in the kitchen that Gabriel used as a mirror and grimaced. Mayhap even his bravery had limits. Her hair, matted with mud, hung in clumps over her shoulder. Streaked with filth and moisture, her kirtle and surcoat clung to her skin.

She went to the heavy door, released the catch, and waved it back and forth to clear the room of the disgusting smell left behind by the intruder. She scooped up the scraps from his meal and tossed them out into the yard. By the time she'd done both, the water was warm enough to pour into the washbowl. She found a threadbare cloth with which to dry herself, stripped her clothing, and scrubbed every inch of her skin, paying close attention to every spot the man had touched. Though the soap and water could not take away the memories, the act of washing rid her of the worst of her lingering reaction to the attack. Next, she worked her braid free and washed her hair. She had just finished rinsing it when a knock came upon the door.

"'Tis me, Grace." Gabriel's voice came from outside.

She quickly wrung the water from the long strands, tugged Gabriel's shirt over her head, and then wrapped the cloth about her head.

Though covered to her knees, she was aware of her bare calves and feet. The shirt clung to her water damp skin. She stood behind the door as she opened it.

Rain poured from the cottage eaves onto the floor. Gabriel stepped in and shut the door. He tugged free of the sodden tartan that covered his shoulders and hung it on a peg at the door. "Lady Mary sent clean clothes, as you wished."

"Thank you for collectin' them for me, Gabriel." Embarrassed by her lack of dress, Grace went to the fire, perched upon a small stool and pulled the shirt down over her bare legs. Unwrapping her hair, she finger-combed the wavy strands to dry them.

Gabriel strode to the bed, upended the sack he carried, and shook the contents out on the tartan there. He picked up her shift and set it aside, then her kirtle, and snapped up something from among the rest.

Seeing him touch her things with such familiarity brought heat to her cheeks. All she had were plain, serviceable garments she had sewn herself. For once she wished for something softer with fancy trim that would catch his eye.

Water dripped from his dark hair as he approached the fire. "Lady Mary sent some salve for your foot and strips to bind it."

Grace offered him the cloth she had used, though it remained damp from her service. "Dry yourself, Gabriel. My foot will wait."

He set aside the small crock and bundled strips to wipe his face and dry his hair, then draped the rag across the back of a chair. His heavy sword made a hollow sound as he laid it on the table. He unlaced his leather jerkin, peeled it away, and tossed it onto one of the rough-woven seats. His shirtsleeves clung to his muscular arms, still wet. When he knelt before her, Grace straightened in surprise.

"Are you truly whole, lass?" His brown gaze, dark with concern, traced her features.

"Aye. I am. Except for the wee cut on my foot, I am the same as I was this morn when we broke our fast together."

His features relaxed. He sat on the stone hearth and rubbed a hand over his beard-covered jaw. His knuckles were red and swollen from the fight. His hair, still wet, hung against his cheeks. Mud splattered his boots and the knees of his trews. Yet he made no move to see to his own needs.

A wave of tenderness drove Grace to retrieve the washbowl from the small table, and, returning to the fireplace, she poured some of the hot water from the pot on the hearth into it. "Come sit at the table and put your hands into the water, Gabriel. 'Twill ease the soreness and the swelling."

His gaze meander from her bare feet, over her calves, then upward. With every inch, it became harder for her to take a full breath, and her mouth grew progressively drier. A sweet ache blossomed in the secret parts of her body. He rose to his feet and the feeling increased. By the time he reached the table, her body clamored for his touch.

His fingers brushed the hem of the shirt she wore. Her knee tingled at the closeness of his fingers, though he never made contact. It took all her control to remain motionless, though the desire to be closer threatened to overwhelm her.

"You are a sweet sight, Grace. A temptation t' me." Gabriel's voice was soft and husky. "'Twould be best for us both for you to dress while I am thus distracted."

Warmth surged into her face and she nodded. She limped to the bed and found her shift. What would it be like to have a man with so kind a nature share her body? She saw the glow on Lady Mary's face when Lord Alexander was near. Their public expressions of affection were few, but she had observed the way his hand lingered at her waist when they walked together. How he cupped her shoulder when he rested his arm on the back of her chair. In his conduct, his love for her was there for all to see.

'Tis that and more I want. But how can I get it? And what is it they share that brings such a light to their eyes?

Grace drew the shirt up over her head and dropped it upon the bed. She glanced over her shoulder. Gabriel would not dishonor her by looking, but the tense set of his shoulders told her he wanted to. She smiled.

How would she feel if he saw her like this? Warmth flooded her body and the intimate, taunting need he inspired intensified. Such new and wondrous feelings set her hands to shaking and made them clumsy as she slipped her shift on over her head, then her kirtle. Her skin felt tight, the fabric rough against it. When she tugged her surcoat into place she realized, for the first time, how restricting clothing could be.

GABRIEL FORCED HIS gaze to remain on the bowl of water before him. The heat did ease the pain of his bruised knuckles, but did nothing to lessen the taut, aching desire that had settled low in his belly. With every whisper of fabric behind him, he imagined what Grace looked like without it. She had been unaware of how the light from the fire outlined her figure beneath his shirt, showing the curve of her hip. And as she'd bent to fill the bowl with water, it had offered him a glimpse of the womanly shape of her breasts. Her normal, modest dress covered her from neck to wrist, to ankle. The hint of what lay beneath now joined the memory of her nestled in the clump of flowers atop the hill when they had first truly met.

One day they would make love together with the summer sun warming their limbs, the smell of those hyacinth blossoms crushed beneath their weight, and he would touch every inch of her.

"I lost my slippers in the mud, Gabriel."

"They are just outside the door. I will get them for you." He rose, grateful for the distraction. The rain had eased, but the fine mist that now fell cooled his heated cheeks. When he returned inside, she had gathered the salve and bandages Lady Mary had sent. She sat at the table, her skirts tucked between her legs as she attempted to tend the wound on her foot.

"I can do that for you, Grace."

He took the cloth from her, tugged the chair out from the table to sit, and, grasping her ankle, lifted her foot onto his thigh. The wound was not a cut, but a deep puncture in the arch. He cleaned it as gently as possible. Then slathered the ointment on the injury and bound it with the strips. He rested his fingers around her foot while his thumb kneaded the pad just beneath her toes. He looked up. She bit her lip. He moved his thumb again and she jerked her foot free.

"Are you ticklish, Grace?"

She smiled, but avoided his eyes. "I winna allow you to devil me about it." She turned her back to put on her stockings. "'Twill be time for the evening meal. Are you not eager t' sup?"

"Aye, lass." He would have preferred it if they could have shared a quiet meal here together. But the bastard who had invaded his hut had seen to ruining that.

She bobbed up, and, gathering her muddy things, stuffed them into the sack Lady Mary had used to carry Grace's clean clothes. "Lady Mary will be waiting for me." Her fingers flew as she braided her hair into a long tail and tied the end with a wet strip of ribbon lying on the table.

Gabriel wiped her slippers as clean as he could. The leather was saturated from the water, though, and when it dried, would be stiff. He frowned. Did she have another pair of slippers to wear? These needed to be reworked and softened. How could he ask without causing offense?

Grace accepted the slippers from him. "Thank you for cleaning them for me." She dropped them to the floor and pushed her feet in.

"They will need to be reworked, Grace."

She nodded. "Aye, I can feel that."

For the first time he noticed her gown. The dark brown sur-coat leached the color from her skin and hung loose about her figure. Her tan kirtle blended with her light brown hair. Though, now that he looked closely, he could see that light reflected off the strands captured a hint of red in them.

Did she purposely hide herself away? How would she look in a bit of color? Mayhap the same color as her gray-blue eyes. A garment that would follow the slender curves he had discovered this eve, courtesy of a chance bit of firelight.

He wiped the mud from his trews and boots, then scrubbed his hands. Without thinking, he unlaced the neck of his damp shirt, and pulled it free of his trews. He used the garment to finish drying his hair, wadded it and tossed it on the bed. He turned and picked up the shirt Grace had worn earlier. She watched him, her gaze on his bare chest. Then her eyes rose to his face, and hot color stained her cheeks. She lowered her eyes, but not before he caught the avid glow of interest and something more in her expression.

Did it stir her to passion, knowing he donned a garment that had touched her bare skin and still retained the fragrance of the soap she had bathed with, and of her? The depth of his own reaction was evident when he turned aside to unlace his trews and tuck the shirt beneath them. With her standing so close, it was painful to lace them again. How could he respond so to just her scent, when she had not even touched him?

When he turned, he found Grace had wiped the mud from his leather tunic and stood waiting with the jerkin in her hands. She held it for him and he slid into it and did up the laces.

It was when they were astride his horse, with Grace tucked before him, that Gabriel realized how little they had said to one another the whole time they had been in the cabin together. It seemed the passion this shy lass inspired tied his tongue in clumsy knots and stole words from his mind. How was he to court her, if he could not find the words?

THE PRICK OF a knife against her neck and the harsh pressure of an arm against her throat dragged Grace deeper beneath the surface of her dreams. She fought again and again to break free of their hold, but each time she reached toward wakefulness they pulled her back down. She woke to find the dawn upon her and groaned with relief. Groggy and unrested, she dragged herself from bed and dressed for the day.

In the three days since the attack, fear had grown and taken root in her mind. The attack of a fever-crazed prisoner months ago had blended with what had happened at Gabriel's hut and caused the terrible dreams. Mayhap if she faced the reason behind them she could rid herself of both the fear and the dreams.

Lady Mary had at one time faced down the MacDonalds, who had tried to kill her husband. If her mistress was strong enough to confront her enemies, then Grace, too, could do so.

She braided her hair, her fingers made clumsy by nerves. She would speak to Lady Mary about it. The bell rang for her to go down to her Lord and Lady's bedchamber, and she hurried to put on her stockings and shoes.

The shoes were another reminder of the attack, for they had stiffened as they dried. Now they pinched her toes when she walked. She would have to take them to the cobbler in the village for the leather to be reworked and a new pair fashioned.

While she helped Lady Mary dress, Grace broached the subject of facing her fears with her.

"Aye, it may help you to face the man who has caused you such distress, Grace," Lady Mary said after a few moments thought. "Although I winna wish you to do anythin' that causes you more hurt than you have already suffered." She turned to look into Grace's eyes while she laced the front of her gown. She grasped her hands and held them still. "'Tis both terrifying and powerful to face down those who have made you feel less than who you are. I would not be the woman I am had I not done so. I dinna believe Alexander and I would have found the happiness together we have had I not chosen that journey. But there is pain in traveling that path, too." She released her grip and offered Grace an encouraging smile.

Grace nodded and took up Lady Mary's shoes, running a

damp cloth over them while her mistress donned her stockings. Lady Mary had stood up to her own clan, as well as the Campbells she now lived among. The men and women had learned to love and respect her because of her courage and her kindness.

Grace could do the same and perhaps uproot some of her cowardice and sow as many seeds of courage.

Before they left the chamber to go below, Mary said, "There is time for you to decide. I will not be going down to visit the man until after we break the fast. If you decide against accompanying me, Marta may go in your stead, as she did yesterday."

"I am grateful for your understanding, m'lady."

Lady Mary nodded and they went down together.

Two hours later, her decision made, Grace kept her eyes on Lady Mary's back as they descended the stairs to the chambers beneath the castle. For three days she had avoided her duty. She would no longer make excuses.

Dank blocks of stone lined both sides of the narrow passageway. With every step, her breathing quickened and panic built within her. She breathed deep and attempted to push it back.

When they reached the bottom of the stairs, Grace paused to take in her surroundings. She adjusted the heavy satchel, looping it over her shoulder so it did not cut so deep. Pitch torches, set at intervals along the walls, lit the way, but also cast deep shadows. No sound penetrated from above, and silence bounced against the stones, so profound it hurt her ears. The place smelled of damp earth, the oily scent of burning pitch, and an undercurrent of human waste.

"Come this way," Lady Mary instructed as she turned right and proceeded down a wide passageway. The flickering light from the torches danced upon the stone walls, fanned by the air they stirred with their passing.

Grace concentrated on Lady Mary's long, blonde braid, and attempted to block out the fear shoved high in her chest, making her breathing uneven and causing her stomach to cramp. They came out into a large, open room. Along the walls were several heavy wooden doors with small barred windows. In the center of the chamber sat a small trestle table with two sturdy benches.

Two men sat there, but rose as soon as the women entered. Artair bobbed his head in greeting. From the width of his shoulders and his height, Grace recognized Gabriel even before he turned. The tightness in her chest eased. Having him near weakened the fear's power over her.

Gabriel's features blanked at seeing her, then a scowl darkened his features. "Grace, what are you about here?"

The dreams were not something she could share with him. Would he, a warrior, think her a coward for even having them? "'Tis my duty t' accompany Lady Mary when she sees t' the sick."

His jaw tensed and a scowl darkened his features. His gaze shifted to Lady Mary. "'You are here t' see the man who hurt Grace?"

"Aye, we are."

"I would speak to you in private a moment, m'lady."

Mary raised a blonde brow at the request, but gave a brief nod.

His intent to protest her presence here was obvious. Grace stepped forward. "Would you ask Lord Alexander to relieve you of your duty, Gabriel?"

A look of outrage flickered across his features. "Nay. But you dinna need—I would spare you ever seeing the man again."

"You will do that as soon as you escort him from Campbell land. But he must be well enough to ride. I wish to help Lady Mary see to him and speed him on his way."

"You will be there t' see he doesna harm us, Gabriel," Lady Mary said.

His jaw grew taut. "Aye, I will." He nodded. His gaze shifted back to Grace. That he wished to say more on the subject was written in every taut muscle of his body.

He snatched up keys from the table and strode to one of the heavy wooden cell doors. "I will speak to him afore you tend him." Grabbing a torch from outside the door, he ducked inside and closed the door.

His deep voice carried easily to them. "Offer insult or threat

to either of these women, and you will not live t' see the morrow."
The resolve in his tone made Grace's heart stutter.

Lady Mary gave her arm a squeeze. "The man will do nothing
with such a threat hanging over him."

"'Tis not you or me I fear for, but Gabriel. For now the threat
is made, he will be honor bound to see it through."

"Aye, they are both aware of that."

Why did men feel every action had to be connected to their
honor? Gabriel was sworn to protect Lady Mary. He had decided
to protect her as well. And she was thrilled by his choice. But what
price would he himself pay for that decision if he had to kill an
unarmed man?

Gabriel swung open the door and motioned them in. Grace
drew a deep breath and gathered her courage. Her feet seemed
weighted with dread and fear. With an effort, she forced first one
foot forward, then the next, and followed Lady Mary over the
threshold.

The torch Gabriel held shed only a small pool of light around
him. He moved to stand at the head of the small cot and raised the
torch aloft. Lady Mary moved close and placed a hand against the
man's forehead. Grace avoided looking at him as she took a small
basin and waterskin from the satchel, then poured the fluid into
the wooden bowl. Lady Mary bent over the man and bathed his
face.

Grace hazarded a glance and almost gasped. One eye was
nearly swollen shut, the other appeared puffy, and both were
purple with bruising. The right side of his jaw was swollen and
misshapen.

Though in the confines of the hut he had appeared at least
eight stone in weight and a head taller than she, he seemed to have
shrunk in the three days he had been confined.

Lady Mary glanced over her shoulder. "I need the cup and the
willow bark tea we brewed, Grace." She turned to Gabriel. "Can
you raise him so he might drink?"

He stepped forward and with little effort raised the man's
shoulders with one hand. Grace retrieved the small, sealed crock

of tea and poured the fluid into the cup and extended it to Mary. The man groaned and held his side while he swallowed the tea. Grace was moved to pity, for he seemed in great pain.

"This will give you ease," Lady Mary said. She nodded to Gabriel and he lowered the man back to the straw pillow. "We will leave the water and cloth. You may place it over your eyes like a compress and 'twill ease the swelling."

He raised a hand in understanding but did not speak.

Grace set the bowl close to him on the floor and placed the cloth next to his hand on the wooden frame of the cot. She glanced at his face. Though he remained silent, sullen anger marked his expression.

Grace's heart drummed in her throat and the air seemed to grow thick. Her hands shook as she packed away the crock, cup, and waterskin before following Lady Mary from the cell. Gabriel ducked beneath the low lintel and joined them outside the chamber. He shoved the torch into the metal sconce outside, shut the door and locked it.

"Once the swelling subsides he will be more comfortable. He needs t' drink more of the tea. We will prepare it and have one of the servants bring it down." Mary said. "His ribs will take longer to heal."

Satisfaction flickered across Gabriel's expression, then he nodded. "I will see he drinks the tea."

Mary motioned for Grace to follow her.

"Might I have a brief word with Gabriel and Artair, Lady Mary?" Grace asked.

"Aye. I will be in the nursery tending Kieran."

"I will only be a moment."

Grace paused next to Gabriel. She had survived two violent attacks in the last two years. The first man was dead, though his foul deeds had been resurrected in her dreams, and the man they had just tended was injured, but the enmity she had read in his face was not the emotion of a cowed prisoner. "Dinna tend him alone, Gabriel. He is hurt, but a hurt animal is more dangerous than a healthy one."

"Aye he is. 'Twas why I didna wish Lady Mary or you near him."

"I will speak to her and try t' dissuade her from tending him again."

He nodded and the taut line of his mouth relaxed somewhat.

Her attention shifted to Artair. "I will depend on you t' see he doesna risk himself, Artair."

The man grinned. "I will do my best, lass." He shot Gabriel a smirk and earned a narrow-eyed glance in return.

"Come, let me walk you to the stairs," Gabriel said. He looped his fingers through the handle of the satchel that rested on her shoulder and hiked it onto his own.

His large hand rested against the small of her back all the way down the passageway. That coveted gesture of care triggered a warm glow that settled inside her chest and brought a flush to her cheeks.

"What has pleased you so, Grace?" Gabriel asked.

"How do you ken I am pleased?" she asked and stepped upon the first stair.

"'Tis in your smile."

She turned to face him and realized that, for once, they were nearly eye-to-eye. She rested a hand against his leather tunic and felt the strength of his chest beneath her hand. "'Tis you who please me, Gabriel."

Instead of smiling, he grew serious. He dropped the bag upon the step beside her. And when his arm went around her and drew her close, her heart beat a wild tattoo. His fingers lingered against her cheek, while his eyes focused on her face with a look so intent she struggled to get a full breath.

"Will you reward me with a kiss?" Gabriel asked.

Grace bit her lip. She had never kissed a man before. Gabriel had kissed her. Uncertainty brought heat to her cheeks. What if she did it wrong and he were repelled by her attempt?

This was what she wanted. She wanted—She did not know what she wanted. She just knew that when they were together, she wanted to curl around him and get as close as she could. Her hands slid up his chest and her arms went around his neck. She studied his lips. They were not too full, nor too thin, but surrounded by the darkness of his beard, looked so...inviting.

Gabriel's arm tightened around her, aligning her body more closely to his. "Grace."

Encouraged by the husky note in his voice, she leaned forward and pressed her mouth to his. His lips parted and his tongue touched the seam between hers. A trembling heat settled low in her belly and her lips parted, too. Her tongue touched his, and that trembling heat grew into a torrid ache between her legs. The ache intensified as their tongues tangled. She pressed closer. It took all her control not to move against him. Did he feel the same way?

Grace drew back to look into Gabriel's face, seeing that his brown eyes were dark and his cheeks flushed.

"Will you meet me later at my cottage?" Gabriel's lips brushed her cheek, her jaw.

With every touch of his lips the feeling grew more intense. "The nursemaid has delivered a babe, and I must care for Kieran for a week or two." Her voice sounded breathy and weak.

Gabriel groaned and drew back to kiss her long and hard. When he finally released her, Grace swayed upon the step, her legs weak. Gabriel grinned and steadied her. "I have a wee gift for you. I meant to give it to you a few days ago but the time wasna right." He removed a pouch from his belt, opened it, and poured something out into his palm.

Grace caught her breath as he held up the delicate strand of pearls. They seemed to catch the flickering light of the torches and glow with warmth.

"I have been saving these for a while and I took them into the village to Bowen Campbell. He is old as a Druid stone, but he still has a talent for making a pretty strand. Turn around and I will fasten them about your neck, Grace."

"Are you sure you mean them for me, Gabriel?" Something so beautiful must surely be too special for her.

"Would I be offering them t' you, if I didna mean for you t' have them, lass? They are fresh water pearls and not as perfect as some I have seen at court. But they say if you wear them against your skin 'twill keep them shiny and fine."

"They are beautiful, Gabriel. 'Tis truly the most beautiful necklace I have ever seen." She blinked back the tears that blurred her vision and shuffled around on the step to present her back for fear he would see her cry. She held her braid aside as he draped the necklace around her neck and fastened it. His fingers, warm and gentle, rested against her nape for a moment, then dropped away. She turned around. "How do they look?"

"Almost as fine as the woman who is wearing them."

She knew there were shadows beneath her eyes from lack of sleep, but that he said it anyway gave her a sweet rush of pleasure. "Thank you, Gabriel. I have never owned anything so fine."

He cupped her face in his warrior's hands and kissed her gently. "Mayhap when I gather mollusks again there will be enough for a bracelet to match."

"This is enough." She touched the strand with her fingertips. Her arms circled his neck and she held him close then brushed his cheek with her lips. "I must go. Lady Mary will be waiting for me."

"Why did you come down here this morn, Grace?" he asked.

She studied his features for a moment. Would he think her a coward? "I came to face my fear and break its hold."

Gabriel frowned. "And did you succeed?"

"I dinna know, but at least I tried." She smiled. "When will you teach me to shoot a bow?"

He ran a hand down the long braid that hung over her shoulder. "Soon."

GABRIEL WATCHED AS Grace climbed the stairs, the heavy bag draped over her shoulder. As soon as she disappeared around a curve in the stairwell, he pivoted and started down the passageway back to the cells.

She had been pleased with the necklace. And he was well pleased with her courage. But why had she not shared those fears with him? He had oft been able to read others' thoughts and feelings through their expressions, but mostly because they did not hold anything back. But Grace held her thoughts and feelings close.

Knowing of Lady Mary's intended visit, he had made a point of being here. He was doubly glad he had done so since Grace had accompanied her. He had read both fear and pity in her expression while they tended the prisoner. But she had stood fast and faced the man.

"How fares Grace?" Artair asked when Gabriel returned to the table.

"She is well."

"That is good. She's a wee fine lass. You could do worse."

Gabriel raised a brow.

"Now that you have drawn attention to the her, there are others who are showing interest."

Gabriel's jaw tensed. "If you are trying t' stir trouble Artair, I warn you again' it."

"No trouble. Just a friendly warning. The lass has matured, and the men have noticed it. You would do well t' claim the lass and wed her afore you find yourself pushed aside by one more eager t' offer for her."

Offer for her? Gabriel stared at the man. It had only been a few weeks since they had kissed upon the keep steps. Why was everyone so eager to push him to wed?

"Connor has a larger cottage. And Craig has the sheep, and his son needs a *mathair*. All lasses want t' be *mathairs*, lad."

Had those two been hanging about Grace? When? And how had he not noticed?

"'Twould serve you well t' make up your mind whether you are intent on a bit of swivving with an innocent lass, or you mean t' honor her with a more permanent place in your bed and your home."

Heat raced up into his face and his temper flared. "'Twould serve you to mind your own affairs, old man."

"I have a soft spot for the lass m'self. Mayhap I should try my luck, too."

Gabriel stilled the urge to grab Artair by the throat and give him a fearsome shake.

Artair grinned and rose to his feet. "I have no roof t' offer her as you do. But for such a lass, I'd be tempted t' rectify that. She could keep my old bones warm, give me children, and care for me when I grow too old t' care for m'self."

Gabriel made a dismissive gesture with his hand. "She would soon grow tired of the sound of your complaints and toss you out."

"She chose you, Gabriel. But that doesna mean you will win her. Certes, you would do well to keep a sharp eye open and cease meandering about when a more direct route is open to you."

One moment Artair was threatening to pursue Grace himself and the next offering him advice. The man was fickle.

As for himself. Was the promise of bedding an innocent lass what had piqued his interest, or was it because he was at last ready to take a wife?

Grace had made it clear a wife was what she wanted to be. Not a temporary partner in his bed. He had accepted her wishes. But had that truly been what rested in his mind and heart? Which was the point Artair was trying to make.

"Sometimes you are a wily old goat, Artair."

The man grinned. "Lad, I have been called worse." He grew somber. "The lass is too good for the two of us. But she chose you, Gabriel."

"She does have the manners and the bearing of a lady. And she said Lady Mary has taught her to read and write."

"A learned wife would be an asset to any man. And of the lot of us, only you could be an asset to her."

Gabriel frowned at his grim tone. "What do you mean, Artair?"

"You are a leader, Gabriel. And she will have need of that one day."

Gabriel started to ask again what he meant, but Artair waved a dismissive hand. "'Twould be nice to have a real lady in your bed, would it not, eh?"

＊

GRACE SETTLED ON the stairs outside the solar. Lady Mary and Lord Alexander spent time alone with Kieran each evening, and the sound of the lad's laughter blended with the deeper sound of Lord Alexander's. Though it was tradition for noblewomen to hire a wet nurse to feed their children, Lady Mary had decided to feed Kieran herself. And now he had outgrown the need to nurse, no matter how busy her day, she never missed an opportunity to spend time with him as oft during the day as she could and each eve before bed.

Half an hour had passed when Lord Alexander stepped out into the hall and, spying Grace, came to join her. "The lad is on his way to sleep," he murmured, his deep voice a rumble in the stairway as he took a seat two stairs above her.

Though Lord Alexander had been nothing but kind to her, she found it difficult to relax entirely around him. Like Gabriel, he was large and physically imposing. His voice held a note of command even when he spoke of trivial things.

"Have you much experience caring for bairns, Grace?" he asked.

"Aye. 'Twas my duty t' care for all the children of the last household in which I stayed. Before—"

Alexander gave a brief nod. "How many were there?" he asked.

"Five."

"What ages were they?"

"Seven, five, three, two and a babe of only six months."

"And you did this alone?"

"Aye, at night."

"The thought alone exhausts me."

Grace stifled a giggle.

Lord Alexander grinned. "I trust my son is in good hands, then."

"I will care for him as though he were my own, m'lord."

He gave a brief nod. "Aye, I ken you will." He rested an arm across his knee. "I have seen you and Gabriel often supping together."

Should he not approve of their association, and told her to cease, what then would she do? "Aye, we have shared a meal or two together of late."

"Though you havena been raised as you should have been, there is still a possibility you may claim your birthright. When first I returned here I petitioned the king to see you receive your just due, but nothing came of it. I could look into it once again."

Grace caught her breath. Fear coursed through her. Her voice shook when she finally found it. "Since I am a woman, the possibility that I should receive anything but unwanted attention is doubtful, m'lord. You might reestablish my name, but what then would come with it? At best, I would mayhap receive some pittance to live on. At worst, I would have kinfolk coming to claim guardianship and direct my future with no regard for my desires. Is that what you wish for me, m'lord?"

Alexander's frown was grim. "Nay, Grace. I but wanted recompense for all you have lost, or at least a measure of justice."

She shook her head. Would it be justice to be shoved into a world she did not understand, and to be treated as nothing more than a pawn to barter. "That world has been closed t' me far too long. I am content with what I have now." And as another thought came to her she clenched her hands in her lap. "Have I become a burden, m'lord? Do you wish me to leave?"

Alexander's frown toppled over into a scowl. "Nay, lass. Not at all. 'Tis the opposite, Grace. You have more than earned your keep."

She drew a deep breath and tucked her hands between her knees to still their trembling. Tears burned her eyes and she turned her face away.

"'Twas not my intent to cause you distress, Grace. And if you have found contentment here, I am pleased. But should your circumstances with Gabriel become more permanent, I would suggest you tell him of your past. You would not wish for him to be taken unaware, should something come of it one day."

Grace bit her lip. Few people here knew of her family, or how she had been forced to live, until Alexander Campbell had been made aware of it. In sending her here, he had fulfilled a favor, but also saved her life.

"I will tell him if it needs be told, m' lord."

"I trust you will." He rose to his feet. "I bid you good eve, Grace. And should Kieran be overly restless, dinna hesitate to wake us."

"Aye, m'lord."

Lord Alexander disappeared up the stairs. Grace curled into a ball, wrapped her arms around her knees, and held on until her trembling ceased and the urge to weep eased.

A few minutes later, Lady Mary appeared, carrying her son. Grace rushed to follow her up the stairs to the nursery. Mary laid the sleeping wean in his bed and drew a tartan over him. "Should he need me, dinna hesitate to wake me, Grace."

"Aye, m'lady."

"'Tis difficult to part from him."

Grace smiled. "I will keep him safe, m'lady. Just as you and Lord Alexander do me."

Lady Mary touched Grace's cheek affectionately. "I will see you early on the morrow."

Grace stood by the deep ornate cradle and watched the baby sleep. Oh, to be so oblivious to cares and troubles. The bed, suspended between heavy supports at each end, was built to allow it to swing gently to sooth him back to sleep, and to keep him from climbing out. A small trunk held his wrappings and gowns, while a table set against the wall held a basin for water, a pad of soap and a rag.

The narrow cot in Kieran's room was much the same as hers. She placed more peat on the fire and lit the small stub of candle that sat on a table next to a well-padded chair. She drew forth the basket of mending she had brought down from her room and leaned close to the candle flame to thread her needle. Her hand shook so she lowered it to her lap.

A soft tap sounded at the door. She set the needle in the fabric of a shirt, rose and opened the door. Surprise brought a quick beat to her heart and an uncertain smile to her lips. "Gabriel."

"I didna see you at the evening meal," he said.

Grace raised a finger to her lips and stepped into the hall leaving the door cracked. "Kieran wasna pleased his regular nurse had left him. He was fussy, so I remained here with him."

He nodded. He had released his hair from its leather tie and it fell against each side of his face. He looked like a dark angel. And his presence promised her redemption from the fear that plagued her. She slid her arms about his waist and pressed close against him. Gabriel tightened an arm around her while his hand cupped the back of her head. "What has happened?"

She shook her head. "I am glad you came." Just having him close quietened her fears and made her feel stronger. Why was that?

His heart beat heavily beneath her ear. How he had looked with his chest bare, wide and well-muscled and covered by a smattering of dark hair, played through her mind. She leaned her head back to look up at him. His mouth covered hers. She raised her hands to comb back his hair with her fingers while her lips and tongue responded to the slow, sensuous movement of his. His hand slipped inside her surcoat and cupped her breast. His thumb found the budding peak of her nipple beneath the fabric of her kirtle and stroked it. The sweet sweeping pleasure his touch inspired stifled the cautious whisper that named the act sinful. She pressed closer to his touch.

Gabriel nuzzled her neck and buried his lips against the sensitive skin between her neck and shoulder. Grace shuddered as chills raced down her body. She wanted to part her legs and draw him between them to assuage the aching need that tormented her.

A soft sound, part cough, part whimper, reached her through the cracked door. She wanted to ignore it and stay in his arms. She wanted his hands to roam at will, for his touch seemed to feed the emptiness between her thighs.

A full-fledged cry erupted from the nursery. Gabriel drew back, his cheeks flushed, his eyes dark. "You must go to him."

"Aye." It was almost painful to pull away. Her skin felt feverish, her breathing labored. She opened the door and peered in. Kieran grasped the edge of the cradle with his small fingers and was attempting to pull himself up. She rushed to him and lifted him out, finding his wrappings soggy with urine. She grimaced and cuddled him close as she carried him to the chest and retrieved fresh wrappings and a gown for him.

She soothed him as she bathed away the dampness and redressed him.

She heard a noise and turned with Kieran on her hip to find Gabriel watching from the door, his expression closed. "Sweet rest for you both, Grace."

She wanted to beg him to stay, but duty lay in her arms. "And to you, Gabriel."

He closed the door and the sound of his footsteps receded.

FROM ATOP A ladder, Gabriel eyed the angle of his cottage's new daub walls. The workmen had done a fine job. The structure was now three times the size it had been when Grace had last visited, and the main room had been given a fresh coat of whitewash, and the bed moved to another room, making it more spacious. The byre at the other end of the house would be where he could shelter his horse without having to go outside to feed and care for him. Part of that space would soon be divided to use as the buttery for his ale and a pantry for food. The doors had already been cut and set, but the interior walls had yet to be built. The workmen would return tomorrow to see it done.

But it was up to him to finish the framework for the thatched roof on this side of the cottage. He had the men construct a separate chamber for sleep, as well as a loft that hung above all the rooms.

In the bedchamber, though it was an oddity, he had had the

men to construct a stone fireplace. The flue would draw out the smoke and prevent it from staining the walls, as well as keeping the smell from permeating his clothing. But it would also offer him warmth when he was abed.

He said 'him' while he thought 'them.' It was so easy to envision Grace in his bed, in the kitchen serving his meals, but he could not imagine them raising children together. Seeing her holding Kieran on her hip, watching her change his wrappings and cuddle him close, had brought Gabriel to his senses.

Why was he expanding and improving his house, then?

He cut off the thought and raised the wooden mallet to pound another peg into place. Despite the breeze, sweat ran down his back between his shoulder blades and along his jaw. He brushed the sweat on his jaw away with his wrist. Artair extended the next wide, wooden slat from his position on the ground. Gabriel hefted it upward and slid it along the beams that ran from the roof beam to the edge of the wall, then held in place until Bruce Campbell grasped it. The two of them hammered pegs into the holes drilled into the beam to secure it.

"Will you use straw or heather for the thatching?" Artair asked.

"Heather." It would be sweeter and would nestle nicely into the lattice strips they were positioning.

"I would be quicker to question what has spurred this sudden desire to nest," Bruce Campbell commented. "It wouldna be the shy young lass you have been seen holding hands with, would it?"

"Cold weather will be upon us soon. I would have a protective shelter for my horse and a warmer spot to rest my head. 'Twas a drafty hole last season."

"'Twouldna be drafty at all if you had a lass to share your bed," Bruce said. "Or at least you wouldna notice if it was." He grinned.

Gabriel motioned to Artair to hand him the next slat. He was not going to share his thoughts on the subject. It would dishonor Grace to do so.

"I would take care with her, lad. Lord Alexander has been

keeping watch over you. If you dinna make a move soon, he may call you to his antechamber to discuss the matter."

Gabriel hammered harder this time. This constant harping on what he should or should not do with Grace had grown more than tiresome. "Mayhap the two of you should show as much interest in your own affairs as you do mine."

Glancing down he caught the grin Bruce and Artair shared and was tempted to drop the mallet on Artair's head and call it an accident. Instead he said, "What would the two of you ken about welcoming a woman into your home? You still share the barracks with the men at the castle."

"Had you stayed with the rest of us, you wouldna be facing such a quandary," Bruce said.

"Had the lot of you bathed more oft, I might have stayed. The stench was enough to make m'eyes tear." Gabriel looked down at Artair. "And they dinna call you an old fart in jest."

Artair and Bruce broke into guffaws.

"Good morn."

A feminine voice from behind them drew the men's attention. Grace stood with her basket a short distance away. "I have brought food for your midday meal."

Bruce climbed down the ladder like the cottage was on fire. Artair abandoned his post, leaving Gabriel poised on the ladder watching the two of them converge on Grace. She had a smile for Artair, but a more cautious greeting for Bruce. The men settled beneath a tree.

She tilted her head back to look up at him. "Will you not be joining us?" she asked.

"Aye, lass." He had not had the nerve to visit her again in the nursery. The image of her holding the bairn on her hip had been burned into his mind and caused him more than a little discomfort.

Now that she was here he wanted to simply gaze at her a moment. She turned to look behind her, as though she felt his attention, then raised her eyes to his again. The moment it became clear his attention rested solely on her, color rushed her cheeks and a small smile blossomed.

Those special smiles were like the pearls about her neck, precious and rare. Every time he earned one his heart raced and he grew hard.

At least Grace did not constantly harp on whether or not he meant to wed her.

"'Twill do the food more justice if I wash before we eat," Gabriel said climbing down from his perch. He went to the rain barrel, and using a bucket, scooped out some water. He washed his face and hands and liberally sloshed under his arms. He went into the house, dried off, and retrieved his shirt.

Grace had spread a cloth under a tree and set out bread, slices of pork, a wooden bowl of hard-boiled eggs and a small wedge of cheese. Artair reached for the cheese and she slapped the back of his hand. "I dinna wish to eat the dirt you are feeding yourself, Artair."

He studied his hands and with a rueful smile rose and went to the bucket to wash.

Gabriel sat down on one side of the cloth and bit the inside of his jaw to keep from laughing when Bruce rose and followed Artair. "'Twill do them good to have a civilizing influence."

She smiled. "I ken where my hands have been and how many times I have washed them this morn." She took up the wedge of cheese, cut slices from it and set them at Artair's place. "May I serve you some cheese?" she asked.

"I would prefer a kiss, but I suppose I shall have to settle for the food since we are burdened by witnesses."

"Anything I might say would make me seem too eager," she said.

"And if Artair and Bruce werena here?"

Grace bit her lip. "I rather like kissing," she said, her voice soft.

Finally. After weeks of encouragement she was growing bold enough to tell him what pleased her. But then kissing was all they had done. And that wee bit of touching that had set him aflame and left him hard and aching.

For the past two weeks catching another moment with her had been difficult. With her time and attention taken up by Kieran, Lord and Lady Campbell's son, they had stolen only minutes at the morning and evening meals. And they had never been alone. Now he hungered for time alone with her.

Bruce and Artair returned and sat opposite them around the cloth. A short time passed while they shared food and news of Lady Mary's sister's visit to come in a month's time.

"Has the lad's nursemaid returned?" Artair asked.

"Nay. Cara winna be returning. She has her own new babe to care for. But Lady Mary has found, just this morn, a woman to take her place. And Kieran seemed to like her."

"Has caring for the bairn made you long for one of your own, lass?" Bruce asked, an avid look in his eyes.

Gabriel shifted, uncomfortable with the turn the conversation had taken. Men oft complained the village women blathered everything they knew in gossip. Well, his men were no better. Gabriel sent Bruce a warning glare but the man was too intent on Grace's reply to notice.

Grace seemed to examine the piece of cheese she held while she contemplated the question. "Nay."

Gabriel studied her features.

"Nay?" Bruce's brows rose.

"Aye. 'Tis what I said."

"Why not?" Artair asked.

"Because there are other dreams in every lass's heart and mind besides having children. You ken that, of course."

Artair and Bruce nodded, their expressions solemn.

Gabriel had to look away to stifle his need to laugh. What did the two of them know about what lay in women's hearts? Swiving, birthing and cooking were the only things he had ever heard them mention when they spoke of women. For that matter, what did *he* know? His amusement died.

Grace leaned forward as though to share a secret with them. "The most important hope we carry is t' be valued. And what value would I have should I say, as an unwed woman, aye I want a babe and you repeated those words t' others? How many men from the barracks would think less of me and knock upon my chamber door late in the night?"

All of them. Gabriel read the same thought in the other two men's expressions.

"So, I say nay and hold the dream of children at a distance."

"If you have finished eating, would you care t' see the work done on the cottage, Grace?" Gabriel asked rising to his feet.

"Aye, I would. Thank you." She smiled as he offered a hand to help her rise.

He retained her hand, using it to guide her around the side, where the byre had been constructed. As soon as they were out of sight, Gabriel leaned back against the side of the structure and tugged her close. "Well done, lass."

"They are like two magpies tattling."

Gabriel chuckled. He ran a callused thumb over her cheek. "Mayhap you have taught them a lesson about the danger of spreading idle chatter."

"For a day or two." Her gray-blue gaze settled on his face.

She smoothed his hair with the back of her fingers. A fierce need for her reared up inside him and he grew hard as stone. His mouth covered hers. He tasted the inner warmth of her mouth as though sipping nectar from a flower, finding flavors of sharp cheese and apple slices. Grace groaned softly and leaned more heavily against him. He tightened his hold, letting her feel his need, and at the same time slid his hand into the open side of her surcoat and cupped her breast as he had before. Feeling her response, he broke the kiss to look down into her flushed face.

"I want you, Grace."

"Gabriel—" She turned her cheek against his chest, hiding her expression, but he felt the hard, labored beat of her heart. "They will wonder what we are about." She pulled away and stood for a moment studying the large shuttered window built in the daub wall. "Why have you done all this?" She asked motioning toward the house.

"I wanted something more than what I had."

"Is that what I am, too?"

The question, spoken with such directness, tied his thoughts into knots and triggered his resentment. Would she, too, now harp at him? "I dinna know."

She bit her lip and looked away. He saw her throat work as she swallowed, and her fingers went to the strand of tiny pearls around her neck.

"I winna be pushed into more than I am willing to give, Grace."

She frowned and shook her head. "I canna push your heart, Gabriel. 'Twill be open to me or it will not. Only you have the key to it." Her eyes, large and expressive had taken on more gray than blue when she looked up at him. "My heart has always been open to you." She tucked her hands behind her and turned. He followed her around the back of the cottage, his eyes on the taut grip of her hands as they clung together.

What was he to say in return to such a declaration? What did he know of hearts? Or love? "I am a warrior, Grace."

"You are a man first. A brave man. Or I believed you to be."

That insult sparked his anger and hurt his pride. "It makes me wonder if you see me as more than I can ever be. Are you looking at me through a young girls foolish dream-clouded eyes?"

She spun around to face him. "My vision is clear. I have seen you at your worst, when you were too far into your cups to stand, and at your best, when you were swinging your fists in defense of my honor. There is nothing clouding my eyes, nor my feelings. 'Tis you who are blind. Otherwise I wouldna have had to hit you with a basket for you to see me."

She swung about and walked quickly away from him.

When they rounded the end of the cottage, Artair and Bruce leaped to their feet.

"We packed the basket for you, Grace," Artair said.

"Thank you." Her cheeks were flushed and her breathing unsteady. "Mayhap you will finish the food later. Will you place it inside?" She motioned to the cottage.

He frowned. "Aye."

"Thank you for bringing the food," Bruce said.

Grace nodded and without another word strode away, her steps uneven and hurried.

"What did you do, Gabriel?" Artair demanded.

He had angered her and hurt her, and in doing so had hurt himself. "Nothing. 'Tis time to return to work."

GRACE SETTLED UPON the window seat in the solar where the light was the strongest. She draped Lady Mary's new gown across her lap and pinned the hem she had marked earlier into place. Then she took up a needle and forced herself to focus on making small, even stitches, but her mind wandered away from the task. What had she done or said to cause Gabriel to withdraw from her?

Had someone else caught his fancy in the fortnight she had cared for Kieran? The hunger of his kiss and the changes in his body had said otherwise. His murmured words "I want you, Grace" did as well. Her cheeks burned with a combination of excitement and embarrassment.

If he truly wanted her, why had he begun to repeat the old arguments she had thought they'd left behind?

The answer came to her like a whisper, but she blocked it from her mind. Not yet. She would not listen to it yet.

Lady Mary entered the solar. Her cheeks were flushed from climbing the stairs, and her pale hair gleamed like moonlight. The braids Grace had fashioned for her that morning pulled the sides back, baring the lady's high cheekbones. The style suited her well.

If she were as beautiful as Lady Mary, would Gabriel love her? Everyone loved Lady Mary. She was kind and gentle, generous and strong.

"Grace, the evening meal is ready. There will be time enough for you to finish that later."

Grace looked down at the gown and smiled as she lightly touched the woven pattern of tiny flowers in the fabric.

"That color would be very becoming on you," Lady Mary said

when she noticed Grace's pleasure.

"It would not be seemly for a servant t' dress in a manner that would call attention t' herself, m'lady, would it?"

"Only if it displeases the servant's lord or lady. I would not mind, nor would Alexander. There was a small length of fabric left after that dress was finished. You shall have it to fashion a collar or mayhap a sash. Mayhap a ribbon or two, as well."

Grace's pulse leaped with cautious excitement. "You are very kind, Lady Mary. But will you not need it for such things yourself?"

"'Twill give me pleasure to share with you. Come." Mary motioned for her to follow. "I will get it for you now."

Grace set the needle and carefully draped the dress on the window seat so it would not wrinkle. She followed Lady Mary up the tower stairs. The distant sound of voices below marked the gathering of the men for the evening meal. Lady Mary tugged open the door to her bedchamber, strode to the large trunk at the foot of the bed and opened it. She withdrew a folded square of fabric and offered it to Grace.

"'Twould look lovely close to your face. 'Twill call attention to your eyes. You have beautiful eyes."

Grace clutched the fabric to her and half raised a hand to touch the very feature Lady Mary had praised, then lowered it. "You are kind to say so. Thank you, m'lady."

"I am sure Gabriel thinks so, too."

He had never said so directly. Would he say such things if he cared for her? She touched the pearls around her neck. He said she was as fine as they were. Had he meant it?

"Is Gabriel aware of your circumstances, Grace?"

What did her circumstances matter? Grace shook her head.

"It doesna make a difference to you, that he isna high born?" Lady Mary looked into her eyes, as though she could uncover Grace's true feelings. "But it might make a difference to him. 'Twould be wise to tell him before he loses himself in you any further."

He had not lost himself. He worried too oft about their differences already. Should she tell him of her birth, it would only make it worse. Most of the time she was able to forget about her circumstances. But now that Lord Alexander had mentioned petitioning the king on her behalf again, she feared that if anyone knew the truth, someone might come at any time to whisk her away from all she loved.

"We must hurry and join the others to sup," Mary said.

"I would take this to my room first, if it pleases you, m'lady."

"Of course, Grace."

Lady Mary paused on the landing outside the room. "Alexander and I would do more, should you allow it."

"Where would I belong, Lady Mary? I would be too poor to be a part of the aristocracy, and my blood is too rich to be accepted as a servant if it was known. In the one realm, no one would think me good enough to wed. In the other, I would be considered too high of birth to touch. 'Tis better if I search for happiness where I can."

Mary stroked her arm comfortingly. "You will always have a place here with us."

Grace's eyes blurred with tears. "I am grateful for that. But it would be better if I choose one world or the other to live in. And if there's any chance at all Gabriel should want me, I prefer whichever station in life would make it easier for him t' accept me."

"I want only your happiness, Grace. I will do whatever you wish t' ensure that." Lady Mary gave her arm another squeeze, then went down the stairs. Grace climbed up to her bedchamber. She placed the fabric on her narrow bed and ran her hand over it. She would decide later how she would use it. Mayhap she could purchase more fabric for a surcoat and use this lovely piece to accent the color.

She draped the fabric around her neck and raised the small metal disk that served as her mirror. The image was blurred, but she could see how the color suited her hair and skin.

Finding her scissors, she cut a narrow strip from the edge. Next she pulled free the leather that tied the end of her braid and worked her hair free. Although her stomach growled, she ignored it to spend a few minutes brushing her hair. Then she pulled the long locks back from her face and tied them with the strip.

She focused on that small bit of color for a moment. The whisper in her mind grew loud enough for her to acknowledge. Gabriel would not wed her. He wanted her, but he would not wed her. She had lied to Lady Mary through omission. Her throat worked as she tried to swallow against the ache in her chest. She eased down onto her narrow cot.

She loved him. She had loved him from the first time she had seen him standing in the great room, so proud and strong, a head taller than all but Lord Alexander. She had seen how fierce he was during training. And how gentle and caring he was with the children from the village. Her heart had all but been broken when she had watched him with Tira and her son, believing he would wed the woman. After Tira left to return to her family, she feared he might follow her. But he had stayed.

She loved him from afar for well over a year. And now she knew what it was to feel his eyes upon her, his hands. She touched her breast where his thumb had brushed against her, and the sensation he evoked returned. She squeezed her legs together in an attempt to assuage the empty ache there.

She had tasted the caress of his mouth upon hers, felt his beard against her face. The feelings she had for him had grown and were now more deeply rooted than ever. They would not change, whether he loved her or not. Whether he wed her or not.

She would love him whether they were together or apart. But she could no longer bear to be apart from him. If all she could have was one more moment of his attention, one more touch of his hand, one more kiss, at least she would not go another year without them.

She rose, put away her scissors and folded away the rest of the fabric in her small trunk. She left her room and descended the stone stairs. Though the journey was not a strenuous one, by the time she reached the bottom, her heart raced and her breathing was labored. The probable consequences of her decision settled on her mind and heart.

What if she should have a child? Lady Mary had been with child before she wed Lord Alexander. Though the villagers and servants had gossiped and smirked about it at first, no one did any longer. Lord Alexander's features were so firmly stamped upon Kieran's wee face, no one doubted the child's paternity. Had any doubts remained, his red hair and unusual tawny eyes, so distinctive, put an end to them. But it had not been the child who had ended the gossip. The gossip had ended because of Lord Alexander himself, in the way he had stood by his lady, in the respect he extended her, in the pride he showed when she took his arm. They stood together against the gossip.

Who would stand with her?

Who would even care enough, to harp against what she had or had not done?

She had been alone her entire life. She called few of the women who resided here at the castle friend. And even fewer men.

The sound of men's voices reached her long before she opened the door to great room. She paused just inside the chamber. Lord Alexander and Lady Mary sat at their table at the front of the room. The aroma of ham and stewed vegetables wafted to her. She spied Gabriel at the table with the other men.

Her heart ached just looking at him. Where was her pride? In the past, pride had been something she could not afford. But one desperate time, when she could have sold herself for a bite to eat or a roof over her head, she had refused. Was love enough to risk it all?

She wove her way across the room. She paused behind Gabriel. A knot formed in her throat. Should she share everything she was with him and it proved less than enough, what then? She turned to the right and found an empty place at the end of a long table next to one of the young clansmen. She slipped into the small spot at the end of the bench. The boisterous talk bouncing back and forth across the table came to an abrupt halt. Every man's attention settled on her.

Heat erupted into her face in an uncomfortable wave. She

lowered her gaze.

Silence continued a beat then two. "Somethin' to drink, lass?"

She forced herself to look up at the man beside her. She took in pale green eyes, a wild mop of red hair and freckles before focusing on the tankard he extended. Her arms felt wooden, frozen. She forced her hand upward.

A large presence loomed beside her, and out of the corner of her eye she saw the men's attention turn there. "We have made room for you at our table, Grace," Gabriel said, and his large hand came within her line of vision. Her heart beat against her ribs as though it might free itself and fly away.

She thought for a moment to rebuff his invitation. The normal volume of male voices in the room fell. And though conversation at the tables along the walls continued, those close by grew silent. She glanced up to see every eye focused on her. Should she reject Gabriel's invitation it would strike a blow to his pride and embarrass him before his men. She could not hurt him. Her fledgling pride crumbled, and she placed her hand in his.

Her legs shook as she rose and allowed him to guide her to the table. Grace stepped over the bench and sat down. Gabriel tucked her in against him. The long length of his thigh pressed against hers. His arm rested against her back. She wanted to cling to him until her trembling subsided, and stiffened her spine against the need. She had stood alone, apart for so long. She must do so now.

Gabriel ran the back of his fingers against her cheek, which was still hot with color. She forced her gaze upward to meet his. Gabriel offered her a wry smile.

The tension at the table eased with that one small gesture. The servants arrived with trays of food and the trenchers. Gabriel cut the meat and arranged the food upon the flat piece of bread so they might share it. Her earlier hunger swallowed up by nerves, Grace nibbled at the choice bits he offered her with little interest. Was he angry? What would he do and say once they were alone? Had he offered her a place next to him at table to save his pride? Pride and honor were all men knew. But what of love? Tension knotted her shoulders and neck.

The men's raucous humor bounced back and forth across the table. Grace paid no notice.

Gabriel reached for the bow holding her hair back and caught the tail of the strip. "This is the same color as your eyes, lass. Like the sky after a storm has past."

So he *had* noticed her eyes.

"Twould please me to see you in a surcoat of that color."

Hope unfolded inside her like the first petals of a blossom. The knot in her stomach unwound a wee bit and she offered him a shaky smile. "I havena stitched a new gown for myself in some time. Mayhap I should."

He sliced and peeled a pear. She ate half of it while he finished his meal.

She shook her head at his offer of a milk-filled tankard.

"Will you walk with me in the courtyard, Grace?"

"Aye."

Gabriel motioned forward one of the servants who carried a bowl of water and a towel. Grace washed her hands and dried them, then Gabriel did the same. He rose and offered her his hand.

THE SKY, BRUISED by the coming night, was streaked a purplish red as they left the keep through a side door that opened into a small garden. The smell of peat smoke and roasting meat drifted on a subtle breeze to mingle with the scent of greenery. Gabriel chose a well-worn path that led to the curtain wall battlements. He knew every nook and cranny of the castle, knew how to fashion the weapons he needed, how to care for himself, his horse, his men during siege. But everything he thought he knew about women ceased to exist when it came to Grace.

"You could have rejected me before my men, and I would have deserved it," he said, breaking the silence.

"'Tis not in me to hurt you, Gabriel. 'Twould hurt me to do

so."

Another wry smile curved his lips. He had learned first-hand what she meant. All afternoon he had been plagued by guilt. Then, when she had avoided his table—avoided him—it had pierced him. When she had sat down next to Calum to share his meal, and him little more than a boy... His skin burned with outrage. At his table there had been an accusation aimed at him from every man's eyes. Her quiet manner and soft smiles had won their affections.

She paused and turned to look up at the structure behind them, a dark shadow against the fast-dying sun. The light brushed her features with gold and set afire the reddish highlights in her hair. He was struck breathless by her beauty.

"I have been bereft of kin since my second year. I didna have a home until I journeyed here. Artair brought me here from Edinburgh, has he told you?"

"Nay, he said nothing."

She drew a deep breath. "The castle was only half finished when first I came. I lived with one of the stone masons and his wife. She and I cooked food for the workmen and did whatever tasks needed doing. I felt blessed to have the shelter over my head, the food in my belly. I have accepted and am content that I must earn my way and am truly grateful for the small gifts others share with me." She touched the pearls he had given her. "But I canna settle for less when I offer myself, Gabriel. 'Tis the only thing I have to give."

"'Tis right and good for you to feel so."

"If it is your wish, Gabriel," she paused for a long moment, then turned her face away from him, her body taut as a bow's string. "I willna seek your table again to sup, nor approach you in any way."

His chest ached. He sat astride a double-edged sword of his own making. Though he could not say the words, every day he found more about her to admire, to desire. Every time he earned one of her smiles, he wanted her. Wanting to give someone pleasure and receiving it in return...was that love? "'Twould pain us both to be parted so completely, lass."

She turned to look up at him, her features still. "If it is the hand of friendship you mean to offer me, I would as soon you strike me and give me reason to hate you."

The fierceness of her words fascinated him, for in them lay a surprising passion he had not glimpsed, even when they'd kissed. "I could no more strike you than you could hate me, Grace."

"Then what do you want?"

He crossed the distance between them, and with every step the desire fired by her tiny spark of passion rolled through his body. He crushed her close and his mouth moved hungrily over hers. She ran her hands up his back to hold him and rose on tiptoe to press her body tight against his. He braced his feet apart and rocked his hips against hers. Her answering movement tore a groan from his throat.

He wanted everything. All she had to offer. Everything he read in her eyes, but had refused to act on. Everything she thought, but did not speak. He wanted to rip aside her restraint and feel her tremble with need beneath his hand. He wanted to look into her eyes as his body covered hers and she found her release.

But there was a price to pay for all that. He could not have any of it unless he wed her. And if he did not wish to wed her, then he needed to set her free so she might find happiness with another.

Breathless from her response and his own thoughts, he broke the kiss but continued to hold her against him.

Grace rested her cheek against his chest. "'Tis a tempting torment, these feelings you inspire, Gabriel."

"For me as well." His voice sounded rusty.

She drew his hand from around her waist and clasped it in both of hers. She held it tight against her breasts. To have her soft flesh beneath his hand yet not be able to touch her was sweet torture.

"Come sit with me, Grace." She released his hand and he attempted to turn his thoughts away from what he could not have by asking, "Will you tell me of your kin?" He drew her to a wooden bench fashioned against exterior wall of the castle and sat down.

"They died in a fire when I was two. Moira, one of the servants took me as her own. She died when I was ten."

"Where did you go from there?"

"I earned my keep working as a nursemaid's assistant until I was three and ten."

"Was it then you came here?"

Within the bend of his arm her body grew taut. "Aye, after a time." She paused. "And what of your kin?"

What had she meant after a time? "Mine, too, are gone. A fever overtook us all and I was the only one to live." He closed his mind to the memories that threatened to rise.

"I'm sorry, Gabriel."

"Aye, I am, too. I was at least old enough t' care for m'self. You were just a wee girl."

"But we both survived."

"Thanks to Alexander Campbell and Artair."

"Aye. Thanks to them both."

"Tomorrow, after we return from our patrols would you want t' practice with the bow?" he asked.

"Oh, aye. I'd like t' learn."

"Then I will take you down t' the training fields."

"I will be waiting." She shifted. "'Tis full dark, and Lady Mary may need me."

Gabriel sighed. Duty seemed to interrupt when least he wanted it to. "I will walk you back in." He had a desire to see where she rested her head at night.

"When will you be escorting the prisoners from here?" she asked as they made their way back into the castle. Gabriel motioned for her to precede him up the back stairs.

"Two days hence." He would be glad to see them gone. Mayhap he could spend more time with her once that duty had ended.

She turned to face him at the top of the stairs and in the flickering light of one of the torches, her features look fragile and feminine. "You will take care."

"Aye. I will, Grace."

She continued down the hallway, then paused at a door and pushed it open. Darkness rushed out. Without pause, she disappeared into the blackness and reappeared with the stub of candle in a small holder and lit it from the torch outside the door. Cupping her hand around the flame, she carried it back inside and set it down on a short table next to a narrow bed. The candle's flame reflected off the small metal disk, a mirror. A brush lay next to it.

In a glance Gabriel took in the meager appointments of the chamber and was reminded of the barren cells of the nuns at a kirk he had once defended from the English. A round basket filled with clothes stood next to the single chair in the room. A wooden trunk standing knee high pressed against the foot of the bed. There were no rushes nor rug upon the floor, but a garderobe was tucked into the corner. A broom rested against the wall next to the fireplace. Everything was neat and clean.

Grace lit a twig from the candle and knelt to light the block of peat in the fireplace.

"How long have you slept here, Grace?"

"Since Lady Mary chose me as her maid when first she arrived." She rose from her crouched position.

His new bedchamber lay down the hill just below the castle, thrice the size of this small room. His bed would barely fit into this chamber.

During battle he had slept in thickets and glens, beneath wagons, and in caves. Wherever he could find shelter. Grace's room was dry and warm. The gown she wore serviceable, the cloth in good repair. The bed better than the straw pallet on the floor many had.

But he wanted better for her. With every fiber in his being he wanted to sweep her up and carry her down the stairs to his cottage and place her in the center of his bed and see her surrounded by—more.

He wanted to provide for her, to protect her. Was that love? Was it love that made him want to please her?

"What is it, Gabriel?" The dull light from the fireplace cast a buttery wash over her pale skin.

"Come here, lass." His voice worked its way around a knot in his throat.

She came without hesitation. Gabriel cupped her face in his large hands and studied her features in the brighter light of the torch. Her large eyes, thickly lashed, studied him in return. He bent his head and pressed a kiss to her forehead, the narrow bridge of her nose, the slight point of her chin. When his mouth settled upon hers, her breath released in a sigh, and her fingers grasped his leather jerkin as though she wished to draw him closer.

He wanted that too. But that tiny cot would crumble beneath his weight and he would not take her on the barren stone floor. She deserved the comfort of a bed. He raised his head and smiled at the glow on her cheeks and the slumberous look of desire he read on her face.

With difficulty, he released her. "Sweet sleep, Grace."

She swallowed and gathered her composure. "And to you as well, Gabriel."

He felt her eyes follow him as he strode down the passageway to the stairs. He entered the great hall and looked about for Lord Alexander. Seeing him approach the very door he had just passed through, he stepped back into passageway and waited for him.

Alexander thrust open the wooden door and stepped into the anteroom, then pulled up in surprise upon seeing him. "Is there trouble, Gabriel?" he demanded.

"Nay, m'lord. I but wished a moment of your time." His heart beat a heavy, frantic rhythm. Sweat broke out on his body and along his hairline. "'Tis difficult to speak with anyone in private with the men watching."

Alexander grinned. "'Twould seem they live their lives through everyone else, eh?"

"Aye, they do."

Alexander studied him with one brow raised, a smile playing about his mouth. "How may I serve you?"

Gabriel swallowed though his throat had dried to dust. "I

wish your permission for Grace and I to wed, m'lord."

"You have asked her, then?"

"I wanted your blessing first, m'lord."

Lord Alexander nodded. "You have it. With luck, she will accept you."

Gabriel released the breath he had not realized he was holding. He had not doubted Lord Alexander would agree to the request, but the enormous step he had taken with the asking wreaked havoc with his normal calm.

"Breathe, man," Alexander said with a chuckle and slapped his shoulder. "I have watched you face our enemies in battle, Gabriel, and though 'tis just as difficult to face your lady in times of strife, the rewards are much sweeter."

Gabriel smiled. "I shall heed your wisdom, m'lord."

"When do you mean to ask her?" Alexander asked. "Mary winna wish for duty to stand in the way of such an occasion."

"After prayers tomorrow. I would have the priest's blessing as well, and he may post the banns."

"'Tis a good plan. This will set Grace's mind and heart at ease. After her time in Edinburgh, she deserves every happiness, as do you."

Was 'her time in Edinburgh' what she had meant when she said, 'after a time'? They would have time to discuss such things after they were wed. "Thank you, m'lord."

"You must spend some time deciding how you will ask her. Women put much value on what is said at such moments."

It was only in his mind to drop to his knee and ask her to wed him. Simple, direct, and as much as a simple man could manage. "I shall give it great thought."

"I look forward to being there to wish you both well, Gabriel," Alexander said and gave him another hearty whack on the back.

"Thank you, m'lord."

Later, as he left the castle and wandered the short distance to his cottage, his heart finally settled into its normal rhythm and his hands quit sweating. He entered his dark cottage and followed the glow of the hearth fire he had banked before leaving the cottage to light a candle. He carried it into his bedchamber, shucked his clothes, and climbed into the wide bed. The banked fire he had built glowed orange in the darkness and pushed aside the damp chill in the air.

The vision of Grace kneeling to light that one small block of peat in her fireplace played through his mind. She would see to his comfort as he would see to hers. They would share this house and this bed. He grew hard and aching at the thought. There were worse reasons for wedding.

Had he done the right thing? He covered his eyes with a forearm. It was too late now to worry.

In speaking to Lord Alexander, he had pledged himself to Grace. He could not in honor retreat.

THE SMALL CHAPEL smelled of incense and damp. The priest's words droned on in the background of Grace's thoughts. She should have told Gabriel everything about her past when he'd spoken of his own kin. But his moods swung like the counterweight on a catapult. One minute he was kissing her until her heart and head swooned, and the next he was striding away as though the jaws of some ferocious beast were snapping at his heels. If she had told him, he might have walked away forever. The way he had kissed her—Her chest felt full, as though her heart had expanded and there were not sufficient space left for her to breathe.

Britta, one of the scullery maids standing next to her, grabbed her hand and tugged. Grace glanced around to see everyone kneeling and eyeing her. Embarrassed heat stung her cheeks. She gripped the bench before her and lowered her knees to the floor.

She truly tried to keep her mind focused on the priest's message. But there had been such tenderness in Gabriel's kiss. She had known he was capable of such feelings. But what did it mean?

Lord Alexander and Lady Mary rose and settled into their

seats at the front of the chapel. Grace hastened to do the same. A murmur at the end of the bench drew her attention, and she turned and beheld Gabriel standing there, his hands folded behind him.

The priest usually said prayers every fortnight with Gabriel and his men in the great hall before they broke the fast, a shortened version of the ceremony he was about to finish here now. Was there trouble? Gabriel would not interrupt the service unless the need to speak with Lord Alexander was dire.

Her heart beat high in her throat.

With a brief prayer the priest ended the service and Gabriel moved forward to speak with Lord Alexander and Father Dillion when they gathered to confer. The servants around her broke into whispers as they, too, speculated on Gabriel's presence.

Father Dillion stepped forward. "Grace McNab. Will you come forward, please?"

A sinking feeling invaded her stomach and she pressed a hand there. Had the inquiries Lord Alexander sent long ago unexpectedly borne fruit? Had they come for her? Might Gabriel stand against them, or would he bid her go?

Her legs shook as she forced herself to her feet and shuffled sideways down the narrow space between the benches to the aisle. Her eyes sought Lord Alexander's face first. His smile eased her anxiety a little. Her attention shifted to Gabriel. His expression was grave, and once again fear stole her breath. Her steps lagged.

She dragged in a breath when she stood before the three men, struggling for a calm demeanor. Gabriel stepped forward and took her hands. His smile was strained. "You need not look so frightened, Grace. All is well."

"What has happened?" she asked in a hoarse whisper.

Gabriel's gaze focused on her face with an intensity that once again made it difficult for her to breath. Maintaining his grip upon her hands, he knelt upon the stone floor. His throat worked as he swallowed.

That small action caught at her heart and hope carried it forward.

Gabriel's husky voice rumbled through the chapel. "My cottage is empty without you, Grace. My heart is empty without you as well. I ask you to wed me and fill them both."

His words triggered relief and joy and a quick rush of tears that ran unheeded down her cheeks. "Are you certain, Gabriel?"

"Aye, lass. I wouldna be on my knees afore you if I were not."

His tone earned chuckles from among the worshipers.

Grace's throat was so clogged and raw with tears that her voice deserted her, so she nodded her assent.

"You must speak the words aloud, Grace," Father Dillion urged.

She nodded again, fighting for composure "I love you, Gabriel Campbell. 'Tis my heart's desire to wed you."

A shout erupted from the audience. Gabriel rose to his feet, drew her close, and kissed her.

The priest raised his hands to quiet the congregation.

"I publish the banns of marriage between Grace MacNab of this Parish and Gabriel Campbell of this Parish. If any of you know cause or just impediment why these persons should not be joined together in Holy Matrimony, ye are to declare it. This is the first asking."

To Capture a Highlander's Heart

The Wedding Night
A Highland Moonlight Spinoff

Teresa J. Reasor

Chapter 1

Scotland, 1330

GABRIEL'S VISION SWAM and pain throbbed behind his eyes. He gripped the front of the saddle with his good hand, and willed his head to clear. He had never fallen from a horse in his life, but with every step his mount took, the ground seemed to reach up to drag him down. Had he not already killed the man responsible for his injury, he'd do it now.

His arm pulsed with the beat of his heart. The limb, swollen and inflamed from the cut carved into his forearm, felt tight as a waterskin. He could barely feel the leather reins clutched in that hand.

Though the injury was bound, it wept sluggishly, turning the bindings reddish gold with blood and pus. The wound was festering, and there was nothing he or Derrick Campbell, their healer, could do for it. One minute chills wracked his body, and the next heat pressed against his skin as though he was boiling from the inside out.

His thoughts dwelt on Grace, waiting for him at *Caisteal Sith*. She was depending on him to return to her. They would be wed within the month.

She and Lady Mary would see him well from this. But until he reached them, he must endure.

An hour later, the pounding in his head was relentless, and his stomach pitched. He clung to the knowledge that they would arrive at the castle by midafternoon. If he could stay on his horse. And for the first time in his life, there was some doubt he had the strength left to do so.

James and Robert Campbell rode up abreast of him, one on each side, their red hair bright enough that even through his blurred vision he could identify them.

"'Tis but a league more, Gabriel. If ye hand me yer reins, I will lead yer mount whilst ye rest your arm," Robert said cautiously.

Never had he handed over control of his horse or his men. But should they be attacked before they arrived at the castle…

"James, I would speak t' Derrick."

"Aye. I will get him." The man fell back while Robert maintained his position beside him.

Derrick rode forward, his bay horse rubbing close to Gabriel's chestnut gelding. "What is it, Gabriel?"

"Take the lead until we reach *Caisteal Sith.*"

Derrick's lips tightened, but he nodded and kicked his mount forward.

Gabriel lifted his hand, his fingers so swollen he could not release the reins. Robert reached over and tugged them free of his grasp. Gabriel shoved his injured arm into the heavy fabric hanging over his shoulder and secured beneath his girdle. It held his arm stationary to keep it from being jarred, and the pain eased a small degree. He closed his eyes against the bob and sway of the horse's movement in hopes of keeping down the bile creeping up his throat.

They would arrive at the keep soon, and Grace and Lady Mary would put him right.

THE LAST OF the clansmen breaking their fast crowded out the keep's heavy wooden door. After a momentary silence, the servants rushed in to clean away the debris from the meal.

Grace turned her attention to the large woman waiting for her. "How may I serve you, Matilda?"

"I have brought the two of 'em to see if there be somethin' t' give me to put on their bruises."

Sitting on a bench against one wall were two lads. Both held his shirt in his lap wadded in a ball. They looked alike enough to be twins, but one had a shadow of beard darkening the edge of his chin, while the other was as clean-cheeked as a bairn.

Grace set her basket of herbs on the bench next to them and eyed the purplish bruise that discolored one boy's shoulder. His brother had an identical injury on his ribs, but did not seem in as much pain.

Their mother, a laundress at the castle, said, "They beat each other black and blue. Fight and bicker like two roosters guardin' the same hen. 'Tis a wonder they havena put each other's eyes out—or worse."

If she could discover what had caused the injuries, it might be helpful. "And what were the two of you about when this happened?" Grace asked. The marks had a defined shape to them. Had the boys been throwing mud bricks?

The two eyed each other, then looked to their mother. The laundress, Matilda, was tall and rawboned, her arms as muscular as any man's. Grace had seen the work in the laundry, and it was hard, heavy, and hot. Any woman who did such labor had to be strong. It appeared the two lads were not afraid of each other, but based on the anxious looks they cast behind them, they had a healthy respect for their mother.

"It started—" the younger boy began, only to have his brother poke him in his bruised rib with a well-placed elbow. The boy doubled over and groaned aloud.

Grace suspected he had broken ribs and started forward to chastise his brother with a shake. Matilda beat her to it when she thumped the older boy hard on the back, nearly unseating him. He barely saved himself with a hand on the floor. He grimaced in pain and retracted the injured arm.

"Go on, Edwin," his mother encouraged the younger son.

"We thought t' fashion a slingshot like David's. Father Dillion mentioned him in his sermon."

Matilda eyed the two. "Fashion it from what?"

The older boy glared a warning at his sibling.

Matilda laid a warning hand on his uninjured shoulder. "Ulric," she breathed a warning.

The boy answered, "From a pair of stockins from the laundry."

Matilda straightened, her expression one of first shocked anger, then concern. Her throat worked as she swallowed. "Ye stole from the castle laundry?"

"Nay, we borrow't them, then put 'em back."

Matilda relaxed somewhat, but folded her impressive arms before her, looking only slightly mollified.

"What did you use as slingstone for your slingshots?" Grace asked.

The older boy turned to look over his shoulder at Matilda. "Different thin's. Stones and bits of wood. But we couldna keep them in the bend of the stockin'. So then we borrow't two blocks of soap, but we had nae more luck with them."

"And then...? Grace urged, though she had already surmised what happened.

"Edwin put the bar into the stockin' and was swinging it around. He let it fly and hit the quatrain and spun it about. So we tried it some more, until—he hit me in the arm."

"'Twasna with intent," Edwin said, his voice just short of a whine.

"I only took one swipe at ye, same as ye did me." Ulric folded his arms in a facsimile of his mother, then thought better of it when his abused shoulder objected.

Grace shook her head. The two of them had too much time to get into mischief. It was time to put them to work before they killed each other.

She called Matilda aside. "Do your boys help in the laundry?" Grace asked, low-voiced.

"Now and then, but for the most part they help m'husband with the crops."

"Edwin has broken ribs. I'll bind them, as I will Ulric's shoulder but—Mayhap they need focus their...curiosity on somethin' more tirin'. If they are too worn out to fight, they canna harm each other. Or mayhap...there's a discipline to training to fight. 'Tis not just slashing at whatever moves. If they are goin' t'fight, let them fight for a cause."

Matilda nodded her understanding. "Aye. I will think on it. How long before they heal?"

"At least a month. But both will need to take care; at least their aches may dissuade them from harming each other for a time."

"Good." Matilda nodded.

Grace mixed up some salve of pork grease, willow bark, yarrow, and a touch of peppermint. She applied it to the bruises before binding the boys' injuries. Next she created a small packet of yarrow flowers for Matilda to make into tea. "'Twill soothe them if they drink this at night before sleeping."

"Thank you. I will see they drink it," Matilda said while she eyed her sons with a fixed determination. The woman removed a coin from her pocket.

Grace shook her head. "'Tis not your debt to pay, but theirs. I will think of something they may do in return. Mayhap harvesting some peat for m'fire when they are healed."

Matilda smiled. "Consider it done, ma'am."

Matilda gripped each boy's arm and marched them out of the hall. Grace spent some time returning the herbs, flowers, and bark to their packets, and put everything back into lady Mary's basket. She climbed the spiral stairs, passing her room, then the solar, Lord and Lady Campbell's bedchamber and, coming to the storage room, opened the door and placed the basket inside, close to the door.

She paused to look through one of the arrow slits toward a small plume of smoke. Nay, it was not smoke, but dust, which meant horses were fast approaching. And the only group expected was Gabriel and his men. Grace's heart took flight, as well as her feet. She raced down the back stairs and through the wide corridors to the great room.

It had been seven days since her betrothed left *Caisteal Sith* to escort violent trespassers from Campbell land. Seven long days.

Two more days and the banns will have been posted a fortnight, and they could marry at any time. She had bartered to acquire the fabric for a new dress, and cut the pieces soon after the announcement. At night, to pass the time, she stayed busy stitching it while she waited for Gabriel's return. The gown was close to finished.

The desire to rush toward her future triggered an impatience she fought hard to suppress. The sweet, exciting things Gabriel made her feel when he touched her were a pleasing torment. She wanted to discover how it might be to have those longings fulfilled.

Grace rushed through the great room to the heavy wooden door of the keep. Several other servants stood in the entrance peering out. The early autumn breeze brought with it the scent of animals and fresh-cut grass. At sight of the first horse entering the curtain walls Grace's heart plummeted. It was not Gabriel and his men, but a group of travelers. And from the standard they traveled under, it was the retinue of someone of importance.

A single man on horseback entered the bailey and spoke to Alexander Campbell, lord of the castle and chief to the clansmen of his territory.

Alexander nodded, and the man rode back across the courtyard to the curtain wall.

Alexander turned to scan the crowd of servants and men who had congregated in the courtyard. His gaze settled on Grace, and he strode to the door.

"Go t' your chamber, Grace, and dinna come down until I send for ye."

She searched Lord Campbell's features, and his grave expression made her heart race with anxiety. "Has something happened t' Gabriel, m'lord?"

"Nay. This has naught t' do with Gabriel. Not yet. What you hoped t' avoid has come to pass, and someone from your past has come calling."

There was no one left of her family, and the only ones who might remain were Lord and Lady Ramsay, the couple who took her in after her nursemaid died. She had been no more than a servant to them. It had been Lady Ramsay who banished her to the streets of Edinburgh with only the clothes on her back. She had been but ten and three. All that kept her from being preyed upon was that she had appeared frail, plain, and much younger than her true age. She also had been good at hiding from those who meant her harm.

"Go now, Grace. I would ken their purpose before ye meet them."

"Aye, m'lord."

"Tell Lady Mary we have guests. She is in the solar with Kieran."

"Aye, m'lord."

With her thoughts afire with anxious imaginings, and her stomach cramped with dread, Grace rushed back the way she had come. She found Lady Mary in the solar playing with her young son. Kieran laughed and bounced upon his chubby legs, and he grinned at Grace as soon as she entered the room. His tawny eyes gleamed a startling amber, as unusual as his father's. The wean's rust-colored hair lay in curls close to his head, gleaming like polished copper in the light from a nearby window, which fell across him and the woman who held him steady by his chubby hands.

"Guests have arrived, Lady Mary. Lord Campbell bid me alert you."

"Who is it, Grace?" A smile lingered on Lady Mary's face as she tilted her head back. She was so full of love and joy, delighting in her husband and child, it spilled over into her every word and expression.

"I dinna ken. But Lord Alexander said—'tis someone of importance." Just saying the words aloud sent a fresh fission of anxiety through her. There were so few people from her past who would still be alive. Who could it be?

"Please take Kieran to Amera, Grace. I will go down and greet our visitors."

Grace rushed forward to take the bairn. She hiked Lord Kieran onto her hip and extended a hand to help Mary to her feet.

"He also bid me stay in my room until he called for me. Mayhap it may be someone who knows of me." She struggled to keep her alarm from her voice and expression.

"Be at ease, Grace. Alexander and I stand betwixt you and any harm."

GABRIEL CLUNG TO the front of the saddle, and tightened his legs against the horse's sides when they quickened their pace and cantered through a field, then the village.

The gray stone walls of the castle had never been a more welcome sight. The sky seemed to tumble and twist above him when he leaned his head back to look up at it. Blackness threatened to take him, and only through sheer will did he beat it back. If he held on for just a wee moment more, he'd see Grace, and all would be well.

The heavy wooden gate in the curtain wall swung open and they entered the courtyard. Strange men and horses milled about the bailey, and his warrior instincts sang. He squinted to try and identify their clan, but could not focus his eyes. Robert pulled his mount to a halt. Derrick and James appeared below him.

"Dismount and we will help you inside, Gabriel."

He heard the words, but it was damned difficult to comprehend what Derrick said above the ringing in his ears. The castle keep stood before him. Grace would be inside, and she would see to his hurts. He pictured her small, heart-shaped face and dark gray eyes and roused himself to kick his foot clear of the stirrup. He leaned forward in the saddle to swing his leg over, and would have tumbled over the animal's neck had someone not grabbed his calf and tugged it down. The step down seemed an interminable distance. When his foot hit the hard-packed dirt he staggered back. James caught one arm, Derrick the other. He almost cried out at the pain when Derrick jostled the injured limb by dragging it up and over his shoulders.

"Get Grace, Robert," Derrick ordered.

Robert bounded up the stairs and jerked the door open. Two others held it while Derrick and James manhandled Gabriel up the steps to the opening. The floor seemed to pitch and roll beneath his feet. The pulse in his arm had turned to fire eating his flesh. He gritted his teeth against the pain.

They had reached the antechamber leading to the upper floors when the scuffing sound of steps sounded on the stairs. Grace appeared, and the speed with which she navigated the narrow, curved stairwell made his heart rate soar. Her face went in and out of focus, as though he had partaken of too much ale.

"Have a care, lass," his words sounded slurred. If only he had a drink to moisten his cracked lips and parched throat.

"Gabriel—" The catch in her voice and the panicked fear he saw in her eyes spurred his attempt to rally.

He forced his muscles to respond and straightened to his full height. "I'll be better soon, Grace." Then blackness swamped him, and he tumbled into unconsciousness.

Chapter 2

GRACE RUSHED FORWARD to touch Gabriel's fever-flushed brow and cheeks. If the heat pouring off him in waves was not enough to frighten her, the way he toppled like an oak cut free from its roots drove a stake of panic through her chest.

She barely glanced at Derrick and James. "Bring him upstairs." She gripped Robert's arm when he meant to follow. "Go t' the great room and ask Lady Mary t' come at once."

"What of the visitors?"

"I dinna care if St. Michael has traveled through the gates of heaven t' visit, Gabriel is more important." Her voice shook, but she staved off her tears.

"Aye." Robert strode through the door leading into the great room.

"Bring him this way," she instructed Derrick and James.

Her bed would be too narrow for Gabriel, but they were readying chambers for visitors in the west wing, so a bed would be available there. She paused to wait for them on the landing above, afraid to watch them navigate the narrow, curved stairs with Gabriel hanging slack between them. As soon as they reached the landing, she opened the door to the passageway and directed the men to the first open door.

The bed was already made with fresh linens and warm pelts. The fire already set. Derrick and James staggered through the doorway with Gabriel's limp body hanging between them.

Grace jerked the pelts down and made room for him. "What happened t' him?" she asked.

James answered. "The second day out we were ambushed by a

band intent on freeing the prisoners. One of them would have run me through, but Gabriel blocked the man's blade. Another caught his arm with the tip of his blade. It is festering."

Grace placed a hand against Gabriel's forehead and cheeks, which were ruddy with fever. Heat radiated off him in such waves she gasped. She moved to bare the arm wrapped in a dressing soiled from several days on horseback. Fluid had seeped from the wound and crusted the dressing to it.

She worked it free gently. "Oh, merciful God." The words were wrenched from her in a raspy whisper, her throat closing around them. Though not large, the injury was deep, raw, and angry, and his arm was swollen, as well as his hand. Red streaks ran from his forearm to his elbow. Her heart clenched. She'd seen men die from such injuries. Her tears blurred Gabriel's beloved face.

Lady Mary was calling her name, the sound carrying through the doorway. "Derrick, please show her where we have placed him. James, help me remove his clothing. He's burning up with fever, and we'll have t' bathe him with cool cloths t' bring it down."

The men jumped to do her bidding. Grace unbuckled Gabriel's heavy girdle. James caught her wrist. "Derrick and I can do this, Grace. He's too heavy for either you or Lady Mary t' lift." The tears she'd fought so hard to suppress ran unheeded down her cheeks. She nodded and stepped aside.

Lady Mary entered the room and frowned when she saw Grace's tear-streaked face.

"You will need your basket of herbs and fresh water, m'lady. I will go for them." Uncertain of her composure, Grace rushed from the room. She ran downstairs to the great room and met Robert coming up. "Go t' the kitchen. We'll need a large skin of wine, some vinegar, salt, and fresh water, and a large pot t' heat it in. See they bring it immediately."

Turning, she took the narrow stairs two at a time past her chamber, the solar, Lord and Lady Campbell's chamber, and reached the next level, which served as storage for clothing and weapons. She gripped the basket that held Lady Mary's things just inside the door, and another of dressings.

By the time she returned to the chamber, Gabriel had been stripped and placed beneath the covers. Fever had taken over and he shivered. Grace set the baskets aside and rushed to the bed to pull up more pelts to warm him.

Several servants arrived with the things she ordered, and Grace busied herself with heating the water at the fireplace while Lady Mary set out herbs and balms. Derrick stood watch while Grace bathed Gabriel's face and shoulders with cool water to soothe his fever, and Lady Mary washed the debris from the wound.

Lady Mary's silence, and her careful composure while she studied the injury, frightened Grace as much as her own thoughts. "We will do what we can, Grace. Gabriel is strong and fit. I have seen men fight their way back from such injuries."

Her heart quailed inside her as though from a blow.

Derrick broke the silence. "If we take the arm, he may yet survive," Derrick said. His voice sounded as though a fist was clamped around his throat. "'Twill keep the poison from spreading farther."

"Take his arm?" Grace repeated, her voice stolen to a gasp by shock. Gabriel was a warrior. He depended on both hands, both arms, to survive. Without his arm he could not protect himself.

How many times had he spoken in warning to her about expecting him to be anything other than the man he was?

She had chosen him to love despite knowing he might die in battle.

"We have time enough t' make that decision, Derrick," Lady Mary said.

"The longer we wait, the weaker he will be. He must be strong t' survive having the limb removed."

But to expect Gabriel to live as anything less—Without his arm, he could not even plow a field, swing a hammer, hunt, or chop wood. It would destroy him, and he would hate them for it.

"'Twould be a kinder service t' kill him now than to take his arm." The pain of saying those words nearly brought her to her knees.

Derrick turned on her. "Gabriel's life is more important than his arm."

"Aye, t' me, t' you." Before she proclaimed her love for Gabriel, she never had the courage to stand her ground for what she believed, or to voice it. Lady Mary led her to this by example. Gabriel had encouraged her strength. She reached deep for that well of resolve and courage now, though every limb shook as though they might crumble beneath her. "But in the taking, we would end his life as surely as if we had thrust a blade into his heart."

Derrick took a step toward her. Lady Mary gripped his arm. "She speaks the truth, Derrick."

His dirt-brown eyes swung from one of them to the other, boring into their hearts.

"After we have tended his wounds for a short time, let us see how he fares," Lady Mary said.

Derrick wrenched his arm from Mary's grasp and stomped out of the room.

Leaving the women little time to recover from the confrontation, Gabriel groaned and thrashed beneath the covers, attempting to kick them off. Grace gripped the sheet and pelts that covered him and held them in place while talking to him soothingly. She thought of everything she had learned from Lady Mary about healing in the last few years. Determination beat back her uncertainty. No matter what it took, she would not lose Gabriel.

She scooped heated water out into a cup and sprinkled ground willow bark and coriander in to steep. She dipped more out into a bowl and added some vinegar, yarrow and herbs to it. While Lady Mary bathed Gabriel's wound with the mixture, Grace bathed the dust and grime from his body.

His body was a forge, radiating an alarming heat and warming the cool cloth as soon as it touched his skin. Grace spooned the willow bark tea into his mouth and continued the compresses.

"If only it were winter, we could pack snow in around him t' cool him," Lady Mary said after they had worked in silence for almost an hour.

"He is strong. He will survive this." Grace had to believe that. The thought of losing him numbed her heart and mind and made it impossible to think.

After several more minutes, Lady Mary straightened, grimaced, and stretched her back. She went to the door to James, who sat just outside. "Go t' the kitchen and ask Fia t' come up."

"Aye, m'lady."

"I dinna wish t' leave you or him, but I must return t' our guest, Grace. Fia will be here to help you."

"Thank you, Lady Mary."

Mary rested a hand on her shoulder, her blue eyes intent. "Should he worsen, send for me."

"Aye, I will."

"You have learned much at my side, Grace. We have learned more together. Have faith in yourself and God. Gabriel will overcome this." Her fingers tightened for a moment, then released.

Mary was almost at the door when Grace asked, "Who is the guest, Lady Mary? Lord Alexander said 'twas someone I knew."

"'Tis Lord Davis Ramsay. Do you remember him?"

The blood seemed to drain from her head, and Grace braced a hand upon the small night stand to steady herself. Everything in the room took on a grayish, smoky hue, as though a veil had dropped between her and what stood before her. The shock slowly receded and her vision cleared. "Aye, Lady Mary. 'Twas his wife, Aundeen, who set me out on the street at the age of ten and three."

She had no doubt why the woman had banished her from their house. She had witnessed too much and shared what she had seen in hopes of protecting sweet Elspeth. She touched her cheek where Lady Ramsay's hand had bruised her face.

Caisteal Sith had proven a welcome haven from her guardian and the mean streets she had survived for nearly a month. "Lord Alexander found me and sent me here."

Lady Mary's jaw clenched. "Lord Ramsay is a widower now."

And what had become of Elspeth, their daughter? Who had been there to protect her once Grace was gone?

"For what purpose has he come?"

"He has not yet mentioned his purpose. When he does, should it concern you, be assured I will tell you."

"Thank you, Lady Mary."

When her mistress turned aside, Grace's anxiety for her rose, and she said her name. Mary paused at the door to look over her shoulder.

"Dinna ever be alone with him, or allow any of the maids t' serve him in his chambers," Grace warned. "He is not t' be trusted. Especially with the younger lasses."

Mary's features froze, and she searched Grace's face. With a nod, she said, "I appreciate your counsel in this matter, Grace."

Gabriel began to shiver once again, and Grace jerked her attention back to him. She dragged the covers up over him, pressed her cool cheek to his hot, beard-stubbled one, and whispered words of love and encouragement.

FIA, ONE OF the scullery maids, came to help, and the two of them worked together to make Gabriel more comfortable.

Grace placed the vinegar-soaked compress on his arm to draw out the poison, and he groaned. The sound struck a blow to her heart every time.

Derrick returned near midnight to check on Gabriel's progress. Gabriel's arm was still swollen, but the red streaks seemed less angry. The wound was clean and less inflamed. But his fever raged on. Derrick raised him so Grace could spoon the willow bark tea into his mouth, and rubbed his throat to encourage him to swallow.

Derrick glanced at Fia, asleep in a chair with her head resting on the edge of the bed. The lass had nodded off nearly an hour before. "Ye canna continue like this, Grace. I will take over for a time while you rest."

"I winna leave him."

"Then lie before the hearth and rest." Derrick pushed her out of the way to wring a cool compress nearly dry and place it against Gabriel's forehead, with another across his throat.

Grace nearly groaned aloud when she straightened from her bent posture and stretched her back. Exhaustion weighted every muscle. When she lay down, the thin mat before the fire did little to cushion the hard wooden floor. Her hip dug into the unyielding surface, and she rolled onto her back. When the ache in her back receded, every muscle trembled and slumped in relief. She threw an arm over her eyes. Tears welled, and she turned her head so Derrick would not witness her weakness. If Gabriel could bear this illness, she could bear it, too.

Mayhap they should take his arm. Fear and worry crouched waiting inside her...waiting to rip her resolve to pieces...but she beat it back. He would hate them all. Even if it saved his life, he would turn away from her, from them.

Though she had never felt so tired, she could not sleep with such fears and doubts circling through her thoughts. As soon as her eyes closed, another concern rushed back to torment her. Lord Ramsay. Why had he come? She prayed it had nothing to do with her.

She did not remember how she had come to be in his household. She did remember Mam, her nursemaid, the only person who had given her affection and care. After Mam died in her bed—of what, Grace did not remember—Grace had been sent to his manor house in the lowlands. She remembered the long ride on the small wagon, but little else.

She had worked for several months with the children as a helper to the nursemaid before Lord Ramsay, an absent guardian, came to the nursery. He had been imposing, dark, and had brushed aside his children's attempts at affection for fear they would scuff his boots or soil his shirt.

She'd been glad he was not any kin of hers, for he had looked at her as though she was less than mud upon his boots. She felt pity for the children, especially the three older lads, for they had been so eager to please the man.

She remembered Blair, two years her senior, and one of the servants' oldest girl. She had stood tall, her straw-colored hair curling about her shoulders and down her back. She assisted the nursemaid, Mistress Beatrice, and had been patient and loving with Grace and the children, her voice sweet and soft. It had been she who slept in the nursery with them to tend to their needs at night.

Grace shifted upon the hard floor while the pain of her memories triggered a need to curl up like a hedgehog. If only she had understood much sooner. But would it have made any difference? Blair would have still been just a servant's daughter, and Grace the unwanted orphan. Why had he done it?

Lord Ramsay had ignored them all until that one visit to the nursery. At Christmas they were directed to bring the children down to the solar to spend a few moments with him and his wife. His gaze once again fixed on Blair in a way that made her color and fidget. Just remembering the hungry look in his eyes made gooseflesh to break out on Grace's arms now, and she shuddered.

He ignored Mistress Beatrice and directed his many questions about the behavior and care of the children to Blair. She stammered her way through the answers, her panicked gaze fastened on the nursemaid, as though begging for her to intercede. "Very good. One day you will have a nursery of your own t' run," he said lightly, and even Mistress Beatrice sighed in relief.

A week later Lord Ramsay appeared in the nursery. He visited for a few moments with his children, and spoke to Beatrice, but his attention strayed again and again to Blair. He grew so bold as to touch her hair and curl a piece around his finger. His tone jovial, he compared her locks to spun gold. But there had been more behind his words, his looks. Mistress Beatrice had been as shaken as Blair when he left.

His visits grew more frequent. He called Blair out of the nursery at times to talk to her in private. Grace remembered well the day when things changed. Blair returned from their discussion barely able to walk, her hair and clothing disheveled and her eyes glazed and red from crying. Mistress Beatrice had taken her aside and comforted her, her voice soothing, but having a tone to it Grace would never forget.

"Say nothin' about this t' anyone, Blair. 'Twould mean you and your *máthair's* lives."

Grace led the children in a game to distract them while Mistress Beatrice helped Blair straighten her clothes and bathe her hurts. Blair was silent, her face white and expressionless. She sat before the fire the rest of the day with a faraway look, as though she had gone deep inside herself to escape what had happened.

She was never the same. And after each visit from Lord Ramsay, grew more and more despondent.

Grace threw an arm across her eyes, hoping to block out the memories, but now the lid had been forced open by the man's appearance, the pain came flooding back.

One night Blair's soft moans awakened her to find Blair twisting and turning next to her on the narrow bed they shared. Grace rushed to light a candle and felt something sticky on her arm and shift. In the flickering light it had looked like ink. Closer to the fire it had shown scarlet.

Grace held the candle high and jerked aside the bedclothes. A red-brown stain spread beneath Blair's hips. Grace smothered a scream, and leapt up to get help.

Mistress Beatrice accompanied her back to the room, but sent her to fetch two others. The stairs were cold beneath Grace's bare feet, the blood on her nightshift sticking to her hip and leg. Blair's blood had dried to a crust on her arm.

When they peeled back Blair's shift, it was plain the blood was coming from between her thighs. The shock on the maid Alice's face turned her expression stony. "She is losing a babe."

The other maid, Rose, shook her head. "She's too young t' be with child."

In her pain, Blair latched onto Grace's arm. Her blue eyes looked pale and glazed. "When he comes for you, run, Grace. Dinna let him touch you."

"Who has come for you, lass?" one of the maids asked.

Blair's grip weakened and her voice was remote. "Lord Ramsay. 'Twas he who hurt me. He is a devil. He forces me down upon the floor and tears at my clothes. I fight him with all my might."

The two maids exchanged a glance.

A sudden gush of something dark spilled from between Blair's thighs, and her hand would have fallen away from Grace's arm, had Grace not continued to grip it.

After only a moment or two her cheeks grew pale and her breathing slowed. At first Grace thought perhaps the pain had eased and she was over the worst of it. Her eyes focused on Grace, but there was an unseeing distance in them. "Dinna let him touch you, Grace."

"I winna do so."

"Never be alone with him."

"I swear it."

When she stopped breathing, Grace cried out and clasped the girl's hand against her. "Dinna leave me, Blair." After so many losses already...

Even now the pain drove her to her feet. She could not lose Gabriel. Happiness was within their grasp. Just two short weeks away. She loved him more than life itself. Should he die...

If Lord Ramsay's purpose for being here had anything to do with her, Gabriel would be her only defense.

She moved to the bed and shook Fia from her slumber. "Go t' the kitchen and fetch bread and gruel and some wine. We need food. Gabriel needs food."

"Aye, Grace." The girl stumbled from the room still half asleep.

"How do you propose t' feed him?" Derrick demanded. "He winna wake."

"I can wet the bread until it creates a soup. I will sit behind him and hold him while you spoon it into his mouth."

"He may choke."

"He needs his strength t' fight this, Derrick. I winna lose him."

Chapter 3

HE RAN THROUGH the mist, his heart racing with panic. He had lost something of great importance. Something he could not go on without. It was the key to everything. He had to find it. The mist was like a blanket, thick and gray, determined to hold him back. He was tangled in it like a fly in a spider web. He had to tear free.

He twisted his body back and forth until one arm wiggled clear of the bindings. He ripped at the mist, his fingers like claws, and though it drifted away like smoke, he could not break free. It stood like a gray wall between him and what he sought.

Gabriel woke to a sense of urgency, his chest heaving with every breath. His head pounded and his eyelids felt too heavy to lift. Had he partaken of too much wine or ale? If he had, it had not been enough, for his mouth was dry as a forge pit and tasted of one, too. Just where was he? And was it Bruce Campbell or Derrick making such a racket that a man couldna finish his rest? Whoever 'twas, he'd see him booted far away, then he would finish his sleep.

But first he must open his eyes. It was a struggle to do so, and afterward he felt too tired to do much else. Every muscle seemed drained of strength. His body ached everywhere. The high ceiling above was not his. Where did he lie?

It all rushed back to him at once. His arm had throbbed with pain in rhythm with the beat of his heart. Derrick and someone else had carried him into the hall where the blackness had taken him.

His head felt heavy, but he rolled it on the pillow and spied Lady Mary asleep in the chair next to the bed. Where Lady Mary led, Grace would not be far behind. Where was she? He needed to see her, speak to her. He had not treated her with complete honesty, and it lay on his conscience as heavy as the mist in his dream. But he could not keep his eyes open for the heavy weights attached to each lid.

BRIGHT SUNLIGHT STREAMED through a window high in the wall and beamed on the floor next to her to reflect onto her face. It pierced Grace's closed lids and she threw up a hand to shield her eyes. She rolled to her knees, then staggered to her feet. Every muscle protested, and she bit back a groan. The wood floor felt cold beneath her feet, her thin stockings providing little protection.

Derrick lay in front of the fireplace as though he had dropped there. His snores rattled through the room like thunder. Fia once again lay asleep with her head on the foot of the bed. Lady Mary dozed in a chair, her hands folded in her lap as though they had dropped there in exhaustion.

Grace crept close to the bed, her attention focused on Gabriel's large body. He lay still, his face so pale his beard looked like soot against his skin. Shadows like half moons discolored the skin beneath his eyes, and his lips were dry and cracked. In the three days she had been caring for him, hollows had formed beneath his cheekbones.

Dear God, how much more of this could he take? Grace bit her lip to stifle the cry of pain working its way up her throat. Instead, she raised the cloth folded over his injured arm to study the injury. It looked less angry, and the red streaks had receded.

Gabriel's eyes opened and she gasped.

"Grace." His voice escaped, barely the sound of a breath.

She sat down on the bed and grasped his hand. It was warm, but no longer burning with the fever that had blistered his lips. Relieved tears trailed down her face. She released his hand to cup his face and pressed grateful kisses on his forehead, his cheeks, and his chapped lips.

Was that a small smile she caught curving his mouth?

He needed water. She reached for the cup on a small table next to the bed and, using a wooden spoon, dribbled water into his mouth as she had been doing for hours on end. After only a few swallows, he shook his head.

"Sleep." The one croaked word seemed to require a monumental effort.

Grace nodded.

"You." He brushed his hand along the heavy tartan next to him.

He wanted her to lie beside him. The idea at any other time would have seemed shameful, but after the past three days, she would gladly give him anything that brought him ease.

She moved around the bed and touched Fia's shoulder. The girl woke with a start, her young face creased by the tartan she'd bunched beneath her head and used as a pillow.

Grace pressed a finger against her lips and whispered, "You may go to bed. Gabriel's fever has broken."

Fia's features lit with a relieved smile, and she clasped her hands together against her small breasts, her eyes bright.

Grace and the girl shared a quick hug. "I am grateful to you, Fia." Grace whispered against her ear.

Fia's thin arms tightened about Grace. "You and Lady Mary care for us all."

Her eyes on Gabriel's still form, Fia crept across the room and out the door, closing the heavy door quietly behind her.

Grace eased upon the bed, stretched out next to Gabriel, and rested her head on the soft pillow. The surface was much more comfortable than the narrow cot in her room. She had not shared a bed with another person since being in the nursery, and it felt both strange and right to take her rest next to Gabriel.

His eyes opened and he turned his head.

Heat touched Grace's cheeks, but she could not resist caressing his scruff-covered jaw. The fever had truly left him. She pulled the wool tartan up over his chest.

With a brief smile, he closed his eyes. His breathing returned to the steady, even tempo of slumber.

Grace tucked her hands beneath her cheek. Overcome by relief and exhaustion, she fell into a dreamless sleep.

It seemed only moments later she was being awakened by Lady Mary.

"You must rise and dress, Grace. Lord Ramsay has requested an audience with you."

Groggy from sleep, Grace first turned to check on Gabriel and realized she was in her own bed.

"I asked Derrick to carry you to your chamber."

She heard no censure in Lady Mary's tone, and turned aside to avoid seeing any in her pale blue eyes. "What time is it?"

"'Tis noon. One of the maids will bring you a meal."

"For what purpose has he asked to see me?"

Lady Mary's expression was grave. "The king's regent has seen fit to charter you a tract of land with a manor house. A modest income comes with it. 'Tis the same tract of land that belonged to your family at one time. But there is an issue. You must first wed and have a husband in order to claim it." Lady Mary paused to grip Grace's hands hard. "Lord Ramsay has told Alexander he wishes to extend to you a proposal of marriage."

"But I am already betrothed."

"Lord Ramsay has contested the betrothal on the grounds that Gabriel has no title, and thus 'tis against the King's law for the two of you to wed."

Grace's heart seemed to stop, as did everything else. The memory of Blair's pale, still, bloodsoaked body rose up to inflame her emotions. "How did he learn of the betrothal?"

"The priest announced the banns, and one of his men told him."

"Today is the last day." Tears burned her eyes and she covered her face with her hands. She wanted to scream and tear at her hair in a passion of denial. Gabriel had fought his way free of the fever, just in time for their happiness to be ripped away.

Love held no value in noble games or struggles for money,

property, and power. She had seen it happen when Lady Mary's father abducted her and threatened to kill her and baby Kieran. Lord Ramsay's petition would hold sway over Gabriel's because of his noble birth.

She rose from the bed. "I should confer with Lord Alexander first before I have an audience with Lord Ramsay. There are things I must share with him."

"Alexander is waiting in the chapel for you, as is the priest."

"I will go to them now."

Grace stumbled to her feet and rushed to drag the ribbon from her braid. She tugged her hair free and gave it a cursory brushing. She secured the length of it at the base of her neck, cleaned her teeth, then washed her hands and face at the basin. Although her surcoat was hopelessly wrinkled and bore salt stains from the dripping cloths she'd used to bathe Gabriel's injury, she ignored both problems, merely giving the surcoat a hard tug to straighten it while she shoved her feet into her slippers. Once she was reasonably groomed, she and Lady Mary took the back stairs to the chapel in the west wing.

Lord Campbell and Father Dillion rose to their feet at the front of the chapel just before the altar when she and Lady Mary entered the room. A chill hung in the air, for the space stood in shadow during the morning hours. Only the tall candle-trees standing at either end of the altar provided a pale light. No fire had been set, since services were not in session, but a faint hint of incense and hot wax hung in the air.

"Grace," Lord Alexander greeted her with a nod. His masculine features were set, and his lips compressed into a taut line.

"I would beg your indulgence for continued sanctuary in your household, Lord Alexander. I winna be dragged from this place again' my will."

"No one will force you to do anythin' again' yer will, Grace. Ye have my oath."

For the first time in what seemed an hour, she drew a complete breath, though her throat continued to feel as though an iron band encircled it. She and Lady Mary sat in one of the wooden pews.

Grace gripped the seat on either side of her, her mouth dry and her breathing ragged. "Father Dillion, is your Bible at hand?"

"Always."

"I would ask you to fetch it."

The priest went to the altar and returned with it.

"Might I hold it?"

"Certes, you may do so." He extended the book to her.

"I've asked to hold this holy book so all of you will ken I speak the truth. I will not marry Lord Ramsay. Not because my love for Gabriel presents too firm a barrier to such a union, though it does, but because he is an evil man who defiles young lasses. Lasses too young to ken what he is about."

She hugged the bible to her, hoping to gain comfort and strength from it. Then she placed it in her lap. "When I was a lass of ten, I was orphaned and taken to his home. My duty was to help care for Lord Ramsay's children, along with their governess and a young lass of ten and two. A servant's daughter. She slept there in the nursery with us, and waited upon the children's needs at night so the nursemaid wouldna be disturbed. Her name was Blair."

Grace tried not to stumble over words while she imparted everything she remembered, her eyes focused on the Bible in her lap, her hands gripping Lady Mary's. To speak of such matters would have been difficult with only Lady Mary, but to reveal them before Lord Alexander and the priest was painful.

"Blair died losing the babe he had forced upon her. She was too young and frail to carry it. She named him to me and three other witnesses as the man who had hurt her. Though she was dying, she warned me to run, should he wish to ever be alone with me. To never allow him t' touch me."

Grace forced her gaze to meet both men's. "When I was ten and three, he began t' come to the nursery more oft." Lady Mary's hands gripped hers almost painfully, and Lord Alexander shifted in his seat.

"'Twas not me he came to see. 'Twas his...his daughter. She

was ten. I caught him in the nursery one night pulling the covers back to look upon her in her shift. When I made my presence known, he pretended t' settle the bedclothes around her, but I knew. By then I had heard things from the other servants, things I would not have understood had I not born witness to Blair's death. There were others he harmed."

"I took Elspeth into my bed, thinking it would hold him at bay. He came to my room, removed her, and carried her back to her bed. I armed myself with my dagger and followed him. He left her unscathed for the night, but brushed against me in a threatening way when he left. I began t' sleep in the nursery so I could hear him come in. Each time I let him see I was awake and watching."

"A fortnight later, Lady Ramsay threw me from their home. She believed 'twas I he was coming to the nursery t' see. When I tried to explain, she struck me hard and knocked me to the ground." Her gaze jumped to Alexander's face. "It left a bruise I carried for almost a fortnight." She touched her cheekbone in memory. 'Twas probably what saved me from some of the harm that could have come my way. It made me most ugly t' look upon."

Lady Mary laid an arm about her shoulders and gave her a hug, her face wet with tears. "You did all you could to protect the child, Grace."

"I have always wondered ..." Had she had the courage to do more...to strike the man down. They would not be sitting here now. Nor would she. She'd been a child herself, ten and three, but had looked younger. No one would have believed her had she spoken out. Only the other servants.

Lord Campbell rose and came to sit on the other side of her. She was shocked when he took her hand. "'Twas Lady Ramsay who sent me to search for you, Grace. Mayhap her conscience tasked her, mayhap she discovered your accusations were true. But 'twas she who sent for me and asked me t' find you."

He gave her hand a squeeze. "I am going to ask several things of you that will be most difficult."

She swallowed hard and forced herself to look into his grave, amber eyes. "Aye, m'lord."

"First I would ask you to tell me the name of the women who witnessed Blair's death and heard her…confession."

"'Twas Rose and Alice. One worked as Lady Ramsay's chambermaid, the other in the kitchen. The nursemaid was Mistress Beatrice. She was still there when I left."

"You said Blair was one and three. The age of consent is twelve, Grace. You are sure she said she fought him but he used force on her?"

"Aye, she said he hurt her more than once. I saw her afterwards many times, as did Mistress Beatrice."

His jaw worked several moments, his features hardening. His voice seemed dangerously quiet when he spoke.

"The second thing I must ask of you, a hard thing, is, should Lord Ramsay propose, you must give him leave t' plead his cause."

Shock took her breath. "My Lord?"

"In pretense. 'Tis time I need, Grace. Time to find these women, and perhaps others who have witnessed Lord Ramsay's…" His gaze traveled back and forth between her and Lady Mary.

"Sinfulness," suggested Father Dillion, his cheeks ruddy, as though he had been standing too close to a fire. A light burned in his eyes, and his fists were clenched at his sides.

They believed her. The relief lifted some of the weight from her and made it easier to breathe.

"Can you do as I ask?"

"I dinna wish to ever be alone with him."

"Ye winna be. I will enlist some of the men to accompany ye about the castle."

Grace remained silent. Could she keep her silence before the others? "What if he should harm a lass here?"

Lord Alexander squeezed her hand. "He will be watched closely, Grace. I give you my word."

Could she play the part of a woman debating her future between two men? Could she be convincing?

Had Lord Ramsay forgotten their battle of wills in the nursery? Was that perhaps why he had come to propose marriage? As his wife, she would never be allowed to stand witness against him.

As for before, there would never have been any other outcome. Had she attempted to strike him, he would have killed her or thrown her out himself. He hadn't needed to. Instead he had his wife to do the deed for him.

Grace was no longer the innocent young girl standing again' him alone. She had her wits about her. But could she do this? "Will this end his hold o'er me, m'lord?"

"If we are able to find witnesses willing to speak again' him, aye, it will."

"And if ye are unable t' do so?"

"He may petition the crown for yer hand, since ye have no other male relatives to contest or agree to the match. I will be sending such a petition on Gabriel's behalf."

But it would not carry the weight of a Lord. And what if Lord Ramsay had already done so? "I winna wed him, Lord Alexander." 'Twould be better to live unwed and in poverty and to die a free woman than to live with a monster.

Lady Mary exchanged a look with Alexander and placed an arm about her shoulders. "'Twill not happen, Grace. Even the regent would be reluctant to force ye t' wed a man ye despise."

"His only interest is the property the king's regent has chartered to me. Might I give it to him so he will go away?"

"That is not possible, Grace," Lord Alexander said with a sigh. "'Tis a gift from the regent, and thus from the King, and to show so little regard for it would be a direct insult to both." He took her hand again. "And yes, the property would mean much to him. There is word that since the Bruce's death the English are once again a threat to Scotland's independence. Lord Ramsay is looking for a safe haven since his holdings lie close to Edinburgh. So, aye, he wants you to accept the charter as quickly as possible so he might claim it through marriage." She had never seen Lord Alexander look more solemn. "'Tis my action that wrought this, Grace. I attempted to set things right for you and have caused you much distress. I will see this resolved if 'tis in my power to do so, I give you my oath. But you must stand strong."

With his tawny eyes gazing directly into hers, Grace had no other choice but to nod. "Aye, m'lord. I will do as you ask." But his reassurances did nothing to ease the sick burning in the pit of her stomach. Should all be lost, she would defy her King and lose her life, because she would not wed anyone but Gabriel.

LORD ALEXANDER DIRECTED her to an antechamber just off the great hall. It was where he ruled on disputes between his tenants or men. Grace had been in the room only thrice in all the time she lived at the castle, and only because she had been tasked to bring him food.

A large table surrounded by heavy chairs dominated the space. Behind it, close to the fireplace, stood Lord Ramsay. He turned to face them when she and Lord Alexander entered.

Nearly eight years had passed since she had seen the man. Gray was sprinkled through his dark hair, but it still lay thick against his head and waved back from his forehead. His deep blue gaze raked down her form, and his jaw tightened.

"I have been waiting for some time, Lord Alexander."

"I am the one at fault," Grace said. "I have been three days in the sickroom, and had just found my rest. I needed a wee time to wake."

She watched the struggle behind his face. To say more and insult her would not provide the right tone for the conversation he wanted. "I am sure the man you have been nursing is grateful for you care."

Lord Alexander motioned to him. "You remember Lord Ramsay, do you not, Lady Grace?"

She wanted very badly to grip Lord Alexander's hand. She remembered doing so when first he found her on the street, dirty, frightened, battered, and bruised. Half starved from hiding in the deepest alleyways, too frightened to ask for food. Did Lord

Ramsay think she would forget any of that? Anger gave her strength, and she straightened her shoulders. She would not be browbeaten or cowed by the likes of him.

"Aye, I remember him." She forced herself into a brief curtsy.

"It has been some years since we have seen each other. You have blossomed from the small, shy girl I remember."

Did the man think her daft? She kept her eyes directed at the floor to hide her distain. "Thank you."

"Lord Alexander has told you why I am here?"

"Aye, he has."

"Since we have a past connection through your father, and I offered you shelter in the past, I want t' offer my protection and support during this time."

"Thank you, but since I have resided here for some time, I have asked Lord Alexander to act as my advisor and protector for now."

Lord Ramsay glanced in Alexander's direction with a frown.

"You have a missive for me from the lord regent?" she asked.

"Aye. I was asked t' deliver it. I thought we might peruse the documents together, so I might counsel you on their meaning."

The idea of being trapped in a room alone with the man made her skin crawl. "I am grateful for the offer, Lord Ramsay, but I prefer t' read them myself. Should anythin' be unclear t' me, I will seek your counsel."

His brows rose. "I was not aware you had been taught to read, since you have been living beneath your station for some time now."

"I have received much in return for my service t' my lady, sir. She and Lord Alexander have been most generous."

Lord Ramsay folded his hands behind his back, his gaze sharp while he studied her. "You are not at all as I thought you would be, Lady Grace. 'Tis most pleasing to see all you have accomplished despite the challenges you have faced."

Grace ignored his attempt at flattery. "Might I have the papers now, Lord Ramsay?"

"They were put in my care for a reason. Should something

befall them and they were damaged or destroyed..."

Lord Alexander broke into his excuses. "The regent will have a copy of them, Lord Ramsay. 'Tis to Lady Grace the property has been chartered. She has a right to see the documents. If it will set your concerns t' rest, I will take possession of them and hold them in trust for her. Since she has asked me t' be her advisor, I will wish t' read them as well."

An expression of impatience flickered across Lord Ramsay's face, and his cheeks reddened. "I will send for them now." He strode to the door and spoke to his manservant, who stood just outside the door. "While we wait, there is something else I would like t' speak to you about, Lady Grace. 'Tis the matter of your betrothal."

Lord Alexander shifted closer, and she felt the heat from his body align itself along her side. The urge to grip his hand once again threatened to overwhelm her.

Ramsay fixed his expression into lines of sympathy as he moved close. "I only sought to spare you and the man you were betrothed to embarrassment and possible punishment. 'Tis against the King's law for you t' wed beneath your station."

Rage flooded her, and for a moment it took all her strength to overcome the urge to lash out at him. Her head pounded with the effort to smother her emotions and maintain a serene expression. "Since my circumstances have changed so suddenly, I think it my duty, as a recognized subject of the King, t' learn more about the King's law. Thank you for suggesting it, Lord Ramsay."

"'Twould please me to share my own knowledge on the matter, Lady Grace," Lord Alexander said. "I may even have a book on the subject."

The quick tap on the door could not have come soon enough. When a thin, fine-boned-young man—nay, he was closer to a lad—entered the room, Grace watched him cross the room to the table, for he carried a leather satchel. His featured looked more than familiar. It wasn't until Lord Ramsay took the satchel from him and they both stood in profile that Grace recognized a resemblance between them. Was this perhaps one of his sons? No, he was too old for that. They had been weans when she was there. A nephew, perhaps?

Lord Ramsay removed the heavy papers from the case. "Please allow me t' point out the royal seal and the signature. They are all in order. All you must do is sign them before witnesses, Lady Grace.

"Why must they bear my signature, Lord Ramsay?"

"In acceptance of the charter and the terms therein, Lady Grace."

Grace reached for the top sheet that held the seal. The crest with the lion clearly marked the paper with the word *Defense* above. She placed it carefully atop the others and lifted the seven or eight other sheets along with it.

"You must sign it before taking it from the room, Lady Grace."

Grace smiled. "I winna sign anythin' I havena read, Lord Ramsay."

"Then read them here and now."

"Nay. I would read them at my leisure and sign them when I am through."

"That is not the way of it, my lady."

She lay the narrow sheaf of papers back on the table. If she did not sign the contract, she did not have to abide by it. "I will wait until Lord Alexander has had time t' read the charter. It has been a tiring three days, and I am not at my best."

"Lady Grace, it will be an insult t' the King t' refuse such a gift."

"This is not a gift, sir." Shackles and the loss of her meager freedoms where what these papers represented. "A gift is given freely without demand for anythin' in return. I will wait until I ken what terms the regent has set for my signature."

"Does it matter? You will still have t' sign them." He turned to Alexander. "You must impress upon her the seriousness of her actions, should she refuse."

"Lady Grace is a loyal subject of the King. She will do her duty when she must. But 'tis not unreasonable for her t' want to ken what is expected of her in return for such an honor." Lord Alexander stepped closer. "Surely you recognize how difficult the last three days have been. A valued member of our clan has been near death, and has just this morn drawn back from it. 'Tis because of Grace's care he is still alive. You must rest, Lady Grace."

"Thank you, m'lord."

"Lord Ramsay is able to counsel me, should I have difficulty understanding the contract. You and I will read the charter together, perhaps tomorrow."

"Thank you, m'lord." Grace bent her head in deference. "Lord Ramsay."

Though ignorant of most of the strange protocols governing the congress between lords and ladies, Grace was well aware of the insult when she did not ask Ramsay's leave. But to chastise her for it would appear ungentle. He nodded, but his voice was gruff with impatience when he said, "Of course."

She walked out the door and climbed the steps to her room. By the time she reached the door, she was breathing hard and shaking all over. Lord Alexander had saved her from refusing the King's gift. With his quick understanding, he had granted her time to consider all aspects of the situation. Should she reach a moment where she would have to openly refuse, she might find herself at the end of a rope.

Once again curled upon the bed with a sleepless day stretching before her, she mulled over what recourse she might have.

She was trapped like a fly in a web, and now she understood what Lady Mary went through when first she had been forced to wed Lord Alexander. But he was a man of strong character, and his love was true.

'Twould be better to hang than to give up the man she loved and be wed to another against her will.

Chapter 4

GABRIEL FORCED HEAVY lids open and focused on the shadow sitting next to his bed. When he attempted to say something, the only sound that emerged was a groan.

"So you have decided t' rise from the dead, my friend." Derrick's familiar voice drew his eyes upward, and finally they cleared.

"What has happened?"

"You have been wracked with fever for three days, Gabriel." Derrick lifted his head and urged him to swallow some liquid from a wooden cup.

"Where is Grace?"

"Her duties have torn her away from your side, though it was with great reluctance."

Gabriel frowned. Something in Derrick's tone brought more clarity to his fuzzy thoughts. "What duties?"

"Lord Alexander has a visitor who has demanded her presence. 'Twas he and his company in the courtyard when we arrived." Derrick sat in the chair so Gabriel did not have to look up at him, then leaned forward and rested his elbows on his knees. "There is no easy way t' say this, so I will just say it. The regent has chartered property t' Grace, but she must wed in order t' claim it. Lord Ramsay has challenged your betrothal because you hold no title. He says you canna wed Grace without one."

Shock robbed time of its movement. It took great effort for him to drag breath into his lungs. "She is of noble birth?"

"Aye. 'Twould seem so."

"Why would she agree t' wed me, if she could marry a lord or duke?"

Derrick eyed him with a frown. "Certes, ye dinna need me to point out what has been plain t' ever'one else for months."

Because she loved him. She had told him so from the beginning.

He had proposed out of pity and a sense of obligation. But since he had been injured and suffering with fever, he realized he did not want to leave her and why. He had realized too late. He had withheld his feelings from her—from himself—when he could have been sharing so much more with her than the tepid passion he had doled out so sparingly.

A man of her own station could provide her with a great deal more than his small hut with its narrow buttery.

But she would already have more in her own right.

"What has she t' say about this?"

"She has not taken me into her confidence." Derrick's dung-brown eyes were dull and solemn. "But she has not been herself. She has gone into herself like a turtle into its shell. 'Tis the only way I can describe it."

It had taken her too long to blossom. He would not see her retreat into herself again.

Gabriel gripped the pelt covering him and flipped it back. But when he threw his legs over the side of the bed, the room spun sickeningly. His gorge rose. Derrick lunged and braced a hand against his shoulder when he would have pitched face-first to the floor.

"If you wish t' fight for her, you must first build yer strength, Gabriel."

The pain was rising, and with it a sense of betrayal. Why would she want him now when the promise of property would clear the way for her to make a better union? "Why did she not tell me of her birth?"

"Perhaps because it has never meant anything to her. Clan MacNab lost their place at court long ago. She had no family, no property t' bring to a union. She had found her place here without it. She has found her place with you, Gabriel. Do you think she will throw you aside for a manor house and wee bit of land?"

He could not fathom Grace behaving in such a manner. She was humble and sweet. He had always wanted more for her. At first out of pity, and then out of love.

"Grace needs you. The rest of us do as well."

Gabriel raised his head despite the urge to bock. "What do you mean?"

"Alexander has posted Artair and Robby to watch over Grace while Lord Ramsay and his men are here, and has ordered the others to be alert. He has posted men throughout the castle and around the man's own chambers. There is something more afoot than just the visit of a lord."

Aye, there was, if Alexander was acting with such caution. But Gabriel was unable to even stand. He needed to regain his strength. Quickly.

"I need food and drink. Something more than that tasteless swill you have been pouring down my gullet."

"That tasteless swill kept you alive and has helped your arm. Had it not been for Grace, you would now be waving about a stump."

Gabriel studied his swollen right arm. It was still red, but the wound looked less inflamed and was no longer weeping.

Derrick continued. "She said ye'd sooner be dead than crippled."

"Aye, I would. What use can I be if I canna defend myself or her?"

Derrick grinned and shrugged "She kens ye well."

She did, despite his attempts to maintain a distance between them. "After I have eaten, will you ask Lord Alexander if he has time to talk wi' me?"

"Aye, I will. And I'm sure he will. There is much you need to ken if you still intend t' claim Grace as your own."

"Aye, I do. I wanted her before she had a manor house and a bit of land. I would want her still if it disappeared into the mist all over again."

Derrick grinned. "I kent you would say that."

※

THE GREAT HALL was quieter during the meal than it had ever been before. Sitting at the head table with Lord Alexander and Lady Mary seemed foreign and uncomfortable. She glanced longingly at the table where Gabriel's men sat. Did they feel betrayed because she had hidden the truth from them? Would Gabriel? If they turned away from her now...

Davy Campbell flashed her a grin and nod and the tight knot spindling inside her unwound a wee bit.

Grace took a sip of wine from the tankard, though she would have preferred water or ale. Her throat almost closed around the liquid, and she suppressed a shudder. Her stomach pitched at the thought of sharing anything with the man who sat beside her.

"I'm told it has been one of your duties t' minister to the sick since you have been here," Lord Ramsay said while he cut apart the slab of pork he had placed upon the trencher. He cut it into slivers, but when he offered her a piece on the end of his knife, Grace shook her head.

He had changed little since last she had seen him. What a cruel irony it was that his strong jaw and piercing blue eyes were so pleasing to the eye, yet the inner man harbored such evil. His sharp gaze still pried and probed, searching for any weakness. And the cruel set of his mouth was still there behind his smile.

Grace kept her back straight with an effort, determined never to show him anything of her inner thoughts. He would use them against her. "Aye, 'twould be my duty, as Lady Mary feels it is hers."

"Will you do the same when you take residence at *Tasgaidh*?" He held out another bit of meat on his dagger and she shook her head again.

Tasgaidh. The word sent a chill coursing through her. It meant a deposited treasure. She would be locked away inside a fine house and live in torment, should this man have his way.

Realizing he was waiting for her reply, Grace cleared her throat. "Should I live there, 'twould be my duty t' do so. None of us are able t' survive without the help of others. The people who till the fields and raise the animals supply us with food. Those who stand fast against our enemies protect us. 'Tis for the good of the clan to assure that all are strong and well so they may perform their duties."

"That is a noble belief, Lady Grace."

She flinched from the name. She was just Grace.

"Not noble, Lord Ramsay. 'Tis the right thing to do."

"You may call me Davis if you wish, Grace."

He took a deep swallow of the wine. "How is the man you were betrothed to?"

He never missed an opportunity to remind her of his attempts to break her betrothal. As much as he wished to annul the contract, he could not. Only death would do so as far as she was concerned. "Gabriel's fever has broken."

"I realize you feel indebted to him and his men for the protection you have received whilst under Lord Campbell's roof, but honoring your betrothal t' him is no longer prudent. You are of noble birth, Grace. Your duty as a woman stands with those of your own station. Marriage between you and a commoner isna sanctioned by the crown."

"Nobility is not determined by blood alone, Lord Ramsay, but by one's actions as well. William Wallace was knighted for his efforts, was he not?"

"Aye, he was. But such honors are awarded rarely."

Gabriel had fought at Robert the Bruce's side. He had spilled the blood of both the Bruce's enemies and Lord Campbell's. He had proven himself brave and true on the battlefield and off. And his Campbell blood had been spilled defending Lord Campbell's men and his land. Was he not as noble a man as the likes of Davis Ramsay?

"Who is that blond man over there who smiled at you?" He pointed at the table where a number of Gabriel's men sat. Where she had eaten beside Gabriel until now.

"'Tis Davy. He is the blacksmith's apprentice."

"And the man there." He pointed at the table closest to them.

"'Tis Fergus. He builds things here at the castle."

"Do ye ken them all?"

"By name, most of them. Most of the villagers as well."

His eyes narrowed. "I ken you have lived the life of a servant too long and have grown too attached to those with whom you have associated."

Her face flushed hot with anger. "When I resided in your household I also knew most of the names of your servants. In truth, I was one of them. Or have you forgotten?"

Color flared across his cheeks, and his expression changed to one of wariness.

She was never going to be able to do this. She harbored too much animosity toward him.

"'Twould seem you hold that again' me, but not Lord and Lady Campbell."

"There is no shame in earning one's way in life, Lord Ramsay. I have chosen t' do that instead of living off the charity of others. Lord and Lady Campbell have encouraged me t' take pride in my service and pride in myself. If you will excuse me, I have duties I must see to now."

When she would have risen, he laid a hand on her arm to hold her in place. Grace controlled the urge to jerk away from his touch. "One of your duties is seeing t' the entertainment and comfort of Lord and Lady Campbell's guests, is it not?"

Grace shook her head. "You dinna understand my place here, sir. My duty is to see t' Lady Mary's needs alone, as her maid and companion."

His brows rose. "So you have never served other visitors here?"

Grace ignored the question. She knew the custom of female servants attending the male visitors, but Lord and Lady Campbell had never practiced it. Lady Mary found the men's behavior toward the servants ungentle. Male servants served their visitors. "If you have a need for anything, you must address Lord and Lady Campbell, and they will see to it. I bid you good eve, sir."

"You may cling to the ways of a servant, but the lady you are is there for all to see. Your place is with those you share *this* meal with at *this* table, not those beneath us."

"I see no one beneath me here, Lord Ramsay. I see people who have embraced me as part of their clan."

"But you're not of their clan, Lady Grace. You represent all that is left of the ruling class of the MacNabs. The property the King has chartered t' you would allow you to help your own clan reestablish itself. I could help you do that."

If he spoke the words directly to her, she would be forced to pretend to consider him. Grace rose and stepped back from the table, breaking free of his grip. "When I am allowed t' read the documents, I will make a decision."

Grace moved to curtsy to Lady Mary and Lord Alexander and ask their leave. Mary nodded her permission, but motioned for Grace to come close.

Lady Mary's frown mirrored concern. "Has Lord Ramsay said something untoward t' you?"

"Nothin' unexpected, my lady. But I canna bear another moment with him."

"Derrick sent word that Gabriel was much improved and is eating."

Relief relaxed the tightness in her chest and shoulders. "I am grateful for such welcome news. Thank you."

"Go to him and see for yourself."

Grace smiled. "Aye, I will."

On her way to Gabriel's room, Grace passed men positioned along the corridor. The farther away from the great hall she traveled, the more her anxious tension fell away.

She reached the junction where the stairs met the hall to the west wing and heard a step behind her. She gripped her small dagger and whirled around to face the threat. Artair stood behind her, hands raised, wearing a sheepish grin. "I dinna mean t' frighten ye, lass. Lord Alexander has asked that I accompany ye while you go about the castle."

Her heart raced against her throat and made it difficult to draw a full breath. She resheathed her dagger. "'Tis grateful I am to have ye watching over me, Artair."

Artair fell into step beside her on the narrow steps and cupped her elbow. "Bruce Campbell and a small group of men have been sent t' Edinburgh to do Lord Alexander's bidding. He wouldna tell me what he was meant t' do."

Mayhap Bruce had held his own council because of Artair's gossiping ways.

"Young Robby will be following ye about like a lost pup when I am not here."

She would not have the boy teased if he was to see her safe. "Artair, any lad Lord Alexander trusts to put himself between me and harm is not a lost pup, but a man."

His grin showed the appropriate chagrin. Grace nodded and continued down the passageway.

She dragged in a deep breath outside of Gabriel's door while her anxiety flooded back. Gabriel was a proud man. Would the change in her station nick his pride and give him reason to pull away from her further? Was she holding on to something only she wanted?

She had tried to believe in his love, but there was a part of him he withheld. She had believed if she could love him enough, his feelings would warm. She knew he desired her. She felt the changes in his body when he held her close. But was it enough to be wanted? Would those feelings be enough reason for him to give up everything he had to stand by her side in a distant place among strangers?

She would be the lady of the manor, and he... With no title, he would be her husband, and always viewed as lower in rank. *If they were allowed to wed.* As Alexander's *buannachann*, Gabriel owned property given to him for his service, but he held no title, and only the King could honor him with one. The chances that would come about were...

Without a title he would be forever trapped between the men he led and those of higher rank. And now she was one of them. Such a situation would surely hurt him.

"Go ahead and knock, lass," Artair urged. "Since waking he

has done little but ask for ye."

At Grace's quick tap, Derrick opened the door and stood aside to allow her entry.

Grace's attention moved past him to Gabriel. For the first time in days, he wore a shirt. Seeing him partially dressed brought the intimacy of caring for him to the forefront of her mind and emotions. She had been protective of his modesty. Though she had tried to maintain decorum while she had bathed him to cool his fever, there were times she had seen more than was proper. She felt shy and uncertain as she approached the bed.

His voice sounded a bit weak when he said, "'Twould seem I have caused ye much concern in the last few days."

"Aye, a wee bit." A sudden rush of tears stung her eyes and she fought them back.

"If you dinna mind, Lady Grace, 'twould be of great help should ye keep Gabriel company until my return," Derrick said.

Grace offered him a smile of gratitude. "Of course."

Grace barely heard the door close, for her every sense was trained on the man she loved.

Gabriel grasped her wrist and pulled her down on the bed beside him. She looked into his face. The fever had left its mark upon his features. Dark shadows hollowed his eyes, and his cheekbones cut a more prominent edge beneath. His finely shaped lips were dry and cracked. But his eyes focused on her face with such searching intensity, her heart raced. He had never looked more handsome.

Her arms went around his neck and she held him. With his arms about her, even in his weakened state, she felt secure. She drew strength from his nearness.

GABRIEL TIGHTENED HIS hold on her and breathed in the clean scent of the soap she used. "On our ride back, my thoughts were of you, Grace. I have never had anyone of my own waiting for me. Ye kept me on my horse when I didna feel I could continue on another step."

Grace's fingers combed through the long hair at the base of his neck, and then she drew back, her gray gaze shadowed by uncertainty.

Gabriel pressed a brief, tender kiss to her lips and rested his check against hers. "Lord Alexander has told me of Lord Ramsay's intent t' offer for yer hand." He leaned back to look into her face.

She grasped his hand and held it between both of hers. "He has yet t' speak of it t' me, though he stated as much t' Lord Alexander. 'Tis my hope t' avoid any moment alone with him that might provide him with time to do so."

"Why did ye not tell me of yer birth, Grace?"

"In every household I have been a part of, I have been more servant than lady. With no family, no connections, I chose the path I wanted, Gabriel. The one that leads to my happiness. Lord Alexander understood and accepted that."

Gabriel's throat thickened with emotion. "I canna give you riches or visits to court."

"Can you hold me in your arms with true affection, Gabriel?"

He cupped her cheek in his large hand. "Aye, I can. I do. And more, Grace."

Her cheeks colored. "Then you have already given me more than Lord Ramsay is able to do. 'Twas he who threw me out onto the streets of Edinburgh to die. 'Twas his wife who did the deed, but 'twas at his behest. What do you think he would do to me, should I be forced into such a union?"

"No one will force you to wed him, Grace."

"If he has petitioned the king, and the king agrees, I will have no choice, Gabriel."

The fear he read in her face triggered a rush of protective possessiveness. "I winna allow it. You belong t' me, Grace."

"We both ken ye canna, nay, winna defy your king. You would have no more choice than I." She reached for his hands and gripped them. "Lord Alexander has set into place the means t' free me from this. But I must pretend, when the time comes, t' give Lord Ramsay's offer as much thought as I have yours. I dinna wish to. To be in the room with him gives my stomach an ugly turn." She shuddered.

He would not lose her. He had been foolish not to proclaim his love for her. But to do so now would make the declaration seem less than sincere.

To imagine her in another man's arms triggered such pain and rage he wanted to pound the man to dust. And to know that she might be in danger, and he could not protect her...

"Derrick said Lord Alexander has posted guards throughout the family wing. If he is showing such caution, he must believe there is some threat. You must take great care, Grace. Dinna give Ramsay or any of his men quarter."

"I will not. But you must do the same. His chambers are just down the passageway from here. Derrick will stay here until you are stronger. And there will be guards posted outside."

He silently cursed his weakened state.

"Let me see your arm. I will tend it, and then I must go." She rose to retrieve the small earthenware pot of water laced with herbs and vinegar Derrick had used on the wound earlier. It had burned like a hot coal, but the wound felt better afterward. She gathered fresh bandages from a small table.

He extended the limb and watched while she gently unwrapped it. The dressing came away easily. The discharge was clearer, and the wound less inflamed, but he would still have to pamper the limb until it healed completely. The scar it left behind would be a reminder of the moment he was injured, and of this one. He leaned back against the pillows to rest, and cursed the fever, for it drained his strength when he needed it most.

"Derrick said you stood again' him when he wanted to take my arm."

"I knew you would never forgive us, should we maim you so terribly." Her throat worked as she swallowed. "I pray I am never forced to make such a decision again."

He tucked a stray strand of hair behind her ear with a fingertip. "I will do my best, *a ghràidh*."

She glanced up from the task of wetting a cloth in the briny water. Gabriel steeled himself against the sting when she laid the rag over the injury before quickly cleaning and bandaging it.

Her gray gaze, darkened by the candlelight, focused on his face. "Dinna promise somethin' ye canna give, Gabriel."

"Do you think me incapable of such feelings, then?"

"Nay. But with all that has happened... I would ask you t' be certain of what you want. You are an honorable man. Lord Ramsay is not and will not behave as one. You may find what you feel for me is not worth such a struggle. Not worthy of such a sacrifice."

It was his own fault she doubted his affection for her. A hollow ache built in the pit of his stomach at the pain he read beneath her careful composure. "Grace..." He wanted to take her in his arms and kiss away her doubts, but the stiffness of her demeanor prevented him from doing so. "I've wanted very badly t' take you to me. To lay claim to every part of you, and show you how much you are wanted, needed. I have wanted to carry you from the castle to my wee hut... and see you there sharing not just my bed, but all that I have, holding a wee babe we have made together t' your breast. Those are na the visions of a man who doesna hold you in the highest affection."

Tears glimmered in her eyes. "If we could remain here and share those things, 'twould be my fondest wish, but Lord Alexander said I canna refuse the gift, for it would be an insult to the king. And because the crown has acknowledged my noble birth...we may only wed through special permission from the crown.

"I have refused to sign the charter. 'Twill grant us some time for now, but should Lord Ramsay press the matter, I will be forced t' sign it. And with my name upon it, the regent will have the power t' choose my husband. And Lord Ramsay, though he has not broached the subject with me, has made his wishes known t' Lord Alexander. He wishes to wed me to gain the MacNab holdings."

How was he to fight this enemy who could win the battle because of his heritage? He had fought beside his king and asked for nothing, but he would now. And what if he still could not win? Pain pierced him far worse than his arm ever had.

"Did Lord Alexander tell you of other things?"

"About the wee lass who died? Aye." They had talked then about the age of consent, too. Lord Ramsay was wily about what he was doing, waiting for them to reach the age, then choosing only those who would be too afraid to speak out. Those who were subject to his power.

"'Twill be a difficult thing for those he has so ill-used to come forward, Grace. And then... 'Tis a common thing. Accepted and ignored."

"Aye. He sees all those without noble blood as there for his use. His boots and gloves have more value to him."

Her eyes gleamed dark with passion and her cheeks flushed with color. Gabriel leaned forward and pressed his lips to hers. "My sweet, wee warrior," he murmured and tucked another soft strand of hair behind her ear.

"Do you mean t' distract me, Gabriel?"

"Aye. There is little we can do until I am strong enough to ride."

"And then?"

"There are those who owe their lives to me. I mean to ask for something in return."

Grace smiled, and some of the fearful tension in her shoulders and face eased, but her eyes clouded and she pulled away from him. Her hands balled into fists at her side. "You must think first of all you will be leaving behind, Gabriel. Your clan will no longer be your own. I winna hold you to your promise, if... 'Tis too much to ask of any man." She rose and rushed from the room.

Chapter 5

THE DISTANT BAYING of the hounds reached her from just outside the curtain wall gate. Grace was grateful Lord Alexander had arranged to entertain his guest with a hunt. As long as they were chasing deer or other game, Lord Ramsay would be away from the castle, and she would be able to breathe again without the constant feeling of being pursued. He was pursuing her relentlessly, though in subtle ways, for he had not come straight out and asked for her hand.

Campbell and Ramsay clansmen readied their horses and stood waiting for Lord Ramsay to join them. The horses were restless, as were the men.

Why was it men found sport in shedding blood? Everything to them was a battle, or a plan to wage one, against each other, against—everything. It was senseless to put themselves at risk over a wild boar when they had plenty of their more docile cousins in a pen outside the castle.

Grace's attention wandered to the small cluster of women standing close to the gate. It was always the women who paid for such folly. For the women of the clan, worry was their closest friend and their worst enemy.

And the women had included her during such times before. But not today. She was still smarting from their cool response when she approached them.

Every day Lord Ramsay remained here, a wider distance stretched between her and the people she cared about most. It was as though the yett had crashed down between them, immovable and unbreachable. She had been alone for so long, but once

Gabriel accepted her, the men and their wives had, too. They had taken her in and made her one of them. But no longer. She clenched her shawl in a fist and swallowed back the tears that threatened. The loneliness carved a hole in her heart as deep as Loch Awe.

Her time with Gabriel in the sickroom had been limited to short moments, for there seemed always to be some demand on her time now. Was Lady Mary hoping to distract her, or had Lord Alexander decided she and Gabriel needed some distance between them? As if there were not enough already.

"You look bonny this fine morning, Lady Grace," Lord Ramsay said as he paused beside her just inside the open doors of the great hall.

He was as full of oats as a porridge served to break the fast. She looked just as she always did. "Thank you, Lord Ramsay." She drew the tartan shawl around her more securely.

He took some time pulling on a fine pair of leather gloves, so fine she had never seen the like. How much had he paid for them? Probably more than she or Gabriel had ever seen in their entire lives.

"Will you not be joining us?" he asked.

"Nay. I have no stomach for the hunt."

"That is a shame. To ride to the hounds makes the blood pump with renewed vigor."

"As will bandaging the hurts and setting the bones when all of you return," Grace said, her tone dry.

Lord Ramsay at first looked startled, then threw back his head and laughed. "There is more t' you than the shy young lass you allow all to see, Grace. I look forward to discovering more."

Quick alarm sent blood rushing to her head. What had she said to inspire such an interest?

"I'm a simple woman, Lord Ramsay."

"I dinna think so. Even as a child you harbored a defiant streak. You hide it well behind your bent head and softly spoken words, but 'tis there, ready t' erupt. Not many women would have the nerve to reject a king's charter."

"I have not rejected it, Lord Ramsay. I have not yet read it."

His eyes swept down her small frame. "You may sign it or not. There canna be any negotiations with the regent. I will stay a few more days t' make certain you have reached a decision you mean to stand by."

"Until I am afforded the opportunity t' hold the document in my hands and read the words, I will never agree to anythin'. I wonder if the lord regent will understand that?"

"So now you turn it upon me?" He grinned and chuckled softly. "We shall do well together."

Grace swallowed back a rising tide of nausea. Nay, they would not do anything together. Beneath her shawl, she gripped the bone handle of her dagger with fierce determination, and for the first time understood the blood lust that overtook men when they were threatened.

"You havena spoken of your children. How do they fare? And how is Lady Elspeth?

The change in his demeanor was immediate. His features tightened and his eyes narrowed. "My sons are dead, all four of a fever, and Lady Elspeth is locked away, gone mad with grief for her *bràthairs* and *màthair*."

Grace gripped the knife handle tighter. The shock of his words vibrated through her like a bell tolling. Mayhap more than grief had been the cause of the girl's confinement. "I am most sorry for your loss, sir."

When he stalked down the steps and joined his men, she sighed aloud in relief.

Artair moved from his position just inside the great hall. "What was it you said that sent his Lordship into such a rage?"

"I asked about his children. They are all dead but one." She ran nervous fingers over her braid. She must tell Lord Alexander of Lady Elspeth's condition.

Artair's thin, homely face settled into lines of sympathy. "Life is hard for even the nobility. Will you eat a wee morsel before you see t' your duties? You barely touched your food. Gabriel winna be pleased, should you waste away, Grace."

"I canna eat when Lord Ramsay is about. My throat closes up tight, and 'tis all I can do t' breathe. I dinna understand why I must sit at the head table and eat with him."

Artair threw out a hand encompassing the room. "He is not here now, lass."

In that moment she found Artair's wrinkled features more than dear. "You dinna call me Lady Grace."

"I beg pard—"

"Nay!" She cut him off and gripped his arm. "I am not Lady Grace, only Grace, Artair. I will never be Lady Grace."

She read pity in his face. "But you always have been."

She shook her head. "Nay. I have always been a servant, and done what I have been told t' do, or what I've been taught. 'Tis time I thought for myself."

If only she had given herself to Gabriel, she would surely be carrying the child he'd imagined at her breast. And they could not be parted.

She imagined a sturdy son with his dark hair and his features in miniature. Tears threatened and she lowered her face. Gabriel would never abuse his children as Lord Ramsay had done, both through his neglect and later with his base needs.

She flipped the long braid over her shoulder and returned to the great hall, finding a seat at one of the empty tables. "Will you pour me a tankard of mead, Artair? I have a hankering for a drop."

Artair eyed her with a frown. "Drinking on an empty stom-ach...this time of day..."

Grace frowned at him and he said no more, but strode to one of the large barrels against the far wall, found a tankard, filled it, and returned. He set it before her.

Grace raised the cup and took a cautious sip. It was both sweet and bitter to the taste and had just a hint of apple in its flavor. She took a healthier drink and it burned her belly.

"What are you about, lass?"

"Nothin'. Lady Mary has given my duties t' one of the other maids that I might prepare for the men's return. I have finished rolling bandages and preparing the balms. My time is now my own."

"And you intend to sit here and crawl into that cup?"

She turned the tankard in her hand. "Nay, I intend t' go to Gabriel's room and speak plainly about certain matters. We have much to settle between us."

"And ye intend t' do it with a mind clouded by drink?"

God save her from nosy Scotsmen. "I dinna think one cup will cloud my thinking." But she hoped it boosted her courage, for she meant to seduced her betrothed and settle the matter…and she hadn't a clue how to go about it.

GABRIEL KNOCKED DERRICK'S hand away as he attempted to place it on his forehead to check for fever. "Get on w' ye. The fever is gone. Your wife will be harping at me when next I see her. 'Tis been four days since yer return, and ye have yet t' see her or yer bairns."

"She kens I am needed here."

"Instead of tending me like a helpless babe, you need t' be with her making another of yer own. Go see her and the lads and lasses. I will be here when ye return." Gabriel pointed at the door with his chin.

Derrick narrowed his eyes with clear suspicion. "Ye seem eager t' be rid of me."

"Aye, I am. A man can hardly think with you clucking about like a fecking *màthair* hen. I have plans t' make."

"Would any of those plans concern Grace?"

"Aye. I have made a grievous mistake and must make it up to her, if I can." He raked his fingers through his rumpled hair. He was trapped in this bed while his rival courted the woman he loved. He realized he had taken her love for granted, and now he had to prove to her how precious her gift was to him.

His efforts would do no good if they were denied the right to wed. Though Lord Alexander had petitioned the Earl of Moray, the king's regent, on his behalf, it could take weeks—nay, months—before they received an answer. Though he had property of his own, earned through his service to Lord Alexander, he was bound to Alexander by blood, by loyalty, and by his occupation. He was his Lord's *buannachann*, to order as he saw fit. Gabriel had earned everything he had through their kinship.

He had worked hard to make his hut more spacious and comfortable for Grace, but she would have a better life than he could give her on land of her own, with a fine house to shelter her.

Her words two nights earlier had left him reeling. Did she think him too stubborn to swallow his pride and stand by her side?

Or had she decided he was not the man she wanted there?

Or had she decided she was not worth the sacrifice?

If only she would speak plainly about the matter.

Certes, the only thing he knew was she was unhappy.

Derrick broke into his morose thoughts. "I will ask one of the servants t' come stay with you."

"Nay." He had had his fill of people hovering over him, eager to treat him like a cripple. "Should I have need of a servant, I will call one. The guards are just outside the door."

Derrick released his breath on an impatient sigh. "Very well. I will leave you to it. 'Twill give me a chance to join in the hunt."

"Aye. 'Twill be the first I have missed since bearing arms for Lord Alexander."

Derrick grinned. "I'll do clan Campbell proud in your place. We'll be sure to roast a boar for the morrow."

Gabriel raised a brow at his boast. "Dinna let yer desire to show off your superior hunting skills affect yer good judgment. Have a care."

Derrick paused by the door. "Aye, I will." A cheeky grin brought color to his thin, bearded cheeks. "Ye'll be joining me in the great hall to feast on my kill."

"I will be there to eat it, even if ye have t'carry me down the stairs."

"Rest and regain your strength, then." Derrick shut the door behind him.

Gabriel sighed with relief. Finally, he was gone and out from underfoot. Gabriel soaked in the blessed silence and smiled for all of a heartbeat until his mind turned to more pressing concerns. How was he to wed Grace when he had no noble blood to secure her hand? How was he to recover from her loss when she was taken from him? He rubbed a hand over his face, then raked his fingers through his hair again, and gave it a strong tug, hoping the pain would distract him from the one in his chest.

It was time he got a look at the man who vied for Grace's hand again' him. If the judgment went again' him, and he couldna have Grace for himself, he would at least see she was wed to someone who would treat her with kindness and respect. Pain drove him to a seated position, and he cradled his head between his hands.

Lying here alone, dwelling on this all day, would surely drive him mad. He had been wrong to send Derrick away. But he could do nothing until he regained his strength. To do so, he needed to move. He threw back the pelts and tartans and swung his long legs over the side of the bed. His head swam only a little compared to the day before. He braced a hand on the small, sturdy table next to the bed and waited for the weakness to pass. His head cleared and he gathered his strength. He pushed himself to his feet.

He had been bathed like a helpless bairn, and his pride pricked him when he had to ask for the chamber pot instead of seeing to his own needs. That stopped now.

Though his legs were not as steady as he wished, he reached the washbasin. Once again he braced one hand on the table and used the other to pour water into the bowl and rinse the last vestige of sleep from his eyes. He had slept and lain about enough. He would bathe and dress as was his custom, and would break his fast below in the great hall, if he had to crawl down the stairs to do so.

After only a few minutes he realized will alone would not be enough to ease the soreness of his muscles. He felt like his body had been pummeled by angry fists, though no bruises showed.

Derrick said he had shivered so with fever it shook the bed and every inch of his body. It was no wonder he was sore from top to toe.

He rolled his shoulders and neck and stared hard at the wall in front of him to ride through a wave of dizziness. How was he to make it downstairs if he couldn't turn his head without the room spinning? 'Twas lack of a good meal that had brought him low. He would eat his fill and be better for it.

He reached for a small linen cloth next to the washbowl, wet it, rubbed it over the block of black soap, and ran the cloth over his neck and chest. He cleaned the more intimate parts of his body, cleaned his teeth with salt, and, lifting the small pitcher to fill his mouth, rinsed and spit. Though his injured arm ached from its weight, he dumped the bowl into the chamber pot.

A tap came on the door, and he reached for a long blue and white linen towel, wiped his face and wrapped it about his hips.

"Aye, enter."

Grace slipped into the room. She froze just inside, allowing the door to close behind her. As soon as she saw him standing next to naked at the washbasin, color flared in her cheeks and she turned to face the door.

"I beg pardon, Gabriel. I thought you would still be abed."

"Aye, I would be, but I've grown tired of lying about. Derrick gave me nothin' but more gruel to break my fast. I have a hankering for lumpy oats and eggs boiled to bouncing."

Grace's eyes flashed with laughter when she glanced over her shoulder. "I can fetch you some."

He studied her expression. She had kept her distance since he called her his love. Instead of being pleased, she had shrunk far within herself, just as Derrick had described. His Grace was trying to shield her soft heart, even from him. And he was at fault.

Her recent coolness would pass and she would warm to him again. He had to believe that. But would it be a good thing? Would it not be kinder to encourage the distance? The pain the thought triggered nearly brought him to his knees. He was not strong enough to encourage her to turn away from him. He had to hold onto the hope the Earl of Moray would accept Lord Alexander's plea.

"Will you fetch my shirt, lass? 'Tis there on the bed." His voice sounded raspy around the knot in his throat.

"Aye." She scooped up the garment and rushed to his side, eyes lowered.

He could not don the shirt and hold the towel in place too.

Grace's cheeks flared with color, but she bundled the fabric and lifted on tiptoe to slip it over his head. She helped him guide the injured arm into the sleeve. He released the towel and slid the other into place. Since the fabric fell to mid thigh, he was covered enough for his Grace's delicate sense of modesty.

Slipping in close beneath his arm, she put her own around his waist. She seemed so small next to his bulk, he hung back, leaning against the table. If he fell with her, she might be hurt. He straightened his shoulders and gathered his strength, determined not to fall.

Her hand resting against his chest triggered a sharp need for more of her touch. He tightened his arm around her shoulders, and they wove a path to the bed. When he lowered himself to the straw mattress, he gripped her hips and pulled her down with him. With her body stretched atop his scantily-covered frame, nature took its course, and he grew hard against her.

He'd been stiff as a pike for her for weeks, but had refused to act on it. She wanted to be wed before tasting the sweetness of the marriage bed, and he wanted to prove to her she was worthy of the wait.

He dearly regretted both their decisions. He found the tender spot on her neck he knew was sensitive, kissed it, and was rewarded by her shiver.

Her eyes had never looked so dark as when she pushed up to look down at him then said, "Show me what t' do, Gabriel."

All the blood seemed to drain from his head to pool in his groin, despite the weakness of his illness, his need grew rampant. "Grace..."

"I want to be with you as a wife is with her husband."

"We are na' wed."

He wanted to be the honorable man she loved, wanted to treat her honorably. If he took her now, and it was discovered, they would both pay dearly. God help him, as desperately as he wanted her, it would be worth it. But he wouldn't allow Grace to be hurt or shamed. And what of the child they might make together?

She straddled his hips and spread the fabric of her kirtle and surcoat out of the way. Her garters brushed his bare thighs and his breath caught in his throat. The warm, intimate heart of her body was so close. It would only take a tug to bare himself and push inside her. The temptation was torture, and he pushed himself up to lean back against the headboard and bunched the tail of his long shirt over his lap, hiding his display of manly desire for fear of bringing her innocence to a startling end.

The harsh beat of his heart thundered in his ears when she crawled up to touch her smooth lips to his. He smelled the apple mead upon her breath and, with a swipe of his tongue, tasted it. He bit back a groan of frustration and need.

It was fear and defiance he read in her eyes when she broke the kiss. "If you take my virginity, mayhap they winna want me, Gabriel."

It was the possibility of their being parted driving her to recklessness. "Any man would have to be a dead stump not t' want ye, Grace."

"We both ken that isna true."

"Lord Alexander's guardianship made the men cautious. You have the grace and manners of a lady, and you can read and write. It pricks a man's pride when his wife is more learned than he."

"I am not more learned, just versed in a different kind of knowledge. It doesna bother you that I can do those things. Does it?"

"Nay, lass. I take value and pride in your abilities." And he could read a bit and write his name as well as any noble, though he rarely had need of those skills.

She rested her cheek upon his shoulder, and brushed her lips over his neck, then skimmed his jaw.

He swallowed with difficulty. He could not set her aside and risk making her feel as though he had rejected her affection.

They must not consummate their betrothal...but he could give her pleasure and perhaps soothe her panic.

With that in mind, Gabriel pulled the ribbon between her breasts, loosening the top of her kirtle. The lily-white skin of her shoulders beckoned, and he tasted the slope of one with his lips and nipped it gently. Grace's quickly drawn breath made him smile. She was so innocent, yet primed for more. In the past weeks he'd dreamt of a hundred ways he wanted to take her.

When he folded back her kirtle, her surcoat pushed her small, perfectly shaped breasts upward, the peaks showing just over the edge of her shift. It wasn't weakness from his illness that set his hands, his body, to trembling, but the promise of feeling her warm skin beneath his touch.

He kissed her without restraint, his lips and tongue hungry for the taste of her. Her tongue sought his as eagerly. He cupped her breasts and ran his thumbs over her rose-tipped nipples until they beaded. He plucked at them.

They might never again have this time together. He would have something to remember. He gripped her hips, guiding her up on her knees while he bent his head and caught one rosy peak between his lips and sucked. Grace murmured his name in shock, but did not pull away. Instead, her fingers smoothed his hair and kneaded the back of his neck and his shoulders in encouragement. He tasted the other nipple and found it just as sweet.

When he tilted his head back to look up at her, there was nothing girlish about the kiss she gave him, or the way she pressed her bare breasts into him. Her tongue tangled with his in wanton eagerness.

He hardened to the point of pain. He worked his hands beneath her gown, kirtle, and shift and traced a path from her stocking-covered knees, past her garters, to the bare skin of her thighs and hips.

She trembled as hard as he when he cupped her buttocks and

kneaded them.

"Your hands feel hot with fever," she murmured as she buried her face against his neck.

"Aye, lass. I am feverish with wanting you." He nibbled her earlobe, and she shivered.

He ran his fingertips down the inside of both legs. Grace eased back to look into his face, her eyes almost black. "Gabriel?" Her voice sounded whispery and breathless.

"I can give ye pleasure if ye're open to m' touch, Grace."

She rubbed her smooth cheek against his beard-roughened one. "I dinna ken what I want, Gabriel, only that I do. Your touch sets my heart t' galloping while the rest of me aches for— more. 'Tis like I am climbing a high peak and something awaits me at the top, but I dinna ken what it might be."

"I wish I could show you." He stroked his fingertips along the rounded curve of her hip, then ran the backs of his fingers down the tender curve of her belly until he felt the soft hair covering her mons. Her cheeks flared with color. Her breathing grew ragged. With her lips parted and swollen from his kisses and her eyes dark with desire, she had never looked more beautiful. He had never wanted her more.

He kissed her with all the tenderness she had taught him while at the same time finding the intimate heart of her with his fingertips. He traced the tender outer lips and rubbed the tiny nub in a circular motion. Grace's hips jerked and she caught her breath. He waited until she had begun to move in response before delving into her feminine passage. The barrier of her virginity gripped his finger as he eased it inside her only a short way until he felt its resistance. Grace's eyes widened at the sensation, and she instinctively tilted her hips.

He shook with the need to claim her as his own. She was so warm, wet, and ready for him. So small and tight. If he claimed her virginity in this manner, it would be the same as if they'd done the deed. He withdrew his hand.

Regret lay like ash in his mouth, bitter and dry. He clamped her as close against him as her bundled skirts would allow. "I want ye, Grace. More than my life."

She cupped his face in her hands and her gray gaze delved into his, searching, seeking.

"I dinna wish to cease touching ye." His voice shook and he cleared his throat. "But 'tis best that I do."

"'Tis a gift only meant for you, Gabriel. No other."

"Aye, I ken that." It was close to killing him to turn aside from what she offered. He should never have touched her. "You are most precious to me, *a ghràidh*. But 'tis a gift I canna claim without hurting ye, and I will lay my life down before I will do that. 'Tis a gift I will savor later with the word wife upon my lips."

The warm flush of desire drained from her. "Are you sure you still want that?"

With little more to do but lie about and think, he had searched his heart and mind as she had bid him. He could teach her clan to fight and protect their territory, and he could run the estate just as Lord Alexander ran his. It would be a challenge, but he had faced others just as difficult. He could do it. He would share a bigger house, share in the land—and that too would be grand—but... It was the look of such open trust and love she had given him before...all of this. He wanted to see that expression on her face again. "Aye, I do. I want you, Grace. I love you. I want to stand beside you, support you my strength and loyalty."

She pressed a tender kiss upon his lips. "I will never give myself willingly to any other man, Gabriel. Not even under order of the lord regent." He read the unbending resolve in her face.

"'Twill not come to that, Grace."

"Aye, it will. As long as there is a bit of land to be claimed, it always does. If you do not claim me now, they will find a way to barter me to someone else. I am no longer free. I am a ward to those above me."

He could not argue the truth of her words. He was a commoner, and she a noble. He was holding onto the hope Lord Alexander had given him. He had to.

Chapter 6

GRACE PULLED AWAY from Gabriel to sit on the side of the bed and rest her elbows on her knees, although her body still clamored for more of the heated pleasure she just experienced with him. She clamped her knees together against the empty ache within. Gabriel ran a caressing hand down her back, and she closed her eyes. She was like a cat, wanting to arch beneath his touch. Craving it.

"If I took ye, Grace, and it was later discovered, we would both be beaten. The lord regent could separate us forever as punishment for breaking the king's law. He would surely force ye to wed someone else. Your guidesman would be free t' treat ye without respect or kindness because ye wouldna be pure."

She jerked away from his touch. It made it hard for her to think. She left the bed to stand before the fire, tugged her shift back in place and her kirtle up over her shoulders, jerked the ribbon tight, and tied it. She straightened her surcoat.

What he said was true. But her heart knew what it wanted. Her body did as well. "There would be no promise of respect or kindness whether I am pure or not, Gabriel."

She turned to face him and her eyes lingered on his features, much thinner from his illness, but handsome enough to make her heart turn over in her breast. She lingered over the width of his shoulders, the strip of bare chest visible between the laces of his shirt, the ropy strength of the one bare leg that stretched from beneath the blanket. He had a warrior's body. Scarred from injuries, muscular from riding and training for battle. He was beautiful.

"Grace—" Gabriel dragged the tartan high up his chest, pain

flickering across his face.

At least she knew now he was as moved by her gaze as she was his. She had felt the heated proof of his desire pressing upward against her buttocks, the trembling of his body and his hands as he stroked her. She would never forget the tiniest detail of those sweet, intimate moments with him. They might have to last her a lifetime.

Pain clogged her throat, and her words came out in a strangled rush. "I winna be forced to wed again' my will. I winna be used as a thing to be bartered. If either should come to be, I will be forced to leave everythin' I know, everyone I love, to escape it."

"Nay. Not yet, Grace."

Hope leapt to life inside her.

"If it comes t' that—"

His words were cut off by a hard knock on the door before Artair leaned around the edge of the portal. His gaze fastened on Gabriel and moved beyond to her, standing at the fireplace. He scanned her appearance, and a quick look of relief crossed his face. "More visitors have arrived, and Lady Mary is requestin' your presence."

Grace tamed her impatience with some difficulty. "I will send something more filling than gruel from the kitchen," she said, as though they had been talking of nothing more than that.

"'Twill help me regain my strength," Gabriel replied. "'Tis my greatest desire to sup with ye in the hall." He offered her his hand.

Grace laid hers in it. "'Tis mine as well, Gabriel."

He bent his head to place a lingering kiss in her palm and then rested his cheek against it. It was all she could do not to take him against her and hold him. She smoothed his thick, dark hair back from his forehead. "I will return when'er I can."

He nodded.

Artair remained silent until they were descending the stairs. He touched her arm to stop her, then looked up and down the stairs before saying, "You might have a care for Gabriel's well-being, lass. Should things between ye...get out of hand, he'll bear the brunt of the punishment to protect ye. And right now, 'tis doubtful he could survive it."

Gabriel had said as much, but with her thinking clouded by fear and other emotions, she had not understood the full weight of the threat. Her stomach turned at the thought of him suffering because of her. She would rather her own skin be stripped away by a lash than to harm one hair on his head.

"Did anythin' appear to be out of hand to you when ye entered his sickroom, Artair?"

"Nay."

"Gabriel would never behave in less than honorable manner with me."

His voice dropped to a whisper. "So you didna go into the room intent on tempting him t' do so?"

It was her humiliating mistake to bear, not Gabriel's. "Even weak from fever, his mettle is strong. Now, shall we speak no more of this?"

"I only wish you to understand the seriousness of what you both face."

She studied his dear, careworn face, and knew in her heart he offered her his counsel out of true affection and concern for her and the man he'd served under during hard times and good.

Try as she might to wiggle free, the weight of it pressed down upon her with greater force. She braced a hand against the wall while it settled. She had been looking to everyone but herself to resolve this issue.

She looked away for fear any sympathy she read in Artair's face would undermine her resolve. "You needna worry about Gabriel in this matter, Artair. I give you my word I winna bring harm to him in any way. I will stand alone in this, as I have always done in the past."

He frowned, his eyes widening in concern. "'Twas not what I meant, Grace."

"'Tis just what must be."

She continued down the stairs and waited for him to open the heavy door leading into the great hall.

Three tables were filled with clansmen eating a late meal. Grace focused on the small group gathered at one of the huge fireplaces. She recognized both men standing with Lady Mary and quickened her steps.

"Here she is now. Come, Grace, and greet our guests. You remember Lord John Campbell, Alexander's *athair*, and Lord Duncan, his *bràthair?*"

She had met them briefly during visits, but had always happily hidden in the background of family gatherings. To be thrust into the forefront now seemed awkward, and made her feel uneasy. She curtsied before the two men. "'Tis a great pleasure t' see ye both again."

The older Lord Campbell was laird of the Campbell clan and respected by all. He stood as tall and broad-shouldered as his sons, and though his dark auburn hair and beard were sprinkled liberally with gray, his features remained youthful. Or mayhap it was his presence that caused one to think so.

Lord Duncan, the second of his three sons, was just as tall, but slighter of build, his face thinner. His gray eyes, though different than his sire's tawny gold, held a look of sharp intelligence and watchfulness. He offered her an encouraging smile.

"They have come to join in celebrating your change in circumstances, Grace."

Then they would be the only ones. "I am honored you thought 'twas worthy of interest."

"We all ken it has come as a surprise, Lady Grace," Lord John said.

"An unwanted one."

His brows rose.

Grace bit her bottom lip.

"Mary told us Gabriel has been very ill," Duncan said.

"His arm was badly injured, but is healing. He would be pleased by a visit, I am sure."

"I will do so now. Might I have your leave, Lady Grace?"

For her to be asked was a new experience. Once again she felt awkward. "Aye, of course." She beckoned to one of the young male servants close by and asked him to take Duncan to Gabriel's sickroom.

"Might I speak to you in private, Lady Grace?" Lord Campbell said.

She was discovering that every time someone in power asked to speak to her, it did not bode well for her desires. She studied Lord John's masculine features, so similar to his sons'. "Certainly, Lord Campbell."

"Mary, will you excuse us?"

"Aye, of course. You may use the chamber just through that door, my lord."

Mary gave Grace's hand a reassuring squeeze.

Lord Campbell gestured for Grace to lead the way. Her heart raced, leaving her breathless, and worry took root in the pit of her stomach. She was trembling by the time they reached the chamber.

Lord Campbell lifted two of the heavy wooden chairs from beneath the table and positioned them before the hearth, though no fire had been set. "Please sit with me, Lady Grace?"

Quick tears burned Grace's eyes, and she perched on the edge of the chair and folded her hands in her lap. What dire news was he about to impart?

Lord John lowered himself into one of the chairs, but leaned forward to rest his elbows on his knees. "Alexander wrote t' me about everything that has happened. Mary told me of Lord Ramsay's impending proposal and your attempts to avoid signing the charter."

He was the laird of the clan, surely she could speak openly to him.

"He has not proposed marriage to me, my lord. Only told Lord Alexander that he means to. And he will not allow me t' read and study the charter unless I do so under his tutalage. I dinna wish t' be alone in a room with him. 'Tis difficult for me to suffer his presence, even in company."

Lord Campbell's brows rose. "Has he threatened you, Lady Grace?"

Blood rushed into her face. "Nay. But I witnessed things in his home when I was young and have good reason not to trust him."

"Has he done anythin' while here t' make you feel uneasy?"

"Aye." But 'twas difficult to put it into words. "'Tis as though he is certain I have no choice left to me but to accept him. And he gains pleasure in taunting me with it."

Lord John's features tightened. "What age were you when you were last beneath his guardianship, Grace?"

"Ten and three, m'lord."

"Did he ever touch you?"

"Nay." Thank God she had been frail and plain, and his interest had turned elsewhere. She flinched at the thought, a quick flash of Blair's face white in death stabbed at her conscience.

"Is it possible you might have misunderstood what you saw? You were very young."

"I dinna misunderstand the words of a dying girl losing the bairn he forced upon her. I dinna misunderstand when she told me to never be alone with him. I lay next to her every night while she wept in shame and sorrow after he hurt her. I dinna believe I misunderstood his intent when he pulled back the covers and looked upon his wee daughter while she slept, dressed only in her shift, mlord. More than once."

Lord John sat back in his chair with a grimace.

"He has locked his daughter away. He said she was crazed with grief, but mayhap there are other things that have disturbed her." Or mayhap he had a need t' silence her. Or mayhap she was with child. The idea sickened her.

"I ken ye are grieved about the betrothal being challenged."

Blood rushed to her face and her cheeks burned. He did not believe her. She forced herself to remain seated. "Aye. But it doesna change the truth of what I ken, sir."

Lord John settled back in his chair with a sigh. "Aye. I believe you do know the truth. I will find out what character of man Lord Ramsay is myself soon enough."

She subsided into her seat in relief. She had no doubt he

would.

"On the other hand, I do ken Gabriel is a fine man."

"Aye, he is."

"For all that, you must prepare yourself for the possibility that the regent may reject his petition, Grace."

She read doubt in the open sympathy of his expression. He did not believe they would overcome these obstacles.

Pain nearly drove her to her feet, but she gripped the arms of the chair and tried to calm herself. "The charter the regent is offering me lies betwixt yours and Lord Alexander's lands. Do you not wish for it t' remain within Campbell control, my lord?"

"Aye, I do."

"Do you not wish for a man loyal t' ye both to stand at my side?"

"Aye."

Then why would he not champion Gabriel?

"If the regent winna accept Gabriel, Grace, I want you t' think well upon another who could serve you well as husband. He would respect and care for you, give you children, help you manage the property, and offer your clan protection."

Her mouth grew so dry she could not swallow. "Who do you mean, my lord?"

"My son, Duncan."

Shock held her immobile. She continued to study his face, probing his expression. She bit back the immediate words that pushed to tumble off her tongue. This was the laird of the Campbell clan. He had the power to have her escorted from Campbell land, should she reject his son out of hand.

How would this betrayal affect Gabriel? Her throat tightened and ached at the thought. Quick tears rushed up, but she fought them back.

"Gabriel has stood at your son's back protecting him for years. Fought at his side. Shown him unwavering loyalty and devotion. Lain ill, fighting for his life, because he defended Lord Alexander's lands and his men."

"There are two clans at risk, Grace."

"And there is honor and loyalty at risk here as well. Without those, the rest will crumble. The rest means nothin'." She shoved free from the chair, its arms feeling like iron hands holding her prisoner. The room seemed cloying and close. She closed her eyes against it. "We have both served your son for years, out of love and loyalty. We have asked nothing that has not been earned."

The tears she had held at bay gushed forth, blinding her. She attempted to blink them away while she strode to the door, fumbled for the handle, and found it by feel alone. Lord John was but a large, blurred shape when she cast a look over her shoulder. "Gabriel would give his life for you. For me. And you seek t' replace him like a pair of boots. If this is what you have to offer in return…'tis a wonder anyone wishes to follow you."

She jerked the door open and fled the room. The thick, dark walls of the keep seemed too restrictive. She averted her face from the servants clearing the large tables, and crossed the great room. She shoved free of the keep and stumbled outside. There was not enough air or light in the world to beat back the pain.

Without Lord John's support to sway the regent, their union would never take place. Should he ask Gabriel to step aside… It would tear Gabriel apart. Tear them apart. The pain was more than she could bear. Grace broke into a run.

Chapter 7

LORD DUNCAN HAD never followed the strictures of the Campbell legacy laid out for him. Though he had skill with a sword and bow, he was only a warrior when he had to be. But he possessed a dagger-sharp mind hidden behind charm and wit. Gabriel had always admired that about him. And he recognized the advantage Duncan had over Lord John and his brothers.

A man who did not sleep with a sword in his hand was often dismissed as no threat. Until he suddenly held a knife to your throat.

"I have spent more time in Edinburgh than Father or Alexander. Their attention is elsewhere. David is too besotted with Lady Ann to travel far from his hearth. Especially now that she is bairned." Duncan's voice mirrored the teasing disgust in his expression.

Gabriel chuckled. "I will eagerly await the day when ye have finally met yer match, Duncan, and remind ye of yer remarks in just that tone. Or is it jealousy I hear?"

"Nay. I am pleased for my brothers' marital happiness, but in no rush to succumb to it." He crossed his arms and leaned back in his chair. "And what of you and Lady Grace? Is this a love match?"

"Aye, it is. Had Ramsay not appeared out of the ether, we would already be wed."

"I am sorry, Gabriel." Duncan frowned.

"I have petitioned for her hand with the regent. Lord Alexander has given me his support."

"You will have mine as well. You have my oath on it."

"Thank you. Grace will be as pleased as I am." But it would require the laird's championship to tip the scales.

"'Twould please me to find a suitable mate for *athair*. 'Twould mayhap improve his disposition. He has been…unpredictable of late." Duncan leaned forward in the chair and braced his elbows on his knees. "He has been stewing over what has happened. Until the regent chartered the property, he considered it Campbell land. He has lent men for the protection of it and the MacNab families who live there."

"And what have they offered in return?" He would need to know if he was to be the guardian of the territory.

"Beer, ale, and mead in abundance. Nearly every family has hives and grows hops. They distill enough to keep half of Scotland in drink. A stream runs through the valley that is very pure, and the locals protect it, lest a change affect their product."

How much beer had he drunk since he came to *Caisteal Sith*? Enough to float his way to France and back. He had only a basic understanding of the process, but he would learn. And now he understood why Lord Ramsay was so interested in Grace's charter. 'Twould offer huge profits to anyone who held the land. How much of those profits did Lord John depend on?

"Grace prefers wine to other drink, but I have kent her to drink a drop or two of apple mead." He looked away in case his expression reflected the intimate thoughts the mention of the drink triggered. "She is a woman, but she is smart and stubborn. Lord John winna be able to bend her easily to his will."

"And what of you, Gabriel?"

He knew what Duncan was asking him. "Did I not say she is stubborn?"

Duncan laughed. "But you have an advantage."

"Aye, but I wouldna use it. 'Twould be better to approach it with the idea of how it would benefit her clan. She has lived as a servant her entire life, Duncan, but she isna ignorant." Nor was he. "She thinks nothing of her own comfort, but she will think of others."

Duncan nodded. "When will you be joining us in the hall?

Lady Mary says Grace isna happy with your absence, nor are your men."

And how would it feel for Grace to be sitting at the head table and he below her? "I am regaining my strength, and my arm isna so painful now. Mayhap another day or two and I will feel steadier."

"Since you are her betrothed, and your petition has already been sent to Edinburgh, you will share our table, my friend."

"Lord Alexander's company may take insult at that."

"May the devil take Ramsay. He uses his people with less care than he gives his horse. And has a reputation for other, less-palatable dealings."

Gabriel raised a brow. "Grace has shared with me and Lord Alexander her memories."

Duncan frowned in real concern. "Not of her?"

"Nay," He shook his head. "But of others in the household."

"God's blood," Duncan swore and grimaced in disgust.

"Will you act as her *dìonadair* at table whilst I am healing, Duncan? She dreads every meal."

Duncan eyed him gravely. "I noticed the men positioned throughout the castle."

"Lord Alexander is keeping close watch over the man and his movements."

"Good." Duncan raised a brow. "Do you trust me to act as her defender?"

"I trust Grace." He grinned. Though Duncan had a reputation with women, he was a man of honor. "I trust you not at all, but I trust Ramsay even less."

Duncan laughed and got to his feet. "I will try to distract Ramsay, and I will ask Lady Grace to sit with me at table. She will be safe. *Athair* was eager to speak with her in private about all we have discussed. I will see what has come of that." Duncan gripped his shoulder. "Good health, Gabriel. Join us as soon as you may."

"I will."

Gabriel slid down beneath the covers to lie flat. The visit had tired him more than he wanted to admit. Having no duties gave him a time to think through all Duncan had told him, and how it could be used to advantage.

The drink her clan produced had more than paid for Lord John's protection. They had earned their keep. She would be pleased.

But the value of the charter could prove difficult. There was not an unwed lord in Scotland who wouldna be interested in asking for her hand. It would be in Lord John's interests to wed Grace quickly to someone loyal to the Campbell cause.

The regent, Sir Thomas, the Earl of Moray, would not be eager to give her to a commoner when others of higher standing were available.

Gabriel threw an arm over his eyes. The small hope he had been nurturing threatened to crumble until he thought of Grace. She was strong, and stubborn, and she loved him. If they stood together, there was a chance they could convince the Earl of Moray their marriage would benefit him more than a forced union she would resent and fight against.

THE FLOWERS GRACING the path just weeks before had died to dried stalks, leaving the area green with barren patches of brown. Gabriel's hut lay ahead, surrounded by trees, the new thatching on the roof visible through the leaves just beginning to turn. She had watched while sitting on a tartan as he, Artair, and Bruce Campbell built part of the roof. Then he added a buttery, a bedroom with a fireplace, and strengthened the walls of the stall where his horse was sheltered. She had not been inside the structure since he finished it. Gabriel had been away, and, aside from making sure the hut was secure, she had not felt the need to go inside without him.

She retrieved the key he gave her from the small pouch of belongings hanging at her waist and slipped it into the lock. It turned easily. She pushed down on the levered handle and the door swung inward. Leaving it open, she released the wooden shutter sealing the only window in the kitchen, letting in light, then closed and bolted the door. The room seemed larger now the bed no longer took up one side. A new chair sat by the fireplace, large and sturdy.

She moved to the bedroom doorway. In the dim light, she could see pelts and tartans spread neatly upon the bed, the bed they would have shared, had Lord Alexander not written the letter so many months before. She and Gabriel would have shared this house, and she would have been content, giving him her love, giving him children, giving him everything she could. Fresh tears rolled down her cheeks, and she sank to the floor, overwhelmed by great tearing sobs of grief.

She cried until her throat was raw and her eyes swollen. Afterward she lay motionless on the wooden floor, hollowed out. She closed her eyes against the broken hopes and dreams. When she woke, shadows lay around her, and a chilly breeze blew into the room from the open shutter to meander across the floor and lick at her. The meager light accompanying it looked soft and gray. It would be near time for the evening meal, and Gabriel would wonder at her absence.

For once obedience meant nothing to her.

She pushed herself up to sit in the bedchamber doorway and rested her head back against the heavy frame.

As she looked around the hut, she once again absorbed everything Gabriel had done to prepare for her to join him here. The wild, uncontrolled grief of only hours before threatened to rise up and swallow her again, but she turned her head aside and blocked out the room until the need to weep subsided.

It was time to drag together all the thoughts that had come to her while she walked the hills surrounding the castle earlier.

Laird Campbell could not cast her out for her insolence. To do so would be an affront to the MacNab clan. Though none of them knew or cared about her, they would be outraged to have their lady insulted in such a manner. Lord John would not wish to antagonize her or her clan. He wanted them to remain loyal.

It was to her advantage as well for that to be so, for the

Campbells were powerful enough to take the land by force. But they could not, because the regent had liveried it to her, and he expected the charter to be honored.

There must be more to this than she yet knew. Why would Lord John offer up his son for such a small holding of land? Aye, he wanted to maintain the bond between the two clans, but there was something else he wanted, something of value there.

It did not matter what it was, only that he desired it.

Now he had shown her how shallow was his loyalty to Gabriel, she would be wary of her dealings with him. She had revered the man from a distance, admired how his clansmen rallied around him. How his sons respected him. But then he would never turn on them.

Just barter one of them to her. She stewed on that a bit more. How would Lord Duncan feel when he learned about it? Did he already ken?

She needed to set aside her emotions and focus on Gabriel. He was her strength. But it was she who had to protect him now. The pain Lord John could cause him with this betrayal would be more difficult for him. Worse than for her. There had to be a way to spare him.

Her feelings solidified into a hot, burning anger, directed straight at the laird. If he wanted her land, he would have to pay dearly for it. More than he would want to.

She rose from the floor, secured the open shutter, and locked the door. Shadows deepened while she climbed the hill to the village, casting everything in a fine, blue-gray light. She was aware of Artair's presence following her from a distance, as he had done all day. What had he thought of her behavior, of the sounds of her unrestrained grief?

When she reached the great hall, she waited for him to catch up to her.

"Are ye better, lass?" he asked, his features folded in lines of worry.

Grace touched his cheek. "Aye. I will be."

He opened the door for her and they stepped inside.

The aroma of roasted meat and beer rolled over her, thick as smoke, and her stomach cramped.

The second thing she noticed was the quiet. Though the room was filled with clansmen, they were not talking, and their normal boisterous behavior was absent. Only Lord Ramsay's men talked among themselves in normal tones.

As soon as she saw Grace, Lady Mary rose, concern crimping her smooth brow. She rushed around the table and came to her. "Are you well, Grace?"

"Please forgive me for leaving you to tend the men alone."

Mary shook her head. "All is well. No one came back bleeding." She touched Grace's brow with the back of her hand.

"I am not feverish."

"You must eat, Grace. You are very pale." She urged her into a chair at the table.

Lord Duncan took a place on one side of her and Lord John on the other. Lord Ramsay took a place beside Duncan. He cast curious glances her way, but, aside from a short greeting, did not attempt conversation.

After a brief greeting, Lord Duncan said, "Tell me about the hunt, Davis. I am eager to join you on the morrow." Ramsay proceeded to expand on his prowess with a bow and the number of stags he had killed during past hunts, though he had gotten none today.

Lord Alexander declared, "We will try again on the morrow for a boar and give Lord John and Duncan the opportunity to join us."

The familiar feeling of being ignored and unseen soothed Grace. In silence, she drained the better part of a tankard of ale, for she found herself parched. She accepted a small wooden bowl of hodge-podge and slowly spooned the stew into her mouth. The cramping emptiness eased.

"Whither did you away, Lady Grace?" Lord John asked, his resonant voice a rasp.

Grace stilled herself against the quivering dread his voice triggered and latched onto her anger. "I sought a more tranquil clime in the forest so I might think."

"And did you come to any conclusions?"

"Aye. I think I shall cast my net and see what other fish rise to my bait. After all, I already have two lords nibbling at the edges. Others may take interest in my wee bit of ground. And if I canna have the man I truly want, 'twill not matter." She shrugged one shoulder and did not attempt to keep the bitterness from her voice. "After all, one would be as good as another." She looked up into his face and allowed him to see the depth of her anger.

Lord John's face remained completely devoid of expression.

"'Twould require time t' decide upon just the right man, mayhap years. The charter says I must have one, but it doesna say how quickly I must choose."

She forced herself to take another bite of the stew. It had lost its taste, the flavor leached away by the fear-driven dryness of her mouth. She set the bowl aside. "I would ask you to excuse me, Laird Campbell. I am very tired and fear I am not good company."

"You must seek your rest." He shifted back to allow her room to rise. "I shall look forward to sharing your company after the hunt on the morrow, Lady Grace."

Would he then give her an answer to her jibes? Or attempt to push her in another direction?

"Thank you." She rose and murmured a quick good-night to the table at large and slipped away.

Cook had told her wine would build Gabriel's blood and give him strength, so she poured a small pitcher, got a wooden cup from the many left on the table next to the casks, and wove her way through the tables.

She paused as the door closed behind her, and leaned against the wall for support, for her legs—her entire body—trembled with reaction. She had just defied the laird of clan Campbell for the second time in a day.

Chapter 8

GABRIEL SET ASIDE the ink and quill, sanded the words he had just written, and dropped the grains into the chamber pot. He folded the letter and, using the narrow cylinder of wax, sealed the sheet, then stamped a design into it with his ring.

While he waited for it to dry, he once again eyed the closed door with impatience. He had not seen Grace since they broke their fast together. Nor had Lord John been in to visit him, though Lord Alexander came to share news of the hunt and said his father planned to visit later.

Following on Duncan's comment that the laird meant to speak with her, Grace's long absence vexed and worried him. What had they discussed?

When a soft tap came at the door, he quickly bade the visitor to enter. As soon as Grace appeared, relief was his first reaction, then concern.

Her surcoat and kirtle were wrinkled, the hems of both stained with dried mud, as were her shoes. Strands of dark hair had escaped her braid and hung on either side of her face in soft waves. Her gray eyes looked puffy, the skin beneath bruised.

He bit back the urge to blurt out a concerned inquiry and instead said, "I have been waiting for you." He rose from the chair. He had bathed and dressed in a fresh shirt and trews so she would see he was no longer an invalid to be waited on.

She smiled as she came closer and, setting aside the pitcher and cup she carried, grasped the hand he offered. "You look much improved."

"I am. Cook has sent me treats all day t' tempt m' appetite.

And Derrick has plied me with cider and other drinks until I am replete."

"Good."

He drew her to the end of the bed, the only surface large enough for them to sit together. "Have ye been away today?"

"Just to walk in the forest."

"Alone?"

"Nay, Artair trailed behind me."

She kept her head bent and he could not read her expression.

"I went to your hut," she said, voice low. "I hadna been inside since you finished." She gripped the edge of her surcoat and fisted the fabric. "'Tis a fine home, Gabriel."

"While I worked on it, I told m'self I did so because it had grown cramped. But 'twas because I kept imaginin' you there with me, and I wanted ye to have somethin'—more."

She raised her face and her eyes glittered with tears. "If I could choose where we live, 'twould be there." She raised his hand to her lips and kissed it. "Because you wanted me there enough to build me more."

"Is it the house that has caused you distress, Grace?"

She shook her head. "'Tis the loss of it."

"'Twill not matter where we live, as long as we are together."

"Aye." She turned to nestle against him, and sighed when he held her close.

There was more. He could see it in her eyes, in the fragile hollows beneath them. She had been grieving today over more than a house.

His mouth was suddenly dry, despite all that Derrick had badgered him to drink over the course of the day. His throat tightened. What had Lord John said to her? And how would he convince her to tell him?

He breathed in Grace's distinctive fragrance of soap and flowers, melded with the smell of the forest and peat smoke. He smoothed the strands of hair back from one cheek and cupped her head to hold it close against his shoulder.

For a long while they remained silent. He rubbed the soft skin of her cheek with his thumb and she shifted closer.

"Do ye ken about clan MacNab and their holdings?" she asked.

"Some, and Duncan shared more with me today."

"Will you tell me about them?"

"Aye. They have been led by a knight of the MacNab family since the war ended and the Bruce appointed him to guide the clan and see to their interests. His name is Drummond MacNab. I ken him well enough to call him friend." He glanced toward the three letters he had penned so carefully after Duncan's visit.

He explained all he and Duncan had discussed.

Grace remained silent for a moment. "Lord John has been recompensed for their protection through trade and coin."

"Aye. The sale to other clans of the extra barrels of beer and mead alone would produce a handsome profit as well."

Grace nodded.

"Will you tell me what drove you to the forest today, *leannon*?"

"Lord John has not yet agreed to champion your petition with the regent."

He was not surprised, but it was still a blow. He had expected the laird to have reservations but... "He hasna refused outright?"

"Nay."

"I have Lord Alexander and Lord Duncan's support, Grace. They may yet sway him."

Her brows rose in surprise. "Duncan offered his support?"

"Aye. Just this morn."

She rubbed her cheek innocently against his chest. Even through his shirt the contact affected him and he hardened.

"'Tis good news."

"Aye, 'tis."

He softened his tone. "Will you not tell me what has brought this sadness upon you, *leannon*?"

"Aye. But not tonight." She raised her face and ran a hand up over his chest to the back of his neck. She combed her fingers through the tail of hair hanging down his back. "I am in need of a distraction." Her words and actions seemed both shy and seductive.

Every moment that had passed between them just that morn rushed through his mind. He needed no more encouragement. He lowered his mouth to hers and claimed it.

GRACE MURMURED GOOD eve to the guards outside Gabriel's room and wandered down the hall. With every kiss he had eased the pain and banished the issues that had tormented her all day.

The door leading into the main passageway to her room stood open, and she walked through and reached to close it behind her.

And saw a man standing in shadows. She froze, a chill of fear trickling down her spine.

"Good eve, Lady Grace," Lord Ramsay's voice came from the darkness. He stepped into the light of the torch beside the door. "We were unable to converse at table this night. Lord Duncan seemed to be in a cordial mood and wished my attention."

The door closed behind her. Her heart thundered against her ribs, and she drew a deep, calming breath. She folded her arms, pulling her tartan shawl against her while resting her hand upon the grip of her dagger. It was a small blade and would do little harm unless she could direct it to a most vulnerable area. After all the injuries she had helped treat, she knew just where to strike, but could she do it?

But surely he would not try to harm her here in the stairway. There were guards posted throughout the wing.

"You wish t' speak to me?" she asked in dread. What if he chose this moment to propose?

"You canna avoid signing the charter for much longer, Grace. Why do you struggle so?" His dark blue eyes looked black in the dim light, and he seemed truly perplexed.

She remained silent, for to say she did not wish to sign away her soul for a house, that house being a direct gift from the king, would surely be used against her.

He cocked his head. "'Tis more than you have ever had, is it not?"

"Not all wealth can be measured by what you possess. There are other riches." Kinship with those around her. The comfort of a true home.

"Do you not see how rude it is to come to table looking as though you have been digging in the earth? A new gown would not go amiss. You can see that for yourself."

So it was her manner and appearance he wished to address. "What I have, I have earned for myself. When I see a need, I will purchase more fabric and stitch another gown."

"Do you mean t' meet the regent dressed as you are?"

"I am certain he isna blind to how humble folk live. 'Twas his awareness of my circumstances that has caused all this." She could not keep the faintest hint of bitterness from her tone. "'Tis my hope he winna sit in judgment of any man or woman who comes before him as his obedient subject, no matter how they are garbed."

"You could have coin to buy whatever you need, borrowed against the income you will have after you sign the charter. The right clothing will enhance your natural beauty. You will want t' be at your best."

The only man she wanted to be beautiful for was Gabriel. She'd spent hours on the gown she meant to wear for her wedding. A new kirtle and shift. She would not wear them for anyone but him.

"But to borrow against something that isna mine would not be prudent."

"Why must you always be so intractable?" he demanded, finally losing patience.

"I winna be beholden to anyone for something frivolous, when the coin might be needed for more important things later."

"Your husband may have other thoughts, my lady."

"That decision will be made betwixt us."

"You mean yon injured warrior." He threw up a hand to point at the door.

She lifted her chin. "Aye, I do."

He drew himself up and even in the dim torchlight his cheeks looked so red she wondered if he might catch fire. One could only hope.

She bent her head in hopes of hiding her expression, for she was tempted to laugh. Should she do so, he could well react badly.

"Are you well, Lady Grace?" Robby spoke from the top of the stairs. Grace cleared her throat and drew a relieved breath.

"Aye. If you will excuse me, Lord Ramsay, I will seek my rest. 'Twill be another big day for hunting on the morrow."

His grunt was neither aye or nay, and she chose to take it for what it was. She touched Robby's arm briefly in thanks and continued on to her door. She shut herself in then bent at the waist and covered her mouth with her hand to smother her laughter.

If Gabriel or Lord Alexander knew of the game she played, they would be the first to caution her against it. But it was good to gain some small ground against a man who always had more than his share. And squandered it. Aye, if he could get his hands on her income, it would go for his fine gloves and boots, and none of the tenants on MacNab land would see anything for their labors.

Eventually she would get him to reveal himself before witnesses.

Chapter 9

GRACE STEPPED OUT onto the raised stoop of the great hall as the first wave of hunters returned. After their day in the wild, the damp smell of wood, dirt, and animal clung to their clothes, mingling with the distinctive odor of blood.

With murmured words of encouragement and prayer, she had prepared herself all day for her first meeting with Lord John face-to-face since she challenged him. She nodded to him cordially when he and Duncan swaggered up the steps and paused to greet her. "'Twas a good day, and most ever'one remains whole," Lord John announced. His cheeks and nose were reddened by the bite in the wind, but his smile expressed satisfaction.

"Ye had good luck at yer sport then, Lord John?" Grace said.

"Aye, I got a deer and left the boar to the younger lads."

It was a relief he had done so, for if the laird were injured, it would throw the clan into great turmoil. It seemed strange to realize he was no longer her laird to worry about. And even though she was angry, she could not wish him ill.

Lord John gestured toward his son. "Duncan had a hand in bringing the beast down. And it was a beast. 'Twill weigh at least twenty-five stone."

The rust-colored stain saturating the front of Duncan's shirt and kilt attested to that.

"Do you have any injuries that need tending, Lord Duncan?" Grace asked in concern.

"Nay." He grinned, in high spirits. "But I'll need a wash and fresh clothes before I am fit t' share a meal. I will see to it now." He sauntered into the great hall with his father.

Lady Mary's voice came from just inside the door as she greeted them, and then rushed out onto the stoop. "Kieran was restless and didna wish me t' leave him."

"Mayhap all the strangers about have made him restless."

"'Tis more he kens his *daideo* is about and ready to spoil him.

Grace laughed. "'Tis not a bad thing, now is it?"

Lady Mary shook her head.

Lord John thought the sun rose and set in his bairn, and was not above getting down on the floor and wrestling with him. Witnessing his tenderness with his grandson had made her wonder how he could be so caring with the wean and so much less so with Gabriel.

The next wave of men came through the gate led by Lord Alexander and Lord Ramsay. Lady Mary greeted the two men as they climbed the steps and Lord Alexander bent to kiss her cheek.

She laid a hand on his chest and tilted her head back to look up at him. "Are you well, husband?"

"Aye. The lads had a grand time."

"Good. It looks like we only have two who may need some attention."

"Aye. Young Davy took a spill when his horse fell. Cam was punched in the eye with his brother's elbow during all the excitement."

"We will see them well."

The boar the twins, Farlan and Cam Campbell, had killed with Duncan's help rolled past on a litter, headed toward the back side of the castle to be prepared for the feast on the morrow. The men trooped by into the great hall for a round of drinks before the evening meal was served.

Cam's eye was already turning reddish purple and starting to swell, and young Davy, the blacksmith's apprentice, must have hurt his arm, for he supported it with the other hand and his face was twisted in a grimace of pain.

Lady Mary snagged Cam while Grace approached the younger clansman.

"What have ye done, Davy?"

"I didna fall from my horse, though some of the men have been sayin' it. Imagine a blacksmith who couldna stay astride his mount." He snorted in disgust.

Grace thought it more important that they knew how to fashion horseshoes and other useful things from metal than to ride.

She gripped the elbow of his good arm and urged him into the great room. Though they were not walking at a fast a pace, he breathed heavily, as though each step caused him pain.

"Are you hurt anywhere else?"

"Nay."

She remained silent and let him go on talking, for it looked as though he might bock if he did not have something else to focus on.

"I stayed on his back all the way down when he fell. 'Twas good he threw me free, for otherwise he might 'ave crushed me."

She led him inside to a far corner where she had organized bandages and salves, wooden splints for broken limbs, and herbs for pain.

"As it is, I slammed m' shoulder into the ground. Somethin' popped, I felt it. Heard it too." Sweat beaded his forehead and he was pale.

"Was your horse injured?" Grace asked, as though his injury was minor, though the sound of it made her anxious.

"Nay, he was just a wee bit shaken. I canna move my hand or feel it, Lady Grace." He turned sky blue eyes on her, shadowed with worry. "I canna be a smith with only one hand."

There a great many things he would not be able to do with only one. "We will see what must be done. If I canna heal it, Lady Mary will."

She urged him to sit on one of the benches. "I will need you to take off your shirt."

He pulled the laces at his throat but could not pull the garment off his injured arm. Grace pinched the fabric, worked the sleeve free gently and pulled the shirt from beneath the girdle about his waist. She bunched the material and raised it over his head and laid it aside on the table.

The muscular sturdiness of his shoulders and arms caught her attention. The many hours he hammered away at horseshoes and other metals had honed his body into fine form. Grace started at his elbow, checking to see if the bone was broken. The look of his shoulder caused a dropping sensation in the pit of her stomach, a mixture of dread and concern. The skin around the joint looked swollen and painful. A bruise the size of her fist discolored the large muscle at the top of his arm.

"I ask your forgiveness for any pain I may cause you, Robby."

He looked a little green when he glanced up at her. "It hurts enough on its own, Lady Grace. Anythin' you can do t' ease it will be better than it is."

She ran her fingers over the joint and her stomach twisted. She felt the ball at the top of the bone pushed back out of the socket. She thought she might bock in sympathy at the sudden flow of saliva flooding her mouth. She swallowed and wished she could spit instead.

Even though he did not complain about her touch, his face took on the color of porridge.

She and Lady Mary had seen numerous injuries, some too horrible to dwell on without either bocking or descending into blackness. At least there was not blood to stem and no bone to pull back beneath the skin. Not yet, anyway.

Lady Mary, finished with her ministrations for Cam, came to see what Grace was looking at and frowned in concern.

"Lady Grace, I believe..." Davy's eyes rolled back in his head and he started to fall backwards off the bench. Grace leapt to catch him, fearful he might worsen the injury to his shoulder by landing on it. Weighing at least half again what she did, and having the loose-jointed limpness of the unconscious, his body fell back against her. She lost her footing and collapsed upon the hard stone floor with a grunt, his whole upper body resting atop her.

Lady Mary's alarmed "Grace!" drew the attention of half a dozen clansmen who rushed forward to help.

Robby, having taken over for Artair as her guard, shoved past the clustered men and bent over her. "Are ye hurt, Lady Grace?"

"Nay." Though no doubt she'd have a bruise on her backside.

One of the men, Josiah Campbell, stepped forward to grip Davy's arm.

Grace lunged forward to catch his wrist. "Wait! If you lift him by his arm you may break it, 'tis out of place. Hold him up so I can wiggle out from beneath him."

Josiah motioned to one of the other men and the two supported Davy's upper body while Robby looped his arms under hers and tugged her to her feet.

Lady Mary spoke close to her ear. "'Tis difficult to put the joint back in once 'tis out, Grace. If 'tis not done right, the arm will break and 'twill be worse than it already is."

With Davy limp and relaxed at their feet and his arm extended to one side Grace saw the solution. If she could do it before he woke it would save him much pain.

"Josiah, put his legs down and straighten them." She removed her shoes.

She pointed to one other man. "Get down here with him and help. I need you to hold him down so he doesna move. I will pull his arm and stretch it out until it eases back into place."

Grace sat down on the floor, placed her feet against Davy's ribs just beneath his armpit, and gripped his forearm with both hands. The men hurried to take position on the opposite side and pressed their weight down on him.

Davy's lashes began to flutter, and color was fast returning to his face. Grace leaned back and tugged with steady pressure against the counterbalance they provided. Grace's stomach muscles tightened and her legs shook from her efforts. The joint distended.

Davy's eyes flew open when the pain revived him. When he tried to pull away from it, the knob of bone beneath the skin shifted and slid back into place, and he gave one sharp yelp of pain. Grace released his arm.

There were several crude exclamations voiced in sympathetic reaction from the men who stood watching.

"What is about here?" Lord Ramsay's voice cut above their

comments as he shoved his way through. His features set in a sneer of distaste when he spied Grace sitting in the floor, her stocking feet visible and her shoes kicked aside.

"Lady Grace, what are you doing rolling about in the floor with that man?"

"Savin' a lad the use of his arm," Gabriel spoke from behind her. "And doin' a fine job of it."

Grace's cheeks flushed with pleasure as she twisted around to look behind her.

Lord Ramsay's head whipped in Gabriel's direction and his eyes narrowed.

Grace accepted Robby's hand and scrambled to her feet. Gabriel, now standing between Derrick and Artair, looked a bit stronger than he had even that morn when they broke the fast together in his room. He still had the hollow look of someone who had gone through an illness, but he was considerably improved. She wanted to urge him to go back upstairs and take his rest, but the men surrounded him and began to slap his back and greet him with obvious relief at his recovery.

After a quick smile Grace turned her attention back to Davy, though her eyes were drawn back to Gabriel again and again.

The two men helped Davy to his feet. Grace urged him back onto the bench so she could test the joint. "Is the pain better?"

"Aye." He started to raise his arm and she pressed it back down.

"Dinna do that. 'Twould be wise to rest it a day or two. 'Tis swollen, and will be sore for some time. I'll bind it to you so you won't be tempted to raise it or overuse it."

Lady Mary gave her shoulder a squeeze. "You did well, Grace."

She exchanged a look with the woman. Now the worst was over, she was shaking and almost panting with reaction.

Lady Mary smiled, then laughed and hugged her. "Aye, I ken." For a moment they clung together in mutual relief.

Now the worst was over, Grace said, "Davy did the hard part." She offered the man an unsteady smile. He rested his hand atop hers. "Ye're a blessing, m'lady. I've had hurts before, but nothin' so bad as this."

"Can you feel your hand now?" she asked.

"Aye." He shrugged his shoulder carefully, then wiggled his fingers. Relief settled over him, relaxing the taut line of his body. He smiled.

Grace took up a roll of bandages, and, positioning his forearm against his waist, she began binding the arm to his body with the strips.

"The worst is past. After two or three days, we'll take the bandages off and you may move it with care."

Lady Mary helped her wrap the bandages around him and tie them in place.

"Is your blood rushing now, Lady Grace?" Lord Ramsay propped a boot upon the bench next to her patient. He raised a tankard of ale and drank.

Grace stole a glance in Gabriel's direction, concerned with how Lord Ramsay might react to his presence.

Remembering their conversation of yesterday morn, Grace raised a brow. "'Tis different from the hunt. Whenever someone is in pain, you do your best to ease it quickly."

He eyed Davy's bandage-wrapped torso. "Aye, I can see that. I can also see how your skill will win over your own clan whenever you take possession of *Tasgaidh*. 'Tis a good strategy."

Grace looked down at Davy. It was not a strategy to care about people. Grace reached for his shirt, eased it over his head, and helped him work his one good arm through the sleeve. "Would you mind getting Davy a cup of ale, Lord Ramsay? I think he has earned it."

The man straightened and stared at her, affronted by the idea of waiting on a man beneath his station.

Grace smiled wryly. She had already kenned how he would react.

Lord Alexander chose that moment to weave between the clusters of clansmen filling the hall, a tankard of ale in each hand. He offered it to Davy. "How is the shoulder now, lad?"

Lord Ramsay scowled and his jaw worked.

Grace and Lady Mary shared a secret smile.

"'Tis better."

"Good. You must follow Lady Grace's orders until 'tis whole again."

"Aye, I will, m'lord."

"Might I go now, Lady Mary, Lady Grace?" Davy asked, looking nervously from one to the other of the four of them. Grace understood well how he felt.

"Aye. Have a care for the shoulder, though. You dinna want to undo all of Lady Grace's labors," Lady Mary said.

Davy smiled and rose to his feet. "I will. Your lordships." He nodded and wandered away into the crowd clutching his tankard of ale.

Lord Alexander motioned to someone behind them. At Gabriel's approach, Grace bit her lip and fisted her hands at her side. Lord Ramsay was sure to do something to provoke him. Every protective instinct in her came to the fore, and she moved to stand as close as she could.

LORD ALEXANDER RESTED a hand upon Gabriel's shoulder. "Lord Ramsay, this is Gabriel Campbell, my *buannachann.*

Gabriel bowed slightly. "Lord Ramsay."

Ramsay's sour expression made it clear he did not appreciate the introduction, nor the fact that he had to look up at Gabriel.

Gabriel had studied the man from afar since he had forced his way through the clansmen and taken Grace to task for helping young Davy. What he saw was not pleasing. Offering a tankard of ale to an injured man was beneath him, as was standing amongst the clansmen surrounding him. As though their proximity might taint him.

Ramsay spoke to Alexander instead of Gabriel. "I dinna think there was need for a war chief now the conflicts with the English have ceased."

"If only that were true. Less than a month ago, clansmen came into our territory and attacked some of our people. Gabriel and his men captured the thieves and escorted them off my land."

Ramsay tilted his head back and eyed Gabriel. "You are the man to whom Lady Grace was betrothed."

Sensing Grace's movement next to him, Gabriel nodded briefly. "Until we hear otherwise from the regent, I remain bound t' her, Lord Ramsay."

Ramsay's lips compressed, but at least he did not spout the phrase, "'Tis again' the King's law," as Grace had told Gabriel he was wont to do.

"Do you read and write?" Ramsay asked instead.

"Aye, I do."

His brows rose, "How did you come by such learning?"

"You fight shoulder to shoulder with all sorts of men during war. There was a learned man, I think a barrister, from the MacClennon clan, bound t' ours for a time. I had an eagerness t' learn, and he was hungry for a distraction during times when we waited for orders from the Bruce."

"I am surprised a man of law would march into battle."

Gabriel raised a brow at that. It was plain to see that Lord Ramsay had not raised a sword to fight for Scottish freedom. Instead, he had spent his time preying on young, innocent lasses while the rest of them fought. "When the Bruce called for clansmen, they came."

"And how long have you trained with Lord Alexander's men?"

"Sixteen years. I was ten and three when I took up the sword." Gabriel glanced at Alexander, acknowledging the wealth of history between them expressed in those few words. "I wasna as tall or braw then, but was on m' way."

Alexander smiled. "He was still taller than most of the men, and agile. I couldna allow all that brawn t' be wasted when we needed men to fight. And he has a talent for it. Has a talent for training others as well." Which was tremendous praise, indeed.

"I follow the way ye trained me, m'lord."

"Even a bear can be taught to dance," Lord Ramsay sneered.

Gabriel steadied his stance and reached for patience. "He didna teach me t' dance, but t' fight when 'twas needed to protect the King or others. Have you been trusted with such an honor?"

Lord Ramsay remained silent, his jaw working.

"Nay, I can see ye have not." Gabriel's attention shifted to Alexander. "If you will excuse me, m'lord."

When Gabriel would have stepped past him, Ramsay gripped his arm. "And how many bastards have you fathered among the women of this clan and others?"

Lady Mary gasped.

Rage flooded Gabriel like molten iron, bringing with it a rush of energy. Gabriel imagined picking up the wee man by the throat and letting him dangle until his breathing stopped.

A small hand slipped into his and clung. He skimmed Grace's face, which was pale with shock. He gave her fingers a gentle squeeze. "None." He turned his head to rake the man with contempt. "You are welcome t' ask others if ye like. If I had, they would have been claimed, fostered, and trained within m' clan. I am not a man who shrugs aside my responsibilities like some."

He looked down to stare directly into the man's face. "I may not have a title, Lord Ramsay, but I do ken how t' speak with courtesy before ladies." He jerked his arm free of the man's grasp and strode away, taking Grace with him.

His temper was still high when he escorted Grace into Lord Alexander's antechamber. He drew away from her to go stand at the fireplace until he could calm himself.

"I meant what I said. I dinna have any weans that I am aware of. But if I did, I would claim them quick enough."

Grace took a seat in one of the large chairs before the fire. "I ken ye would, Gabriel."

A husky voice came from the open doorway, "Lord Ramsay has enough for both of you. Unrecognized, unfostered and ignored. I know, because I am one of them. That he has given me a position as his manservant isna a blessing, I can tell ye."

The young lad looked to be mayhap thirteen. He was thin as

an oatcake, and with no beard, he looked more lass than lad. There was something feminine in the way he moved as well. His hair was as thick as his father's, and gathered in a short queue at the nape of his neck, leaving his features bare. The resemblance to Lord Ramsay was enough to prove who begat him.

Grace rose to stand before the boy, who was a head taller than she. "Have ye met Lady Elspeth? Do ye ken if she is well?"

"Aye, I know Elspeth. I canna say she is well, but she is alive."

Grace flinched and gripped the boy's arm. "Has he truly locked her away?"

A sudden, bleak look crossed his face. "Aye, he has. She has been locked away for some time now."

Grace stepped closer to him. "Where? If you tell us, mayhap we can free her."

"She can never be free, Lady Grace." There was a knowledge, a surety in the way he said it.

A sickness filled Gabriel's stomach. "Does he treat you well, lad?"

Bitterness flickered across his face. "He feeds and clothes me, which is more than the other bastards he has spawned can expect of him."

At least he was not misusing the lad. "Do you not have any other kin you can go to?"

"Nay." He shook his head and looked away. "There is no one left."

Gabriel sought something hopeful to say. "You will be old enough to strike out on your own soon."

The boy remained silent a moment. "No one escapes his grasp once they are in it." He turned to look at Grace. "Only you, Lady Grace. Take heed. Dinna trust him, for he will find a way to drag you back if he can. He has not forgotten that ye slipped away before he was finished with ye."

Gabriel rested a hand on the boy's shoulder and felt how truly frail he was. "What do ye mean?"

"I dinna ken how, but he plans to have you, Lady Grace."

He bent sharply at the waist, turned, and strode away.

"Wait!" Grace called and he hesitated at the door. "What is your name?"

"I am called Logan."

Grace nodded. "There are those who will take you in and offer you shelter, Logan. If you escape him, you will be welcome."

He paused for a long moment, studying her face, then giving a brief nod, turned, and continued up the stairs.

Gabriel reached for Grace and rested an arm around her, but she did not lean against him, and there was no fear in her expression. "You have Lord Alexander's protection, Grace. He canna harm ye."

"Nay. I winna allow him to." There was a steady determination in her expression, and a burning anger he had never seen before. "Should he harm me or mine, he winna live to enjoy it."

Chapter 10

GABRIEL PAUSED IN the entryway of the great hall to scan the chamber. The lively chatter that usually accompanied a visit from Lord John, the Campbell laird, was absent. Derrick had mentioned the men's strange behavior at table during meals, and his curiosity was tweaked. For the group to be so quiet after the second day of a successful hunt was truly odd. The men seemed focused on their food and nothing else.

The tables filled with Lord John's men appeared almost as subdued, their attention now and then directed at the head table. Gabriel wondered at their interest and walked farther into the chamber. His muscles protested only a wee bit as he limped across the room to join his men. After four days in bed and any number of small meals pressed upon him, he felt stronger, but not yet fully himself. The trip across the great hall siphoned off some of his reserves, but did not deplete them. Aye. He was regaining his strength and was on the mend.

He murmured his thanks when young Robby Campbell bobbed up and offered his place.

Artair slapped his back, and Gabriel suppressed a grimace when every muscle protested the abuse.

The man's grin stretched his well-worn features. "'Tis about time ye showed yer ugly face and rejoined the fight."

"Aye." Séamus Campbell grinned from across the table and gripped his wrist. "'Tis glad we are to see ye still above ground and not on the brink of cocking up yer toes."

Robby returned from the barrels along one side of the hall with a tankard of ale and placed it at his elbow. Several servants appeared. Artair placed a meat pie on the corner of the trencher Robby had abandoned, while the young clansman spooned some stew into a wooden bowl and set it before him. A young lad holding a wooden platter of roast pork paused beside him and Gabriel waved him away with a word of thanks.

Gabriel looked down the length of the table to find smiles directed at him, but no one spoke.

"Eat, lad," Artair urged in a whisper. "Ye will need yer strength soon enough. I'd swear ye have dropped two stone in the last four days."

His men's concern had him eyeing the food. His appetite had not yet returned, but though he had eaten a wee meal in his chambers, Gabriel took up the pie and bit into it.

While he chewed, he risked a glance at the head table. Grace sat between Lord John and Duncan, but her gaze was fastened on Gabriel. She sent him a smile, then returned her attention to Duncan when he offered her something from the trencher before them. She shook her head, and instead took up the tankard they shared.

Gabriel had last seen her in the early morn, when she brought a meal of porridge and eggs to him and lingered to share it. The memory of how his last request for eggs and porridge had led them down a pleasant path triggered a smile even now.

Sandwiched between Lord John and Lord Duncan, Grace looked fragile but at ease, and actually gave Lord Duncan a brief, polite smile.

Artair leaned close. "The lass seems steadier at Lord Duncan's side than she did Lord Ramsay's, and doesna look like a frightened hare, as she has these few days past. The laird asked to have a private word with her yesterday noon after he and Lord Duncan arrived. She has been shut in on herself ever since."

Not shut in exactly, but in a state of despair. What had the man said to her?

A young male servant came to stand at his side. "The laird has asked for your company at their table, Gabriel."

Mayhap he would learn now. He rose from his seat, and leaving the food, attempted a normal stride as he approached the table. The longer he was on his feet, the more quickly his muscles would recover. He was grateful when Duncan shifted his chair down the table and rose to get another.

"Come sit beside me, Gabriel," Lord John demanded.

"I would be pleased to do so, m'lord."

Gabriel paused to greet Lord Alexander and Lady Mary.

Lady Mary smiled. "'Tis very good you feel well enough to join us, Gabriel."

"Thank you, m'lady."

Gabriel nodded to the man next to her to acknowledge him. The blankness of the Lord Ramsay's expression said more about his displeasure than a frown.

He turned his attention to Grace. "Lady Grace." He touched his heart in deference and offered her a smile. "Lord Duncan."

A place had been set between Grace and Lord John. He moved around the table and gratefully took the seat. The trencher set before him had roast venison already sliced, stewed apples, and one of the meat pies he had partially eaten.

"I have been told the fever brought on by your injury laid you low," Lord John said.

"Aye, m'lord. Lady Mary, Lady Grace, and Derrick Campbell saved my life."

"'Tis a blessing you were spared. Your work is not yet done, Gabriel," he commented. "'Tis what Father Dillion said this morn when I spoke with him."

"Since Father Dillion is oft seen having conversations with a power most high, I shall accept his word as truth."

Lord John chuckled. He filled a tankard from a pitcher and placed it before him before topping off his own cup. "Eat and drink heartily, so your strength may return."

He had heard that more than once. "Thank you, m'lord."

Gabriel turned to Grace. "Mayhap you will allow me to serve you a bite or two from my plate, Lady Grace." He removed his dagger and cut the venison into pieces.

Her concern for him lay in the depths of her eyes. "Certes, are ye truly well enough to be here, Gabriel? You must not tax yourself."

"I have rested and am on the mend. You must eat, too." He sliced the meat pie in half and handed her the spoon.

"Lord Duncan has shared his plate with me. I have eaten my fill, but I will drink some of the wine Lord John poured for you."

The men at one table began talking, then another, until the noise built around the hall until it reached the normal rumble.

"'Twould seem the temper of the room has been improved by your arrival, Gabriel," Duncan commented, his gaze directed at his father.

Lord John raised a brow, his expression wry.

"Do you support such shows of rebellion, Lord Campbell?" There was a challenge in Lord Ramsay's tone as he directed the comment at the laird.

Lord John raised a thin sliver of pork to his lips, chewed it, then swallowed. He raised a hand, his gesture taking in the hall. "Do you see men brandishing swords, Davis? Any men standing atop tables, shouting their displeasure? Do you see anyone in the castle refusing to do their duty?"

Lord Ramsay's features flushed. "Nay."

"Then I see no fires of rebellion. Nor do you." He bore down on the last three words. He rested an arm upon the table and leaned forward to eye the man. "Would you have one or all flogged for making their wishes known in a peaceful manner?"

"Nay." Lord Ramsay subsided. "But you may wish to be wary of such support being shown to one of the rank. Trouble will surely follow later when all doesna go as they wish."

At Grace's restless move beside him, Gabriel grasped her hand and held it tightly in his. The arrogant certainty in the man's tone was hard to shrug aside. It did what he intended it to do, forced out the fragile feeling of hope until all that was left was helplessness. How oft had Grace been subjected to the man's jabs since his arrival?

Lord John leaned back in his chair and reached for his tankard. He took a long drink, then set it aside. "'Tis a laird's duty to look to the well-being of the clan as a whole. I can promise you, there will be no trouble—now or later."

With a scowl Ramsay subsided back in his chair.

Lord John turned, and Gabriel tensed, ready to defend his men, but he spoke to Grace instead.

"'Twas this you spoke of to me yesterday, was it not Lady Grace?"

"Aye, m'lord. 'Tis like having a hungry rat nipping at your heels."

Lord John covered his mouth and coughed several times, the sound suspiciously like a laugh.

Gabriel wished such humor could lighten his own mood. Because he was a soldier, he had learned to take each moment as it came. But he could not wait and hope all would be well if he wanted Grace to be his wife. Lord Ramsay had already proven his determination to prevent their union in any way possible. Though Lord John had just defended him and the men, there was no promise he would support his plea with the regent.

"I have finished my letters. Will ye return Lady Mary's quill and ink, Grace?"

"Aye, I will."

Gabriel nodded.

Duncan asked about the skirmish when Gabriel was injured. Battle was a frequent necessity, and though Gabriel wished to protect Grace, he could not shield her from his way of life. She had lived through violent struggles and accepted it.

"'Twas three days out when we became aware we were being tracked. We picked up our pace while we moved through a deep ravine leading onto Campbell land. They were lying in wait for us ahead, while a group of four came at us from behind. One of the horses took an arrow in the left haunch and came up lame. We fanned out and sought cover.

"The four in the rear were dispatched easily, but there were six more. We charged at them head-on. Derrick took the leader, whilst the rest of us took care of the others."

"But he didna take him alone," Grace added.

Surprised, Gabriel swung his attention to her.

"Derrick told us you saved him by taking the strike. Ye could have been killed, Gabriel. Yer arm…"

"Derrick is our healer when we are away from *Caisteal Sith*. He cares for us all."

"Are we now measuring every man's worth by what he brings to the clan? If so, they are all precious. You are Lord Alexander's man at arms. The leader of his men during times of trouble. What would we do, should something happen to ye?"

The words *what would I* did not have to be said. They were there to read in her expression.

"I couldna let him fall."

"Aye. I ken." She rested her hand on his wrist, acceptance warring with the love in her gaze. He longed to kiss her and offer his comfort, but he satisfied his longing by covering her hand in the only gesture open to him.

Gabriel glanced up to find Lord John's attention fastened on her.

Lord Ramsay moved from his seat and crossed in front of the table. Grace withdrew her hand and settled back in her chair.

"If you are finished with your meal, I would ask a word in private, Lady Grace."

Grace eyed the man as she would an adder about to strike. She turned to Lord John. "May I be excused, m'lord?"

"For only a moment, Lady Grace," Lord John said, his eyes on Lord Ramsay. "There will be music to enjoy shortly."

Lord Ramsay bowed. "I wouldna wish to delay our enjoyment of the entertainment. I will be brief."

Chapter 11

GRACE ROSE AND took up her tartan shawl. Gabriel having risen as she did, draped it over her shoulders and she took the time to slip his larger dagger beneath her wrap. She murmured her thanks. Dread dragged at each step while she walked around the long table. Artair was waiting for them at the door and opened it.

"You winna be needed," Lord Ramsay said.

"I have been ordered by Lord Alexander to accompany Lady Grace where e'er she goes," Artair answered.

The man's features tightened with anger. "Does your master always guard the womenfolk of the castle with such caution?"

"Aye, m'lord. Certes, when strangers are about."

With a sour look Lord Ramsay stood back to allow Grace to precede him into the hall.

He motioned her inside of Lord Alexander's antechamber. Artair stood just outside the open door. Grace took a place behind one of the large wooden chairs and gripped the back of it with one hand. Her fingers, icy with nerves, shook upon the wooden spindles that decorated the frame.

"I ken we havena had much time to renew our acquaintance, Lady Grace. When last we saw each other, it was during a confusing time. I hope you realize I had nothing to do with my wife's actions. 'Twas madness that caused her to act without kindness toward you."

Aye, a madness brought on by his actions. A madness that had caused his daughter to be confined. How did he live with himself?

"I hope you will not hold her transgressions against me."

He had enough on his own account without adding his wife's. "Nay. I do not."

Lord Ramsay smiled and for a moment she recognized a fleeting charm in his expression, but it had no affect on her. "I am pleased to hear it." Satisfaction radiated from his smile. "Lord Alexander said you have had time to read the charter."

"Aye, I have."

"Tomorrow would be a good time for you to sign it? Lord Alexander suggested after we break the fast together."

There was nothing in the document dictating who she must wed in order to accept the charter. She had studied it carefully, and Lord Alexander had also scoured it to make certain. But Lord Ramsay's eagerness to have her signature on it made her uneasy.

With Lord Ramsay's son's warnings running through her head, she eased from behind the chair, caution in each step. "To be the lady of Clan MacNab, and to take possession of a manor house and the property, is a fiercesome responsibility, is it not?"

"Aye, but with the right guidesman 'twill prove an easier task. I—"

Grace cut him off for fear of what he might be about to say. "Before I sign the charter, I would like to travel to the valley and meet with some of the clan."

Ramsay's brows rose. "For what purpose, Lady Grace?"

"If I am to live amongst among them, 'twould be better to be accepted as one of them than looked upon as a stranger."

"You are the last of the ruling class of their clan. You are their lady. 'Tis their duty to obey you and the regent's edict. Acceptance has nothing to do with it."

It had been his arrogant abrasiveness, his belief that he was above everyone, even God's law, that bred resentment in his household. If she could but use that against him in some way. As a lord, he had all the power, and those around him had none. Even his wife could not raise questions about him. But Grace—as a lady with no connection to him—she might do so.

"Acceptance has a great deal to do with it, Lord Ramsay. 'Tis easier to guide than to force. Easier to expect loyalty once it is earned through kindness and respect. 'Twill be a great change for them, and 'twill ease the way, should they meet with me."

"You have been too long among those beneath you, Lady Grace. Mayhap I should insist you travel with me to Edinburgh so you might be introduced to your equals and learn their ways."

"Are Lord Alexander and Lady Mary not my equals, sir? Are not Lord John and Lord Duncan? I have been Lady Mary's companion since her first days here. I have learned how to conduct myself at her side. Are you saying she has failed me in some way?"

Over Lord Ramsay's shoulder, Grace glimpsed Lord Duncan standing in the doorway. She dragged in her first full breath since entering the room.

Frustration worked its way across Ramsay's features. "Nay. But clansmen are like children. You must rule them with a firm hand. To show them weakness in any way is to invite rebellion."

"The man with true power is the man who doesna have to wield it," Grace said with more assurance.

"Like the clansman you insist on clinging to. 'Tis an embarrassment how you cleave to this Gabriel and refuse to share anyone else's plate. Do you have no pride?"

Grace raised her chin at the insult. "I didna mind sharing Lord Duncan's."

Ramsay's jaw tensed and his face flushed a burning red. "You should be more aware of who has the regent's ear, Lady Grace. 'Twould take only a word from me to have your beloved Gabriel thrown into the deepest, darkest hole."

Grace's heart shuddered inside her chest.

"If you wish to keep him alive, you will give my proposal of marriage your utmost consideration. In fact, we should return to the festivities and announce you have accepted it. You have no other prospects."

Panic brought numbness to her hands and face, and it took all her wits to keep from backing away from him. "But I do have other prospects, Lord Ramsay. Lord John has already spoken to me about them."

His look of shock gave her some satisfaction.

"I have put his aside, just as I will yours, until the regent has ruled on Gabriel's petition. I signed a betrothal contract before God and a priest. Lord and Lady Campbell witnessed it, as did others in the chapel, nearly all who reside here. 'Twas a solemn promise. 'Tis not for you to say it means nothing."

"'Tis again' the law," Ramsay shouted.

"When the regent himself tells me there isna hope, only then will I believe it."

Lord Ramsay stalked toward her, fists clenched, his voice close to a growl, but still loud enough to carry. "I will see Gabriel Campbell dead if you dinna surrender this madness. You will wed *me*." He thrust a thumb back toward his chest.

She caught her breath in alarm and rage. She drew the dagger. Should he attempt to strike her, he would regret it.

Duncan strode into the room with Artair a step behind him. "Nay, she will not. Should you raise a hand again' Gabriel or any other Campbell clansman, you will be delivered to the regent a piece at a time."

"Would you threaten the regent's officer?"

"You are the regent's messenger, and no officer. 'Tis no idle threat, Davis. I will testify before the regent that you threatened death upon a valued member of our clan in an attempt to force Lady Grace to end her betrothal and accept your proposal. That alone will see it done."

Grace's legs shook as Duncan purposely cut between them to shield her.

Lord Alexander, with Gabriel at his side, rushed into the room, the Campbell laird behind them.

Lord Ramsay threw out an arm and pointed at Gabriel. "You will never wed that baseborn warrior. I will see to it."

"Certes, I winna wed you, Lord Davis Ramsay. If you were my only choice, I would still rather spend the rest of my life barren and alone."

Ramsay lunged forward and would have struck her, had Duncan not thrown up a forearm, striking him beneath the chin and knocking him back.

Lord Ramsay staggered, but would have saved himself from an ignoble tumble had it not been for Lord Alexander's booted foot helping him the rest of the way to the floor. The man went down hard onto his back, and Alexander planted the same foot in the center of his chest with more than a little of his weight behind it. It drove the man's breath from him with a whoosh.

Ramsay squirmed and kicked but could not shove it aside. The man was gasping like a netted salmon before Lord Alexander stepped aside and motioned Artair and Gabriel forward. The two of them lifted Ramsay to his feet and set him in a chair none too gently.

"You have insulted my hospitality, Davis, threatened one of my clansmen with harm, and attempted to strike Lady Grace and my brother. Explain what has brought about these events, Duncan."

Lord Ramsay hugged his arms against his chest and glared up at Lord Alexander through red-rimmed eyes. "You will regret this," he hissed. When he attempted to rise, Gabriel and Artair shoved down on his shoulders, holding him in place. Ramsay sent a look of such venom at Gabriel, Grace was tempted to draw his dagger again.

Lord Alexander sucked in a long breath. "I dinna believe so, but, certes you will, Davis."

Duncan stepped forward. "He threatened to have Gabriel killed in an attempt to force Lady Grace into accepting his proposal of marriage. When she would not bend to his threats, he attempted to strike her."

"Is this true, Grace?"

"Aye, m'lord." She braced a hand upon the back of the chair to steady herself, for now the fray was over, she trembled with relief.

"Was that what you heard as well, Artair?"

"Aye, m'lord. Certes, I warrant ever' man in the stairwell heard it as well. He were shoutin' it."

Lord Alexander shook his head. "There are witnesses who will testify you have tried to force Lady Grace to accept your proposal again' her will." Alexander glanced up at Grace, and a flash of humor lit his tawny eyes and a quick smirk touched his lips. "You have broken the king's law, Davis."

Chapter 12

GABRIEL LEANED AGAINST the stone curtain wall and narrowed his eyes against the early morning sun while he watched the last of Lord Ramsay's escort disappear around the bend some distance away. "'Tis useless I have been these many days. I canna join my men to patrol around the castle. And I was too late to offer Grace protection or comfort last night. I am grateful you were there, Duncan."

Duncan shrugged and rested an arm against one of the taller blocks that formed the crenellation atop the wall. "She seems to have weathered the storm well enough. And you didna see the bloodlust in her eye when she drew your dagger. I have no doubt she would have used it."

"Lord Alexander must ha' thought the same, for when I discovered it was missing he leapt to action more quickly than I have seen him move in some time."

Duncan chuckled. "Mayhap in future you will wish to keep such sharp weapons well hidden when she is angry. 'Twas as though she meant to goad Davis into revealing himself. And her stubbornness could rival Lady Mary's."

Gabriel grinned. "Aye. 'Tis grand, is it not?"

Duncan laughed.

"They have been cut from the same cloth. Lady Mary and Grace have a way of standing their ground, as though their feet are planted deep in conviction, although they never raise their voices."

"I wouldna say never. Do ye not remember when Mary decided t' separate Alexander's head from his shoulders, and mine, with the wooden service from the aumry?"

Gabriel chuckled. "Aye, I do. But she would take a pike to anyone else who threatened him."

"Aye, she would. And in the next moment heal the hurts of those with whom she is most angry." He touched the small scar over his eyebrow.

Gabriel smiled at the memory. He had seen the injury when first it had happened. One of the wooden bowls she'd hurled had grazed Duncan and split the skin. Lady Mary bandaged the gash after she had calmed, and apologized most sincerely.

Gabriel stepped away from the wall, and Duncan fell into step beside him. Gabriel wondered at the other man's purpose for inviting him to walk the battlements, since he did not seem eager to walk them at all. There was more to it than just a wander through the many memories they shared. And there were many.

Gabriel's life had been entwined with Lord Alexander's since he was a boy. Because of his strength and size, there had never been any other path to him but to raise his sword in defense of his country and his clan. Alexander himself had trained him. He had never wanted more than that before. But he wanted it now. He would be grateful to be able to stand next to Grace in whatever way he could, and serve her as a husband.

Duncan laid a hand on his arm midway down the planking between the north and south towers. "There is something I wish to share with you, Gabriel. I wouldna treat your loyalty to our clan, to all of us, with anythin' less than the respect it deserves."

'Twas bad news, then. There had not been time for the regent to address the petition Lord Alexander had sent. But what else could it be?

"Should the regent rule again' you, my father has asked Grace to consider marrying me to ensure the area remains friendly to the Campbell clan. In return, we would offer our protection to her clan."

Grace was right. Whenever there was a bit of unprotected land about, there was always someone anxious to claim it.

This was his clan.

He had sworn fealty to Laird Campbell and loyalty to Lord

Alexander.

But to see the man next to him holding his Grace, serving as her husband...

He braced his hands against the top of the stone and bent at the waist while a war of emotions raged through him. His cheeks burned with anger hotter than the fever from which he had just recovered. A knot the size of a clenched fist lodged in his throat.

It was several minutes before he could speak, and still he could not look at Duncan for fear of losing his composure and possibly doing something he might later regret. "Does the laird mean to ask me to step aside?"

"Nay. We are all hopeful the regent will rule in your favor, Gabriel. Father has written a letter commending your service to our clan and to the Bruce. He has stated his support of your marriage to Grace."

Gabriel nodded. The tightness in his chest began to recede, and with it the sense of betrayal. "I have written my own letters to those I have served with in the past and asked their support."

Duncan slapped him on the back. "Good. In order for you to wed Grace, the regent will also have to offer you a knighthood or more. He may also ask for you to adopt her clan as your own, and for you to take the MacNab name."

He thought about the sacrifice. He would be losing a part of himself, a source of pride that was woven into the fabric of his being, as tightly knitted as his kilt. His blood was Campbell. But had Grace not accepted the Campbell clan with an open heart? Would their children not be a blend of MacNab and Campbell, and carry the blood, the heart of both clans. "There is naught I wouldna sacrifice to stay with my lady, Duncan."

Duncan nodded. "Even a blind man can see Lady Grace's feelings for you, Gabriel. They are as fierce as Mary's for Alexander. At the moment Grace canna see beyond that. But there are other concerns.

"The MacNab clan isna large enough to protect itself against an outside attack, and, though they have Drummond as their leader in other ways, he canna train them to wage battle. Grace's place is at the head of their clan. There is no doubt you could be the leader they need to take his place. Once the regent meets you, 'twill be up to you t' sway him to that same belief.

Duncan looked at him now. "As soon as you are strong enough, we will all accompany you to Edinburgh to meet with him face-to-face. Lady Mary has suggested two days hence."

Gabriel remembered many months before when Artair told him Grace would need him to fight for her one day. He had not understood what he meant at the time, but he did now. "I will be ready."

"I am depending on it, Gabriel."

He had never seen Duncan look more serious, and somehow that eased the lingering remnants of pain.

"As comely and sweet as Lady Grace is, I would be honored to be held in her affections, but I fear I would always fall short. 'Tis you who have won her heart. No man should have to overcome such an obstacle with his bride."

"You would give up your Campbell name for her?" Gabriel asked as they continued to walk.

"I would do it for my clan because I would have no other choice. But love must surely make the sacrifice easier to bear."

"Aye."

"You will want to give some thought to what you wish to say to the regent."

Gabriel nodded. He came to a halt before they reached the tower. After a couple of steps Duncan turned to face him.

He could not even imagine what it would be like to never see Grace again, to be forced to deny his feelings for her. They could not go on always wanting each other and never being together. But it would be worse than death to see her with another, sharing the joys meant to be theirs. He would have to leave this place, offer his sword to another clan's laird to escape it.

It had always been his custom to envision victory in every battle before they entered the fray. He would not allow doubt to take root now. Grace needed him. He would not fail her, or himself.

❊

"I HAVE WRITTEN the letter, signed it, and had it witnessed by Lady Mary, Father Dillion, and Séamus Campbell." Lord John unfolded the document and placed it in her hands.

Grace read the letter carefully and rested her fingers on the Campbell seal at the bottom. After everything else that had happened she hardly knew how to feel, but relief and joy were in the mixture. "Thank you, Lord John. I am most grateful."

"'Twill take more than a few letters to convince the regent that Gabriel is the best man for the task, Grace," his deep voice rumbled. "Should he reject Gabriel, you will be faced with many who will wish to fill his place."

"I do ken." She had thought long on the possibilities. "Lord Alexander and Lady Mary made me a part of their family when I had none, Lord John. I winna forsake their love and trust in me. Whatever decisions I make, I will make with them in mind as well."

Lord John took the letter and sealed it with wax and stamped the Campbell seal in place. He handed it to Alexander.

Lord Alexander laid it aside and took up both copies of the charter and laid them before her. "You must sign them, Grace. Your clan needs your guidance."

She bit her lip hard.

"I would like Gabriel to be here to witness the signing. 'Tis his shoulders the burden will rest upon as well."

"'Tis not a burden, Grace, but an honor," Lord John said.

She was doing her duty; that should be enough. She did not need anyone telling her she had to enjoy it. "You have always rested in the bosom of your clan, embraced and accepted by all, m'lord. I dinna remember anythin' about my time with clan MacNab. Had I been beloved by anyone there, I would have been taken in by someone when Mam died. In light of that, I will reserve my opinion of whether 'tis a blessing or a curse."

Lord John's frown deepened, but he said no more. Lord Alexander went to the door and instructed that Gabriel be found and brought to the antechamber.

Grace wandered to the large fireplace and relaxed a bit in its heat. She pressed a finger against the bridge of her nose. Plagued by thoughts of what her life would be like from this moment on, she had slept little. She was paying for it now with an ache behind her eyes.

She would be responsible for clan MacNab, as Lady Mary carried the responsibility for her husband's clan. Lady Mary had trained her well; she could do it. But not alone. It had to be Gabriel. She trusted no one else to stand by her side and look after her interests.

Long, slow minutes passed while they waited. With Lord Ramsay's exodus, the fearful feelings triggered by his presence had eased. But still worry clung to her like frost on the grass, clammy and brittle.

She cleared her throat. "Excuse me, m'lords."

They both looked up.

"The same thoughts keep twisting about in my mind, and I would share them with you so you may offer me counsel." She straightened her shoulders and faced them both. "Are you certain Lord Ramsay winna petition the regent for my hand, Lord John?"

Lord John shook his head. "'Twould do him little good, Grace. Duncan and Artair witnessed his threats. The guards up the stairs heard him as well."

"But they will not be there to testify, and he will arrive in Edinburgh long before Lord Duncan and Artair will."

She turned to Lord Alexander. "Lady Ramsay wouldna have wished to speak again' him because of the shame it would bring to her and her daughter. If she sent you to find me, mayhap she had begun to wonder if what I told her was right and true. Then as soon as I was found, she died. Did a sudden illness come upon her, or did some mishap take her life?"

"I dinna ken, Grace, but once we reach Edinburgh, I will make some inquiries."

"She died shortly after you sent me here. Does that not seem…" she searched for the right word, "…fortunate for him?"

Alexander's heavy brows crimped into a frown, and the creases in his cheeks deepened as his lips firmed. "Why did you not tell me of this earlier before he left?"

"There was much confusion last eve, and this is the first moment I have had to speak to you, m'lord. He says his daughter has gone mad with grief for her *màthair* and *bràthairs,* but would she not be ten and eight now, and mayhap rebellious enough t' speak out?"

Seeing that she had both the men's attention, she decided to lay all her thoughts and fears at their feet.

"I was of no interest to him until the regent recognized me. As a servant, I had no voice, but as a lady with no connection to him, what I might say and who I might say it to could prove most troublesome to him." She said the most difficult thing quickly. "Incest is a crime punishable by the crown. But if he could silence me...through a bond of marriage demanded in the king's name..."

Alexander and Lord John exchanged a glance.

At the sound of booted feet in the hall, the discussion broke off abruptly.

Grace was glad to see more color in Gabriel's cheeks when he entered the room with Lord Duncan close behind. His gaze rested on her first before he turned to Lord Alexander.

"Lady Grace wished you to be present while she signed the charter," Lord Alexander explained.

Gabriel crossed the distance between them in three strides and offered his hand. She gripped it with both of hers. Her throat was dry, and she swallowed. "Lord John has given us his blessing and written a letter of support."

"Duncan has told me. I am grateful, Lord John."

"'Twill be up to you and Grace to do the rest."

"We winna fail, m'lord."

His attention swung back to her.

"'Tis my fondest wish for you to be my husband."

He held her gaze as he said, "As it is mine for you to be my wife."

"I winna take another, Gabriel." As hard as she fought them, tears streamed down her face. "There is no man who could take your place in my heart, and 'twould not be honorable to expect another to accept less."

Gabriel's fingers tightened around hers, drawing her attention. His steady gaze soothed her. "You have to sign the charter, Grace. To refuse to do so would anger the regent, and turn him again' our cause before we ever plead it."

But to sign it might separate them forever. Tears blurred her eyes again, and he gripped both her hands. "I will be yer husband, and I will serve you and yer clan for as long as ye need me."

"'Tis a lifetime I'm asking of you."

He brushed her forehead with his lips. "Do what you must, *a ghràidh.*"

Though tears continued to fall, Grace dipped the quill in the ink and set it to the paper, scrawling her name without care across both copies of the document. After it was done, she laid aside the quill and studied her handiwork. Inside her rose such a feeling of panic, it required all her resolve to keep from grabbing up the heavy sheets and ripping them to pieces.

She stepped aside for Lord John and turned away to avoid watching while he and Lord Alexander signed them. She returned to Gabriel, for having his arm about her was the only solace open to her. "Sign them, Gabriel. I would have your name upon them as well."

He nodded and moved to the table, signed the documents, and returned to her.

"How long might it take you to gather your things and prepare to leave for Edinburgh?" Lord Alexander asked, the question directed to them both.

"Only a short time, m'lord," Gabriel answered and Grace nodded.

"Do it now. We will leave within the hour."

Grace's heart pounded at the base of her throat. It was not just her fears and imaginings running away with her. If Lord Alexander thought they needed to leave right now, he believed the things she feared were real.

Chapter 13

GRACE RUSHED TO place small bits and pieces of herbs, dried flowers, and barks in small bundles, then placed them all in one of the traveling bags Lord Alexander gave her. If any of the men were hurt during the journey, she would have need of them.

Lady Mary hovered next to the blue gown Grace had made to wear for her wedding. She touched the delicate flowers Grace had embroidered into the bodice with thread only a shade lighter than the fabric. "You will need to take your wedding gown, Grace. You should wear it for your audience with the regent."

"I stitched it to wear for Gabriel."

"Aye, and he will be with you before your audience with the regent, and see you then. All will go well, and you will wear it before a priest as soon as the meeting is over."

Grace searched Mary's face. "Do you truly believe the regent will rule for Gabriel and me to wed?"

"Aye, I do." Mary expertly folded the gown, rolled a piece of linen around it, and tied it with string. "Gabriel is willing to make sacrifices to do what is right for your clan and for you. He is strong enough to be their leader. Lord Ramsay is too entrenched in Edinburgh to wish to live in the Highlands or take an interest in what is right for your people. You must point that out to the regent when you speak to him." She rolled the kirtle and shift up in the same manner. She stuffed the package into the leather bag as well, and buckled it closed.

"Aye, I will, Lady Mary."

"Not lady to you any longer, Grace. Only Mary." She smoothed back wavy strands of hair that had escaped her braid, a frown wrinkling her brow. "You finish here. I've thought of a few other things you may need along the way, and I will bring them to ye shortly."

Grace's eyes stung with emotion. "Thank you, Mary."

Mary hugged her and rushed out of the room. Grace had just finished putting her brush and scissors in the bag when she returned.

"You must take my cloak as a gift. 'Twill be cold at night, and 'tis lined with fur to ensure yer warmth."

"I canna take such a gift, Lady Mary."

"Only Mary, now, Grace. And aye, ye can and must. I had Alexander t' share his warmth."

And as much as he would want to, Gabriel would not be able to share his. She would be alone among the men. The trip ahead would be difficult.

Would she ever return to *Caisteal Sith*? She looked around the room. There were precious few items left. Two gowns, a kirtle and two shifts. The basket Gabriel had given her. She moved to it and touched the handle.

"Should I pack the rest of my things?" Grace asked.

"Nay. I dinna think I am ready for that yet, Grace." Lady Mary's eyes filled with tears, and she leaned close to embrace her.

Her friend's loss of composure triggered Grace's own tears, and for several minutes they clung to each other. "You must return to celebrate. And when you are ready to travel to *Tasgaidh*, if you wish it, I would like to visit there with you."

"Aye, I do wish it." Knowing she would be missed, that she was loved, helped her face what lay ahead in Edinburgh.

She fought to regain her composure. "There is not enough time for me to say what is in m' heart. Not enough time for me t' thank ye for all you have done for me."

Mary's arms tightened around her. "Ye didna have to say it. What is in yer heart is in mine as well." She took a step back and brushed at the tear tracks on her cheeks. "My hopes and prayers go with ye, Grace. And now ye must hurry to the bailey. They will be waiting, and we both ken men dinna wait well."

Grace attempted a smile and straightened her shoulders. "Aye. We do."

SÉAMUS CAMPBELL TOOK point and guided the company up the hillside trail that ran along the opposite side of the loch, away from *Caisteal Sith*. Lord Alexander followed close behind him. It had been some time since he had needed to ride farther than a league, and Gabriel understood his look of anticipation. Marriage, family, and the responsibility of running the clan kept him close to the castle. It must seem a mundane existence when compared with being a leader in battle.

Lord John took position five horses back, his dress and demeanor much like any of the clansmen. He, too, was dressed in simple clothes, but his bearing set him apart, even if his clothing and horse did not.

Lord Duncan rode in front of Grace. He had covered his hair with a hat and blended in a little more easily than his father and brother.

Gabriel felt humbled that the three most powerful men in the clan rode to defend him and Grace, and to stand by them.

Gabriel fell in behind Grace, alert for trouble. She would not be used to the pace or length of time in the saddle, but they had little choice. Lord Ramsay had more than an hour's lead, and they would have to push hard to overtake him and stay ahead.

Orange, yellow, and red leaves floated upon the jagged, rock-strewn shore of the loch. Fall had touched the trees with glorious color, and their finery as well as the distant mountains were reflected in the water's surface. Gabriel would have lingered atop the ridge and shared the view of the castle nestled in such beauty with Grace, but there was no time.

The twisting path beaten through the woods by their frequent patrols followed the loch for a distance. After more than an hour's ride, Gabriel caught sight of a glint of sun on metal and shouted, "To the east."

Lord Alexander signaled behind to Séamus. He saw the same glint. Being further west, they were already ahead of Lord Ramsay and his escort.

After two hours in the saddle, Lord Alexander called a halt to give the horses and men a break. The smell of mud, crushed vegetation, and the strong scent of horses hung in the crisp air, while heat rose from the animals.

Gabriel dismounted and tested his legs. They were a bit shaky, but would do. He strode forward to stand beside Grace's mount and help her down. She had difficulty swinging her leg over the horse's withers, but slid down off the animal's back easily.

Her legs buckled, and he used his good arm to catch her close against him. His hand rested on her bound hair, which was pinned around her head. With her cheeks and nose reddened by the cold air, her gray-blue gaze intent upon his face, it took everything he had not to kiss her.

"Rest again' me until you feel steadier," he suggested, his voice husky.

With her cheek pressed against his chest and her arms about him, the balance between them seemed to settle into place. He had been content to see to her comfort, not the other way around. Having her see him helpless, his strength drained, had given him more than a few moments of discomfort. A foolish idea. If things should ever be reversed, he would want to be by her side.

"My legs feel as shaky as a willow branch in a gale. They shall be well broken in by the time we reach Edinburgh."

Gabriel smiled at her attempt to make light of her discomfort.

She looked up at him, and though there was an edge to her smile, there was humor in it, too. "We will be moving again soon." She pointed to a nearby clump of brush and then tottered off to see to her needs. Artair moved left, Robby to the right, while Gabriel took position just in front of the brush.

When one of the men started up hill, Gabriel, mindful of Grace's privacy, shot him a frown and, with a quick gesture, motioned him downhill. The men down line wandered off the path in that direction.

Grace reappeared and moved to her mount, where she removed a small roll of canvas from one of the leather bags hooked to her saddle. She unrolled it and pulled free a linen square which was already wet, wiped her hands, and rolled it back up.

She took out another bundle, a piece of cloth folded around something, and opened it. "You need t' eat and drink often, Gabriel. Cook gave me these for you."

He raised a brow and reached for one of the oatcakes liberally filled with currents, one of his favorites. Had she asked the cook to fix them for him to tempt his appetite? "I will thank her when we return." He bit into the treat and chewed.

"'Twould please her if ye did." She offered him the bundle, and he shook his head.

"Keep them with you. The others winna be so quick t' liberate them from you."

Grace smiled and tucked them back into her satchel. He guided her to the slope and spread his cloak so she would not have to sit upon the damp ground.

They were only two hours into a journey promising to last five days. It would be difficult for them both, but they were pulling together, seeing to each other's comfort. When Grace tucked her hand into his, he gave it a quick squeeze and kissed her knuckles. "Are you warm enough, lass?"

She nodded. "Aye. Lady Mary's gift is keeping me warm." She ran a hand over the fine material of the cloak.

"Have you kent what you will say to the regent once we have gained an audience?"

She shook her head. "Nay. I only ken I must speak from the heart and hope he hasna been too hardened by the many other considerations he must face from those hoping for more."

"Aye. To run a kingdom must be as divine a calling as Father Dillion's."

"And a labor of love, depending on how close he and the Bruce were."

"The two were like brothers, though Moray is the Bruce's nephew. He was always at his side. He will support King David to the death, as will we all."

"What was it like to fight at a king's side?"

In the past he had shied away from discussing those times with her. It seemed to make her anxious.

He remained silent a moment, debating how much to share. "Battle isna about glory, Grace. 'Tis bloody, and loud, like a hundred anvils being pounded at once. But ye are na poundin' a metal block. Yer poundin' men just like you. There are the screams of the horses. The screams of the injured and the dying. The screams used when trying to drown out the fear the others strike in yer heart."

She squeezed his arm, and rested her head on his shoulder. The wee pressure comforted him.

"There were many of us. The Bruce had a way about him. He had a vision for us, and for Scotland, and words enough to inspire ye t' want to help him fulfill it. Lord Alexander and the others are much like him. Sir Thomas, the regent, is a warrior. He ran campaigns for the Bruce. Continues t' do so when need be for King David."

"Mayhap ye may speak t' him as one warrior to another?"

"Mayhap." Or one chief to another. Only Campbell interference had kept MacNab territory from being taken over. With a few of his men, he could lay claim to it and to Grace. Territory was only taken and held by those strong enough to hold it. How would Grace feel about being taken like chattel? A smile worked its way across his face. And with it came an idea.

Lord John strode down the path and came to stand close to Grace. "Ride beside me for a time, Grace."

Her eyes met Gabriel's for a moment.

"You changed his mind about backin' me as your husband, lass. He could have asked me t' step aside." Her eyes widened, and he knew he had guessed right. "You have nothin' t' fear from him. He's committed now."

She nodded and moved to her horse. Artair rushed forward to hold the reins while she mounted, but instead she took the reins from him and touched his arm briefly in a show of affection. She fell into step behind Lord John and guided her horse past the others.

"Do you have pride in who you are, Grace?" Lord John asked.

Confused by the question, Grace eyed him with wariness. "I took pride in the work I did helping Lady Mary care for the sick. I took pride in finding a place among your clan, though I dinna bear the Campbell name."

"Do you not have pride as a MacNab?" he asked.

"Ye canna have pride in somethin' ye have never kenned. I only remember Mam, the woman who cared for me until she died. To her I was Grace. I didna know I was from clan MacNab until someone took me t' Lord Ramsay's home, and I was told then."

His features grew harsh with a frown.

"For eight years I have served your clan. I thought t' earn the right to be one of ye. To find a place for myself among ye."

Alexander spoke for the first time. "You winna be banished from our clan, Grace. Ye will be a part of ours and her own. And ye will be close enough to come t' us whenever ye wish."

But it would never be the same. And what of Gabriel? How would he feel, being banished along with her? She had been thinking only of herself when she asked him to travel this path with her. If she truly loved him, she should have encouraged him to stay with his Campbell kin.

"You will make your place among your own people, Grace," Lord John broke into her thoughts.

"Mayhap I am just some wean Lord Ramsay was given along the way." She voiced a fear, or was it a hope, she'd harbored for years. "Mayhap I am not a MacNab at all."

"Nay, lass. Ye canna deny your heritage. 'Tis written upon your face. I knew your *máthair*. You have her smile, though I have only caught fleeting sight of it. And you have your father's temper, and his quick way with words."

She flashed him a look. "'Tis a talent I have only discovered in the last few days."

Lord John chuckled.

After a moment's silence she asked, "What were their names?"

Lord John pulled his mount to a stop, his shock evident. His gaze swept to Alexander.

"I didna ken she had not been told."

Both men's features hardened in identical expressions.

"Your *athair's* name was Lord Boynton Fergus MacNab. And your *màthair* Lady Annabell Grace. She was from clan MacKinnon."

Grace nodded. "Thank ye for tellin' me."

"When there is time, I will tell you more about them. You will need to know, if you are t' represent your clan before the regent."

Understanding struck her, and she smiled at him, she realized for the first time. "Thank you, Lord John."

When the two men quickened the pace, she kicked her own mount forward. The sooner they got to Edinburgh, the sooner this torment would end.

Chapter 14

IT WAS DUSK when Lord Alexander halted beside a stream and announced it was time to make camp. For several hours, sentries had dropped back to follow the progress of Lord Ramsay's company, then ridden forward to report. He and his escort were close, but far enough behind they could not overtake them unless they pushed further into the night.

Gabriel found himself in an odd position. He had been in charge of making those decisions for some time. With his illness, many things had been taken from his hands. He did not care for the feelings of impotence and frustration, but they gave him an understanding of what Grace was experiencing.

After her moments with Lord Alexander and the laird, she had eventually fallen back to ride between him and Duncan. Her eyes had gone to Artair several times, as though to check on him. She had grown close to the older clansman. No, she had always been close to him. Had he known about her lineage all along? He must have, since it was he who brought her to *Caisteal Sith*. Gabriel would ask him about that later, when Grace was asleep.

He dismounted and moved to help her off her horse.

"How do ye fare, lass?"

Her cheek was streaked with dirt, her clothing covered with dust as heavy as the rest of them. "Might I just stand here and sleep? 'Twill save time on the morrow."

Gabriel chuckled. "Do ye not wish for him to seek his rest, then?" He gave the horse a pat.

She attention slid in sympathy to the animal. "Aye," she sighed. "Artair, will you turn him so when I fall off, no one will see?"

Artair bit his lip, then bent his head to hide his smile. "Aye, m'lady." He led the horse in a quarter turn.

Gabriel gestured with his left hand. "Just slide off, lass, and I will catch ye."

Grace leaned forward against the horse's neck, kicked free of the right stirrup, and seemed to gather her strength. When she swung her leg over the horse's haunch, she caught her breath and stood in the one stirrup. Gabriel stepped forward, looped his left arm about her waist and took two steps back, lifting her free of the animal.

She stiffened, then gradually relaxed.

"Do ye think ye can stand?" he asked.

"Aye. 'Tis not my legs that hurt, but other parts. Though no doubt my legs will join those other parts soon."

He lowered her feet to the ground, but kept a steadying arm about her waist.

"'Twill ease off if ye walk about, lass," Artair offered with some sympathy.

Grace nodded and took a tentative step, then two, back toward the horse.

She seemed to have her legs beneath her, though she was stiff, so Gabriel released her. She rested against the animal again, stroked the side of his jaw and patted his neck before removing her small water bag, the rolled piece of canvas, one of the larger bags, and a tartan tied with a strip. "Let him seek his rest, Artair."

"Aye." Artair gathered Gabriel's reins as well and walked all three mounts toward the others.

Gabriel took her things from her and found her a place outside the hub of activity until camp was set up. "Is there anything I might do to help?" Grace asked.

Gabriel eyed the activity around them with some satisfaction. He had trained the men well. Pack animals were relieved of their burdens, the fire built, water bags refilled from the stream. Two of the men were watering the horses. Others were gathering firewood. "Nay, lass."

"Might I go to the stream and wash, then?" she asked.

"Aye." He signaled to Robby to follow her.

She handed him the tartan and tottered down the hill to the stream. Had he been her guidesman, he would have offered to rub her back, but as it was, he could not ease her aches. He stood watch while she took off her cloak and gave it a vigorous shake, sneezing as dust flew through the air.

She was used to climbing the hills and valleys around the castle, gathering herbs, bark and flowers for medicines. She climbed the stairs a hundred times a day going about her duties at the castle. She sometimes walked long distances to visit a sick wean or a new mother. But she had been in the saddle for the better part of the day, and it showed in her slow, careful movements. It would be worse tomorrow.

Duncan sidled up to him, "She's faring better than I thought."

"Aye." Mayhap he could purchase a horse and cart at the next village so she might be more comfortable.

"She will have more purpose than caring for the sick once she is with her own clan," Duncan commented. "They have had Drummond, but his strengths lie in negotiation and the accounts."

Gabriel nodded.

"You will have a different purpose as well, Gabriel. Are ye sure yer ready to step away and follow this different path?"

Gabriel paused to give it some thought. Until now he had depended on his sword for everything. He would have to rely on other strengths once he found his place within Grace's clan. "Aye. I have watched Lord Alexander change from a warrior to the chief of his people. I will try to follow his lead."

Duncan nodded. "You will be the MacNab chief. 'Twould be my suggestion to give her a bairn as soon as ye can. 'Twill seal your place in their clan to have a child."

Gabriel raised a brow. "Not everything is about my place, Duncan. 'Twill be my pleasure to give Grace a child, but 'twill be because I care for her and she wants it, not for any political purpose."

He turned to check on her, and found her standing just beside him. Her expression brought back every moment of their intimate encounter in his sickroom. His blood heated in a second and, had it not been for his sporran positioned just so, he would have embarrassed her and himself, for even a kilt could not hide everything. She blushed and lowered her eyes before taking the bundled tartan from him and slipping past them.

He turned to find the other man grinning and poked him none too gently in the ribs.

Duncan grunted.

"I dinna need ye putting ideas into m' head," Gabriel complained. "I have enough of my own."

Duncan laughed. "But it doesna harm to plant the seed elsewhere." He looked toward Grace.

GRACE CURLED UP in the midst of the clansmen on her tartan pallet, achingly grateful to rest. She pressed her legs together to try and quell the tempting emptiness inspired by the thought of making a babe with Gabriel. She had been around farm animals long enough to understand how it worked. She had happened upon a man and woman in the woods once. Their groans had drawn her and, thinking someone was hurt, she had gone to help. Mortified, she fled before she saw more than movement, but not before she learned that their sounds had not been cries and moans of pain. Her cheeks heated at the memory.

She had seen the intimate parts of Gabriel's body. She had felt that part of him stiffen and grow when they were close. Was it wrong to wonder how it would be between them once they came together in that way?

One of the clansmen opened the large basket of food prepared for the trip, and Grace went to help serve the meal, hoping the work would loosen her muscles. Her legs no longer felt like soggy laundry, but now cramped if she remained still for long. She passed out the small loaves of bread, each with a sausage tucked inside through a hole cut in the crust. Robby passed out cheese.

When she returned to her place, she found a wedge of cheese and a one of the rolls in the center of her tartan. She gathered the food and sat beside Gabriel.

She glanced about for Artair, for she had not seen him in some time.

"What is it, Grace?" Gabriel asked.

"Artair is not here."

"Mayhap he is part of the watch and will return shortly."

She nodded, but bit her lip, still looking around for the older man. Finally she sighed and nibbled at the piece of cheese. She had grown used to Artair's protective presence, and missed him whenever he was absent. What would she do when she did not see him every day?

"You feel a great affection for him."

"Aye. He brought me t' *Caisteal Sith* from Edinburgh. He was kind t' me." She had never told Gabriel how she came to be at the castle. "I was alone on the streets for nearly a month. I was—" she closed her eyes against the pain "—very dirty, and very weak. I hadna had enough food or water." She swallowed. "There were men there. They would offer me food t' try and coax me to them." She shuddered and fell silent at the memory. The way they had looked at her, even with her bruised face and dirt-stained dress…had been the same way Lord Ramsay looked at Blair.

"I was…afraid of ever'one and… hid away wherever I could. A wee lad I found…I thought I was protecting him, but he stole my shoes the beginning of the second week…my feet were…I wrapped them in strips from my shift t' cover the cuts. They were so raw and swollen, I could barely walk." The less she could walk, the more she was in danger of being taken. She had been terrified, unable to sleep lest they came for her.

"I once slept inside a rabbit hutch. 'Twas warm, and the animals were gentle. Their owner not so much." He had nearly torn her hair out dragging her out of the structure until his wife intervened long enough for her to get away.

"There was a babe I found laid in a bundle on the street. There was somethin' wrong with its mouth and it could not suckle. It sounded like a wee kitten when it cried. I stole milk and dipped a scrap from my shift into it and dribbled it into its mouth." She swallowed. "It died in my arms the next day." She fought the need to rock against the pain. She looked down at the bread and cheese in her hands. Queasiness attacked her, and she set aside her food.

Gabriel gripped her hand hard, and she curled into him and held on. "It was a blessing. The poor wee thing was suffering so. I left him on the steps of a church and waited until one of the nuns found him."

They sat in silence for a moment. She was grateful he did not speak, for the urge to wail out her pain was strong.

"When Lord Alexander came, I didna believe him when he said Lady Ramsay had sent him t' find me. I tried t' run, but Artair caught me, and I fear he had more than a few scratches and bites by the time he subdued me. It took some time for him to convince me neither he nor Lord Alexander meant me harm."

"How did they find you?" he asked, his voice husky.

"They paid other street children t' look for me and bring word to them if they saw me. They searched the waterfront and the— other places. 'Twas a miracle from God they found me."

"Artair took me to an inn and paid a woman there t' wash my clothes and help me bathe and bandage my hurts." She gave a deep, relieved sigh at the memory of that miracle. To be clean and warm after so long. She had wept and decided if he forced her to serve him it would be worth it. But he hadn't. "He bought me a new shift and shoes, but I couldna wear the shoes for a while." On the long trip to the castle he had held her, and comforted her when she awakened whimpering in fear every night. He stroked her hair until she fell back to sleep. She would not have survived without him.

He had talked about his wife and bairns, long dead of a plague before the war. The grief had been sharp on his face. She had slipped her hand into his and leaned her head against his shoulder, offering comfort in return for all he had given her.

She looked up to find Gabriel holding his bread and cheese in one hand but he had touched neither. He had been too busy comforting her.

She pulled away. "You must eat."

"You, too, Grace. 'Twill be a long day tomorrow."

A weary acceptance settled upon her like a weight. She drew her knees up and rested her cheek upon them. "Do you suppose he will come to see me at *Tasgaidh*?"

Gabriel's throat worked as he swallowed. "Aye, *leannan*. I believe he will."

Chapter 15

GABRIEL'S GAZE WAS drawn to the quarter moon high in the sky, and then to Grace. She had fought sleep, wanting to wait until Artair returned, but sleep finally claimed her. He had pretended a calm he did not feel to soothe her, but worry lay like hunger gnawing at his stomach. Those pains could not be quieted by anything but action.

Artair had witnessed Lord Ramsay's tirade and attack. With him gone, Duncan would be the only other witness to his threat. Grace's word would be shrugged aside as the whinings of a reluctant bride.

He rose from his place next to the fire, gathered his weapons, and wandered behind a tree to strap them on and then to relieve himself.

He approached William Campbell, who was posted at watch. "There has still been no sign of Artair or young Robby?"

He shook his head, his blond hair catching the weak light from the fire. "Nay."

"I will take a wee ride and see if I can find them."

William frowned. "Ye have just healed from the fever and ridden all day. Do you nae wish one of the others to go?"

It was the fifth day since he had awakened from the fever, and though he still felt a wee bit sore in spots, he felt almost himself again. "I wouldna put my life at risk if I didna think I was able. I have more to lose now." His glanced back to Grace.

William nodded.

If something had happened to Artair and Robby, it would be he who would have to break the news to her, and it was the last thing he wished to do. He trusted his men to follow their training and do what needed to be done. But staying behind and waiting would drive him mad. "I will urge Lamont to accompany me. He knows where the camp is, and is as stealthy a warrior as we have."

"Aye. 'Tis a good choice."

"Should Grace awaken while I am gone…"

"I will tell her."

He walked quietly to where Lord Alexander lay and rested a hand on his shoulder. Alexander woke instantly. "They are na back," he said, as though their absence had troubled him as well.

Gabriel shook his head. "I dinna think he'll harm Rob, but…Artair can bear witness again' him."

"How many men will you need?"

"Only one. I only mean to scout out the camp for now. If we can get them free, we will."

Alexander nodded.

It took him very little time to find Lamont among the others, for as stealthy as he was at other times, his snores would rival and mayhap overtake Derrick's in ferocity. He laid a hand on the man's shoulder, and his eyes popped open, alert as though he had never been asleep. "We are two men down and need to take a wee stroll to see where they might be."

Lamont gave a nod and swung to his feet.

Gabriel looked up into the distant glow of a quarter moon. The light would be with them. He quickly peeled off his leather jerkin, stripped off the white shirt, and exchanged it for the one of dull brown Lamont handed to him. It was too small through the shoulders and chest, but would do until they returned.

"Who has already been on patrol?" he asked as he slid the protective vest back on and fastened the toggled wooden buttons.

"Cameron," Lamont answered.

Gabriel buckled the leather girdle fastening his sword in place on his right side. He could fight left-handed if the need arose. "Has Lamont left the wrappings on his saddle?"

"Aye."

"I'll take his."

It took only moments for them to saddle their mounts. Gabriel fastened strips of fabric over the metal parts of his horse's bridle to cover the shine and silence any noise they might make.

Going to the weapons cache stacked in the center of camp, he chose a bow and looped a quiver of arrows over his shoulder. Lamont did the same.

He paused before mounting his horse to look back at Grace's small, still form, now wrapped in both her cloak and a tartan. He would not allow himself to think what would happen should he not return.

This was what he was. Who he was. She understood and embraced it. She had survived the streets of Edinburgh, and was stronger than even he had suspected. She would have the Campbell lords with her to see her through.

He swung into the saddle and turned his mount north. The dull thud of the horse's hooves was the only sound on the hard-packed dirt road. They left the smell of smoke and the sound of snoring men behind with the campfires.

Chilled air crept through his shirtsleeves and made his breath a misty cloud. He ignored the cold and focused on every sound around them. With a shuffle of leaves off to the left, a deer exploded from the brush. It leapt across the path in front of them, and crashed through the underbrush on the other side. Lamont's horse danced while his own ignored the disturbance, attuned to his master's response.

How many nights had he ridden like this to rescue, attack, or defend? Too many to count. Had he died, his men would have grieved. Was that not the measure of a man? Not the men he had killed, but the number who respected and accepted him with loyalty and friendship.

The closest of them was Derrick. More brothers than friends, they had fought back to back. Shared food when it was at its most scarce. And Derrick had shared his family, because Gabriel had none of his own. He dwelt upon the last time he had visited Derrick's hut. The weans had climbed and clung to him like squirrels on a tree. The lasses wanted a kiss and a cuddle, while their brothers had wanted to wrestle.

He would leave that behind when he and Grace wed. And they *would* be wed. He would not accept anything less. They would have bairns of their own. And they would have their Campbell kin to visit oft, and share their hospitality, as they had with him. 'Twas not so verra far to travel.

Tiny flickers of light appeared ahead, and a faint whiff of smoke carried on the breeze. They left the road and rode into the cover of the trees. When they reached a copse of blackthorn, Gabriel pulled his mount to a stop. They dismounted, tied their horses to the brush, and in single file zigzagged a path toward the camp.

Spying a sentry walking the perimeter, Gabriel signaled to Lamont behind him. Gabriel slid in behind a tree and froze. He tracked the guard's progress until he was a safe distance away, then dropped to all fours and crawled closer.

A tent had been erected toward the back of the site, no doubt for his lordship's privacy and comfort. That it had been pitched outside the circle of protection was telling. The men with him either sensed his character, or were paid and did not care for him.

The young lad who served Lord Ramsay, Logan, exited the tent wrapped in a tartan and went to one of the fires to squat before it. He spread the blanket to gather in the heat. He folded his arms atop his knees and rested his head upon them.

After only a few minutes, he rose to dip water from a bucket and drank. He filled the gourd once more and moved to one of the men sitting close to the flames. It was Artair. His hands were bound in front of him and tied to a wooden stake hammered into the ground. Robby sat next to him in the same position. The lad held the dipper so that each man could drink, then dropped it back in the bucket.

Instead of returning to his rest inside the tent, he took a seat beside Artair.

Gabriel focused on Artair and Robby. They looked in good health, though Robby sported a black eye, and Artair some bruises on his face. Their capture did not bode well. What did Davis

Ramsay intend to do with them? Certes, nothing good.

A man who believed everyone was there to serve his pleasure had no respect for anyone's life but his own. Ramsay had already proven what he was capable of with his threats of murder. But he would be too cowardly to do it by his own hand. He would offer money to those desperate or greedy enough to be bought. Or he would use deceit and his political power to accomplish it.

But at the moment he held two men, one of whom was at grave risk because he had witnessed the man's true nature.

Gabriel returned his attention to studying the camp. It was set up much like theirs. Men, five in a group, lay asleep around each fire. There were three built. That left five men on sentry duty.

In the center, surrounded by the sleeping men, extra weapons were cached. The horses were tied in a group to one side, where one of the guards stood. The bundles from their pack animals were stacked neatly between two groups. The cart they used to transport Lord Ramsay's possessions was set to one side of the tent.

Gabriel fell back, and almost immediately Lamont eased up beside him. "With a distraction we can set them free," Gabriel whispered. "'Twould suit me well to give Lord Ramsay reason to sleep on the ground among his men." He explained what he planned to do.

Lamont smiled. "Aye. They will notice you because of your size. You make too big a target. I will be able to pass among them without notice. I will wander over for a drink and cut their bindings afore yer wee distraction."

"If you can, avoid damagin' the lad sittin' with them. I dinna believe he will raise the alarm."

Lamont raised a brow.

"There isna love lost between the lad and Lord Ramsay. No doubt he would be grateful should the bastard burn. He may just be his only heir." But Gabriel doubted it.

Lamont nodded. They settled in to wait, and heard the guard's progress before he ever reached them. The man chose just a short step or two away to seek the privacy of a bush to relieve himself.

Lamont edged forward. Gabriel shook his head in admiration at how silently the man moved. His own bigger feet and bulk made it difficult, but he managed to get within striking distance just as Lamont popped up beside the man. The guard started, shot urine down the front Lamont's kilt and turned to flee. Gabriel swung and gave him a tap beneath the jaw that lifted him clear of his feet. He landed with a thud and lay still.

"Had ye not already put him to sleep, I'd give him a thump or two myself," Lamont complained with a grimace as he swiped a hand over the front of his kilt, then wiped it on the ground. "He winna be happy when he wakes. Have a care." Lamont melted away.

Gabriel squatted next to the man to keep one eye on him and one on Lamont's progress.

Lamont kept his head down and meandered directly across the campsite to the water bucket. He lingered there, pretending to drink, then dropped the dipper back into the bucket. He paused behind the Ramsay lad, Logan. Logan got to his feet, and Gabriel tensed.

The lad walked over and lay down among the men next to the fire and turned his back to the blaze.

Lamont, after a brief comment to Artair, wandered back to his position and continued on to the path the sentry had walked.

While he waited for Lamont to double back, Gabriel busied himself cutting strips from the guard's kilt and shirt. He tied the man's hands and feet and fashioned a gag. The guard groaned softly and shifted, but did not awaken as he secured him.

Next he stripped a long piece of pine bark from the base of a tree and used some of the sap to dampen the ends of the fabric.

Lamont appeared as though out of thin air, giving Gabriel a start. Lamont chuckled. "Ye were right. Their bindings were already cut."

"Good." He reached for the bow and quiver of arrows.

They left the guard and, moving quickly, fell back, working their way around to the back of the camp.

"I told Artair and Robby not to wait if the opportunity arose for them to slip away."

"They dinna have a guard posted to watch them," Gabriel, said shaking his head. Every instinct was screaming for him to escape. "And they dinna show much concern for Lord Ramsay asleep in his tent. Either this is a trap, or the company of men guarding him have no fondness for the man."

Either could be true. They needed to get on with this and away quickly. Gabriel wrapped the tips of two arrows with strips from the guard's shirt while Lamont started a wee blaze with a flint. The fabric caught with a slight sizzle. Gabriel drew back the bow and let fly the first arrow. It struck the tent, the point penetrating the fabric close to the top, where most of the resin would have been painted onto the fabric. The burning strip of shirt came loose and dangled against the side of the tent. The heavy fabric began to smolder, and then caught fire with a sudden rush. He lit the second arrow and aimed at the base of the structure. The bolt pierced the tent, the arrow still burning.

Lamont stomped on the meager fire he'd lit, grinding it out. They turned and melted farther back into the trees, then ran full out toward the horses. Gabriel paused to look back and saw Robby running hard toward him, but Artair was pinned to the ground by a burly clansman. Gabriel reached for an arrow, set it in the bow, drew back and fired. The arrow struck the man in the thigh and he crumbled atop of Artair before rolling away.

Artair struggled to his feet and staggered to a run, only to be tackled by another man.

Lord Ramsay staggered from the tent, roaring orders.

Men raced toward the copse, weapons in hand, while others scrambled to put out the fire.

Gabriel swore in frustration. If they captured him, he'd be dead by morn, and it would clear the way for Ramsay to claim Grace and her land. Though the desire to stand and fight to free Artair burned as hotly as the flames eating at Lord Ramsay's tent, he had no other choice. He turned and ran.

The sound of the men crashing through the underbrush remained close behind as he reached the horses. Lamont was already mounted, with Robby behind him. "Where is Artair?" Robby asked.

Gabriel shoved his foot in the stirrup. "He didna get away." He urged his horse forward before he was in the saddle. The first arrow shot past so close he felt its breeze whip by his face. A steady volley dogged their progress until they rode out of range.

It was not until they were far away and slowed their mounts, he let himself dwell on the failure. "We will lie in wait for Lord Ramsay and his men and get him back."

"And if they should kill him?" Robby asked.

Since Artair had been captured in Campbell territory, they would have cause to deal with him. "Should Ramsay kill him, 'twill not only be Artair buried on Campbell land."

Chapter 16

GRACE GRIPPED THE reins more tightly than necessary, and her horse tossed his head and champed at the bit. She eased her hold and patted the gelding's neck in apology. A chill still clung to the air, giving it a sharp bite that stung her ears and nose.

Worry for Artair gnawed away just beneath her breastbone. What would Lord Ramsay make of them breaking camp and moving on without him? Would he take his rage out on Artair? She prayed not. The older clansman had endured a hard enough life, having survived horrible injuries and the loss of his wife and children years before.

She was certain Ramsay had captured Artair because of her affection for him.

Gabriel had ridden for a long while in silence, which of itself was not unusual, but the hard set of his jaw and the flinty light in his eyes spoke of frustration and anger.

"You tried, Gabriel."

"I shouldna have tried. I needed more men. I was blinded by the need to prick Ramsay."

"You freed Robby, and without bloodshed."

"Ramsay wants you, and he wants the charter. He wants to silence you, and the only way he can do it, now ye have rejected him, is through death, Grace. Should he want to make a trade, once he and his men catch up to us, you will want to exchange your life for Artair's. I winna let you."

His expression set her heart to beating in her ears and wrists, not from fear, but with an answering passion. Relief and joy sang through her veins. If she had any doubts about his love, his expression wiped them away.

"All I have known are battle and bloodshed. There have been women. I am not a monk, nor ever thought to be one. I have known passion, but I have known little of tenderness and care. You have given me my first taste of it. I winna sacrifice you."

He turned his attention farther afield, as though to settle himself. "We will be stopping soon. Just on the other side of the valley is where your territory begins." Gabriel pointed toward a wooden bridge fording the stream in the distance. "The water is down now, but 'twill rise and move so swiftly in the spring 'twould seal the clan off if the bridge werena there."

Her gaze rested on him, not the bridge, and he seemed to sense it.

"We will get him back, Grace, in some other way."

If it was possible, he would see it done.

Gabriel's expression changed and he straightened in his saddle. Grace followed his line of sight to the bridge he had just pointed out to her. Where it had been empty only moments before, a large body of men on horseback were crossing it. Every man in the line reached for a weapon. Lord Duncan fell back to ride on her right, and Derrick and Robby rode up close behind.

She wished for the hundredth time in the past week that Gabriel had taught her how to fight. She did not care for feeling helpless when faced with a threat. She reached for her dagger and rested her hand on its bone handle.

Lord Alexander raised a hand and called a halt. At his signal, Gabriel rode forward. Derrick slid in beside her to take his place. Grace's mind and body tensed and focused.

Two men broke away from the group blocking the road and trotted slowly toward them. Lord Alexander and Gabriel urged their mounts forward.

The four dismounted. When Lord Alexander strode forward and gripped the lead man's hand, she relaxed and released the breath she had been holding. The man greeted Gabriel with an outstretched hand and pounded his back enthusiastically, sparking her curiosity.

After only a few moments, Gabriel raised an arm to signal the company to come ahead.

When Derrick held her horse steady while she dismounted, she murmured a word of thanks.

Gabriel wove his way through the men and horses to come to her side. "'Tis a group of your clansmen wishing to meet with you, Grace."

Surprise, then dread, held her in its grip for one moment then two. Gabriel's reassuring smile eased the feeling. Though she had told Lord Ramsay she meant to meet them before taking her place among them, she had hoped to avoid it until she was wed. Her steps lagged uncertainly, and Gabriel matched his progress to hers. Lord Duncan and the others fell in around them, a show of protection and support for which she was grateful.

Lord John had already greeted the man, and the two men were conversing energetically when she and Gabriel joined them.

Their leader broke off what he was saying. His bushy brows nearly met above gray eyes so pale as to be colorless. His hair, grizzled and bushy, curled out from his head thick as sheep's wool. A terrible scar ran from the outer point of his right eyebrow to his jaw.

It was a warrior's face, but she read no anger or aggression in his expression.

"Lady Grace," Lord Alexander beckoned her to come close. "This is Sir Drummond MacNab. He is your cousin."

The man came forward on crutches, and leaned heavily upon them.

Grace offered him her hand. "Thank you for coming to greet me."

A smile softened his features. He grasped her hand and bent over it awkwardly. "Your servant, Lady Grace. Ye look ver' much like yer *màthair*."

To be told she looked like someone other than herself twice in the last two days was a bit disconcerting. "Did you know her?"

"A wee bit. There is a painting of her in the main hall at the house. If I didna ken better, I would believe 'twas you."

"Mayhap I will see it soon." She placed a hand on Gabriel's arm. "You know Gabriel Campbell, my betrothed?"

"Aye. He is the reason we are here. We have come t' accompany you t' Edinburgh and show our support of the match."

Grace caught her breath and smiled, her grip on Gabriel's arm tightening. "Thank you."

The sound of horses coming on fast came from the north reached them. They turned to see two clansmen racing toward them full out.

"Lord Ramsay and his men are near, Lord Alexander," one called out.

"How far behind?"

"A league—by now maybe less."

"Cousin." Grace tasted the word so foreign on her tongue. She had never had anyone to call kin before, and was torn between confusion and a small, niggling happiness she was afraid to believe in. She squared her shoulders. "We have a wee bit of trouble riding on our tail."

Drummond grinned. "How may we serve you, m'lady?"

GRACE SHIFTED IN her saddle for the second time in as many minutes. "They will be here soon, m'lady," Drummond said from beside her.

She nodded her attention, riveted at the hard-used road before her.

Gabriel eyed the stocking knotted at the top and looped about Grace's hand. She had slid a bar of soap inside the garment, saying she would use it as a weapon if need be. Having tried unsuccessfully to imagine how to use such a makeshift invention, he asked, "What do you hope to do with that, Grace?"

"Break a rib or two of anyone who threatens harm to me or mine."

Every man's head turned in surprise. Duncan laughed.

"There are two clans between you and harm, Lady Grace,"

Drummond said, his tone reassuring, but with laughter lurking beneath it.

"I dinna fear for myself, Drummond. But if Lord Ramsay has harmed Artair..." There was a threat in her tone and her jaw was set.

Lord John turned to look at Gabriel as though to say, *See to your woman.* Though his lips twitched suspiciously.

"As soon as we are wed, Gabriel, I will ask you to teach me to fight. I dinna like feeling helpless and unable to defend meself."

Drummond grinned at him over her head, then quickly sobered when Grace looked his way.

Lord Alexander covered his mouth with a fist and cleared his throat.

Gabriel studied her small, earnest features. During the attack on their village, when he had come upon her covered in mud and the man atop her attempting—the image would forever be embedded in his mind.

"Aye, I will teach ye, Grace." He grinned at the other men's quick, wide-eyed reactions as much as her satisfied smile. "But first you must give me yer word ye winna use any of it again' me."

The men broke out into guffaws. Their merriment was cut off suddenly as the first of Lord Ramsay's company appeared around the bend in the road.

The likelihood that the man would turn Artair over without a struggle or an attempt to negotiate some form of revenge was slim. With three times the number of men hidden on either side of the road, it could easily turn into a slaughter. The loss of Ramsay clansmen would be a waste, and could also put them at odds with the regent, depending on his personal connection with Lord Ramsay.

The company halted some distance away.

"'Twould seem Davis has finally learned some caution," Lord John commented.

"Or he is as wily as Lady Grace has said he is," Duncan added.

Lord Alexander nudged his horse forward, and the rest of

them followed his lead. He pulled his mount to a stop only a short distance from Ramsay.

"Good day, Lord Alexander," Lord Ramsay greeted them, his attitude jovial. The leader of his men sidled up beside him.

"Davis." Alexander bent his head in greeting. "It seems you have one of my men with you. I have come to ask for his return."

"Indeed. He and another were spying on our camp last eve."

"They were reporting to me on your progress while you still traveled across our lands."

"Why did you feel you needed such reports?" he asked. "I had come in good fellowship, at least until you saw fit to demand that I leave."

Gabriel sensed Lord Alexander's bid for patience. His shoulders rose as he sucked in a breath and, though his features remained composed, his hand tightened on the reins. "I am sure you dinna wish to discuss why I was obliged to ask you to leave, Davis. 'Tis not common knowledge among your men, but we may make it so, if you wish."

Lord Ramsay's features tightened into a scowl.

"I am asking for Artair's return," Alexander said, his tone measured.

"And I am asking to be recompensed for my tent. We were attacked last night by two of your men." He lifted his brows challengingly while he focused on Gabriel. "My tent was burned, and one of my men received an arrow to the thigh."

"If you hadna taken two of my men prisoner, there would have been no cause for any of this, Davis." Alexander reached into the pouch at his waist and removed a small purse. He tossed it to the man at arms next to him. The man in turn presented the purse to Lord Ramsay.

"Where is my man?" Alexander asked.

Lord Ramsay nodded and his man at arms signaled to someone behind them. Two men came forward carrying Artair by the arms. He hung limp between them, his head lolling.

Grace made a small sound as the men stopped before them and laid him at her horse's feet. She backed the animal away.

Gabriel grabbed her arm when she would have dismounted and gone to him.

"He is only a wee bit harmed. No more than I would have been inside a burning tent."

"Coward!" Grace yelled. "You have only the courage to prey upon those too weak to defend themselves. How many men held him while you beat him?" She narrowed her eyes, and if looks could have slain him, Gabriel was certain Davis Ramsay would be dead. She cocked her head. "Nay t'wouldna have been you. Ye are na man enough t' face him alone."

"Every drop was spilled in your honor, Lady Grace. I still havena taken t' heart your rejection. You would be wise t' surrender and accept our union. The Earl of Moray will rule in my favor."

"If you were the only man left in Scotland, I wouldna allow you to touch me. I will reveal your secret while standing in the front of every church in Edinburgh. And write to every lord and lady of your acquaintance to warn them to hide their weans from you."

She stood up in the stirrups. Gabriel gripped her arm tighter for fear she might leap from her mount and attack the man. "You men who serve him. Dinna let him near your lasses. He will defile them. Ask your sisters, your wives, your daughters if they work inside his fine house in Edinburgh, about how he preys upon those who have no voice. How he uses children instead of fully grown women."

"Silence!" Lord Ramsay yelled at the top of his lungs, his face white and twisted with rage.

"I am not a wee child, Davis Ramsay. Climb down off your horse and face me alone." Grace drew her small dagger and the intent in her face was plain. "I will carve out your heart and feed it t' you before you can draw your last breath."

Ramsay kicked his mount forward and would have trampled Artair's crumpled body, but Duncan charged forward and blocked his mount. Ramsay fought the reins and swerved around Lord Alexander, and whipped his horse into a gallop. For a long moment his men remained stationary, mounted, and silent.

His man at arms nodded to them all, but his eyes remained on Grace. He touched his forehead with his fingers to her and slowly kicked his mount forward.

"They know," Duncan said as they filed past in a steady stream.

"Aye," Lord John nodded.

"Then why will they not do somethin' about it? Why winna you?" Grace demanded. Lord Alexander and Lord John exchanged another glance, their expressions grave.

Gabriel dismounted, intending to help Grace down. But she sheathed her dagger and was out of the saddle before he could grasp the reins.

She fell to her knees next to Artair and gently smoothed his sparse, stringy hair back from his face.

His swollen eyes slitted open at her touch and his voice was a rasp. "If yer goin' to make such grand threats, ye need a bigger dagger, lass. Ye can use mine."

Gabriel smiled despite his concern.

Tears streamed down Grace's cheeks. "Where are you hurt, Artair?"

"Everywhere, *lass*. But I dinna think anythin' is broken. I was playin' at bein' more hurt than I am."

She dried her face with her sleeve and ran her fingers over his bruised arms and legs, his bony shoulders and chest. When she touched his ribs, Artair flinched.

Gabriel knelt next to him on the other side. Guilt and rage churned inside him, making him ill. "I am sorry, Artair."

"Ye did yer best. He would have killed ye had he captured ye, lad."

Knowing Artair was right did nothing to ease the regret of his failure. He looked down the road where clansmen had come out of hiding to fall in once again, his jaw working in frustration.

"Did they leave the lass behind?" Artair coughed, and he curled in on himself, his jaw clenched in pain.

"Lass?" Gabriel said sharply.

"Certes, the young lad who serves, Lord Ramsay is no lad." He spit blood. "He figured out 'twas she who cut our bonds. While his men beat me, he beat her with his fists and left her bleeding on the ground. They put her in the cart with me."

Grace's face went taut with horror. "It has to be Lady Elspeth. We must go after her."

Gabriel was loath to tell her. "We canna do so, Grace."

"Why not?"

"Because she is her *athair's* property. She is his to do with as he likes."

Her features went still, as though turned to ice. "Do you believe that, Gabriel?"

"Nay, lass. But—'tis the way of it," he sighed. Even saying the words was distasteful to him. "Unless she comes forward and asks for our help, there is nothin' we can do."

He read more than disappointment in her expression, but it was not only directed at him, but at the Campbell lords as well.

"I have failed to protect her once again," she breathed. "She was right there before us and we didna see."

He understood well how she felt. There were two more important concerns they had to face, though. Artair would not be able to travel to testify to Lord Ramsay's threats, and Ramsay would be well ahead of them by the time they saw to Artair's comfort and healing.

Chapter 17

GRACE CLOSED THE chamber door quietly. Artair was clean, fed, his ribs bandaged, had been drinking willow bark tea, and now he was easing toward sleep. Gabriel had volunteered to sit beside his bed and watch over him until he drifted off.

Grace kneaded her aching back and wandered down the wide hallway to the staircase that wound its way down to the first floor. She had caught a glimpse of the painting Drummond mentioned when they first arrived, but she had been too busy seeing to Artair's comfort to dwell on it.

Now she had time, she intended to discover if the painting was a close likeness. Was it proof enough she was her mother's daughter?

She rested a hand upon the highly polished banister and descended the stairs to the wide entrance hall, savoring the smell of beeswax and the lingering aroma of the pork they had supped upon while she crossed the flagstone floor to the portrait.

Grace stood close to the painting and, in the failing light, studied every line of the Lady MacNab's face. The woman was not beautiful, but comely. The stiff posture in the other portraits that hung on the walls of the gallery above had been discarded in this one. She sat in a high-backed chair with a babe in her arms. Was the bairn her, or a brother or sister? Had she had a brother or sister? It seemed so wrong not to know, but there had been no one to ask.

Her attention shifted back to the woman. Were her own eyes as large, her chin as pointed, her brow curved as gracefully? She ran her fingertips over the structure of her own face, seeking the answers.

She had been a child of two or three when the house, this house, had burned, leaving most of it a hollow shell. She was the sole survivor of the family. If only she could remember some wee thing about this woman, her mother.

Her first memories were of Mam, stooped and gray, her hands knobbed, and her joints stiff. Her grandson had lived with her as well. What had been his name? Donnel?

Was he still here? She would have to ask Drummond.

She turned her head at the sound of heavy boots coming down the curved stairs that led up to the second story. It was grand stairway, each step wide enough for a man's foot to rest easily. Even a foot as big as Gabriel's. He stood tall and proud, and carried himself with the confidence and balance of a warrior. His hair, released from its normal tie, fell against the sides of his face in dark waves to his shoulders. Even in his tattered tartan and dust-stained shirt, his bearing was regal. He looked as though he belonged here more than she.

"He is finally asleep," he announced when he reached her. "He wanted us to leave tonight instead of on the morrow. I have assured him we will be no more than a day behind the others, and Lord John will work to get us an audience with the regent in our absence."

"Ramsay had him beaten so he wouldna be able to ride." She had decided she would no longer refer to the man as lord, for he did not deserve the title.

He came to stand beside her. "Aye, the thought crossed my mind. And he knew you wouldna leave Artair until you were certain he would be well again."

He turned his attention to the portrait. She waited for him to voice his opinion.

"You do look a wee bit like her." He slipped an arm about her and drew her close. "But she doesna have your wide cheekbones." He tilted her face up and kissed each cheek.

Every bone in her body seemed to melt at the gentle brush of his lips against her skin. She rested against him.

"Or the wee peak of hair dipping here." He kissed her forehead. "Or the freckles across the bridge of your nose." He tapped the tip of her nose with a quick kiss. "And she couldna have your passion, Grace."

When his lips touched hers, she was more than ready for them. He tasted of the berry jelly Drummond's wife had brought them as a sweet to go with the bannock bread and pork. She raised a hand to cup his face and feel the springy softness of his beard. She was moved to touch every inch of him and discover what it was to claim him as her husband. The thought brought a flare of heat to her cheeks and a tempting ache in intimate places.

"You make me forget everything, even m'self, when you kiss me, Gabriel," she murmured when he broke the kiss.

His smile flashed in the dim light of the entrance hall. In the few moments they had stolen here together, evening had arrived.

She had had time to think about her outburst on the road and cringed each time it came to mind. Where did this well of anger come from? She had never known it before. "Were you ashamed of me today, Gabriel?"

His brows rose in surprise. "Nay, lass. Why would you think so?"

She drew him to the stairs to sit down. Tipping back her head, she studied the towering ceilings crisscrossed with beams, carved with designs. A huge, circular chandelier hung unlit overhead.

"In the past days, I have uncovered a wealth of anger inside me. And I canna seem to control it. Everythin' that comes to mind during those times flies out my mouth."

He chuckled. "You hit me with a basket the first day we met, lass. I knew you had a temper."

"But I have never lost it so readily before. And I have never wanted to bring harm to anyone ever before."

"Everythin' ye have ever kenned is changin', Grace. Ye have a right to be distressed."

"I have been selfish and havena thought enough about you, Gabriel. Have I played upon your honor and forced you to stand beside me?"

He rested his elbows on his knees. "I have been a soldier for most of my life, Grace. Slept on the ground more than I ever have a bed. I had no place to call home until we settled at *Caisteal Sith*. When you have no past left t'look back at and your future is never certain, you welcome each day as it comes."

A great need to hold him close and comfort him rose in her, and she rested a hand on his arm.

He swallowed. "When you look at me as you are doing now, I ken I am fortunate that you hit me with your basket and woke me to everythin' I had been too blind to see." He looked up at the ceiling as she had earlier. "This place is as good as any t' rest my head." He smiled. "Better than most I have kenned." His hand covered hers. "And as long as you are with me, 'tis where I hope t' be."

She felt humbled by his loyalty and his love. Tears blurred her eyes. She stretched up to plant a soft kiss on his mouth and then looped her arm through his. She rested her head against his shoulder and sighed with profound contentment.

The dull tap of shoes preceded the appearance of a young maid. Her gown was shapeless and brown, her hair pinned at her nape. The spotless white of her kirtle drew Grace's attention.

She looked down at her travel-stained appearance and grimaced. She had one clean gown besides her wedding dress left until their arrival to Edinburgh. She would wear it tomorrow. But it seemed her betrothed had never seen her in anything but the drab brown or gray gowns, and half the time they were stained with mud or blood or other things she did not want to think about.

"Do you wish me to light the chandelier, Lady Grace?"

"Nay. The candle-trees will be enough. What is your name?"

"'Tis Nessa, ma'am." She gave a quick bob.

"Is there a chapel here, Nessa?" Grace asked.

"Aye."

"A priest?"

"Nay. There is Father William who passes by now and again."

To have a priest in permanent residence was rare. "Who presides over your marriages and burials?"

"Sir Drummond, ma'am. Or Father Birk now and then. He is ninety at least and is deaf as a bucket. But he still leads mass now and again."

"Thank you, Nessa."

The girl bobbed again, collected the heavy candle-trees and left.

Gabriel's hand rested atop hers. "What are you thinkin', Grace?"

It would do little good to cover the same ground again. She shook her head. "I had thought to ask for blessings to speed our way on the morrow before we leave."

She wanted to be wed, here, now tonight, before their fate could be decided by men who believed that one man was as good as another as long as he had a title.

Lord Ramsay believed it. Lord John believed it. The regent would believe it, too. He was one of them.

She swallowed back the pain. As hard as they might struggle against it, they would be parted, and would never know what it was to hold each other through the night, or share themselves as husband and wife.

She would carry the pain and regret of it for the rest of her days. She knew Gabriel would, too.

Knowing there was no way for her to shield him from that pain, it broke her heart all over again.

She wanted to sit here on the stairs with him all night. And breathe in his special scent blended with the musky smell of sweat and horses.

She knew she smelled no better. It did not matter. To touch his hand, his face, to feel his body resting close against hers, was more precious than anything she had ever known or ever would.

Nessa returned with the lit candles, interrupting their peace all too soon.

Grace grasped at the need to care for others to help ease the desperate chaos of her thoughts.

"Is a chamber readied for Master Gabriel?"

"Aye. 'Tis in the west wing, the second door on the right." She pointed up to the gallery above them to the left. "The fire is lit."

"I must speak with Drummond about the morrow. Would it please you to come with me, Grace?"

"Nay. I will bathe. 'Twill be a pleasure not to smell like a horse for a night at least."

"Aye. Me as well," he agreed with feeling. "Mayhap I shall find a trough between here and there." He rose from the stairs and offered his hand. Once she was on her feet, he cupped her face, bent his head, and gave her a chaste kiss. "Restful sleep, *a ghràidh.*"

"And to you, *a ghràidh.*"

She turned to see Nessa following his progress as he wandered out the door. Her cheeks reddened when she realized Grace had caught her staring.

"Will you take me to the chapel, Nessa?" Mayhap prayer would ease her panic and uplift her mood.

"There is no fire lit to take the chill from the room, m'lady."

"It doesna matter."

The chapel lay at the back of the house, past the kitchen. Even after the maid slipped away and closed the door, the aroma of freshly baked bread blended with the faint fragrance of incense. The room settled around her, dark, quiet, and cold, the only light the candles on the altar.

Grace sank to her knees before the altar and spoke the only words that encompassed all her hopes. "Please, God."

Chapter 18

GABRIEL LENGTHENED HIS stride, for dusk was quickly rushing toward dark. If he didn't find the hut soon, he might end up stumbling around until daylight. Following the directions of the blacksmith on the property, he crossed a short bridge and came upon Drummond's hut nestled back away from the stream that ran along the well-traveled path.

The sound of children giggling went silent when he knocked upon the door.

A wee lad opened the solid wood portal. His eyes widened while his eyes trailed up and up to Gabriel's face. Gabriel smiled to put the lad at ease.

The clumping sound of Drummond's crutches came from within until he reached the door. "Is somethin' amiss?" Drummond asked, his wiry brows twisted together in concern.

"Nay. But I am here to ask somethin' of ye, Drummond."

"Something more than sleeping on the ground for three days and goin' to Edinburgh?"

"Aye, a wee bit more." He did not really know what kind of punishment might be doled out if someone broke the King's law and performed a marriage joining him and Grace. But since Grace's rejection of Lord Ramsay had been witnessed by both his men and her MacNab clansmen, surely that would nullify his challenge. "How attached you are to your skin, your neck, or both?"

Drummond stepped out the door and closed it firmly behind him, cutting off the golden glow that had temporarily lit the yard. "I am a wee bit partial to both of them since I need them, but since I owe them to ye, I will be askin' you to explain." He motioned for Gabriel to follow him, He came to a stop a distance from the house. "The weans have better ears than my favorite hound, and they tell their *màthair* everything they hear."

He had no right to ask it of the man, ask it of anyone, but the need to lay claim to Grace had taken hold of him with a vengeance. It was not just the desire to meld her body to his, but more. They were meant to be together, and no force on earth was going to prevent that. "I've come to ask you to see Grace and me married on the morrow."

He sensed rather than saw Drummond's quick look in his direction. The man remained silent.

It took some time, but Gabriel told him everything that had taken place since his illness and Ramsay's challenge of the banns, up until today's confrontation.

Drummond leaned against the wooden railing on the bridge. "You'd think the man would be afraid t' be in the same room with her. She would have sooner cut him from bollocks to throat than look at him today."

"Aye."

"With great reason, from what I heard as well. Are ye certain he didna harm her?"

"Aye, I am certain he did not. And even if he had, I would still be here beside her. Grace believes he is determined to wed her to silence her, but 'tis my belief he is just as determined to gain control of her livery. His own property lies close to Edinburgh, and now that the Bruce is dead, 'tis only a matter of time before the English try once again t' regain their hold over Scotland. The first place they will attack will be Edinburgh.

"If I am not wed to her, and he convinces the regent to force her t' accept him, he will be visiting here at the manor house only long enough t' reap the profits from the clan's work. Certes, Grace will be locked away somewhere your clan canna reach her."

"And his daughter was traveling with him dressed as a boy and acting as his servant," Drummond cleared his throat and spit in disgust. "That alone should be reason enough to send him to hell."

"If it can be proven. 'Twould take the lass testifying again' him. And then it would still be her word again' his."

Drummond muttered a curse.

"Do you think you could convince the old priest to wed us, Drummond? Grace has rejected Lord Ramsay, before your clan. The banns have run their course."

"It could be dangerous for you both, Gabriel. Do you mean t' hide the marriage until he rules, or admit to it?"

"We will admit to it, if you and the clan will agree to my challenge."

"A challenge?"

Though he could not see Drummond's expression, the surprise in his voice made him smile.

"Aye. We will delay our journey to Edinburgh for three days. You must call the clan together and choose nine of your best fighters. Should I beat all nine, those nine, and any man who follows them, will swear fealty to me as their chief."

In the dull light of the quarter moon, Gabriel could only see the whites of Drummond's eyes. "If ye are wed to Lady Grace, ye will still be the leader of our clan. The clan is already in support of the marriage."

"But only because you have vouched for me."

"Not only me, Gabriel. There are others here who have fought beside you. They are already ready to follow you. They have heard from us all ye are an honorable man."

"But 'twill take their loyalty sworn t' me t' force the issue. If the regent sees they will follow me of their own accord, and I have taken possession of both the land and your lady, there winna be anythin' left t' debate."

Drummond shifted on the crutches. "'Twill not require nine. Five will do. There are only fifty called upon to protect the clan. The rest are farmers and brewers, and their training is in need of improvement."

Gabriel heaved a mental sigh. Five men. He could face that many and win. He'd killed more than that in a day while feeling less hearty than he did now.

But they, too, had not been at their best.

He would do what he had to do.

If he could sway those five, the rest would follow.

During the three days the clansmen came together, he would have time to meet with groups of the others.

"You are taking a big risk, Gabriel. In the three days ye tarry here, Lord Ramsay will be beatin' on the regent's door to be heard."

"Aye, and Lord Alexander, Duncan, and John will be doing the same on my behalf. And nothin' can be settled until Grace is there. She asked to deliver the charter to Sir Thomas herself. Until it is in place and accepted by the regent, neither of our petitions will be ruled upon."

"When do you mean to do this?"

"Morning prayers. I dinna wish to put any more of the clan at risk than I must, and at the moment there are only two women serving us at the house."

"There could be safety in numbers," Dummond suggested.

Gabriel remained silent thinking it through. "Should this fail, I winna have it so the entire clan can be punished, Drummond. Only me."

"But you would see me?"

"I thought you could claim to have gone mad for a moment or two."

Drummond's laughter sounded loud in the silence.

"Nay, you will have done enough if you can arrange for the priest to be at the house by daylight. Artair wishes to have his name on the contract. I have already spoken to him about it. Mayhap two widows. The women may say I ordered them to attend Lady Grace. If they can sign their name, 'twould be best."

Drummond grunted. "I will see it done."

Gabriel fell in beside him as he tottered his way back to the house. "This will save you and many of the men a trip to Edinburgh."

"Ye have to survive this challenge first, my friend. Though

there are na many of them, the men have been trained."

He knew the danger of being too confident. There was always one warrior who thought he was the best and would want to prove it as well. "If I canna teach them to be better than they are, I dinna deserve to be their chief."

Chapter 19

INSISTENT TAPPING INTRUDED on Grace's slumber. The room was dark as pitch, the fire gone out. When the door opened, the bright yellow glow from a candle-tree with three candles in it preceded Mistress Moire, the housekeeper, as she stepped over the threshold. Save at the front, her dark hair was bundled under a white muslin cap. She moved immediately to the fireplace and relit the fire. One of the candles proved sufficient to ignite a fresh stack of twigs and peat.

Grace rubbed her eyes and stifled a yawn. She blinked at the woman while she walked to the bed. "I beg pardon for interrupting your sleep, Lady Grace. Master Gabriel has requested your presence in the chapel at daybreak. There is an important personage there he wishes you to meet. He asks that you wear your very best gown for the occasion. The one you have been savin'. He said you would ken what he means."

Grace pushed herself up and tugged the warm tartan up to cover her, for the room was chilly. "Who is it, Mistress Moire?"

"I dinna ken. He asked that I help you dress and do your hair."

Grace's brows rose. "It must be someone of great importance." She wiggled free of the bed and dragged the tartan with her to stand close to the fire.

Nessa appeared at the door with a tray and set it down onto the bench next to the fire.

It held some of the bannocks from the night before, some of the berry jelly, and a small bowl of porridge. Grace reached for the wooden cup among the other dishes and sniffed it. She recognized the spicy scent of mulled wine and sipped the drink while Mistress Moire unpacked her gown and kirtle from the leather satchel. They were wrinkled, and she strode out of the room with them both over her arm.

By the time the housekeeper returned with her clothes, Grace had roused herself enough to use the chamber pot, wash her face and hands, and clean her teeth. Not since childhood had she shed her clothing in front of another person, and now she held her new shift against her, unable to bring herself to stand bare before them.

"Do you need help, m'lady?" Nessa asked.

"Nay." She bit her lip. "Could you turn your backs so I may change?"

Mistress Moire sent a look in Nessa's direction and the two turned their backs. Grace rushed to tug the garment she'd slept in over her head and put on the other one. She had chosen the softest muslin she could find, and relished the way it felt against her skin. Next came her stockings, the finest she could make. She smoothed them up her legs past her knee and tied the garters to hold them in place.

She had never been pampered before, and it felt strange when the two women lowered first the kirtle over her head and then the surcoat. The embroidered flowers on the bodice, a shade lighter, gave the gown a richness beyond anything she'd been able to wear in the past. It had taken hours to do the stitching, but the result was worth it. She pulled the laces tight. The fabric hugged her ribs and pushed her breasts up.

"You have a fine shape, Lady Grace," Mistress Moire said. "And the color of your surcoat suits you well."

"You are very kind, Mistress."

She donned her new girdle, but left her dagger by the bed while wishing for the tenth time she had purchased a new one. She shoved her feet into the new slippers, butter soft and made just for her feet. It hardly felt like she was wearing shoes at all.

Nessa brushed and braided her hair, using the ribbons Grace had saved for so long, a gift from Lady Mary for Yule. The maid proved she had a way with the work when she looped the long braid at the back of her head and pinned it in place.

"You look bonny, Lady Grace," Nessa said with a smile. "Master Gabriel will be more taken with you than he is already."

Grace hoped he would be. She wanted for him to think her beautiful just once. She touched the maid's arm. "Thank you."

She removed a tiny, cloth-wrapped bundle from the pouch, folding back the fabric to reveal the pearl necklace Gabriel had given her. The pearls seemed to gather lustre from the warmth of her touch. Wearing them made her feel like a queen. That Gabriel had gathered the pearls himself and had them strung for her made the gift even more precious. She had never owned anything so beautiful. With them fastened around her neck, she felt ready to face anything.

The women followed her across the gallery and down the stairs. Grace's breathing came in unsteady gulps while excitement and nerves warred with each other just beneath her ribs.

"May we watch until Master Gabriel sees you?" Nessa whispered just outside the chapel door.

"Aye. If ye really wish to."

The two women nodded in unison. Mistress Moire opened the door.

The candles in the chapel had all been lit. An arrow bank of stained glass windows cut across the back of the room directly behind the altar, and ran all the way up to the ceiling. The blue and red of the panels reflected the candlelight like stars. Gabriel stood with his back to the door, head bent, talking to a short, portly man in a black cassock. The priest's cloud-white hair haloed his head like dandelion fluff.

Grace stepped over the threshold. Gabriel looked up and straightened. The white of his shirt looked like snow against the darker tone of his skin. He had tied back his hair, baring the angular masculinity of his face. His kilt was new, and had a strip of dark blue woven through the tartan fabric that almost matched her kirtle.

He murmured something to the priest and strode toward her. His gaze slid over her, starting at her hair and slowly moving down, touching her everywhere. A wolfish gleam flared in his brown eyes, possessive and intent.

Heat rushed into her cheeks. Her breasts felt full, the nipples beading beneath her kirtle and pushing against the fabric.

She was barely aware of the door swinging shut behind her and the excited whispers traveling through it.

When they met at the door, Gabriel took both her hands in his. "You will be my wife in every way before this day ends if you wish it, Grace."

She dragged in a breath, but she was so addled by emotion, the words were hard to find. "'Tis everything I want, Gabriel, but should we defy the King's law...?"

"There is more than the law, *leannon*. There are hundreds of years of custom that will carry just as much weight. Will you give your trust to me?"

He had regained his swaggering confidence with his strength. The determination she read in his face, the set of his shoulders, filled her with hope. "Tell me what you mean t' do."

"I mean to take you, Grace."

Yearning, fervent and enticing, nestled between her thighs in a sensation so ripe she found it almost impossible to draw breath.

"And I mean t' take your clan with my sword."

Her heart shuddered inside her. If he were maimed or killed before they could build their life together...

"'Tis not a fight to the death, *leannon*. I dinna mean to spill blood. Only show them I mean to be a strong and fair leader."

He sounded so sure. But men always were. "But what if 'tis blood they want, Gabriel? They have been beneath Campbell rule for some time. You may be a handy buckler at which t' direct their resentment."

"Aye, that may be. Drummond and the others who back me will away with me to speak with all the men. I mean to use Ramsay as the threat we need t' end, and my loyalty and love for you t' sway them. Then I'll fight their best for their fealty as well."

The strength of his resolve was reflected in his expression, avid and passionate. "I want you t' be my wife because I love you,

Grace, but I need you t' be my wife as the *lynis pin* from which the rest will swing. I have no title, but if I go before the regent as the MacNab chief, 'twill end it all."

Ramsay would have to attack her clan to take it from him, and go across Campbell lands to do so. And none of the Campbell lords would allow it. It was a bold strategy. A warrior's plan.

But what could she do to aid him? "'Twill take more than a marriage, Gabriel. 'Twill take the women as well. Or do you think we dinna have a place in this? The lasses who cook their food, share their beds and birth their bairns will wish to ken their lot in life winna be worse, but better for all this."

His brows rose and he nodded. "Aye. I have been a warrior too long and think as a warrior." His eyes held an invitation that brought heat to her cheeks. "You will need t' teach me what 'tis t' think like a husband, lass."

She tucked her hand through his arm. "I mean t' start very soon."

His quick smile and husky chuckle sent a shiver of anticipation through her. With every step down the aisle, the rightness and certainty of what they were about to do built inside her.

For the first time, she noticed Artair sitting in front of the altar between two older women. He was hunched forward, his hand holding his ribs. "Ye look bonny, Grace. Just as ye were always meant to. I am here t' bear witness while you say your vows."

"I am pleased to have you are here, Artair, but you shouldna be out of bed."

"If ye get on with it, I winna be for long."

Gabriel grinned, then moved on to introduce the two Mac-Nab women. "'Tis an honor t' be here to bear witness, m'lady," one said, while the other nodded her agreement.

"'Tis an honor t' have you both here t' share this occasion with us," Grace said and pressed both their hands.

"Father Birk," Gabriel spoke loudly, and close to the priest's ear. "This is Lady Grace."

"My lady." He took her hand in his, which was rough with

calluses, the fingers knobbed at every joint. He was only a wee bit taller than she, his face craggy with age and brown from the sun. Almost lost in the folds were pale blue eyes as sharp as a sparrow's. He might be hard of hearing, but Grace doubted he allowed anything to slide past without notice.

"I have waited years t' perform a wedding such as this. A lady from the MacNab clan and the *buannachann* from clan Campbell…'tis a good match. Your heirs will be strong and bold. They will carry the MacNab name, will they not? There are more than enough Campbells about, but not near enough MacNabs. We dinna wish the line to die out."

Gabriel leaned close and spoke directly into the Priest's ear. "Aye. I give you my word, Father."

Father Birk nodded well pleased. "Let us begin, lest the good Lord takes me before 'tis done." He flashed Grace an impish, gap-toothed smile.

Grace shoved aside all the worries that threatened to cloud the moment. She had prayed for this last night in this very chapel. It had to be a sign from God that it was truly happening.

Her excitement from earlier returned, tempered by the seriousness of the ceremony. She wondered if perhaps the whole clan would hear them when they shouted their vows loud enough for Father Birk to hear. She had to quell the urge to laugh more than once.

"I, Grace MacNab, daughter of Boynton MacNab, now take thee, Gabriel Campbell, son of Calum Campbell, t' be my husband. In the presence of God, and these witnesses, I promise t' be a loving, faithful, and loyal wife to thee, until God shall separate us by death."

Gabriel's voice held a raspy undertone of great emotion held in check as he said his vows, his deep, resonant voice carrying more easily than hers. "I, Gabriel Campbell, son of Calum Campbell, now take thee, Grace MacNab, daughter of Boynton MacNab, t' be my wife. In the presence of God, and these witnesses, I promise t' be a loving, faithful, and loyal husband to thee, until God shall separate us by death."

"By the power invested in me by the holy church and God our Father, I pronounce you man and wife." Father Birk made the sign of the cross. "You may now kiss your bride."

Gabriel wrapped her in his arms, and his lips settled on hers in a kiss rife with possession and passion, but also love. The die was cast and they could not go back. Their future and the future of her clan lay in Gabriel's hands.

Chapter 20

THE SUN WAS setting, and a purplish haze promising rain hung over the distant hilltops. Though they had not shared the wedding with the rest of the clan, they shared themselves afterward.

Grace had talked more in one day than she often did in a week at the castle. She had learned about her mother and father from some of the older women of the clan who remembered them. They'd been eager to share with her. She used the opening to explain the kindness and care she had received at Campbell hands.

She tried to plant several seeds during the conversations, both of confidence in Gabriel and concern regarding Lord Ramsay's attempts to claim her or their land, and the real possibility of him contesting their marriage.

She came away with several gifts in celebration of their wedding, the finest a woven tartan of red, green, and blue. 'Twould make a fine kilt for Gabriel when she had time to stitch it.

Behind Gabriel's horse ran a pup of about three months. His long, gangly legs bounded along, his ears flopping like bits of rag, and his tail wagging constantly. The man who had given it to him swore he would make a fine hunting hound. At the moment he seemed the most ferocious toward sticks, for he pounced on one, bit it in half, let the pieces fall and then bounced after the next. How something so small could make so much noise was a wonder. He caught a scent and made a sound somewhere between dying and singing and tried to follow it. When he ran out of rope and came up short, an expression of such affronted frustration crossed his face, Grace laughed aloud.

They paused outside Drummond's hut to say good eve to the man. The knight had been helpful and supportive in ways too numerous to count. "'Tis a shame you have spent your weddin' day with everyone but each other. But the good done this day will show on the morrow. News will spread of how you spent time with each family."

"We will have a lifetime to spend together. These few hours have been not just a necessary sacrifice, but also a pleasure," Gabriel said. "We will do the same tomorrow."

Grace was reminded there was only one more day to win over the clansmen before the coming challenge. While distracted she could forget about the coming danger. But now it was rooted again firmly in the forefront of her mind.

Eventually they approached what could become their new home. The structure resembled a small castle much more than a manor house, for it had a curtain wall that housed a small bailey. The metal spikes of the yett, which could be lowered in case of attack, were visible overhead as they rode through the narrow gate.

"Lord John repaired the house after it burned and added the curtain wall. One of the women told me about it today. Lord Duncan has passed a week at a time here during a hunt or when he journeyed away to Edinburgh or other places."

"Aye. I have been here a time or two with them both, and once with Lord Alexander. But I never slept in the house."

Mistress Moire's nephew Angus appeared, the only stableman they had. He held the horses steady while Gabriel dismounted and came around to help Grace down.

While she gathered the small gifts she'd received, Gabriel paused to give the boy instructions. "Put the pup in one of the stalls in the barn with fresh water. I'm sure Mistress Moire will have scraps for him."

"I'll see to it, sir. And happy weddin' day t' ye both."

"Thank you," Grace murmured. He dipped his chin as he walked the horses around to the stables.

It was no longer dusk, but coming on to night. A sudden

nervousness attacked Grace's stomach as she thought of what lay ahead. Gabriel took the packages and offered his arm as they mounted the steps that led to the front door.

Mistress Moire and Nessa stood in the main hallway waiting for them. "Good eve, ma'am. sir." They bobbed a curtsey in concert.

"Would you like me t' take those?" Nessa started forward.

"I can take them up," Gabriel said.

"Have ye had a meal?" Mistress Moire asked.

"Aye." He patted his stomach. "We have been fed all day."

Mistress Moire smiled. "'Tis good t' hear ye have been welcomed as ye should be."

"Everyone was very cordial," Grace said. Her cheeks heated, and she looked away. Standing together, newly wed, with both women knowing what would come about as soon as they went upstairs, made her feel as though she stood naked before them.

"We moved yer things into the master's chamber," Mistress Moire said, her neutral tone that of a good servant. "I will show you the way." She mounted the stairs. Gabriel held out a hand and Grace grasped it, her eyes downcast.

They crossed the gallery and followed Mistress Moire down the east wing. At the end of the hall she came to a halt. "The fire has been lit, and the candles. And we left you some wine t' drink and a wee bite to eat. Your travel gown and shift are cleaned and there for you as well, ma'am."

"Thank you, Mistress Moire. You are most thoughtful." She forced a smile, though nerves made it difficult.

Gabriel lifted the lever and pushed open the door, and then stood back and waited for her to enter.

The room was warm, the fire blazing. Grace fumbled at the ties that fastened her cloak, her fingers clumsy, and finally got them free. Gabriel laid her bundle on a nearby chest and lifted the cloak from her shoulders to hang it on a peg behind the door.

The bed was much like the one she had slept in the night before, large and sturdy. The tartans and pelts were folded down, showing spotlessly clean sheets. Her heart was suddenly racing and her breathing coming in nervous pants.

A tray of cheese and bread and a pitcher with cups stood on a side table.

Gabriel's fingers brushed along her sleeves, and he slipped his arms around her and held her back against him. "Are ye afraid of what will happen between us, *leannon*?" He spoke softly against her ear, and she shivered.

She rested her hands on the muscular arm encircling her. "Mayhap—a wee bit. 'Tis more... they ken what we are about." She covered her hot cheeks with her hands.

Gabriel chuckled. "But only you and I will ken how we please each other, lass."

He pressed a kiss to her temple, then moved to the tray to pour the wine. He offered her the cup, his gaze steady. "I am in no hurry, Grace. This is too important to rush."

He strode to the washbasin, washed his hands and face, and blotted them with a towel.

This was her Gabriel, her husband, the man she had fought to wed. Had prayed to wed. The man she had loved for two years. She would not allow her innocence and nerves to stand in the way of pleasing him.

He sat at the foot of the bed, loosened the laces running down the sides of his boots, and tugged them free. She went to the basin and washed the dust from the day's activities from her hands and face before removing the hairpins so her braid fell over her shoulder.

After a small, bracing sip of the wine, she left the cup on the washstand. The buckle of the new girdle was stiff, and she had to struggle with it for a moment. Once free of it, she draped it across the back of the one chair in the room. Her soft shoes slipped easily off her feet. She joined him at the foot of the bed.

She had been waiting for this moment for months, as had he.

She studied his large, stocking-covered feet next to her own small ones. She raised the hem of her gown, bundling the fabric in her lap and baring her garters. Her breathing hitched with nerves and excitement. "Would it please you to unwrap your gift, husband?"

Gabriel's eyes rested for a brief moment on her naked thighs. The wolfish gleam she had glimpsed in his eyes in the chapel flared again. His strong throat worked as he swallowed. "Aye, wife. Very much.

Chill bumps rose on her legs in anticipation of his touch. He braced a hand behind her on the bed and rested the other on her leg just above her stocking, curling his fingers along the inside of her thigh. He pressed a kiss against her throat while he brushed his fingertips upward in a tempting caress, then skimmed them back down. Her body remembered the pleasure she had experienced from his touch. When he started back up again, the closer he drew to the intimate heart of her, the more fevered the wild throb of need became. She tilted her hips forward in anticipation and nearly groaned aloud in disappointment when he withdrew.

"Will you stand, *leannon?*"

She had to gather herself, but did as he asked, dropping her skirts to the floor. He reached for the lacings on her surcoat. "Ye look bonny, Grace. The color suits you. Will ye wear the gown again on the morrow?"

"If ye wish it."

"Aye. I do." He peeled the garment down her arms and laid it carefully over the chair. He made short work of the single tie between her breasts at the top of her kirtle and eased it down until it fell to the floor.

The room had felt comfortable when they first arrived, but the shift was thin, and she shivered. His hands went around her waist, splayed against her back to cradle her against him. He bent his head to press a kiss upon her bare shoulder. "I will keep you warm and safe, Grace."

His tenderness nearly undid her. She raised her arms to encircle his neck, tugged the tie from his hair and raked her fingers through the thick waves. "I dinna doubt it, Gabriel." She lips found the heavy pulse at his throat, and a tender spot behind his ear. He shivered.

He reached for his girdle and with quick, practiced moves unbuckled it. He shrugged aside the fabric gathered over his shoulder so the kilt dropped to the floor. "Hold onto me, lass." He lifted her so she was straddling his waist, his hand hot against her buttocks. He knelt upon the bed and lowered her to the mattress.

His mouth was hot and urgent when it covered hers, his tongue dipping forward to chase hers in a way that created a maelstrom of sensation, starting in the pit of her stomach and spreading outward. His callused palms and fingers, so used to gripping the handle of a sword, cupped and kneaded her breasts with gentle reverence.

He moved against her, and she felt the change in that part of him, thrusting against her like a bold blade wrapped in flesh, hot yet soft.

She ran her hands up and down his back while a fever of need overtook her. She wanted to tear away his shirt and feel his skin against her own. She dragged it up and he rose up on his knees, loosed himself from it and tossed it aside. She caught her first glimpse of his erect member, long and thick.

It was not fear that made her breath grow ragged and her throat dry, but something more elemental.

Gabriel's breathing was as rough as hers, and two bright spots of color rode his cheeks. "I must have ye, Grace."

She had no thought to deny him. "Aye."

He gripped himself and rubbed the tip against her intimately, allowing her to feel the strength and heat of him. The feelings she had experienced in the chapel when he said he would take her returned. She parted her thighs wider. He pushed with steady pressure against her and entered the first small bit. Her body resisted the intrusion, then surrendered with a sudden bite of pain. The sensation of being filled where she had been empty and aching before was part pain, part pleasure.

Gabriel grasped her hand and guided it down between them, urging her to explore where their bodies were joined. "We are one, Grace." His voice rumbled just shy of a growl, his features honed smooth and sharp from strong emotion held in check. His hair lay against each side of his face, and she reached up with one hand to smooth it back and draw his lips back to hers.

Her fingers traced the connection between them, his flesh taut and buried far inside her. They were bound by God, but this would bind them as husband and wife. She would never again be alone, nor would he.

The heavy beat of his heart thudded against her. His lips captured hers again and again in soft, sweet, lingering kisses. She withdrew her hand to trace the strong slope of his shoulders, then his chest.

The longer he tarried, the more aware she became of every small movement he made and how it affected that physical bond between them. When he withdrew a little, she murmured, "Dinna go." He came back to her, and she lifted her hips against him in welcome.

Gabriel caught his breath, and made a sound somewhere between a sigh and a groan...or was it a whispered "God" she heard?

Each time he moved, at first intermittently, then with less and less time between, he unleashed another pulse of wild, sweet pleasure.

When his movements became more measured and intent, she was caught up in a quest, seeking to capture that irresistible sensation. It promised more and urged her on, building to a tantalizing sharpness.

Just when she thought she could stand no more, he reached between their bodies and touched her in a spot so exquisitely sensitive her hips jerked, and she tightened around him while shattering pleasure crashed up and over her.

Gabriel thrust one last time and rolled his hips, burying himself as deeply inside her as he could, sparking another delicious quake in her.

With her bones turned to mush and her muscles to quivering jelly, a luscious lassitude invaded her body, and even her eyelids felt too heavy to lift.

✳

GABRIEL GRADUALLY RECOVERED his breath. When he moved to ease from her, Grace roused herself enough to nestle against him. She was slender and fine-boned, her hands and feet tiny, but the shift she wore revealed the fullness of her breasts. Though he'd had brief contact with them before, he meant to bare them the next time they were together where he might enjoy them more fully.

Had he been patient enough?

"Are ye alive, then, *a ghràidh*?" he asked in some concern when she continued to lie motionless, her eyes closed.

"I dinna ken yet." Her small smile reassured him.

He laughed. He traced the curve of her shoulder with his fingertips, then brushed a kiss against it and felt her shiver in response. This was his woman. She would be no one else's. He had branded her with his body. Promised before a priest to love and care for her until his death. He would kill to protect her.

And he was well pleased with what had just happened between them. Hidden beneath her soft-spoken, humble demeanor was a strong woman. When she bared her thighs and offered herself to him, he discovered a bold one. When he had taken her, there had been no fear in her face. She had welcomed him.

Everywhere her kirtle covered was soft and white. He wanted to explore every inch of her.

Claim every inch of her.

Grace's eyes opened. The storm gray color with just a hint of blue hid well the passion of which she was capable. But not from him. "Is all as you would have it, Gabriel?"

Was she concerned he was not pleased with her? He bent his head and gave her a long lingering kiss. "Aye, most assuredly, Grace." He breathed against her lips.

He settled the pillows against the heavy headboard and drew her up, offering his shoulder for her to rest her head.

She snuggled against him. Gabriel folded one of the tartans over her and brushed a kiss upon her temple.

"It has been tiresome being denied the time to talk with you today. Will you tell me what argument you used to secure Lord

John's support for me?"

"'Twas... He betrayed you by denying his full support. And I told him so."

"Duncan told me of Lord John's request for you to consider wedding Duncan, should the regent reject my petition."

"Aye. I was very distressed for you. And insulted. I have lived as a servant, but have been treated most kindly by my lord and lady. Because of their generosity, I am not ignorant to the differences that separate us from those we serve."

She spoke as though she were still a servant, though her title made her one of the aristocracy. He suddenly realized how difficult it must have been to have one foot in each world, and never be able to claim either completely.

"They, not Lord Alexander and Lady Mary, but others, dinna believe they owe the same degree of loyalty to the common folk as they expect them to give.

"I told Lord John that if he couldna show a man willing to give his life for him any more loyalty than he had, I didna see why anyone would follow him."

Dear God, she did not realize the danger in what she had done? Had she been a man, Lord John might have struck her down for the insult. Being a woman and a lady had saved her. "What did he say?"

"I didna give him time to reply, but left him. I was in a temper, and not fit to be near anyone."

"Then later?"

"He asked if I had decided. I told him I would cast my net and see what other lords might be interested in serving my clan. That it might take me years to decide on a suitable match. I didna say as much, but I made it plain t'would not be his son."

His Grace had defied the laird of the Campbell clan for him. Being the lady of clan MacNab had given her leave to do so. Had he done the same... The punishment did not bear thinking about.

"What could lead a man, the leader of a clan, to believe that one man is as good as another in terms of sharing a marriage or a bed?"

The outrage in her tone, the flinty look in her eye, and the color staining her cheeks was warning enough that she had not fully vented her spleen on the matter. If that was what set her on the course she had taken, he was grateful for it. But he would not spoil his wedding night by saying the wrong thing.

"We are sharing both because of what ye did, Grace." He ran a soothing hand down her arm.

She she made a visible effort to rein in her temper. "I shall never trust him again. Nor should you."

She slipped from the bed, padded to the small garderobe in the corner of the room, and disappeared behind the curtain.

He rolled onto his back and stretched.

There was more difficulty in separating loyalties from one matter to the next. The situation was like the roots of a tree, burrowed far into the ground, and so entwined it could not be sorted easily.

He had sworn his loyalty to the Campbell laird because Lord Alexander followed him. Through his ties with Lord Alexander, he had been privy to the reasons behind many of his decisions. Often his lord's innermost thoughts were made plain to him through sharing a glance. He had been his right hand in many matters.

But as chief of her clan, his loyalty would lie with the clan who followed him. The binding oath he had taken would no longer stand with his change in circumstance.

But only if he were chief.

And only if he was not hung for defying the regent and marrying Grace.

She slipped from the guardrobe and moved to the washbasin, poured water and turned her back to him. Small bloodstains marred the pristine white of her shift, proof the marriage had been consummated. They could not turn back, and even if they could, he would not wish it. He would not change one moment of this night.

Gabriel rose from the bed and wandered into the guardrobe to see to his own needs and give her some privacy.

Grace averted her face as he stepped from the guardrobe. Was her shyness because her new husband stood naked before her, or because she had cleaned herself and seen the evidence of their lovemaking? He decided both were true while he went to the basin to wash himself and his hands.

"Did all go well with the men today?" she asked.

He would not lie to her. "'Twas hard to tell." The MacNab clan had been at the mercy of Campbell rule until the Charter, and Gabriel had been a part of it. Clearly many still harbored resentments.

He flipped a tartan over his lap to put her more at ease and adjusted a pillow behind him.

"What can I do to help, Gabriel?"

He smoothed the hair around her face loosened from the braid by their lovemaking. "You are already doing it. You are standing by my side."

"If enough clansmen dinna sign and we go before the regent, I winna allow you to bear the brunt of what we have done. We will stand together. And we will share what punishment there may be."

He had lived his life balanced on the edge of death in one way or another. While recovering from his recent injury, he'd realized he wanted some peace. He wanted to make love with Grace and live a life that consisted of more than constant patrols against attack. He wanted to wake each morning to her sweet face and watch her suckle their children at her breasts.

"Ye canna shield me from the worst, Gabriel." Grace sat up to face him. "He may strip me of all this." She gestured around the room. "Since I have lived without such finery, 'twill not be a great loss. He may give the charter back into Lord John's keeping or another's, and the loss will be borne by the clan. But should he try to take you from me... Even the King is not above God's law, and to kill you so another may take your place, will be morally loathsome to the church."

If he lost his life it would be because *he* had flaunted his disobedience of the King's law. But he could not remind her of that and take away her hope.

He flipped back the tartan and patted the bed beside him. "Come lie with me, *a ghràidh*. We have talked long enough of serious things, and I am in need of a distraction."

His use of her words when she wanted a kiss brought swift color to her cheeks.

"I have a strong desire t' see you lie beside me in nothin' but your stockings and pearls, Grace." Just the thought had him hardening.

She touched the pearls at her throat and bit her lip. When she reached for the hem of her shift he smiled.

The dark stains upon the fabric caught his attention again. Mayhap they would just kiss and caress one another. It would be enough for now.

When she lay bare beside him on her side, he ran a hand over her narrow waist to the curve of her hip. She was as beautiful as he had imagined her, her breasts full, the nipples as pale pink as the wild roses that grew behind his hut. Her skin was smooth and pale.

Her gaze flicked down, then back up to his face. "Again?" Her eyes were wide.

"Aye. As often as ye wish. As long as it gives ye no pain."

A wash of color spread down her throat and across the top of her breasts. "They say a gift that is well-used is one much appreciated." She ran a palm over his chest.

He wanted to crow aloud. Gabriel turned against her and tucked her close. "They do say that. 'Twill be my pleasure t' show you how treasured ye are," he murmured, and his lips claimed hers.

Chapter 21

GRACE WANDERED OUT of the bailey through the front gates. Once she was outside the air stirred with unseasonable warmth and came alive with sound. At least two hundred clan families had descended on them. Wagons and carts of every shape and size were arranged in a large fan facing the manor house. Gabriel stood in the midst of it all directing the care of the horses, which were tied to long leads along the tree line.

When last she had seen him, he and a group of ten men were digging cesspits along the perimeter of the field. Each one was marked by a wagon turned on its side to provide privacy and ensure no one stumbled into them while in their cups.

Nessa appeared with a basket. "Will this do, Lady Grace?"

"Aye. Thank you."

"Mistress Moire has bid Angus to go with us."

A welcome idea since, so many people unknown to her were about.

"He is familiar with plants and such, and may be able t' help ye find what ye need."

"I only need a bit of willow bark and sprigs from yew bush, mayhap a few others. We will need be prepared should anyone be injured during their visit."

She still hadn't recovered from the heartache of nursing Gabriel through his fever. The possibility of him being injured again weighed on her heart and mind.

She had brought along small amounts of several herbs, plants, roots, and bark, but should she suddenly need more… She had to have something soothing to do, otherwise she would go mad with uncertainty and worry. The challenges would not start until midafternoon, and the wait was already wearing on her.

Angus proved most helpful, knowing exactly where to look for the willow trees. She harvested some of the bark, as well as heather, dandelions—though the flowers had long since died, but the leaves and roots were still hardy—plus she found wild thyme, oak bark, and tansy. She stored each plant in cloth packets so they would not mix together, and planned to hang them to dry once she returned to the house. Angus dug up the garlic they discovered in a large patch of dried leaves with his small wooden shovel.

She spent the time explaining to Nessa what each bark or leaf would be used for.

"And the garlic?" she asked.

"That is for Mistress Moire. 'Twill add flavor to meat and stew, and can be used as a poultice for thick lungs, though it should have been harvested earlier for it to be at its most potent."

"How did you learn all this?"

"From Lady Mary. She taught me to read and cipher as well, she and Father Dillion." A sharp wave of homesickness assaulted her. If they were there, Gabriel would not be facing five men who would be determined to draw blood, even if he was equally determined not to.

When men were caught up in the excitement of battle, even in practice, horrible injuries could occur. She had packed and bound more than a few. Had seen fingers hacked off to nubs, and other things she locked away from her thoughts with stubborn determination. Gabriel would be fine. No one had yet bested him with a broadsword. She believed in him.

It was still early morning when they returned to the house, but already both pork and beef were roasting on huge spits above well-established fires.

She and Nessa sorted the herbs and bundled them for drying. They cut strips of linen for bandages and rolled them. While Grace steeped some thyme to be used to clean wounds, she also made willow bark tea to ease pain. A paste of the tansy would soothe any open sore. She covered the bowls and placed them in the basket along with scissors, a small knife, and the bandages. And last she filled a small waterskin with vinegar.

Wagons holding barrels of beer and ale had been placed close to the curtain wall in the shade. Next to the containers of drink she found Drummond sitting behind a table provided from inside the house. He had propped his crutches against the wall within grabbing distance, and a tankard of beer, a quill, a stoppered bottle of ink, and a parchment document sat before him.

"How do ye fare, cousin?" she asked.

"I am well. And you?"

"I shall do." She wanted very badly to look at the parchment but fought the urge. "Might I bring ye somethin' to eat?"

"Nay. I have broken the fast and am waiting for the feast later."

"Is your family with ye?"

"Aye, just there." He pointed to one of the wagons down the hill. Grace could not make out the woman's features, but she held a babe in her arms and three others ran in circles about the wagon.

"I shall greet your wife and introduce myself." She held up the basket. "I have prepared some balms and tinctures."

"They will be needed. With this many clansmen about, there are bound to be a few knocked heads."

She was grateful he avoided mentioning the coming conflict. "There always are."

He chuckled at her dry tone.

Now that the social amenities were over, Grace moved closer to read the document before him. Ten signatures stained the skin. Ten out of two hundred. Fifty more would follow when Gabriel won the challenge, but one hundred and ninety would be needed to convince the regent. She struggled to keep the anxiety and fear from her expression, but her skin felt clammy with it. Though women rarely signed such things, she pulled the stopper from the bottle, wet the end of the quill, and placed her signature on the sheet.

Drummond studied her. "'Tis a difficult thing ye have taken in hand. That he is a Campbell and was Alexander Campbell's *buannachann* works again' him."

"He is my husband. I have chosen the best man to lead the clan. He has sacrificed his home and his clan to be here. Is that not proof enough of his commitment?" She sternly beat back the tears that threatened. No more tears! She had to remain strong. Men only respected strong.

"Aye. I believe it does. But it takes more than that to convince the others the two of ye have the good of the clan at heart."

"Have we come with our hands out demanding anything from you or them? Everythin' I have, I earn myself. I will continue to do so by seeing to their good." Grace braced a hand upon the table. "This will be the the MacNab clan's only chance to break free of other influences and stand with strength and pride. I hope the men will think well on that."

"The only chance?" he repeated. His brows blending into one.

"I am a stranger. Neither they nor you have reason to trust me, nor I them. You dinna ken me. But ken this." She stared directly into Drummond's eyes so he would know she spoke the truth. "If they dinna follow us now, and it costs Gabriel his life, I winna return here to claim this place or this clan as m' own. I will die by my husband's side rather than be branded a whore and see my marriage made null. With my death, the charter will be dissolved, and all will return to the way it was. Let them think about that."

She gripped her basket hard, straightened her shoulders, and strode away before she said more.

GABRIEL STUDIED THE layout of the practice field. There were some changes he would make. He had watched the men practice with both bow and sword this morning, and they were skilled, but could be better. Their weapons could be better, too.

The leader of the men at arms was a muscular man, shorter than Gabriel, and two score years in age. From his battered appearance, he had seen battle often. No doubt he would be one of his opponents during the challenge.

When the time came, he would find a way to approach the man and offer his suggestions in a way that would not bruise his pride or challenge his skill.

He did not want to take over here as the *buannachann*. There were other tasks that would demand his attention as chief. He would lend his sword to protect the clan, but it would not be his main purpose anymore.

The idea of such a wide-ranging change brought forth many emotions. It would be less taxing, and Grace would be pleased that he was no longer in danger so often. But he would miss the comradery with the men. His men. In fact, he already did.

It might take many months—or years—to gain the MacNab clansmen's trust. He had never shied away from a challenge, but this one, certes, would prove the most difficult. He would be attempting to win the respect of a clan with swords always threatening at his back.

He left the practice field and hiked around the curtain wall to the front entrance to the manor.

Drummond sat behind a table, a deep scowl darkening his features. Gabriel paused to speak to him.

"How stubborn is yer wife, Gabriel?"

"Very stubborn."

"How stubborn?"

"She defied Lord John and bested him on my behalf."

Drummond's eyes widened. "Will ye tell me how she did it?"

An itch started between his should blades, an instinctive awareness of danger. "What has she said t' ye?"

"She spoke most eloquently of what will happen should the men not follow ye, and what she would do, should anythin' happen t' ye because of it. Should she repeat it t' anyone else…"

His breath caught inside his chest and his heart beat like a drum against his temples. "Tell me ever' word she said, Drummond."

As Drummond repeated her words, he agreed that his wife was eloquent. And he would count on it later, after the challenge was done. She could drive a sword right to the heart of every matter with only a few phrases. She had spoken out of love and fear for him. Had she said it to anyone but Drummond...

A dropping sensation struck the pit of his stomach and a fine mist of sweat broke out all over him. Should the man decide to turn on him now...

"Why have ye told me? 'Twould have been as easy to spread the word and be done once and for all with any Campbells on yer land." He paused. "For the time being"

"'Twould have been just as easy for you to leave me lying in my own blood and piss and let me die, but ye didna. Ye carried me from the field and protected me. And though I cursed you at the time because of my legs, I wouldna have had the joy I ken now, had I died." He motioned toward the wagon where his wife and Grace sat talking.

"Also, I figured if I backed ye, I would only have t' deal with one Campbell instead of them all."

Gabriel laughed, though he felt a wee bit queasy. "I am grateful to ye, Drummond. I shall speak t' her now."

The man nodded. "Did she mean it? Will she stand to the death with ye?"

To his grief and his pride. "Aye. She will."

The longer he thought about what she had said, the more it fed his impatience. He lengthened his stride when he saw her leave Drummond's wife and wander down to the next group. He caught up to her just as she was greeting the man and his wife and grasped her arm.

She turned in surprise, then smiled. "Gabriel." She placed a hand over his. "This is my husband." The pride he heard in her voice brought him pleasure, yet also doubt. If she believed in him so strongly, why would she feel the need to constantly defend him before he had a chance to defend himself? He would not hide behind his wife's noble skirts, not even for her.

His anger was building.

The woman was stout and jolly and smiled a great deal. Her husband was thin and short, his expression dour. She chattered a like a magpie about her weaving and laughed a great deal. Her husband could not get two words in, not that he tried. Finally Gabriel interrupted by saying, "Lady Grace and I are needed at the house, mistress. May we ask your leave?"

She blinked in shock that he asked permission, going silent. She recovered and bobbed a curtsy, but did not speak again. She curtsied again when Grace took her hand and said, "I am glad we met."

Her husband smiled and spoke for the first time. "Aye. You must have many tasks t' complete before the challenges."

"Aye, we do."

"I feel a need for a drink. I will walk with ye a wee bit. I havena made my mark upon the oath." He grabbed a tankard and fell into step beside Gabriel. "I will be pullin' for ye during the challenges. Any man who can bring Shara's chatter t' a close deserves it."

Gabriel laughed because it was expected, not because he felt it.

"And because ye showed m' wife respect when so many dinna do so. She talks a bit, but she has a grand heart."

The three of them came to a stop before the table. Gabriel offered his hand. "I will be grateful."

The man shook his hand, bobbed his head to them both, and turned to Drummond. "Ye ken who I am. I would have ye write my name, and I will make my mark."

Gabriel guided Grace up the front steps.

"What is amiss, Gabriel?"

"I would have a word with you, Grace. In private." He dropped the basket on a small table in the entrance hall.

When he glanced at her anxious expression, he was tempted to reassure her despite his anger, but thought better of it. He was a man, and she, his wife, not the other way around. They climbed the stairs and passed the many doorless rooms, for they had been borrowed to create tables for the food all the clansmen's wives brought to feed everyone. Their door was shut, and he raised the latch and shoved it open, then closed it firmly behind them.

"What has happened?" An anxious pallor crept across her cheeks.

He shoved aside his first instinct to choose his words with care, "Do you wish me dead, Grace?"

Her mouth shot open in shock. "Nay. Why would you think it?"

"Had Drummond shared yer feelin's among the men instead of with me, ye wouldna have to worry about the regent hangin' me. Certes, I would be killed inside the practice field, and you wouldna be able to hold the clan at fault. Or should I survive, meet my end by some misadventure."

He paced for a moment. "They harbor resentment enough again' me because I am a Campbell, Grace. You canna use a threat to force them to support me. They will only resent you as well."

She began to tremble and tears stood in her eyes. "But they're not signin', Gabriel." Her voice shook.

"'Tis not over yet. And ye canna stand like a shield between me and harm. 'Tis an insult, and one I winna stand for. If you make me look weak before the men, 'twill work again' me, Grace. If not now, then later. And if I am t' dwell here with you, I will have to fight for my place. They will expect it, and I do, too."

She clenched her fists at her sides "Ye canna die because you love me. I winna stand for it."

Pierced by those words, his anger lost its impetus. He placed his hands on her shoulders. He could not soften.

"If my sword isna enough, I will allow ye to use yer reasoning to shame them, Grace. But ye must wait. Will ye give me yer word that ye will do as I say?"

She rubbed away her tears with the sleeve of her kirtle. "Aye." Her eyes looked as rain-washed as forest ferns, her lashes clumped with tears. He was moved to wipe them away, but stilled the urge.

If he gave in now, she might once again speak out, and this time to the wrong man. "I must away to prepare, Grace." He needed to warm his muscles with movement. "The men will want to exact a wee bit of revenge before 'tis over. You must be prepared."

After a brief pause she nodded. She turned away, mayhap to hide her distress from him.

He closed the door between them and paused for a moment. The silence behind the door did not bode well. He had not offered words of forgiveness to her before taking his leave. Should something happen to him, he wondered which of them would that omission torment most?

Chapter 22

SWEAT STOOD OUT in beads upon Gabriel's skin and rolled down his chest and back. He raised the dipper of water and drank deep. His muscles felt loose and warm, and though his right arm was not completely healed, it had stood up well to the rigors of his practice.

If it broke open again, it would bleed, and he would not go into the challenge already bloody. He would have Grace bind the cut before they began.

Clansmen and their families were already arriving at the practice field. Children ran about, their high-pitched laughter at odds with the seriousness of the occasion.

He spied Grace in the crowd. Her wren brown surcoat and pale gray kirtle blended with the others. She had worn her finery while visiting their homes, but now she wished them to realize she was one of them, the same as they, despite her title.

She wove her way through the people to stand on the edge of the field within his sight. She looked pale, and her features schooled in the careful composure of the servant she had been. She busied herself with spreading a tartan upon the ground.

He retrieved his shirt and leather jerkin, which he'd hung upon one of the quatrains with the length of fabric he had cut from his kilt, lest they impede his movements during the fight. He wiped his face and the back of his neck with the length of cloth as he approached her.

He laid his sword at her feet and dropped the other garments next to it. He took his place beside her and for a moment, then two, silence reigned between them even as the hectic activity around them continued.

He was ripe with sweat, and he reached for the scrap from his kilt and wiped beneath his arms lest she be offended.

"Have you forgiven me, Gabriel?" she asked softly.

"Aye. Before the last word was spoken, *leannon*."

A shadow of concern still lurked in her eyes. He cupped the back of her head and brought her mouth to his in a quick, fierce kiss. "Were we not surrounded by others, I would hold ye and show ye how deep my forgiveness and my contrition are for speaking to ye as I did, Grace."

The stiffness left her shoulders and she drew a deep breath. "I would never do anything to hurt you, Gabriel."

"Aye. I ken."

"Will you forgive me as easily when I tell you I set the pup free to play with Drummond's weans in the bailey, and they've carried him off and claimed him for their own?"

He threw his head back and laughed, and with that tossed aside the last of his worry over the argument. "He will be happier sleeping in their bed than in the barn, and no doubt will be verra well fed." He brushed the back of his fingers against her cheek. "We will get another when we return from Edinburgh."

She nodded, and he could see the shift in her demeanor, a sort of bracing he did not understand until she asked, "Do you wish me t' bind yer arm?"

"Aye."

She reached for her basket, and after the task was done, they once again fell silent. He focused on the fight ahead, for to think of anything else would be a distraction. He left the rest to her, because there was nothing he could do to ease it.

Drummond appeared and laboriously made his way down the bank into the practice field. Gabriel rose, offered Grace his hand, and tugged her to her feet. She placed her hand against his chest and raised her eyes to his face. Her features were stiff with the effort to control her expression, but her gaze remained steady. "I will be waiting here for you when yer finish."

He nodded and pressed a kiss to her forehead. "'Twill be over soon." He retrieved his sword, shirt, and jerkin.

While he dressed, the company of fifty men moved with some precision to take position just beyond the archery targets. Five separated from the group and came to stand beside Drummond.

Drummond, acting as sergeant at arms, eyed the group. "We winna abide any dishonorable actions. There are five men watching, all experienced warriors, who will act as *rèitear*. This isna a fight to the death, but a challenge of skill. Should a man be knocked off his feet, combat will end. Should he be disarmed, 'twill end as well. Otherwise, each duel will end when one of the *rèitears* signals. Is it clear?"

The men nodded.

"You five will draw to determine in what order ye will fight."

Gabriel stepped back and waited. The urge to see how Grace fared was strong, and he glanced briefly in her direction. Mistress Miore, Nessa, and Artair sat with her on the tartan. His tension eased, knowing she was not alone.

The five *rèitear* were all older MacNab clansmen who had survived the war but no longer bore arms with the younger fighters. While they took position around the practice area, he pondered the wisdom of his own choices. He stood alone on MacNab ground, one of only two Campbells among them. And he was depending on MacNab men to judge fair or foul in this venture. He was either the boldest warrior alive or a fool.

His first opponent stepped forward, leaving him no more time to worry the problem.

This clansman appeared younger than the rest. He had a loose-limbed grace in the way he moved that reminded him of Duncan Campbell. A war axe or mace would have better suited him than the long broadsword.

Drummond introduced him. "This is Duff MacNab, son of Leith MacNab. We fought with him."

"Aye, I remember him." The man had died in battle and been buried on the move at Sterling. Gabriel met the young Duff's gaze. "We will talk later of your *athair*."

Duff inclined his head. "I will look forward to it."

After raising their swords to one another in recognition, they stepped back. Gabriel gripped his broadsword two-handed and took up a fighting stance. At Drummond's signal, Duff advanced and swung. Gabriel tested his strength with a weighty return and felt the give in the lad's control. He fell back, encouraging the lad to go again. After several more parries, he held back long enough to save the lad's pride. He lunged in close and locked the guard of his sword against his opponent's. With a twist and jerk, Duff's weapon flipped up and away and landed in the dirt a short distance away.

In good grace, the lad retrieved his weapon, signaled his defeat, and returned to his company.

His second challenger sauntered forward with the watchful wariness of a seasoned warrior. Drummond introduced the man as Parlan MacDuff.

As soon as Drummond signaled, Gabriel went on the offensive, beating Parlan back with a variety of thrusts and strikes. Next he disengaged and allowed the man to advance so he could see what he was made of. Gabriel blocked several thrusts that came closer than he liked, the clash of their swords ringing out in a familiar cadence. With a shout that made the other man jump, Gabriel went into full-fledged attack, moving in a swift combination of thrusts, slashes, and strikes that drove him back. Parlan, in full retreat, stumbled, lost his footing and fell.

Gabriel was already backing away when one of the *rèitear* called an end to combat.

His face red, Parlan glowered and spit, then stomped off the field.

Gabriel strode to the water bucket, took a shallow drink, and wiped his face with his sleeve. He studied the crowd of clansmen and attempted to judge their reaction to the men's defeat. The stoic way they sat and watched offered him no insight, so he turned back to the field.

Though he had defeated the first two easily, the next three would decide his fate. He reached for calm and turned back to face the next challenger.

The leader of the MacNab forces stood waiting.

Drummond said simply. "This is Evan MacNab, leader of the fighting force protecting us."

Gabriel nodded. "They look to be a bit young and green. They will season well with more practice."

"Aye. Better weapons wouldna go amiss, either."

"Aye. I noticed the need this morn while I watched the lads at practice."

Drummond raised a brow and shot him a look cautioning him. "Are we negotiatin' here? Or are ye goin' to fight?"

MacNab shrugged a shoulder. "Since we be here, we might as well ge' on with it."

They took their places and raised their swords.

MacNab leapt at him the moment Drummond's arm dropped, his sword arching. Gabriel blocked the downward swing and felt it all the way to his shoulders. The second blow was only a wee bit weaker. What the man lacked in skill he made up for in strength. He hacked, thrust, and swung with all his strength, every strike, strike after strike.

The men downfield, beyond the targets, rose to their feet and yelled their encouragement.

After several minutes of the same, Gabriel decided had he fought to kill the man it would have been easier. Evan left himself open to strikes that could have been deadly. To continue on the offensive and parry his thrusts and slashes would not end the fight. He waited for an opening to get in close. At the man's next swing, Gabriel leapt back, and without Gabriel's parry to stop the blow, the weight of the sword threw MacNab off balance. Gabriel lent his weight with a shove, and MacNab fell to his hip.

The *rèitear* signaled combat had ended.

Gabriel backed away, giving MacNab room to rise. He gained his feet, then rushed forward to reengage with a thrust aimed to kill. Gabriel turned with the movement and thought he had avoided it until the blade bit through his jerkin, shirt, and then skimmed his side and tore away. In defense, he swung his sword backhand, his blade angled flat. It struck MacNab in the back of the head, and the man went down and lay still.

Drummond motioned to one of the *rèitears* to check him.

"He is still alive," the man reported.

"Leave him where he lies. Let the rest of his men fight around him while we finish," Gabriel bit out, his tone sharp.

His rage burned hot, setting fire to his cheeks as he retrieved MacNab's sword. If the man awoke and decided to continue the fight, he would be forced to kill him. Why would he risk his life for a taste of revenge?

His anger and frustration built, and he gripped the pommel and threw the sword. The weapon spun hilt over blade until it struck one of the archery targets. The blade sank deep, and the weapon shuddered, then swayed back and forth.

"You are bleeding, Gabriel. Do ye mean t' see to it before we continue?" Drummond asked.

He looked to Grace. She was on her feet, her face white. Artair stood next to her.

"Nay, I winna wait any longer to end this."

Drummond beckoned to the next man.

He was older, a seasoned warrior, from the wary look in his eye. "My name is Broc MacNab," he introduced himself. His gaze lingered on Evan MacNab's prone figure, then leapt to Gabriel's face.

With a brief nod, Gabriel raised his weapon.

Broc balanced his sword on his palms, and offered it to Gabriel in a gesture of acceptance. "Ye could have killed Evan a dozen times had ye wished. All the men saw it." He nodded toward the crowd. "They saw it, too. He was dependin' on ye t' be too honorable t' draw blood—and ye were, but he was not, and he shamed us all." He swallowed. "I winna raise my sword again' ye, even in challenge."

Gabriel lowered his sword, his muscles relaxing in surprise and relief, for now the heat of confrontation had passed, his side throbbed like an angry tooth. His shirt, sticky with blood beneath the leather tunic, clung to his skin. His kilt showed a growing bloodstain as well.

He ignored it all while he offered his hand.

The man gripped it. "My name will be on the oath, as will all the men who follow me."

"You winna regret it."

Broc stepped back and motioned toward the company behind the targets. Twenty men cut away from the group and broke into an easy lope.

Shaw MacNab, the last challenger, came forward. He was stouter than the rest, but slower. Though he put up a hearty fight, Gabriel had him disarmed in a short time. Afterward, Shaw approached him saying, "Do you need a hand up the bank?"

"'Twould please me to say no, but I won't," Gabriel said through his teeth.

Shaw grabbed his wrist and guided his arm over his shoulder with a grin. Gabriel nodded, and they headed for his waiting wife.

Chapter 23

THE DINING HALL table was littered with bloody cloths, a large wooden bowl of bloodstained water and her small sewing kit holding scissors, thread, thimble and needle. The wound was finally closed and no longer bled, but she doubted her shaking would ease as quickly. To cover the weakness, Grace brushed back a wisp of hair with her wrist and bent to rinse her hands in the bucket of water at her feet.

"Ye have done fine stitching there, lass," Artair spoke from the other side of Gabriel, who lay prone on the table. He dipped a cup of the willow bark tea she had steeped and offered it to Gabriel. "Finer than Lady Mary had time to do on m' arm."

At Artair's and Gabriel's insistence she had stitched the gaping wound closed, though it was customary to pack such injuries. Artair had cited Lady Mary's care of his arm, insisting he would have lost it had she not done so. Having seen the scar and the injury, Grace had to agree.

When offered the choice, Gabriel had agreed with Artair. "I have t' ride on the morrow, 'twill be easier without an open wound t' hinder me." To his credit, once he was committed to the plan, he had gritted his teeth and made no sound. Had he done so, she would have never been able to finish.

She rinsed the bone needle off with water and handed it to Nessa to place it back into her sewing kit. The girl had worked silently beside her while Grace struggled to get the bleeding stopped, but she had turned her head aside while Grace had secured the skin tight together with stitches. "You may clear the mess away, if ye would, Nessa."

"Aye, ma'am." The girl emptied the pink water back into the bucket it had come from and scooped the bloodstained clothes into the bowl. She carried it all away, leaving the table looking none the worse for its use.

"'Tis not as bad as I thought 'twould be. 'Tis shallow across the front, but the tail of the cut bit a wee much," Gabriel commented.

He could make light of the injury all he wanted, and though the mark across his belly was little more than a scratch, the wound at his side had been deep enough that she could see beneath the surface of his skin.

She drew several breaths now to controlled the rising need to bock, and shifted her attention back to him to quell it. "I didna cause you too much pain stitching the wound?"

"Nay, lass." He rolled his head back and forth on the table.

"Do ye wish to sit up?"

"Aye."

She narrowed her eyes in warning. "Then allow us to help you, so ye dinna undo my handiwork."

With a meekness she suspected was only for her benefit, he said, "I will, Grace."

With Artair on one side of the table and Grace on the other, they helped him to a seated position at the edge of the table. The smell of sweat, thyme, and the coppery scent of blood still lingered on him as they leaned in to wrap the bandages around his waist and pull them tight.

"Dinna fash yersel' over this. 'Tis but a wee scratch, Grace. 'Twill heal like all the rest."

She paused in the task to shoot him a frown.

Artair laughed, but swiftly cut it off when she turned the same look in his direction.

"Now all the excitement has passed, I mean t' find some food, and hobble off t' bed." He gave Gabriel's shoulder a squeeze. "Ye did well, lad. Had that—" He cut off what he started to say and cast a glance at Grace. "Though there was one man shy of enough honor to fill a thimble, doesna mean the rest follow in the same vein. Dinna judge them all by his actions."

Gabriel looked up from watching her pin the bandage. "I dinna mean to, Artair. But he drew blood, and I mean to use it again' them."

"Good," Artair said with feeling.

Grace interrupted. "I will have someone bring you food if ye wish to seek yer bed now, Artair. 'Twould not do for yer ribs to grow worse while I am away."

"I will see to m'self, lass. I promise to mind m'self while ye are na here. Ye have enough to do seein' to that one." He pointed at Gabriel and wandered out of the room.

Grace returned to the conversation Artair had interrupted. "It could have been worse, much worse. And it could still fester."

"Aye, and I could stump m' toe risin' in the middle of the night to use the chamber pot, and fall and break m' neck," he replied drily.

She stifled her laugh. "Certes, I shall insist we leave a candle burnin' so you dinna do so." She checked the bandages' tautness.

"The candle could fall and set the house aflame," he replied, suddenly serious. "Dinna borrow worry, *leannon*."

She did sigh at that, but when she moved to step back, he tugged her between his legs and held her face between his hands. His mouth took hers with a ferocity that left her heart racing and other parts of her aching for his touch. Her arms went around him and she clung, her heart swelling with gratitude and relief. He was *alive*. When Gabriel finally broke the kiss, she pressed her cheek to his and stroked the back of his neck.

"We must make an appearance and reassure the clan the wound isna serious. And to see how many are signing the oath." His hands moved restlessly up and down her back in a soothing motion.

"You need to rest, Gabriel."

"Aye. And I will. I give ye m'word. But we need to do this too, *leannon*."

She rested her forehead against his shoulder and wished with all her might this night could be done. She straightened and scanned his features. Lines of pain bracketed his mouth and drew his brows tight, but his eyes were clear and full of stubborn determination. "I will fetch ye a shirt."

"Nay." His jaw worked. "I will go as I am. Let the bandage be a reminder."

"Are you trying to shame them as you accused me of attemptin' t' do?"

"Aye." His expression turned flinty with rage. "Those who wanted Evan MacNab to succeed need to be reminded of his failure."

She now understood what he meant by using the blood against them. "Aye. They do." She backed away so he could ease down off the table. His kilt was stained with blood, as was her surcoat. She would wear his blood as a badge, but she would never forget or forgive the moment she saw Evan MacNab thrust his sword at his back.

"Where is Evan MacNab?" she asked. Should the man make an attempt again, Gabriel was in no condition to defend himself.

"He was lying on the practice field. Mayhap he still is. I will send one of the men to see." He guided her arm through his. "Be at ease, lass. No doubt his head will be hurtin' worse than my side." He moved gingerly while they left the dining hall to go back out the front entrance. The bailey was filled with clansmen and their families. At their appearance a cry went up.

Not feeling especially trustful, she held tight to Gabriel's arm. They moved through the crowd, accepting people's good wishes, but Grace searched every face now for any hint of a threat. She wished they were back at *Caisteal Sith*, safe and surrounded by Gabriel's men. She had come here against her will, but, once they arrived, had hoped to be accepted.

She realized the blood running through her veins did not constitute belonging here any more than it did at *Caisteal Sith*. She wished she could say Gabriel would not be stabbed there either, but he put himself at risk every time he raised his sword there as well.

A line of men had gathered at the table where Drummond sat.

Gabriel sent two of the men into the house for something to sit on, and they returned with two large chairs. Gabriel urged her into one while he sat in the other. His pride kept him from showing his pain, but Grace could see it. She slipped away and made more willow bark tea, and he sipped it instead of the ale someone brought him.

As the men streamed past, he shook each one's hand after they made their mark, and thanked them.

As night fell, torches were lit, and one of the women brought them food and drink. Grace cut the beef in small pieces for him and urged him to eat.

"How many came?" Gabriel asked when the last wandered back to the others.

"All save one," Drummond answered.

The two of them shared a moment of heartfelt grins and a handshake that turned into a hug. When they broke apart Gabriel asked, "Is the one still alive?"

"The man I sent said he wasna there in the field and his things werena in the barracks."

Grace relaxed in relief at the news.

"Send men out to search for him. I would rather ken he has gone from here than wondering if he lies in wait to try again."

"Aye. Agreed. I will see to it."

Drummond rolled the parchment up, but when Gabriel reached for it, he pulled it back. "'Twas earned by your skill, sweat, and blood, but by Lady Grace's as well. Will ye come around, lass, so I might present it t' ye?"

Quick tears pricked her eyes at Drummond's generous gesture. She gathered her composure, rose, and walked around the table.

"I ken it doesna seem it, but when you must away on the morrow, ye will go with every clansman's and woman's hope that all goes well for ye both. Gabriel has done his part, you have done yers, and the clan has done theirs. Surely the regent winna stand in yer way beneath the weight of all of that." He presented her the parchment on the palm of both hands, much as Broc MacNab had offered his sword in fealty to Gabriel.

Grace's reserve broke and she bent to kiss Drummond's cheek and hug him. "We couldna have accomplished this without ye," she murmured. "I will forever be grateful to ye, cousin."

His eyes were suspiciously bright in the torchlight when she straightened and took the roll of animal skin carefully in her hands.

"Will you hand me m'crutches, lass? 'Tis time I gathered yon wife and weans, and the fine dog they have claimed, and made m'way home."

Grace held them for him until he struggled to his feet and got them beneath his armpits. Gabriel slipped an arm around her waist and they watched Drummond totter down the field toward the wagon.

"We will do this, Grace." Gabriel said, confidence and determination in every word.

His belief never wavered. After all he had accomplished, she would not allow any doubt to taint it. "Aye, I believe we will."

Chapter 24

THE AFTERNOON WAS traveling into dusk when Gabriel spied a sprawling, two-storied structure on a street of other similar buildings. A sign hung over the door that read *Ram's Head Inn*. He beckoned to the men behind him and rode through the arched portico into the courtyard where the strong smells of manure and peat smoke hung. He waited for the men to gather and checked Grace's position among them before he dismounted.

Once his feet were planted on the ground, he allowed himself a sigh of relief. He had not given thought to being injured during the challenges. To consider such things before a battle tried a man's nerves and tempted unfortunate things to happen. He had expected the slight nicks and cuts that came with close order practice. Those he would have shrugged off easily. But his side caused him discomfort every time he moved, though thankfully was not festering, thanks to Grace's careful care. It needed rest to heal, something none of them had gotten in the past three days.

When he entered the common room and breathed in the aroma of roasted meat, garlic and beer, his stomach growled loud enough to be heard. The stench of manure tracked in from the courtyard hung beneath the more pleasant smells. A man approached him from behind the counter. "Is Laird John Campbell residing here?" Gabriel asked.

The man, beefy with muscle and fat, frowned. "Who might be askin'?"

"Gabriel Campbell, chief of clan MacNab. I am here with m' wife, Lady Grace. They have been awaitin' our arrival."

The innkeeper's frown cleared. "Aye, he is here. He asked for someone to be sent to fetch him when you arrived."

While they waited, Gabriel and the innkeeper settled on an amount for housing for three nights for his men and their horses.

Drummond had given him an account of the moneys available to him now he was wed to Grace and chief of the clan, and had furnished him with enough for the trip, and more to purchase needed supplies for their return.

With his own coin Gabriel meant to purchase some bolts of fabric for Grace so she might replenish her wardrobe. After seeing her in her wedding gown, he wished to encourage her to continue wearing vibrant colors.

Since it was customary to share the rooms with other travelers, Gabriel inquired about a room to themselves.

"Ye will pay for both the beds?" the innkeeper asked.

"Aye. We are newly wed and my lady is most modest."

The innkeeper shrugged and set a price. Gabriel paid it. If tonight should be their last together, he would not share it with strangers. He tucked the key in his sporran.

He returned to the courtyard. The men gladly abandoned their mounts to the stable hands and filed into the common room for food and drink. He handed Broc MacNab a small purse to pay for the men's food and drink for the next three days.

Then he gathered Grace's bags and his one. Two young lads came running to take the bags when they entered the common room, and he handed them over with the key and a coin to pay for their service. The leather case with their marriage contract and the parchment he did not trust out of his sight, so instead tucked it carefully beneath his arm.

He had just begun to guide Grace to one of the heavy tables when Lord John, Alexander, and Duncan descended the stairs at the end of the room. The three men strode toward them looking determined. Lord John reached them first and greeted them with, "What do ye mean by chief of the MacNab clan, and that ye are wed?"

Afronted by his tone, Gabriel straightened and placed a soothing hand over Grace's when hers tightened on his arm. "'Tis true.

The clan signed an oath of fealty to me four days ago. Grace and I were wed in the chapel at *Tasgaidh* six days past, before a priest and witnesses."

Lord Duncan laughed with exuberance and pounded him on the back hard enough to hurt. "Well done, Gabriel!"

He did not miss the warning glare Lord John tossed in Duncan's direction, nor the hard look he turned on himself. "D' ye ken what a risk yer takin'?"

Had his laird held out the hope he would be denied the right to wed Grace and claim her lands? Aye. He probably had. And now he knew about the revenue the clan generated, he understood the why of it.

"I believe I undertand well, since I am the one takin' it, Lord John." Facing an audience with the regent, Grace did not need to hear warnings of doom, but of hope. "I will share my thinking on the matter after we have had a meal and somethin' to drink."

He guided Grace to a table and the other three followed. He laid the leather case on the table between them. The lad returned with the key to their room and he secured it. A woman approached and he ordered drink and food for all, since there was only one choice of fare for a meal.

"How many signed the oath?" Duncan asked once she was gone.

"All but one. He was not to be found before we came away."

Lord John shook his head as though he felt addled. "How did you sway them?"

"Grace and I stood together as we will do on the morrow." He told them briefly of the visits to the many clan homes, and the challenge, playing down his injury. The food came served in wooden bowls instead of trenchers, and for a time they focused on assuaging their hunger.

"What of Bruce Campbell's inquiries?" Grace asked.

"It has gone well, Grace," Lord Alexander replied. "We have urged several witnesses to come forward, and they have agreed. They will attend on the morrow. One is the nursemaid who cared for the children. Others are lasses Lord Ramsay harmed."

"And Lady Elspeth?" she asked.

"There is no news of her or the lad Logan."

She subsided, her expression crestfallen.

Gabriel offered her encouragement, for he knew it mattered greatly to her. "We will continue to ask after her, Grace. Mayhap she will seek you out."

"If all goes well, she may not have to," Lord Alexander said. "She will be freed of her father without having to come forward. No one need know of her treatment at her father's hands."

"I will pray it will be so. 'Twould end any hope for her happiness, should word be spread."

"'Twill not be from us, Lady Grace," Duncan assured her.

She offered him a sweet smile filled with warmth.

After his earlier thoughts, the sight of that smile directed toward anyone but him gave Gabriel a quick pinch.

He gave Duncan a warning glance, only to receive a bland smile and a shake of his head in return.

Lord John leaned an elbow on the table, and his deep voice rumbled over the others around them. "Ye said ye mean to share yer thoughts about what ye have done."

Gabriel glanced at Grace. Her spine curved with exhaustion from the long ride. Dust coated her gown, as it did his own clothing. The idea of asking Duncan to see her to their room flitted through his mind. She would be faced with the reality of it all soon enough.

Grace spoke before he, her tone flat. "We both ken what we face, Lord John. At worst Gabriel could be flogged or hanged for defying the king's law. Our marriage could be dissolved, leaving me branded a whore and unfit to wed another. But to hang the acknowledged chief of a clan and to shame his wife will be more difficult for the regent and for the rest of Scotland to stomach.

"Should the worst happen, I will meet my maker by my husband's side, and you will once again have control of *Tasgaidh* and all its holdings. No other clan will wish to cross your lands to reach it."

Lord John straightened. Lord Alexander remained stonily silent, as did Duncan.

Gabriel had never seen the laird put in his place before. He held his breath and wondered if he'd have to draw his sword against his own clan, and if he could do it.

"I beg your pardon, Lady Grace, if by my tone or temper ye misunderstood my intent. I have grave concerns for ye both, otherwise I wouldna be sittin' at this table, willing to ride to yer defense. But I also have a responsibility to protect my clan, as big as the one you will have after yer meeting with the regent on the morrow."

"I do understand, Lord John. I have felt the weight of that responsibility since the moment I signed the charter." Her tone softened. "Gabriel knows the weight better than the both of us, for he has given up his home and clan, and has had to fight to earn his place within another. He will continue to fight every day for acceptance and control. I carry the weight of kenning he does so because of me."

For a moment Gabriel thought she might break, but instead she rose and the men came to their feet.

"It has been a long three days, and the morrow will come quickly," he said. "I would see my lady to our chamber so we may seek our rest. If there is nothing more urgent we need to discuss?"

"Nay." Lord John said in a subdued tone. "The streets become crowded from early morn. We will need to leave at daybreak, right after we break the fast."

"We will be ready."

ONCE IN THEIR chamber, Grace hung her cloak on a peg at the door and slipped behind a curtain to use the chamber pot. Gabriel tossed the case on the empty bed and placed the bucket of water next to a small table with a washbasin, then barred the door. The chamber seemed neat and clean, although as sparse as Grace's at the castle. Candles were lit, as well as the fire, and the room was warm.

He sat on the bed and leaned forward to rest his elbows on his knees while he waited for Grace to appear.

She moved to the washbowl, poured water from the pitcher, and washed her hands and face.

"Come sit with me, Grace."

She plucked the laces of her surcoat free, dropped the soiled garment to the floor, and gave it a kick.

He smiled at the gesture, for it reassured him she was regaining her spleen. She took a place beside him and leaned into him when he slipped an arm around her.

"I have a confession t' make."

She leaned back to look up at him.

"Ye canna take full responsibilty for my being with ye at *Tasgaidh*. Aye, I agreed because I love ye, but 'twas for myself as well."

She remained silent, waiting for him to continue.

"Did you notice how Lord John backed off when he kent he was speaking to the chief of a clan instead of one of his clansmen?"

Some of the tension beneath the surface of her expression relaxed. "Aye."

"I have wanted that, Grace. I have led men all my life, but I have always been second in command. And now, I may not be a lord, but I will command respect and be treated as an equal. Because of yer clan."

She leaned against him again, her head tucked into the hollow of his shoulder. "You should have always had it, Gabriel. An accident of birth should not determine whether a man is worthy of being a king, a lord, or anythin' else."

His heart gave a leap and he placed his finger against her lips. "Dinna let anyone else ever hear ye say that, lass. 'Tis treason."

"I winna repeat it. 'Tis between us alone."

"Aye."

He brushed his lips against her forehead and rose.

He grimaced at the dusty spot he'd left on the tartan. He removed his sword and placed it on a small chest, which had several nicks from possibly the same treatment. He unbuckled his girdle and allowed the dirt-stained kilt to fall to the floor. A cloud of dust billowed while he dragged his shirt off and checked the bandage around his waist. His muscles felt stiff after sitting on the bench for so long, but the soreness in his side was now only a twinge. He poured water in the basin. Slender arms encircled his waist, and Grace pressed against him from behind.

"Let me, Gabriel. Ye shouldna bend."

"Aye, I will. 'Twas in my mind to share the water after we have removed yer kirtle." He tugged at the lace between her breasts, loosening the neckline of the garment.

Grace was slower to bare herself to him, still shy, and when she left her shift on, he did not complain. She lifted the bandage away from the wound and declared, "'Tis healing." She fetched her scissors and cut the strips and unwound them. The narrow cut had already scabbed over. The deeper one looked red, but showed no signs of sepsis.

Grace wet a cloth, rubbed it against the bar of soap, and bathed his face. He sighed and relaxed beneath her care. There was tenderness in her touch, in her gaze, as she wiped the dirt and sweat from his body, just as she had wiped the blood from it four days before. There was love in the way she rested her cheek against his back and pressed a kiss between his shoulder blades.

She emptied the basin and knelt with fresh water to bathe his legs. "Our first night at *Tasgaidh*, when Artair was hurt and we sat upon the stairs, you asked what I was thinking."

"Aye." With her on her knees at his feet, his body heated. The vision of her taking him in her warm mouth flashed through his mind. He would one day introduce her to the idea of sharing the sweet joy of being kissed so intimately.

Her words jerked him back to the present.

"I had a great fear that if we didna wed before we reached Edinburgh, we never would. I thought, should we lose the chance t' hold each other for a night, or t' share even a single loving act, we would both regret it for the rest of our days."

She dried the one leg and wet the other. "After you went away to see Drummond, I went into the chapel and I prayed. I prayed for God to give us our one night, our single moment, if that was all we could have." She dried his leg and rose to her feet.

His throat felt thick with emotion, and his voice emerged rusty and just above a whisper. "And then we wed the next morn."

"Aye. Like an answer to my prayer."

Gabriel urged her against his naked body and found his voice. "I am greedier than you, *a ghràidh*. A lifetime winna be enough." He kissed her softly, thoroughly, not wanting the passion to build between them too quickly, not until after he had cared for her as she had him.

Ignoring his nudity, he opened the shutter, threw out the used bathwater, closed it, and returned to pour more. He took up a fresh cloth and studied the curve of cheek and brow as he wet it and wiped the travel dust from her face and neck. Still shy, she turned her back, pulled off the shift, and dropped it to the floor. The tender, vulnerable curve of her neck and spine lay exposed, and when he pressed a kiss at her nape, she shivered.

He wet the cloth and squeezed the water from it over her shoulders. It ran in rivulets down over her back and breasts. Those on her back he caught with the swipe of the cloth while they trailed over her buttocks.

He eased in close from behind to mold his body to hers, and her damp skin adhered to his. Their size and height difference had never been more apparent as, with a hand against her belly, he held her in place, trapping his erection between them against the small of her back.

Grace shifted, pushing back against him and tilting her head back against his shoulder. Her nipples deepened to red, pebbled like cherry pits when the cloth touched them. He longed to take them in his mouth, and promised himself the sweet later. He wet the cloth again and squeezed some of the water from it before bending his head and caressing her shoulder with first his lips, then his teeth. She caught her breath when he licked the nip and worked his cloth-covered fingers between her legs, brushing back and forth against the tender flesh. Grace reached back to grip his thighs and murmured his name, her tone urgent, her hips moving in response to his careful pressure.

He dropped the cloth to the floor atop her shift and urged her toward the bed, where he jerked the covers back, baring a mattress covered by a thin sheet. She crawled over the footboard and he followed.

Her cheeks were flushed and her eyes almost black with passion when she rolled onto her back to welcome him. She parted her legs, baring the deep rose center of her sex. The urge to take her was strong, but instead, something she had said earlier made him pause. If they had one night together, raw passion was not what he would wish to share with her, but something more, so she might know how much she meant to him.

With that in mind, he bent his head and kissed the inside of her thigh and nibbled gently at the flesh. Grace caught her breath and ran a hand down the back of his neck. He moved upward and first nuzzled, then laved the hollow of her belly with open-mouthed kisses. When his mouth closed over the peak of her breast, she made an endearing squeak of surprise. The look of wonder on her face when he raised his head made him smile, and so he tasted the other one as well.

When he rose over her and sought her lips, she murmured his name on a sigh. He cupped the side of her face and offered her long, slow kisses, their tongues mating in a tender battle neither hoped to win.

Her hands moved in restless caresses up and down his back, then lower, over his buttocks. When she wrapped her fingers around his erect member and stroked it, he groaned against her lips, for she had never been bold enough to do so before.

"Guide me home, Grace," he murmured against her ear while he used teeth and tongue upon the tender lobe.

She did, and he pushed inside her with a gentle thrust. The warm, moist welcome of her body almost undid him, and he balanced on the dagger edge of finding his own completion and leaving hers behind. He practiced thrust and parry positions in his head until the feeling eased.

Grace raised her hips, urging him deeper, and he eased in tight, then backed away. The pulling soreness of his side was forgotten beneath the shaper bite of his desire. As his slow, easy movements were countered by hers, he thought he had never experienced anything as perfect as their union. The pleasure became an irresistible agony, intensifying until he could hardly breathe. When she bowed beneath him and cried out her release, he poured himself into her.

Chapter 25

GRACE WOKE TO darkness. The fire was a glow of embers, but she was not chilled. Gabriel had risen at some point to spread the pelts and tartans over her and blown out the candles. He lay sprawled atop her, his leg bent between her thighs, his arm across her ribs, his warm breath fanning her shoulder. She loved the way he held her, as though both anchoring her at his side and protecting her at the same time. He did both. But not today. They would share whatever came their way, good or bad.

Despite her need of the chamber pot, she lay still, listening to his breathing until dawn crept between the shutters like a sliver of fire, for the light looked red. She could wait no longer to wake him, for nature's call was urgent, and they needed to dress. She wiggled free and padded naked across the floor to the fire to feed it. She found a twig of wood in the basket there, and lit it. Cupping the flame to shield it, she moved to the table next to the bed and lit the two candles, then laid the snuffed twig in a dish there.

Gabriel rolled on his back and stretched. The impressive width of his muscular shoulders and chest, so strong, so virile, caught and held her attention until the familiar lassitude invaded her limbs. She placed a palm over his heart where a patch of hair lay at its thickest and bent to kiss him tenderly.

When he would have urged her down beside him, she shook her head. "Some things winna wait," she murmured, and slipped away to use the chamber pot.

By the time she had finished and come from behind the curtain, he was on his feet to take her place.

She washed quickly and cleaned her teeth, then slipped her

shift over her head and donned her stockings. Next she spread the rest of her clothing out on the unused second bed.

While Gabriel washed, she did the same for him, and they took turns helping each other dress. He tied the ribbon of her kirtle while she did the laces of his shirt. When he approached the kilt she had laid out for him, he tested the fine fabric between his fingers.

"'Twas a wedding gift from one of the clansmen's wives. Her name is Siusan. Mistress Moire stitched the loops for your girdle."

"'Twill bring me good luck to have something given so generously."

"Aye."

"What of you, *leannon*?"

"I have you, and ye'll be wearing it."

He kissed her forehead.

The urge to weep rose up, and she bit her lip and turned away to get his brooch, taking her time in getting it. Once he tightened his girdle around his waist, she helped him position the fabric just right over his shoulder and pinned it in place.

It occurred to her then that they were doing what men always did when they girded themselves for battle. They donned their weapons and rode off to face the unknown.

While she brushed and braided her hair, he donned his boots and brought her shoes. He waited for her to pin her hair in place before fastening her pearls around her neck.

She was trembling by the time he finished, her stomach twisted into knots so painful she thought she might bock. When he laid his hands upon her shoulders, she wanted very badly to cling to him and let loose the maelstrom of emotion building inside her.

It would only make things more difficult for him, because he could do nothing to ease her.

She drew several deep breaths, swallowed back the rising tide in her throat, and settled herself.

"Ready?" he asked while he slid his sword into the scabbard on his girdle.

She nodded. They had their weapons. The two contracts inside Gabriel's pouch. And their love for each other. It would have to be enough.

THE TOWNSHIP OF Edinburgh stretched out around them. The buildings were packed as close together as the hens in a croft. Gabriel found the look and feel of the place distasteful. He felt hemmed in, smothered by too many people, too many structures, some wooden, some stone.

The sight of twenty MacNabs and twenty Campbells riding together encouraged the crowds to keep their distance. His own handpicked force moved as a unit through the wide dirt streets, instinctively placing Grace in their center. They were not as well armed as the Campbell force, but their experienced warrior demeanor was enough to make others wary. Often appearance was enough.

Human and animal waste littered the streets, and refuse lay in the gutters, swarming with flies. A rat as big as a cat dodged between the hooves of their horses and he grimaced.

They passed a variety of conveyances, wagon, cart, and litter, carrying all manner of goods. Open-air markets offered the same. But street vendors hawked their wares everywhere.

He was used to the many smells of the barracks, where a company of sixty or seventy men slept, close-packed and un-washed, for days or even weeks, depending on the season. He associated the castle with the aroma of food from the kitchen, of drink, the lye soap of the laundry, the burning of fires. And within the curtain walls lay trapped the odors of animals, bred, fed, hunted or slaughtered, and, yes, of even less pleasant things. None of them could compare to the foul stench that wafted upon the air here. It reeked like an open cesspit. One that had not ever been cleaned.

He thought of Grace living in these streets, among these peo-ple, a child, alone, hungry, dirty and afraid. Where had she found shelter? In that wide doorway there, beneath that cart loaded with vegetables, or had she huddled in one of the dark, cavelike passages between the buildings? He could not comprehend how she had survived.

They turned west to climb the great towering peak of rock where the castle, only partially visible, perched like an eagle in its nest. The sides of the hill looked jagged, as though chiseled by giants in uneven tiers, their surface covered in scrubby green growth. The horses did not labor up the gradual slope, but it stretched a good distance, the ride taking longer than he expected. Almost at the top they encountered a curtain wall and an open gate. Two guards stepped from a guardhouse and eyed the group of well-armed men.

Lord John was in the lead, so he identified himself, Lords Alexander and Duncan, Lady Grace and Gabriel.

"You winna need your men or your weapons, m'lords. There is a garison of men above t' protect everyone while you are here."

Gabriel handed over his sword and dagger and ordered his men to be at their ease until they returned; the others did the same.

The four of them rode through the gate and up, the grade far steeper here. At the top on the left was a small stone structure with narrow windows, a chapel. The road continued on, spiraling up the hill and curving toward a flat area that opened into a large square. Great clumps of stone still protruded from the ground, great lumps men were working to level with hammer and chisel. On the right stretched two long, two-story wooden buildings, the barracks. Next to them were the mess hall, armory, and the stables. Sentries stood on tall platforms, able to see any movement within the square or in the township below. Well-armed guards were posted along the perimeter.

Across the flat area stood the keep, constructed of enormous logs as big around as a man's body, a structure that looked, if not as solid as stone, as impressive in construction. Instead of having towers, the building branched out on either side to take up the entire north side of the square.

Lord John turned his mount in that direction, and Alexander

and Duncan followed.

Grace's mount sidled up to his. Her features were composed, but he could see the pulse throbbing in her throat. He stretched out his arm and offered her his hand. She gripped it tight. They had struggled and fought to stay together. Should it have all been for naught...

He would not allow himself to think in that vein. "We will have a grand tale t' share after this has passed, *a ghràidh.*"

She attempted a smile, lifted her chin and nodded. They kicked their horses and moved forward, hands still linked.

A stable boy ran forward to grasp the reins. Gabriel dismounted while Lord Alexander assisted Grace down from her horse. "Bruce shall be here shortly with our witnesses," he spoke quietly to them both, his tone reassuring.

"He has done more than I dreamed possible," Grace said. "I shall tell him so."

Lord Duncan held the door to allow Grace to enter first.

She strode forward and mounted the two large steps. After that one moment of trembling weakness in their room, she had regained her nerve, and was moving forward with grace and courage. Seeing her behave so helped him steel himself against his own concerns.

The walls of the formal entrance were paneled with a rich, golden wood, and the high ceiling was crossed with thick beams. Narrow windows placed high in the exterior wall facing the square allowed sunlight in, where it angled down to shine in bright patches on the floor. Guards stood at attention on either side of the two large doors leading into the hall proper.

A man approached them. His hair held back in a tight braid at his nape, he wore a painfully white and spotless shirt which contrasted with his kilt of red and green with a narrow strand of yellow threaded through it. Lord Alexander spoke quietly to him, stating their business, and he guided them to one of the benches placed against the wall. "Good morn. My name is Craig, and I am the earl's personal secretary. The earl will be with you shortly. I will come for you when he is ready. While you are addressing him, you will say, sir, Sir Thomas, my lord, or your grace. He has reserved your highness for only the king."

They dipped their heads in acknowledgment.

✳

AS SOON AS the earl's secretary walked away, Grace sank down upon the bench, her legs giving way. Gabriel took a place beside her and reached for her hand. His were very warm, while hers had grown icy with nerves. He rubbed the one to warm it.

The door opened at the end of the room, and Lord Ramsay entered, striding across the hall directly toward them. Behind him followed two men.

He bent at the waist directly in front of her. "Good morn, Lady Grace. You are looking very bonny. I knew a little color would set off your hair and skin. I hope the journey here was not too trying."

Grace stared at him blank-faced and refused to answer. He tipped his head to Lord John, Alexander, and Duncan. Next he focused on Gabriel, taking in their linked hands.

"It is polite to stand in the company of a lord, *buannachann*."

Gabriel raised a brow. "Would ye care to come over here and make me?"

Lord Ramsay's expression went cold. "You have allowed this man too much familiarity, Lord Alexander, and he has grown arrogant. You would be wise to be wary of him, lest he murders you in your bed."

"I am not worried, Davis," Lord Alexander said blandly.

Ramsay made a sound of disgust in his throat and marched away to sit on a bench down from them. The two men with him followed.

If nothing else, the short conflict had settled Grace's nerves. Lord Duncan slid into the seat beside Gabriel. He murmured, "I would have paid a coin or two t' see him try."

Grace smiled at his humor.

The door at the end of the room opened again and Bruce

Campbell appeared. He remained at the door, and Lord Alexander rose and crossed the distance in long strides. After a brief conversation, Bruce nodded and ducked back outside.

Lord Alexander joined them again. He bent to speak to them in hushed tones. "All is ready. He will remain outside until we are called into the hall. We dinna wish t' give Davis any warning."

One of the men with Lord Ramsay stood and started toward the door Bruce had just closed. Grace tensed. Should the man see the women and report it to Ramsay, he might find a way to block their testimony.

The double doors opened before them and the man halted mid-stride. A man emerged, accompanied by Sir Thomas's Secretary, Craig. The secretary showed the man the door, then approached their party.

"His Grace will see you now." He moved on to Lord Ramsay's party.

The eight of them filed into the hall and approached the regent of Scotland.

Chapter 26

GRACE'S FIRST THOUGHT was Sir Thomas stood and carried himself like a warrior. She recognized the stance. He had a wide face, narrow nose, and a thick crop of dark hair liberally sprinkled with gray. His eyes were a darker brown than Gabriel's and had a piercing quality that triggered a quiver in her belly when he looked at her.

The secretary introduced her first. She curtsied deeply, and the regent took her hand and bent over it. "It is pleasing to meet you, Lady Grace."

She swallowed, though her throat was dry, and her heart seemed to have risen into her throat. "Thank you, my lord. 'Tis kind of ye to see us."

"I believe you have a document to return to me," he said.

"Aye, your grace." Grace walked quickly to Gabriel. He removed the charter Lord Alexander had placed inside the leather pouch and handed it to her. She returned to the regent with the document and handed it to him.

He unfolded the charter, looked over the signatures, then handed it over to his secretary.

"I was told you were reluctant to sign the document."

She felt the spiteful hand of Lord Ramsay in that, and the instant anger fed her courage. "Aye, my lord."

"Why?"

"I had no family I knew of within the clan. I had made my place with Lord Alexander and Lady Mary. Change is difficult when you are facin' the loss of all you ken and love. I didna wish to be alone among strangers."

"And you were betrothed to be wed."

"Aye. To Gabriel Campbell."

"You may take a seat, Lady Grace. We will return t' that."

Craig went down the line of lords with introductions, and each man knelt.

When he introduced Gabriel, Sir Thomas eyed him up and down, taking his measure. Grace tried to read what his thoughts might be, but the man's face was expressionless.

The last two men were barristers, experts in the law come to speak on Lord Ramsay's behalf.

The regent bid them all to sit on wide benches with sturdy backs. Grace perched on the edge of one, for to slide back would lift her feet from off the floor. She glanced at Lord Ramsay. The man was too confident in his manner, considering what he knew they had on him.

"Lord Ramsay, it was you who contested the banns of Lady Grace and Master Gabriel Campbell's betrothal."

Ramsay bobbed to his feet. "Aye, your grace."

"Why did you object?"

"Gabriel Campbell is a commoner, your grace. He has no title, thus it is against the law for him and Lady Grace t' wed. Also, with his close connections to all the Campbell lords, I didna think he would be a suitable leader for the MacNab clan. The Campbells have had control of all MacNab land for many years. It is time the MacNabs are able to take back their land and find their own way."

It was clear the barristers had helped Lord Ramsay prepare his attack.

The regent eyed Ramsay for a moment. "And you think you would be a suitable husband for Lady Grace and a leader of her clan."

The thought brought a sick feeling to Grace's stomach. She would either kill the man or he her.

"Aye, I do, your grace." Ramsay schooled his features into an expression of sadness. "I lost my wife and children some years ago, your grace. I wish t' start anew, and mayhap have a family again. Lady Grace would be a suitable match for me, and I for her."

Grace moved restlessly, and Sir Thomas homed in on it like a hawk after a mouse. "Did he ask for your hand, Lady Grace?"

"Nay, your grace. He *told* me I had to marry him or he would have Gabriel killed."

Sir Thomas's brows rose and he glanced in Ramsay's direction. "Do you have anyone who witnessed his threat?"

Duncan rose. "I did, your grace and there was one other, but he was unable to travel here today. Several others were in the stairwell and heard him shouting."

"I have the other witnesses' statements, your grace, signed and witnessed," Grace said. Gabriel pulled out the letter written at the last moment before leaving *Tasgaidh*. "'Twas written as Artair Campbell told it, and witnessed by Sir Drummond MacNab, sir, since Artair doesna read or write." She carried it to Sir Thomas.

"What was your response to Lord Ramsay's outburst, Lady Grace?" he asked when she reached him.

"I told him plainly that if he were my only choice I would rather spend the rest of my life barren and alone."

When she started to return to her seat, he said, "Stay were you are, Lady Grace."

The regent looked down at the letter for several seconds, then back up. "Sounds like a heartfelt rejection, Lord Ramsay."

"I believe Lady Grace has been affected by her many years with the Campbells, where she has been allowed to consort with those beneath her and has developed unwholesome attachments to them. I believe with time, away from them, she would learn t' care for me."

Liar! He knew well enough she hated him. Grace clenched her hands at her sides. She looked up to find Sir Thomas studying her.

"Gabriel?" Sir Thomas addressed him.

Gabriel rose. "Aye, my lord."

The regent went to the highly polished table he obviously used as a desk and lifted a bundle of documents from its surface. "I have received several letters written on your behalf. It seems you might have been able t' win the war single-handed had the rest of us gotten out of your way."

Color stained Gabriel's cheeks. "Nay, your grace. I was but one of many fighters. We could not have won without men like the Bruce and yerself leading us."

"I was proud t' do my part." Sir Thomas leaned back against the highly polished table. "I have also read letters from the three lords who have come to testify on your behalf as to your suitability to wed Lady Grace and lead her clan."

"Yes, your grace."

"How many years have you served Lord Alexander?"

"Sixteen."

"You fought alongside him?"

"Aye, since I was thirteen."

"He is Lord Alexander's *buannachann*, my lord," Ramsay spoke, and his lawyers shushed him.

Gabriel straightened and focused on Sir Thomas's face. "Not any longer, your grace. I have been called to lend my sword to the MacNab clan."

"Why would you leave your clan to fight for another?"

"Because Lady Grace bid me to do so."

"Have you been released from your oath to Lord Alexander?"

"Aye, I have."

The regent was no fool. Grace saw the man's clever mind working, and when his eyes fell on her, a quiver shook her belly again. "You were fostered with the Campbell clan for some time were ye not, Lady Grace?"

"Aye, my lord. I have lived with them for eight years."

"So you are close to many of them?"

"To Lord Alexander and Lady Mary, and the clan members Lord Alexander leads."

"Do you think your ties to them will make it difficult for you t' do what needs t' be done in the MacNab clan's best interest?"

"Nay, my lord."

"Why not?"

She paused to pray for the right words. "I did what you bid me t' do, I signed the charter. I didna take that lightly, sir. 'Tis not just a bit of land you handed me t' care for, but more than a thousand souls."

Sir Thomas straightened from the table and moved to stand before Grace, his hands folded behind him. The spark of interest in his gaze set her heart to racing. She had reached him.

"You believe 'tis your duty to care for all upon your land?"

"Aye, my lord. Why would I not care for the hands that feed me, the bodies who provide a roof over my head, and the swords that protect me? 'Tis my duty to protect them as well." Her voice grew softer, more intent. "I am a bridge between the two clans, your grace. While I have ties to the Campbells, they, too, have ties to me. I have cared for Lord Alexander's son, just as he cared for me when I had no home, no family, and was alone on the streets here in Edinburgh. He would no more raise a sword again' me than I would again' him. We are small. The weight and strength of the Campbells have protected us. But I would like to see us grow strong enough to be a supporting arm, should the need arise."

"How can you stand alone if you are but an arm?"

"There are only two hundred fifty clansmen, my lord; the rest are women and children. We have not the numbers."

"You have visited the clan?"

"Aye, I have. And they have made their wishes known t' me. They have sent a message t' you."

The strain was wearing on her, leaving her trembling. Gabriel lifted the folded parchment from the pouch and placed it in her hands. He offered her as much encouragement as he could with a glance. The next few minutes would either see him hanged or accepted as worthy to be her guidesman. Her throat nearly closed at the thought.

She was breathing hard by the time she returned to Sir Thomas and placed the precious document in his hands. He unfolded it onto the table.

His head whipped up. His eyes narrowed and settled upon Gabriel. Two spots of color stained his cheeks.

Grace pressed a hand to her midriff, where her heart seemed to have fallen and lodged.

"Craig. See everyone out but Gabriel Campbell and Lady Grace. I will speak to them alone."

"Aye, your grace."

The others filed out, and the last thing Grace saw was Lord Ramsay's spiteful glee at the regent's anger.

GABRIEL CAME TO stand beside her, and their hands reached for each other.

Gabriel's throat was parched and his heart beat like a drum.

"Whose idea was it?" The regent demanded. And it was the regent who spoke. Up until now Sir Thomas had been in the room, but now it was the acting king of Scotland speaking. And he was angry.

"'Twas mine, your grace."

"But I agreed," Grace added.

"And is there a contract of marriage in yon satchel as well, Master Gabriel?"

"Aye there is, your grace. Signed and witnessed, our vows spoken before a priest."

"You thought to lay claim to the MacNab holdings for your Campbell kin."

"Nay. I thought to protect Grace and her clan. Lord Ramsay said he had your ear, that he could make certain she would wed him. He is a leech who would drain the lifesblood from the clan for himself and use their land to hide, should the English cross our borders again. I couldna stand by and see Grace being forced again' her will to wed a man willing to do such as he would do to her.

"I had asked her t' wed me before we ever kent about the charter, when she had nothin' but a basket t' carry her herbs and a few gowns. I would still wed her if that was all she had today."

"You are still a Campbell."

"Aye, but I have pledged my alliance to the MacNab clan as much as they have me."

The regent stepped close and his gaze drilled into Gabriel's. "Would you raise your sword again' your own clan to protect them?"

"I pray God I winna ever have t' make that choice, but they are mine now to lead and protect, and I will do whatever I have to t' see it done."

The regent turned away and moved back to the table. The tension of anger still rode his shoulders, but he had calmed. He raked back the thick dark hair in a gesture more human than royal, and Gabriel hoped the worst had passed.

He turned to face them, his expression once again composed. "I winna acknowledge the marriage."

Grace turned against Gabriel, her nerve finally breaking. He slipped an arm about her waist to hold her. She did not cry but clenched his shirt in her hands.

"I winna demand that it be annulled. But I winna acknowledge it either. Do you understand what that will mean?"

They would be married in the church's eyes, but not in the realm's. The validity of their marriage could be questioned, and their children might or might not be recognized as heirs to *Tasgaidh*. Gabriel's throat burned as he swallowed, the pain of it settling deep inside his chest. "Aye, my lord."

"Do you understand, Lady Grace?"

She nodded, and her voice broke when she spoke. "Aye."

"There will come a time when I may call upon you to lend me your sword and your men, Gabriel. You had best train them well."

"It will be done, my lord."

"Craig, ask the others to return so we may finish."

Grace raised her head, her cheeks wet with tears. "Wait. Your grace there is another matter."

Gabriel gripped her arms and held her away so she might look into his eyes. They had come out of this, not unscathed, but together. They had tried the regent's patience enough.

"We canna deny them their voice, Gabriel. They came here expecting to be heard."

For a second the urge to shake her was strong. Had he ever kenned anyone as stubborn as she?

"What is it?" Sir Thomas asked, his jaw muscles rippling.

"It concerns Lord Ramsay, your grace."

Chapter 27

THE COMMON ROOM was a rumble of voices and laughter, but their table contributed little to it. Grace felt numb after the meeting, her emotions wrung out as thoroughly as the laundress at *Caisteal Sith* wrung out the sheets. Gabriel, too, had the same look about him. He had spoken little. What was left for them to say?

"Did you see Davis's face when the wee lass pushed the bairn into his lap?" Duncan asked. "And when the bairn looked at him, 'twas like looking at a reflection. I thought he might bock. The lass couldna have been more than twelve when she birthed him."

"Every person who has had him in their home will be wonderin' if he has been at their children," Lord Alexander said. "He will be pay a price there."

"Good. The lasses deserve a bit of justice," Bruce Campbell said from the end of the table. He looked thinner and much the worse for the experience. Mayhap hearing their stories had been as hard for him as it had been for her. "You said he spoke of wantin' a family again. If he pays for the many weans he has, 'twill serve him well. How many more does he need to carry on his name?"

"Certes, eight should be enough," Lord John said, his expression grave. "But there are surely more."

"I found four others, but they were too afraid to come forward. Mayhap they will change their minds when 'tis kenned he has been ordered to pay for the weans' upkeep. Had his grace spoken t' me in that icy tone, I'd have either bocked or—" Bruce cut off what he was saying when Gabriel leaned forward and narrowed his eyes at him. "I beg pardon, Lady Grace."

Had Bruce but kent that they, too, had encountered that same tone and look and been crushed by it.

She rallied a smile, though it was hard. "You are forgiven—this time. You deserve some wee consession for all the kind works you have done." She had to know. "Did you find any sign of Lady Elspeth?"

"Nay. He has either hidden her away or she has gone into hiding."

Grace conceded that she had done all she could do. Weary of hearing more of such a dismal discourse when there was nothing to be done about it, she rose. The men came to their feet. "Thank you for all you have done. All of you. I am most grateful."

"You are welcome, Grace," Lord Alexander said. "Lady Mary will be excited and pleased to hear your news. You and Gabriel must return to us as soon as you may."

"We will, my lord."

Gabriel's hand rested against her hip as they walked to their room. With his continued silence, she felt a distance between them that had not been there since before he returned ill to *Caisteal Sith*. After all they had both been through, mayhap this last blow had been too much.

Once in their chamber, she removed her surcoat and shoes. She placed the gown on the bed and ran a finger over the flowers she had painstakingly embroidered on the bodice. She had worn it on the happiest day she had ever known, and now one of the worst and the best at once. How was she to feel when with one hand she had been granted her fondest dream, and with the other, she had seen Gabriel's chance to leave a legacy behind crushed, as well s hers. Without the regent's blessing, their marriage could be claimed invalid, all because of a title.

They were alive, whole. And they would love each other. That was all that mattered.

Then why did she feel this dull, bruising ache just beneath her ribs? It lay too deep to allow tears to cleanse it.

She carefully folded the surcoat as tightly as she could, then removed the one travel-worn gown she had left in the leather saddlebag before placing the surcoat inside. Would she ever be able to wear it again without memories of this day spoiling her pleasure in it? Atop the surcoat she placed the leather pouch of documents Gabriel had so watchfully carried.

She turned to find him sitting on the bed watching her, his elbows on his knees and his hands laced together. He suddenly rose and came to offer her a hand to help her rise. "I must away for a wee time, Grace. Just an hour or so. There is somethin' I must do."

She started to ask what, but subsided. Mayhap he just needed a few hours free of her after—She could not think of it anymore. "I will be here."

He nodded. "I winna be long. Bar the door, lass."

After he had gone, she looked around the empty room. There was nothing to pass the time or occupy her thoughts. No sewing or other small tasks needing to be done. Those terrible moments with Sir Thomas kept running through her mind, until she thought she might scream and rail against the injustice of it.

Hoping to calm herself, she unbraided her hair and washed it—difficult to do in a small washbowl with cold water—then sat before the fire and combed it out, the repetitive motion soothing her.

Time passed slowly, and she rose to crack the shutter and try to determine the time.

A knock came at the door, and she ran to it and lifted the bar. One of the boys who carried baggage stood outside. "There's a messenger in the common room, Lady Grace. He says he canna leave the letter, but that he must deliver it directly into your hands."

If something had happened to Gabriel—Nay, surely more than just a note would be sent in that case.

She grabbed her cloak from behind the door and threw it over her kirtle. Bundling her hair, she twisted it into a messy knot at the nape of her neck.

A young man stood at the courtyard door of the common room, a leather bag hanging across his body that looked to weigh as much as he. On seeing her rushing toward him, he stepped forward. "Lady Grace MacNab?"

"Aye, I am she." She was out of breath, and she was painfully aware her hair had slipped its knot and hung over her shoulders and down her back in flyaway curls.

"I have a letter for you from Sir Thomas Randolph, the Duke of Moray."

Dread hit the pit of her stomach like a battering ram.

He held a heavy piece of paper that was folded and sealed with wax out to her.

She took it and saw her name written across the front, along with Gabriel's, and the royal seal pressed into the wax on the back.

Lord Duncan suddenly appeared at her side. "Lady Grace, is there something amiss?" He handed the messenger a coin, and the lad scampered out the door with the bulging bag.

What if Sir Thomas had changed his mind and meant to dissolve their marriage as further punishment?

In the wake of the messenger's exit, Gabriel elbowed his way through the door with several packages tied with string dangling from his fingers.

His features hardened into a concerned frown. "Grace, what is amiss?"

"'Tis a letter from his grace."

He shoved the packages at Duncan, his masculine features tightening with a black, bitter anger. "Enough!" he murmured against gritted teeth. He tugged the letter from her fingers and broke the seal.

While he scanned the lines, his mouth, a straight, grim line, relaxed, as did the crease between his brows. When he looked up, his brown eyes held the wolfish gleam she loved.

"Sir Thomas has relented and changed his mind, Grace. He says had he listened to the testimony about Lord Ramsay first, he would have understood more fully why we were so determined to use any means to ensure he had no claim on you or the clan. For our sakes, and the sake of our children, he has acknowledged our marriage, and has given us his blessing."

Lord Duncan gave a shout of celebration as loud as any Campbell war cry, causing heads to turn in their direction.

The joy robbed from them earlier came rushing in to fill her heart, and Grace leapt into Gabriel's arms. He caught her against him and spun her around. The noise and confusion of the common room faded as she looked into his face and saw the same joy she felt. "We are free, Gabriel." Free to love, free to live a life together, secure that no man could contest their right to be together.

"'Twould not have mattered, Grace. Ye are m' wife. I claimed ye wi' m' vows, with m' body, and with m' heart. No force on heaven or earth could ever change that."

At the unwavering love she read in his face, her own for him swelled inside her. "As I lay claim to you, husband," she murmured, and kissed him.

The End

Books By Teresa J. Reasor

BREAKING FREE (Book 1 of the SEAL Team Heartbreakers)
BREAKING THROUGH
(Book 2 of the SEAL Team Heartbreakers
BREAKING AWAY (Book 3 of the SEAL Team Heartbreakers)
BUILDING TIES (Book 4 of the SEAL Team Heartbreakers)
BREAKING BOUNDARIES
(Book 5 of the SEAL Team Heartbreakers)
TIMELESS
DEEP WITHIN THE SHADOWS
(Book 1 of the Superstition Series)
WHISPER IN MY EAR
CAPTIVE HEARTS
HIGHLAND MOONLIGHT

Trilogies
A Highland Moonlight Spinoff
TO CAPTURE A HIGHLANDER'S HEART: THE BEGINNING
TO CAPTURE A HIGHLANDER'S HEART: THE COURTSHIP
TO CAPTURE A HIGHLANDER'S HEART: THE WEDDING
NIGHT

NOVELLAS
BREAKING TIES (A SEAL Team Heartbreakers Novella)

Short stories
AN AUTOMATED DEATH: A STEAMPUNK SHORT STORY
CAUGHT IN THE ACT (A HUMOROUS SHORT STORY)

Children's Books
WILLY C. SPARKS, THE DRAGON WHO LOST HIS FIRE